The Perfect Seduction

LESLIE LAFOY

St. Martin's Paperbacks

THE PERFECT SEDUCTION

Copyright © 2003 by Leslie LaFoy.

All rights reserved. No part of this book may be used or reproduced in any manner whatsoever without written permission except in the case of brief quotations embodied in critical articles or reviews. For information address St. Martin's Press, 175 Fifth Avenue, New York, NY 10010.

ISBN: 0-312-98763-3

Printed in the United States of America

St. Martin's Paperbacks edition / December 2003

St. Martin's Paperbacks are published by St. Martin's Press, 175 Fifth Avenue, New York, NY 10010.

10 9 8 7 6 5 4 3 2 1

PROLOGUE

The air was thick and hot and alive with the drone of insects. There was no respite from it, not even in the shade of the veranda. A bead of perspiration trickled slowly down Seraphina Treadwell's back as she looked at the two coins in the palm of her hand. With the other, she tightened her grip on her portfolio. Forcing a smile, she met her patron's gaze and said as politely as she could, "I recall that we agreed on a commission of five pounds sterling."

"True," Cora Matthews said, her chin high and her lips thinned with a smirk. "However, Lord Matthews has pointed out in the interim that you are without formal training or credentials and should therefore be quite grateful for whatever sum I choose to give for your work. I have decided that two pounds is quite sufficient."

And Lord Matthews was quite without a legitimate title; everyone in Belize City knew the pomposity for what it was. Her pulse hammering, Sera tried one more time. "We agreed—"

"It's two pounds or nothing at all, Mrs. Treadwell. Given your circumstances—"

"I am very much aware of my circumstances," Sera interrupted, hastily dropping the coins in her reticule. *I am aware of a great many things,* she silently added, setting her leather case on the wooden planking at her feet. *Not the least of which is that you would have little girls go hungry and shoeless rather than honor your word.*

Carefully extracting the charcoal drawing from the carrying case, Seraphina turned it so that the other could fully see it. "As you commissioned, a drawing of your house. Done, as per your request, with considerable . . . aggrandizement. Does it meet your expectations, Lady Matthews?"

The woman's eyes sparkled for just a moment and then the mask of cold disdain slipped back into place. "It will have to do, won't it? You are the only artist in the colony."

Seraphina smiled. "I am, indeed," she replied while blithely tearing the drawing straight down the center. She handed one half to a stunned, wide-eyed Cora Matthews while adding, "You've paid for half a picture. When you decide to pay for the other half, do let me know."

While the other woman sputtered in wordless rage, Seraphina dropped the remaining half of her work into the portfolio, saying, "Good day, Mrs. Matthews," then turned, lifted her hems, and walked smartly down the veranda steps.

She was halfway down the front path and into blazing sunlight when Cora Matthews found her voice. Sera smiled, ignoring the diatribe. There was nothing Cora Matthews could do to her. They were at the end of nowhere. Actually, Seraphina silently amended as she lifted the hem of her skirt higher and vaulted over a mud puddle, Belize City was beyond the end of nowhere. It was nothing more than a flat place on the mosquito-infested coastline of the Gulf of Mexico. It didn't belong to any country in particular, not even itself. There wasn't a local government, or a constabulary, or anything approaching a definable culture. Belize City simply existed, steaming at the edge of the jungle, day in and day out, year after year after year.

Most people didn't plan to come here; life simply washed them up on the shore. She could count on one hand the number of persons she knew for whom Belize had been their intended destination. Of those five, one had come to his senses and sailed away within a month. Two of them—her parents—had been laid to rest in the cemetery. The other two—Arthur and Mary Reeves—had gone off on yet another exploration for ancient civilizations. They'd planned to be gone for two weeks. The two weeks had become two months; the two months had now stretched to six.

God bless Arthur and Mary—wherever they were. Their house still stood and their daughters were fine—or as fine as three young ladies could be, given that their parents had disappeared without a trace. The Reeveses' money was a different matter entirely, however. It had been gone for the last month and a half.

Seraphina sighed. She'd counted on the pittance from Cora Matthews to buy food for this evening's table. With what had been left over, she'd thought to order the eldest of the girls a desperately needed pair of shoes.

Now, because of the woman's stinginess, shoes were out of the question. The two coins jangling in her reticule wouldn't buy all that much food, but at least it would keep the wolf from tearing down the door for another week. After that . . . After that, their survival was going to depend on divine intervention. It was altogether too much to hope that God would offer her a way to get the Reeveses' daughters out of this hideous place.

A way out . . . Seraphina paused in the center of the muddy roadway. Beyond the half-dozen ramshackle buildings that comprised Belize City proper, a two-masted ship sat at anchor in the bay. Having arrived sometime during the night, it was presently sending a portion of its crew to shore in several small dinghies. Beyond it all, from far out at sea, came the daily bank of rain clouds.

One didn't need to own a watch in Belize, Seraphina reminded herself as she gathered her skirts and strode forward. The rain came at two o'clock each afternoon. And while misfortune wasn't quite as predictable, it did occur far more frequently. The ships that blew into the bay invariably brought a brimming portion of it. She needed to be home with the girls before the captain turned loose his sailors and the sailors turned Belize City into Gomorrah.

Marta de Leon, Sera decided, setting her course toward the small flock of molting chickens halfheartedly pecking the bare ground in front of Marta's mildew-stained tent. Marta would exchange provisions for the two pounds sterling and not mention the ten already owed her. The other traders weren't as likely to be as generous or kind.

"Mornin', Mrs. Treadwell."

Sera started at the familiar voice and quickly turned toward it, unwilling to have Milton Hopkins at her back.

"Got a letter for ya," he said, pulling it from the front pocket of his tattered, filthy dungarees and stepping deliberately close—too close—in order to hand it over.

"For me?" Sera asked, taking the once white packet and then stepping back to put a more acceptable, safer distance between them.

"Well, for Mr. Reeves," Hopkins clarified, his words whistling from between the teeth he had remaining. "But seein' as how he's not here to accept it for hisself and how he and his missus left their girls with ya, it seems like maybe it might be all right to give it to ya for safe-keepin'."

"Thank you," she replied, studying the envelope. It was indeed addressed to Arthur Reeves. The penmanship was excellent. There were no extraneous flourishes and not the slightest sign of wavering. The hand that had written it had been precise, strong, determined, sure. Bold. Definitely male.

"It's from London," Hopkins said. "England."

"So I see."

"Ship sent the mail in a couple of hours ago. I was goin' to bring it out to the house after a bit, but since yer here and the walk's a fair to middlin' one . . ."

Summoning a polite smile, she backed away, saying, "I'm glad I was able to save you the trek. I appreciate your attention to duty, Mr. Hopkins. I'll keep it safe until Mr. Reeves's return."

"Had any word from your husband?"

She froze, her heart tripping as she scanned his face, looking for the slightest sign that he knew something she didn't. "Not since he led the Reeveses off into the jungle," she answered warily. Taking a slow, deep breath to brace herself, she asked, "Have you heard from him?"

"Not a peep."

Sera sagged with relief, then, remembering that she was supposed to be a concerned wife, stiffened her back and mustered what she hoped passed for an expression of disappointment and grim resolution.

"Don't lose hope, Mrs. Treadwell. Folks have been known to walk out of the jungle. And if anyone can, it'd be Gerald Treadwell."

An icy wave rippled down Seraphina's spine. "I pray each night for a miracle," she answered tightly, shuddering as a second chill raced through her.

"Now, it *would* be a miracle if ya ever saw those Reeves folks again. Wouldn't count on it, Mrs. Treadwell. Six months . . ." He shook his head. "Not even their bones is left now."

She choked back a gasp and then did her best to swallow the anger that came in its wake. Still, it edged her words when she said, "And you were doing so well at buoying my spirits."

Oblivious to her sarcasm, Hopkins nodded and openly considered the curve of her breasts. "Ya have to face the facts sooner or later, Mrs. Treadwell. Odds are ya won't be a widow, but those girls is orphans. Pure and simple. Best be makin' some plans for them. Mizz Amanda's gettin' close to the marrying age."

Seraphina's jaw sagged. Marrying age? Amanda, the eldest of the three girls, was all of nine years old!

"And speakin' of the sweet little thing," Hopkins went on, making a production of looking around the little village. "I don't see Mizz Amanda anywheres about."

And Belize would freeze before he did. "She's at home this morning, helping her younger sisters with their arithmetic and geography lessons." And just so that he didn't entertain any untoward ideas, she briskly added, "I'm on my way back there now."

He spat on the ground between Sera's feet and, ignoring her gasp and hasty two-step retreat, said, "You really ought to bring her into town more often, ya know. Girl her age ought to be seein' folks besides the family hens. My Isabel would be right good company for Mizz Amanda. 'Bout the same age, they are. Give or take a year or two."

Three, actually, Sera silently corrected. But a lifetime apart in terms of sordid, worldly experience. And it would remain that way as long she had breath in her body. No decent woman—of any age—should ever know the things that the twelve-year-old bride of Milton Hopkins did.

"I know a man over in Guatemala who might be interested in her."

Seraphina pretended that she hadn't heard the offer— or noticed that his gaze had dropped to her hips. What a loathsome man! She fisted her free hand even as she reminded herself that she had been brought up as a gentlewoman. Good Lord, there simply had to be a way to get the girls out of this nightmarish place. There had to be.

But first she had to get away from Milton Hopkins. And the rudeness of obvious escape be damned; her skin was beginning to crawl.

"I really must be going, Mr. Hopkins. The girls are waiting luncheon on me. Thank you again for delivering the letter," she said, then deliberately turned away and resumed her earlier course.

She didn't glance back; she didn't dare. His leering always brought out the worst in her. The man had so few teeth left as it was. If she were to punch him as she was so sorely tempted to do, he'd starve to death and she'd spend forever feeling guilty. And then, of course, there would be the inevitable talk. *Did you hear what Seraphina Miller-Treadwell did?* Her reputation was tattered enough already; killing Milton Hopkins would be its final unraveling. He simply wasn't worth it.

Marta's chickens—even more pathetically defeathered at a closer distance—squawked in protest and scurried to get out of her path. But once they were away, they fell silent, allowing the low drone of conversation to reach her ears.

Seraphina paused, wondering how much longer Marta would be with her other patron. Should she patiently wait or make her presence known by knocking on the pie tin nailed to the tent's center post? Good manners weren't generally expected or practiced in Belize. She glanced toward the shore and noted the dinghies being dragged up out of the tide line. Time was growing short. Twin beads of perspiration rolled down her back and into the already drenched layers of fabric encircling her waist.

Sera listened again to the conversation inside the tent, noting that it now contained the certain ring of business being concluded. Deciding that she could afford to be polite and wait her turn, she resisted the urge to use her sleeve to wipe her brow and instead considered the letter crumpled in her hand. It took a moment and a bit of shifting, but she managed to tuck her portfolio under her arm and free her hands for use.

She smoothed the wrinkles from the letter as best she could and then reexamined the boldly written address. *Arthur William Albert Reeves. Belize.* Clearly, the sender had no inkling that Arthur had disappeared. Which left her in a quandary as to what to do. Seraphina sighed, wishing this sort of decision hadn't been thrust upon her and yet knowing that she didn't have any choice but to make it. One shouldered all manner of burdens for friends.

The simplest solution would be to file the letter in the box of receipts she was amassing in Arthur's absence, but if she did, there was a possibility that she would be ignoring important business that needed to be addressed. What that business might be, she hadn't the foggiest notion.

But she did know that in the three years the Reeveses had been in Belize, Arthur had never received correspondence of any sort. Mail came so seldom that everyone knew when it did and who had received what. The very fact that a letter had come at all implied that it was of great importance and therefore she was duty-bound to ascertain its contents. And considering that Arthur and Mary had left her in charge of their home, their children, and their money . . . Surely that delegation of authority extended to dealing responsibly with their correspondence.

Of course, there was nothing on the face of the letter itself to suggest that it was of a business nature. It was just as likely to be a personal communication. If it was, to open and read it would be a grave violation of Arthur's privacy.

"You're dithering, Sera," she muttered, frustrated with herself. "Just open the thing and be done with it."

Her teeth clenched, she quickly broke the seal on the letter and opened the folds. Two slightly wrinkled one-hundred-pound banknotes fell out and fluttered down toward the mud at her feet. Her heart racing and lodged high in her throat, Seraphina dropped her portfolio to save them—and the girls—from ruin.

CHAPTER 1

London
1860

It had been damn inconsiderate of Percival to drown in his bowl of porridge. And Arthur was certainly taking his sweet time about assuming the mantle of responsibility. As brothers went, the two of them were pathetic at best. The fact that they were—or in the case of Percival, *were*—half-brothers didn't matter. Between them, they'd managed to top off his well of resentment. Yet again.

"Wallowing in dark thoughts, Carden?"

He continued to stare into the depths of his morning teacup as he honestly answered, "No more so than usual, Aiden. No more so than usual."

Across the table, Barrett Stanbridge reached for a third slice of toast and asked, "And would this be the usual thoughts over the state of the empire? Or perhaps the fact that no one's building railroads in England these days?" Slathering a generous portion of butter on the lightly browned bread, he added, "Or maybe you're dwelling on the rather nasty comments Lady Caruthers offered on your plans for her new conservatory?"

"I was going to get to those items in good time," Carden admitted, wondering if noon was too early in the day to begin drinking. "And I wouldn't be using my talents to design conservatories for silly old ladies if Parliament would get on with the standardization of gauges for the existing rail systems."

"Ah. Very true," Aiden Terrell replied, setting his empty teacup aside and reaching for a cherry pastry.

Barrett nodded in agreement and spooned up a heap of strawberry jam. "Then the black thoughts have to be about his having to endure the privileges of being a peer until his brother returns from God knows where."

"Arthur's in Belize. And there's precious little privilege to offset the tedium of being a peer," Carden snapped, polishing off his tea and setting the cup back into its saucer with a loud clink.

"We'll have to take your word on the matter," Barrett countered, grinning. "Neither of us is ever going to know for ourselves. Which, of course, begs the question of why you continue to associate with us."

"Because you're happy drunks and miserable card players."

Aiden laughed and refilled his cup from the silver teapot. "That and we're most kind about taking the unwanted women off your hands."

Carden momentarily winced. Damn if he hadn't forgotten about dealing with that bit of business. Out of sight, out of mind.

"Speaking of women," Barrett said predictably, momentarily forgetting his toast and making a production of looking around the breakfast room, "where's the lovely thing with whom you left Covent Garden last night? Have you got her under the table?"

The suggestion triggered a mental image. Carden mentally filed it away and shifted in his chair to casually arrange the silk dressing gown so that it concealed his physical response to it. "As far as I know," he answered his friends, "she's still upstairs, still abed. I haven't checked recently."

"It's rather late in the morning," Barrett observed before taking a wolfish bite of his toast.

"We were up rather late into the night," Carden replied with a smile, knowing he was expected to say something of the sort. One accommodated friends in such things. And, being friends and gentlemen, he knew they wouldn't press for details on precisely how he'd passed the hours spent in the woman's company.

"Might we take this as a sign," Aiden asked, adding cream to his second cup of tea, "that this one will be around a bit longer than the others before her?"

Carden laughed at the less than subtle—and so very expected—inquiry. "No. And no, I don't care which of you takes her off my hands. Draw straws if you'd like."

"Aiden got the last one," Barrett declared. "It's my turn. What's her name?"

"Jenine. Or Joan," Carden supplied. He shrugged and added, "Or something like that. We didn't engage in any prolonged conversations."

Barrett nodded, his eyes narrowed as he looked out the open breakfast room doors and toward the stairwell at the front of the house. "Have you hired a new housekeeper yet?"

Puzzled by the abrupt change of subject, Carden glanced toward Aiden, seeking an explanation. The other shook his head and shrugged his shoulders in silent reply. "All right, Barrett," Carden said on a sigh. "What does my hiring a housekeeper have to do with the woman presumably still in my bed?"

Laying aside his unfinished toast, Barrett brushed crumbs from his fingertips while explaining, "I was thinking that perhaps she might be waiting for breakfast to be brought up. She'd likely be quite grateful should someone think of obliging her expectations. And if there's no housekeeper to see to the task . . ." He met Carden's gaze, grinned and winked.

He saw the direction of his friend's thoughts and settled back into his chair and the usual game. "There's no housekeeper. The advertisement runs in the *Times* today. I imagine that they'll begin queuing up within the next hour."

"Then hadn't you best be getting dressed for the interviews?" Aiden asked. He looked him up and down, cocked a brow, and then added, "Or do you intend to select the candidate least affected by your lack of inhibition?"

"Now there's an idea," Barrett contributed, rising from his seat and beginning to gather items for a breakfast tray.

"Capital one, if I may so myself," Aiden remarked, handing over the teapot. "If he were to hire the right kind of woman, he'd save himself the necessity of finding a new romantic interest every other day or so. There's a great deal to be said for convenience."

Carden snorted and passed Barrett the jam. "There's even more to be said for novelty and the thrill of seduction."

"Boredom is such a bore, isn't it?" Barrett observed, lifting the hastily assembled but well-laden tray. He chuckled and then said, "Give me fifteen minutes to charm your latest before you come up to make yourself presentable."

"Fifteen?" Carden asked. "That's all?"

"Actually, I think ten will be quite sufficient," his friend replied while moving toward the door, "but I'd rather err on the side of certainty. The young lady might be a bit uncomfortable if you walked in just as she's agreeing to slip down the back stairs with me."

Aiden pulled a gold watch from his pocket and flipped open the ornate cover. "How long are you going to give him?"

"At least thirty."

"It won't take him that long," the other replied, placing

the open timepiece on the table so they both could see it. "He can be quite the charmer when he wants something."

Carden smiled broadly. "He's almost as good as I am. And given the proclivities of the woman upstairs, I doubt that it'll take him much more than five minutes to convince her to shift romantic allegiance. I'm allowing another ten for her to ably demonstrate her new loyalty and then another fifteen for them to get dressed and gone. You know how it goes."

Aiden's smile said he did. "Be honest, Carden. Won't you miss her charms just the tiniest little bit?"

Carden considered the center of the now almost empty breakfast table. Aiden was young—just twenty-three—and while able to hold his own when it came to drawing women into his arms, still maintained some of youth's romantic notions about doing so. He'd had them at that age, too. But somewhere in the intervening seven years, they'd been discarded along the roadside of experience. Aiden would let go of them soon enough; Carden could see no reason for him to teach the hard lessons that life and women inevitably would.

"I very deliberately choose women who are . . ." He paused, not quite certain of the best word to use. There were so many qualities that he deemed necessary in his lovers.

"Forgettable?" Aiden supplied.

Carden shook his head. "Utterly disposable."

Aiden pursed his lips and stared at the linen tablecloth. After several long moments, he brought his gaze back to Carden's and asked, "Has it ever occurred to you that you might choose the wrong one at some point and find yourself trapped into marrying her?"

Of course he had. That's why he'd made all but a science of selecting the women for his liaisons. Perhaps, on second thought, he did owe it to the younger man to provide some words of fundamental wisdom. "Only the daughters of peers come with that kind of power, Aiden. I take great pains to avoid them. Pains, I might add, that are every bit the equal of those they take to avoid so much as conversing with a third son like myself."

"So, in short, the answer is no."

"I have no intention of being married. By either choice or force."

Aiden smiled, his earlier tension obviously ebbing away. "Marriage would put something of a crimp in your social life."

"Not in the least," Carden countered as the front bell chimed. "Which means, of course, that making any vows of fidelity would be extremely hypocritical of me. And I firmly believe that there's a sufficient number of hypocrites in the world already. I refuse to add to the problem."

"Very decent of you."

"Thank you. I think so."

The bell chimed again and they both looked out of the breakfast room doors.

Aiden leaned forward for a better look down the hallway and wondered aloud, "Isn't Sawyer going to answer the door?"

"He went to run errands for me," Carden explained, pushing himself up from his chair. "Obviously he hasn't yet returned."

"You're not going to answer it yourself, are you? Dressed like that?"

He looked down at his silk dressing gown, realizing that he was barely covered and a far cry from decent. The bell sounded yet again. He considered the expanse of hallway and the door at the other end. "Would you prefer to listen to the bell ring incessantly?"

"Not really."

"Neither would I," he admitted, drawing the sides of the gown closer and giving the waist sash a quick yank. "And, the matter of preserving our sanity aside, the advertisement was clear that interviews are to begin at two. It's just now noon. If the woman's brassy enough to repeatedly ring the bell two hours early, then she fully deserves to have her sensibilities shocked to the core."

He was moving to the door when Aiden said, "I'm dressed. I could get it for you."

"It's not your house," Carden declared and then left his friend at the table. The bell sounded again as he reached for the knob. His teeth clenched, he wrenched open the thick mahogany panel and immediately stepped into the opening, prepared to serve up a scathing lecture on good manners.

He stopped breathing instead. She was without doubt the most exotic, lusciously curved beauty he'd ever seen. The fact that her clothes were hopelessly unfashionable, faded, and wholly insufficient for the spring weather did nothing to detract from the essential elements of her. Tall, blue-eyed, and—judging by the curls peeking out from under a battered bonnet—brunette, she was an almost perfect picture of genteelly impoverished English womanhood. But where most Englishwomen of some quality had skin the color of fine porcelain, this creature decidedly departed from the norm. She was finely featured and delicately boned—which only served to make the softly burnished hue of her skin all that much more intriguing. Her hands were the same delectable color, her fingers long and graceful and without the slightest evidence of a wedding ring.

And her demeanor . . . It was a curious mixture, as well. She'd flinched as he'd flung open the door, but then stood her ground and looked him up and down without the slightest squeal of surprise at his state of virtual undress. At present her gaze was fastened on his shoulders and she seemed to be searching for a beginning, an explanation of her presence. He didn't really need one, he decided. She was standing on his doorstep and that was enough. He was sufficiently resourceful; if she gave him just half a chance, he could take their relationship from here.

"Good day, madam," he drawled. She started and met his gaze as a blush swept into her cheeks. She hadn't been searching for a beginning at all, he realized. She'd been absorbed in consideration of his physical person. And judging by the guilty look in her eyes, her mental attentions had bordered on indecent. Carden only barely managed to keep his smile contained as he added, "How may I be of service to you?"

She softly cleared her throat, squarely met his gaze, and answered, "I've been told that this is the residence of Mr. Carden Reeves."

"It is." God, her voice was just as exotic as she was. Definitely British but with a very slight, gently rolling foreign accent that he couldn't place. And in that instant he knew that he'd hire her regardless of her references. Maybe there was something to convenience he'd been overlooking all these years. It was certainly worth a try.

Carden smiled and leaned his shoulder against the doorjamb, saying, "The interviews are to begin promptly at two. You're welcome to wait on the walk until then. It would be unfair to the others to begin early."

She blinked those incredibly blue eyes of hers and looked sincerely puzzled as she said, "Interviews?"

Most actresses dressed better, but he had to admit that she had talent. Willing to play his part, he blithely supplied, "For the housekeeper position advertised in this morning's *Times*."

For a second, anger flashed in her eyes like ice in the sun and then it was gone, replaced by a kind of tattered resignation that made him want to reach out for her, to take her face gently between his hands and ask her to tell him how she came to be standing on his doorstep. She'd cry and he'd kiss away her pretty tears and draw her inside, assuring her that all would be—

"I'm not here to interview for employment," she said,

shattering his fantasy. "I have personal business to discuss with Mr. Reeves. Is he perchance at home and receiving callers this morning? It's very important."

She thought he was the butler? In what corner of the British empire did butlers answer the door at noon dressed only in a silk dressing gown? Amused, he crossed his arms over his chest and inquired, "What sort of personal business?"

"I'm sorry, sir, but 'personal' implies that it would be inappropriate to discuss the matter with anyone but Mr. Reeves."

She'd said it kindly and softly, but the notes of censure were there nonetheless. One needed a housekeeper who fully understood and was willing to hold the line of propriety. At least in public. "I'm Carden Reeves. And I'm certain that I'd recall having previously met you, madam. What personal business could there be for us to discuss?"

She drew back—not as though repulsed by any means, but in apparent shock. He couldn't tell whether it was because she'd suddenly realized that she was speaking not to the butler but to the master of the house, or because the masters of the houses in that far corner of the empire didn't answer their own doors in dressing gowns. As her gaze skimmed him from hair to toes, he decided that it must be the latter; she seemed more curious than embarrassed. He liked curious women.

"Madam?"

"Forgive me," she said somewhat breathlessly as she met his gaze again. "It's just that you're nothing at all like Arthur."

If her intent was to give him a turn at rocking back on his heels, she succeeded. "You know my older brother?"

She nodded. "Your brother was a wonderful, kind, and considerate man."

He felt the earth shift under his feet and he straightened

his stance, desperate to hold his equilibrium. "Was? Did you say *was?*"

She too shifted on the step, squaring her shoulders and lifting her chin slightly. "I regret having to be the bearer of such news, but nine months ago your brother and his wife departed for a brief expedition into the interior of Belize. Since they haven't returned or sent word, they're presumed to be dead."

"Presumed?" he repeated, knowing even as he did that he was grasping at straws. "Then he might still be alive."

Her smile was tight, and deep in her eyes he saw the tiniest, briefest flicker of irritation. "You know nothing of the jungle, do you, Mr. Reeves?"

"He can't be dead. He simply can't be."

"I'm afraid that is the most likely of all the possibilities."

Christ on a crutch, this was the very last thing in the world he wanted to hear. First Percival and now, apparently, Arthur. He was cursed. And damned. If word got out of his change in status, his every waking moment would become a living hell. He didn't deserve this. Nothing he'd ever done in his life had been rotten enough to have brought this kind of divine vengeance down on his head.

"Mr. Reeves?"

He quickly scrubbed his hands over his face and then dropped them to his sides as he tried to focus his vision on the woman standing in front of him. The beautiful messenger of ugly news. Proof that God had an extremely twisted sense of irony. And a mean streak as wide as the Thames.

"While I'm sensitive to your upset and grieving, Mr. Reeves," he heard her say kindly but firmly, "there are, unfortunately, matters which simply must be dealt with immediately."

He should ask her in; discussing personal matters on

the front steps was definitely outside the bounds of social protocol. "Such as?" was all he managed to choke out.

"I am Mrs. Gerald Treadwell," she began, her smile weak and strained. "Your brother and sister-in-law left me in charge of their affairs. It was to have been a very temporary arrangement, but the circumstances changed. I thought it best to bring what was left of their lives to you. Since your sister-in-law was an only child and orphaned, you are the only living relation of whom I am aware."

His brain wasn't working properly; he heard her words—each and every one of them—but only one out of three had any sort of significant impact. He couldn't ask her to repeat it all. It wouldn't make any difference anyway. He considered what he remembered of her little speech. She'd said her name was Treadwell. *Mrs.* Treadwell. And something about bringing . . . A dim light flickered in his awareness. Personal effects. She'd brought him Arthur's and Mary's personal effects.

Carden nodded. "Have the boxes or trunks or whatever delivered at my expense."

"I've already seen to the order and the paying of the costs, Mr. Reeves. They should arrive here within a few hours."

He thought that should have concluded their conversation, that with that she should have expressed her condolences one more time and then bid him good day and walked away. But she didn't. She stood there, watching him with huge blue eyes filled with patient expectation. "Why," he wondered aloud, "do I sense that our conversation is not yet done?"

"Perhaps because it isn't," she instantly countered. "I have brought your brother's children home."

"Children?" He all but choked on the word. Good God, the woman was better than any professional pugilist he'd ever seen. She hadn't laid a hand on him and yet he was reeling.

"Were you not aware that your brother had children?"

"Arthur and I . . ." Memories swept over him and with them came the usual flood of anger. In the span of a single heartbeat, the cloud numbing his mind was seared away. "Never mind," he said laconically. "It's hardly relevant. How many children? And *please* tell me that there's a son or two in the litter."

It wasn't either irritation or impatience in her eyes this time; it was anger. She didn't make the slightest effort to conceal or bank it but instead turned her back to him and crisply nodded. A sudden movement out toward the street caught his attention and drew it past her. There was a rented hack at the curb, the driver apparently sleeping in the box, whip in hand. It had been the opening of the carriage door that had drawn his gaze.

He watched as a young girl in a ragged dress stepped down onto the public walk. A second girl, slightly smaller, followed on her heels, her skirts too short by half and exposing far too much of her calves to be decent. A third girl—a very little one—jumped two-footed from the carriage and bounded to a halt beside what he could only presume were her older sisters.

Carden stared at the carriage door and willed a young male—size didn't matter—to come out of the dark recesses. He was still commanding it when the eldest of the three girls turned back and smartly closed the door on his one and only hope of salvation.

It was all but official. He was going to become Carden Reeves, the goddamn seventh Earl of Lansdown.

CHAPTER 2

What doubts Carden might have been able to entertain as to their parentage evaporated as the three girls came to stand beside their nurse on his front steps. They were the very image of Arthur; the same dark eyes fringed with long, thick lashes that had been entirely too feminine on their father, the same full shape of their lower lips, the same way of holding their heads. And damned if they didn't have Arthur's manner about them, as well. All the world was an adventure for them, every person in it subject to open scrutiny and finely honed analysis. And at that moment he felt very much like a bug in a jar.

"Mr. Reeves," their nurse said as they boldly looked up at him, "may I present your nieces, Amanda, Beatrice, and Camille."

Alphabetical. How typically Arthur.

"Darlings, this is your Uncle Carden. Your father's younger brother."

Out of sheer habit, he countered, "Half-brother."

The littlest one looked as though she might cry. The eldest didn't react at all, her face seemingly having turned to stone. The middle one cocked her head to the side and narrowed her eyes as though she were trying to see him more clearly. Their nurse—Mrs. Treadwell, he recalled—

arched a gorgeously shaped eyebrow and softly cleared her throat. The sound reminded him of Sawyer and, belatedly, good manners.

"Won't you please come in?" he asked, stepping back and drawing the door wide with a gesture every bit its equal. Mrs. Treadwell nodded and motioned his nieces forward. They marched across his threshold in alphabetical order and then stopped dead in the center of his entryway. He closed the door, his mind racing.

"Ah . . . This way, into the parlor," Carden said, motioning yet again, this time to the small room reserved for the receiving of guests—not that he ever had any that didn't know him well enough to come in through the back door.

"If you'd like to have a seat, ladies," he offered even as he noted the layer of dust covering all of the furnishings. Someone—probably Barrett—had written "hire a maid" in the stuff that coated the narrow table backing one of the matching settees. Hiring a maid was properly within the housekeeper's duties, of course. And he definitely intended to hire one of those today. In a matter of hours, in fact. "If you'd be so kind as to excuse me for a few moments," he said as the three younger guests plopped down on the upholstery with enough force to raise a choking cloud. "I need to make myself a bit more presentable."

"That would be fine, Mr. Reeves," the nurse said, apparently rooted to a spot in front of the unlit hearth. "And most appreciated," he thought he heard her add under her breath.

He was tempted to point out that she hadn't shown the least little sign of being repulsed by his state of near nudity; that she'd seemed more entranced than anything. He kept his observations to himself, however, deciding that they'd gotten off to a rough enough start without deliberately trying to embarrass her. "Would you care for some refreshments while you wait?"

"That would be most considerate."

"I'll see to it, then. Ladies," he offered, giving them a brief bow as he backed out of the room and pulled the doors closed behind himself.

Once alone and out of their sight, he paused and raked his fingers through his hair. Sweet Jesus. Arthur. Dead. And with daughters his only legacy. What a hell of a mess this was now. How long could he hold things off? How long could he keep up the pretenses and maintain the tidy, uncomplicated nature of his life? Six months? Maybe a year? It all depended on what he did with his nieces and with their exotically tempting nurse. Sending them away would be the easiest, most intelligent thing to do. The rebellion of the Sepoys had made a mess of India. But he had friends still garrisoned in the Transvaal. Maybe . . .

Carden raked his hair one more time and set himself in motion, hoping that he'd have a solution by the time he finished dressing. In the meanwhile, he had something approximating a plan that didn't involve any effort from him beyond giving orders. He could delegate with the best.

He'd no more than stepped into the breakfast room than Aiden looked up from the *Times* and quipped, "You look a little harried."

"There's a crisis of sorts. Have you heard Sawyer come in?"

"No. But then, he could have found something to clear that perpetual lump from his throat."

"Drat and damnation." How long could it take to see the tailor and pick up a new supply of unmentionables? "All right, Aiden, consider yourself pressed into duty. Sitting in my front parlor is a stunningly beautiful woman with an unfortunate case of duty. Accompanying her are three little girls dressed in rags."

His friend laughingly folded his paper. "Your past has finally caught up with you."

He had better sense than that but knew now wasn't the time to undertake a discourse on the subject of sexual precautions. "The urchins are my nieces and the woman who dragged them in here is their nurse. For God's sake, be a good friend and fix a tea tray and take it to them while I dash upstairs and find my clothes."

Aiden retrieved his watch from the table. "It's been only thirteen minutes since Barrett went up."

Which made it less than ten for his world having been set on its ear. "Then he'd damn well better be as good as he thinks he is," Carden pronounced as he headed for the stairs.

"I don't like him."

Seraphina pursed her lips and considered how she ought to reply to Camille's declaration. Honesty was a good thing and yet, on the other hand, the girls' survival was utterly dependent on firmly placing themselves in their uncle's good graces.

"I think we should reserve our judgments for a bit," Sera offered diplomatically. "We have, after all, arrived on his doorstep completely unannounced and it's been a great shock for him to discover that not only is his brother not returning home, but that he has three nieces of whom he was apparently uninformed. People are never at their best when in shock. With time, he may become a bit less . . ."

Sera floundered, mentally reviewing all the observations she'd made in the brief span of her acquaintance with Mr. Carden Reeves. The man had an instinctive disdain for convention. Opening his own door. At noon and wearing only a fine silk dressing gown. A dressing gown which had left precious little to her imagination—especially when he leaned his wide shoulder against the doorjamb and casually crossed his arms and ankles. It had taken every ounce of her self-possession to keep from ogling the long expanse of his bared and well-muscled thigh.

And it was obvious that he made a habit of presenting himself that way to women. He'd been completely at ease, perhaps even unaware of what his stance offered for her perusal. Carden Reeves—every wide-shouldered, narrow-waisted centimeter of him—fairly radiated a sense of confidence.

The man was clearly a rake. A seducer of women. She'd known that the instant he'd opened the door and met her gaze. She'd felt the heat bolt through her from head to toe, stealing her breath and instantly—but, mercifully, only momentarily—scattering her wits. He'd been aware of his instant, powerful effect on her, though. And he'd been amused. She hadn't known whether to be insulted or embarrassed and so she'd opted for wary and businesslike instead. It had seemed to go better after that. Until his callous remark about hoping Arthur had produced sons.

"Uncle Carden might become a bit less what, Miss Sera?" Beatrice pressed, her eyes narrowed in the way she did when puzzling something.

Handsome. Tall. Incredibly well built. Deliciously roguish. Temptation incarnate. "Pompous," Sera answered crisply, deciding that it probably came closest to being the root of all his shortcomings.

As she expected, Camille asked, "What does 'pompous' mean?"

"Full of himself, darling. Your Uncle Carden thinks very highly of himself."

"Why?"

She should have expected that question, as well. But she hadn't and now found herself backed into a corner by her own doing.

"Because he's handsome," Amanda supplied with all the authority of a woman three times her age.

Beatrice, always doubting anything her older sister said, instantly demanded, "Is Amanda right, Miss Sera? Is Uncle Carden handsome?"

Seraphina recalled the well-chiseled features, the blue-gray eyes, the sinfully dark hair with the merest wisps of silver at the temples. And the smile. That dazzling, heart-tripping, sensibility-rattling smile. There was no denying the patently obvious or avoiding a very basic discussion of some essential truths.

"Yes, he's a very handsome man. And while some men manage to go through life without letting their good looks affect their self-opinion, it would appear—at first glance—that your uncle isn't one of them. With time, he may prove otherwise. We must allow him the opportunity."

"He's a ladies' man," Amanda announced.

Seraphina swallowed down her shock and deliberately kept her tone breezy as she asked, "And might I inquire as to how it is that you're familiar with that expression?"

The look in Amanda's eyes said that she knew she'd crossed the line of propriety. But ever undaunted, she smiled bravely and replied, "Everyone in Belize says that Mr. Hopkins is a ladies' man. Surely you heard it, too."

"I have, but I wasn't aware that you had, as well," Sera admitted ruefully. There being no erasing what was certainly dubious knowledge at best, she elected to do what she could in making it as valuable as possible. "Your uncle may be a great many things—a romancer of women among them—but he isn't at all like Mr. Hopkins, Amanda."

"How are they different?"

Amanda and her persistence. Someday it was going to well and truly land her in water far over her head. And hot water at that. Sera quickly sorted through the possible answers, hoping to find one that would adequately inform

Amanda of realities of which she needed to be aware and yet leave her younger sisters innocent.

"Your uncle strikes me as the kind of man," she answered carefully, "who prefers significantly older and considerably more mature companions than those favored by Mr. Hopkins. And we'll say nothing further on the subject. It's a generally inappropriate one for young ladies."

"Then why did you talk about it?" Beatrice instantly asked.

And curiosity will someday kill the cat. But where cats had only nine lives, Beatrice apparently had thousands of them. Which, given her proclivities, was a very good thing. Sera gently smiled at her. "If I don't explain such matters to you, who will?"

"Uncle Carden?" Camille guessed.

Sera's stomach turned to lead even as she maintained her smile. The very thought of entrusting Carden Reeves with the social education of his brothers' daughters was something she would have preferred to avoid contemplating. But she had. Many times. It had been one of her first worries as they'd set sail and Belize had disappeared from sight. Of course, she'd assumed that he would be a man very much like his brother and could therefore be trusted to handle the responsibility ... well, responsibly. But having finally met him, she knew that she'd presumed too much. Carden Reeves was not the kind of man who appreciated prim and absolutely proper women. In fact, he probably didn't know any. And went well out of his way to evade any that might inadvertently cross his path.

She'd considered this possibility in the long days and nights at sea, but she'd refused to dwell on it. The ramifications had been too unpleasant. She hoped to remain with the girls, but was prepared to be thanked and sent on her way. She could endure that fate and had a plan of sorts for her life after that moment. But if she needed to remain with them to protect them, then she might well be placed in the position of having to beg for employment as their governess. She'd been forced by circumstances to beg once in her life and . . .

"Miss Sera?"

She deliberately and gratefully shut away the memories. "Yes, Beatrice?"

"What will happen to us if Uncle Carden doesn't ask us to stay with him?"

"He will, darling," she assured all of them. "You needn't worry yourselves about such things."

"He may ask us to stay," Amanda countered, "but it would be only because he thinks he must be polite. I don't think he much likes the idea of our being here. You could see it in his eyes when we were coming up the walk."

True. He'd have had an altogether different look in his eyes had one of them been a nephew. "As I said earlier, your uncle wasn't at his best in that moment and we must give him time to recover from his initial shock."

"What if he never recovers, Miss Sera?" Beatrice posed. "What if he truly doesn't want us to stay here? Where will we go?"

Men of Carden Reeves's social class did not throw their orphaned nieces into the street. People would speak badly of him for doing so. The girls might not be wanted or appreciated but their being offered a home was a certainty. It might not be what she had been envisioning for them, but it would be a roof over their heads, food on their plates, and clothes on their backs. There were millions of people in the world who couldn't hope for as much and she knew it. She also knew that another reassurance—no matter how sound and rational—would fall on still disbelieving ears. The girls wanted to be certain that there was another road to deliverance.

"My father had distant relations living in Devonshire," she lied. "If your uncle proves himself a complete ogre, we shall go in search of my family and see what we can make of ourselves as farmers."

Camille knitted her brows for a second and then said, "I don't know how to farm."

"Neither do I," Sera confessed, "but I'm willing to try new experiences."

"As we did with sailing," Beatrice pointed out happily, instantly accepting the possible adventure. "None of us—except Miss Sera—had ever been on a ship before we left Belize, but we did well with it after a bit. Remember how the captain told us we were excellent sailors?"

Camille wrinkled her nose. "I didn't like the frowing-up part."

"I wouldn't want to be a sailor," Amanda contributed. "They don't have any teeth."

Camille's entire face wrinkled this time as she added, "And they smell bad, too."

Beatrice tilted her head to the side and stared at the closed parlor doors. "Uncle Carden smells good."

Amanda offered a most unladylike snort and said, "I think he wears perfume."

Sera studied a painting on the far side of the room, pretending that she hadn't heard the comment. She didn't want to explain how Carden Reeves had come to have a woman's scent on him at midday. She didn't even want to think about it.

The realization came with all the power and surprise of a thunderbolt. She'd assumed that he was unmarried! The way he'd looked at her—all but getting himself a spoon—had suggested that he was accustomed to pursuing women for the possibility of conquest. And while some men discontinued the habit after taking a wife, some didn't. She knew that from bitter personal experience. Carden Reeves could be a married rake; the perfume clinging to him might well be that of his wife.

Sera sighed with relief. All the way here—through all

the doubts she'd entertained once it had been too late to change course—she'd imagined passing the girls into the arms of a loving aunt and uncle, of immersing them in a household full of noisy, cheerfully welcoming cousins.

As she'd stood on the doorstep explaining her presence, the dream had evaporated like smoke. Now . . . She strained to listen, hoping that from somewhere in the house she might hear the sounds of children's voices, children's feet. What she heard was the rattle of a tea cart, a moment of complete silence, and then the turning of the heavy brass knobs on the parlor doors.

The doors were pushed open and the cart rolled in. The young man pushing it was no servant. He didn't have the proper demeanor. And he was too finely dressed by half. Tall, well built, and with the greenest eyes she'd ever seen, he met her gaze and grinned before turning his attention to the girls.

"Good afternoon, ladies," he declared jauntily as he maneuvered the cart around the end of one settee. "Carden said he had four pretty callers, but I can see that he was understating things as usual."

He brought the well-laden cart to a halt at the side of a damask upholstered chair and straightened to his full—and considerable—height. His gaze came to Sera's. "I know it's hardly proper, but given the circumstances . . . Allow me to introduce myself. I'm John Aiden Terrell—called that only by my parents and simply Aiden by my friends—late of Saint Kitts and a friend of Carden's. His man, Sawyer, is out on errands and rather than subject you to poor hospitality, I'm taking up the slack in his absence. Tea, my dear ladies, is served."

Remembering the expectations taught in her childhood, Sera graciously moved to the chair beside the service. Seating herself, she quickly counted the teacups. Six. He intended to partake with them and expected Carden to do the same when he returned.

"Thank you, Mr. Terrell. It is a pleasure to meet you. I do hope you'll join us," she added, gesturing to the open end of the settee on her right. "Shall I pour?"

"Please," he said, splitting his coattails and lowering himself to the cushion shared with Camille. "Though it will take a few minutes more for the tea to be perfectly steeped."

Camille peered around him to consider the various items he'd brought. "The biscuits look delicious."

The smile John Aiden—Aiden—Terrell flashed Sera as he reached for the fine china plate spoke volumes and instantly set her at ease. Although a young man, he obviously had some experience with children. Enough to know a politely indirect plea when he heard one.

"And they are delicious," he said, offering Camille her choice from the plate. "Would you care for one, Miss . . . ?"

"I'm Camille," she answered, grinning as she looked up at him, a biscuit firmly in hand. "Thank you very much, Mr. Terrell."

"I'd guess that you're about five years old. I have a sister who's five, you know." He didn't wait for a reply but rose slightly and extended the plate toward the other settee, his gaze meeting Beatrice's as he said, "And you, Miss . . ."

"Beatrice." She took a biscuit and offered her thanks.

"I'd guess you're about seven or eight. Am I correct?"

"I'm seven."

"And I'm Miss Amanda Elizabeth Reeves. I'm nine."

Fighting a smile, and with one dark brow ever so slightly cocked, he offered Amanda the plate of biscuits, saying, "I would have guessed much older, Miss Reeves. You're very grown-up for nine."

"I'm told so quite frequently," she replied, selecting a biscuit of her own.

"I would imagine so," he agreed, his struggle to contain his smile growing more obvious.

The conversation between John Aiden Terrell and the girls continued, but Sera was aware of it only as a dull drone in the back of her perceptions. Carden Reeves, dressed in a finely tailored suit, filled the parlor doorway. Good Lord, he was handsome. Wickedly so. He'd have had to have been a saint not to use it to his advantage. No doubt even nuns noted his presence on the street. The appraising look in his eyes as he met her gaze told her what she already well knew—Carden Reeves was no saint. The slow warmth spreading through her also told her that she was no nun; she was a fool.

Angry with herself, Sera tore her gaze from his and focused it deliberately on the exchange going on around her.

She'd no more than done so when John Aiden seemed to become aware of his friend's presence. He turned toward the door, saying, "Ah, Carden. You're decent. Care to join us? I brought an extra cup."

"Actually," she heard him reply, "I thought I might leave you to carry on the conversation with my nieces while Mrs. Treadwell and I speak privately."

There was no way that Mr. Terrell could politely refuse to do so and no way she could avoid the necessary exchange. She'd have to make the best of it, have to keep her wits about her and her memories near at hand.

"I shall be back shortly, darlings," Sera said, starting to rise. Mr. Terrell vaulted to his feet and offered his hand in gallant assistance. She accepted it, smiling bravely at the girls, and adding, "Please continue to mind your manners."

They nodded. Aiden Terrell continued to smile. And Carden Reeves slowly, openly, measured her from hair to hem as she moved to join him at the doorway. His assessment wasn't nearly as disconcerting as her heart-tripping, wildly hopeful reaction to it.

CHAPTER 3

Calling herself the weakest of fools, she tamped down her emotions and followed him a short distance up the main hallway, silently nodding her thanks when he stepped aside and allowed her to precede him into what was obviously his study. The walls were darkly paneled, the windows of leaded glass and framed by dark green damask draperies. A thick, fringed carpet of Oriental design muffled her footsteps as she made her way to the chair opposite an imposing mahogany desk. Behind it was a wall of shelves containing an odd assortment of miniature structures. There were several bridges and almost a dozen of what she could only think of as tiny dollhouses. The why of it all became clear as her gaze moved to the farthest corner of the room. Propped on an easel was a detailed plan for a home. Notations had been made all around the margins and boldly sweeping arrows indicated where they applied.

Carden Reeves was an architect. She looked back to the models on the shelves behind his desk, this time better able to appreciate what they represented. The lines were clean and uncomplicated, the overall feeling of the structures stately. And while they were generally unpretentious, they were nevertheless unmistakably homes for the monied class.

"Won't you please have a seat?"

Sera quietly situated herself in the visitor's chair and then waited, hands folded demurely in her lap, for him to take up his place on the other side of the desk.

He went only to the corner nearest her, leaned against it, and summoned a smile that looked more painful than anything else. "I find myself in a socially awkward situation, Mrs. Treadwell."

She'd been anticipating the rebuke. "I understand completely," Sera hurriedly assured him. "I would have sent you word of our pending arrival had there been a reasonable chance of any correspondence arriving here before we did. Unfortunately, we didn't have the luxury of delaying our departure from Belize and so couldn't engage in such niceties."

She paused to add emphasis to the politeness of her next words. "I sincerely apologize for having so surprised you. I hope that it's not an altogether unpleasant one."

"Actually," he replied dryly, "it is."

She'd lived all of her life in the backwaters of the empire, and while the limits of good manners were frequently pushed in those environs, they were never completely abandoned. To be in London, in the very heart of Great Britain . . . She'd expected more. In all honesty, she replied, "I truly don't know what one is supposed to say in such a situation, Mr. Reeves."

He snorted, a look of disgusted resignation turning down the corners of his mouth. "I think saying nothing at all would be the greatest blessing for which I could hope."

He expected her to sit there mute and passive? To quietly wait for him to vent his displeasure on her for doing the only thing she could have reasonably done? He was indisputably handsome, but he was too arrogant by half. It wasn't in her to bow to any man. Not ever again. And the consequences be damned. When it came down to it, pride was all that stood between a person and abject humiliation.

"Do you," she asked icily, "like my late husband, prefer your women silent?"

"Your husband's dead?" he asked, his gaze dropping momentarily to her left hand.

"Presumably," Sera supplied crisply. "He was serving as Arthur and Mary's guide when they went off on their ill-fated expedition."

He nodded, knitted his brows, and considered the carpet for a few seconds before quietly asking, "Have the authorities formally declared any of them to be deceased?"

Seraphina sighed softly, her anger melting away. He was calmer than when she'd first delivered the disturbing news, but it was obvious that he was still willing to hope for a happy outcome. "There are no authorities in Belize, Mr. Reeves," she explained gently. "It is a wild, ungoverned place that no empire on earth feels obliged to claim. People rarely go into the jungle. Those that do, seldom come out of it. That is a fact of life and, in this particular situation, death, in Belize."

He raked his fingers through his hair, then stood up and began to pace as he fairly growled, "And a fact of death in England is that a seemingly healthy man of sixty years could fall face forward into his morning porridge and leave the rest of us to muddle through the mess."

Sensing that there was much she didn't understand about his circumstances and that she'd be better able to gauge her own responses if she could get him to explain, she rose from her chair so she could watch him. Gently, she said, "You made mention of this unfortunate porridge incident in your starkly brief letter to Arthur."

He stopped in his tracks and met her gaze with a cocked brow. "You read my letter to Arthur?"

"In his absence, I had no choice but to open it and read it." She decided that there was no point in detailing her reasoning for doing so. Or admitting that she'd appropriated the two hundred pounds he'd enclosed. "I believe you said the man's name was Percival."

It took him a long moment, but he eventually nodded and resumed his pacing, his hands clasped behind his back, his gaze riveted on the carpet passing beneath his feet. "There were three of us," he began. "Percival and then Arthur. Both by our father—the late and very great Lord Gavin Reeves, fifth Earl of Lansdown, and his first wife. I'm the third son, the only child by his second wife."

He stopped in front of one of the windows and, his back to her, continued, saying, "Percival and his wife, Honoria, had no children. Arthur, as it turns out, managed to produce only daughters before his departure from earthly concerns." He sighed heavily and the notes of anger rang clearly in his words as he added, "Which means that if he's well and truly dead, then I have to become the new earl."

"I gather that I'm expected to feel some pity for you," Sera retorted before she could think better of it.

"I don't want to be an earl."

His anger had been replaced by a bleakness that she suspected was founded on the same emotions expressed by the condemned when they said *I don't want to be hanged.* Part of her regretted the twist of fate that had taken Carden Reeves down a road he had no wish to travel. Another part of her, the more pragmatic side, suggested that there were far worse fates that could befall a man than being elevated to the status of a peer. However unexpectedly.

"Life seldom deals us the cards we'd like to have," she observed, hoping that she could balance her sentiments to provide him some measure of consolation. "Given that reality, it is up to each of us to do the best we can with what we have. And forgive me for being so blunt, but I fail to see how being a peer of the realm poses any great hardship on a person's circumstances. If anything, I should think that it would give one an incredible advantage in life."

He shook his head slowly and she couldn't tell whether the sound he made was wry laughter or choked-back tears. "We'll have to agree to disagree on that point," he finally said, turning away from the window to face her. "The subject of my nieces is one, however, on which we will need to come to terms."

So very businesslike; he probably exhibited greater passion about the tailoring of his suits. "Are you willing to take them in?" she asked, silently resolving to be instantly gone with the girls if he so much as hesitated in offering assurances.

"Only a heartless man would turn away children—family—in need."

It was certainly a declaration, but hardly the enthusiastically welcoming response she wanted to hear. "Do you have a heart, my lord?"

Sera barely kept her jaw from sagging in amazement as he appeared to give the matter considerable thought. "Of a sort," he said slowly, somewhat regretfully. "However," he added with far greater spirit, "I am, at the core of it, a bachelor, Mrs. Treadwell. A happily and firmly ensconced-in-my-ways bachelor. My home is not a wholesome place for impressionable children. Especially little girls."

Yes, Seraphina silently agreed, so she'd initially surmised on her own. The hope of a loving aunt and cheerful cousins had been nothing more than wishful thinking. Unless, of course, Carden Reeves was willing to change the general situation for his nieces' benefit.

"More importantly," he added, interrupting her speculations, "I have absolutely no desire to change the way I live. I know nothing of caring for children and I have no interest whatsoever in learning how it's done."

Handsome. Arrogant. And incredibly selfish. "So you intend to provide for your nieces financially, but to have them reside elsewhere?" she summarized.

"Yes. It's the best solution," Carden replied. The way she lifted her chin told him that she thought otherwise. If he had any good sense at all, he'd declare the matter settled and get on with the rest of the details. But, in just the few minutes they'd been alone together, he'd discovered that good sense had nothing whatsoever to do with the feelings she stirred in him. She didn't shrink back from a contest as so many women did and he liked that. He liked that enormously. Almost as much as he liked the exotic accent of her speech—which became more pronounced when she was even the slightest bit irritated.

No, no sensible man would pretend ignorance and ask, "Don't you agree, Mrs. Treadwell?"

"My lord, your nieces have lost the underpinnings of their world," she replied, trying, he knew, to sound calm. She didn't in the least; her *o*s had broadened and he knew that if she continued on, so would her *a*s. It was a fascinating thing to hear. And her eyes . . . Blue fire.

"Their parents have died. They've had to live in poverty and then abruptly leave behind the only home they've ever known. I think it important that they have an opportunity to regain a sense of stability. You are the only family they have left. If you were to send them away, they couldn't help but infer that they're unwanted. They're very intelligent girls."

If they were just half as intelligent as their nurse . . . "I'm a complete stranger to them," Carden countered realistically. "I seriously doubt that Arthur ever uttered my name in their presence. I don't think their little hearts will be permanently broken should I send them to live at the country house."

"To be cared for by servants?" she protested. "Is that

your idea of what makes for a sense of family and a happy childhood?"

No, that had been his childhood and it had been a miserably lonely one. He'd wish it only on his worst enemy. Nevertheless, despite his regrets over it, his past had shaped his present and destined his future; he wasn't any sort of a family man and he knew it. His nieces would be far better off without him as a daily part of their lives. "They'd have you, Mrs. Treadwell. Wouldn't you be able to provide them stability and see that they have happy memories of their childhoods?"

"You intend for me to remain with them?"

"You are their nurse, aren't you?" he responded, puzzled by the unexpected twist in conversational direction. She had thought to be released from her duties?

"I'm a friend of the family, your lordship. I agreed to be responsible for the girls in what was to have been the brief absence of their parents."

Ah, there it was. Mrs. Treadwell was no common servant and she wanted him aware of her social status. And, now that he thought about it, he could see that he'd made an assumption that couldn't be supported by the obvious facts. This woman didn't carry herself as servants did, didn't speak as they did. She was, he realized, a woman of his own social class. Or rather the social class that had been comfortably his until less than an hour ago. Everything had changed since then. Not the least of which was his having acquired the responsibility for the proper upbringing of three young females, a task for which he was wholly unqualified. And if Mrs. Treadwell thought she was going to be allowed to drop them on his doorstep like unwanted kittens and then walk away . . . Not as long as he had breath in his body and money in his pocket.

"Have you made plans or commitments that would preclude remaining with them?" he asked with what he hoped passed for nonchalance.

"No," she said slowly, quietly. "I have not."

Then, if he was reading between the lines correctly, there was no man who could claim her fidelity. Carden smiled. "Is there anything that would prevent you from continuing to be responsible for my nieces' care and education?"

"No, there is not."

"Good. Then the matter is settled," he happily declared. "I assure you that you'll receive generous compensation for your services."

Her smile was fragile and strained. Color flooded her cheeks, turning them a lusciously distracting shade of cinnamon rose. Damn the fashion mavens who thought women ought to be dressed to their necks in the daylight hours. What he wouldn't have given in that moment to see the swells of her breasts flood with color, as well. But there would come a time and soon enough. He'd make sure of it—and that this exotic creature had a gown worthy of her beauty.

"Will we be leaving for the country residence within the hour?"

Carden thought he detected a bit of sarcasm in her words, but quickly decided that he'd been inattentive and was simply imagining it. "I suppose you have traveled a long way and would appreciate a bit of rest, wouldn't you?"

"Our journey has made us quite resilient. We're perfectly capable of soldiering on. I wouldn't want to inconvenience you."

There was no mistaking the underlying tone this time. Precisely when had her feathers gotten ruffled? Although their exchange had been taut a few times as the result of minor disagreements, they'd been doing tolerably well up to now. Hoping to ferret out some clue as to what had disturbed her, he observed, "You have a tart tongue, Mrs. Treadwell."

Her smile was soft but her eyes had darkened to the color of steel. It was a most amazing transformation. "My apologies."

"You don't mean them."

"Of course I don't, but it's what one is expected to say when called out for being impolite. The other half of the expectation is that you are to accept the apology without comment and change the subject of conversation."

"I don't like playing by the rules."

And I don't enjoy being appraised like a plum pudding, Sera silently countered. Unwilling to openly censure a man on whose benevolence the girls largely depended, Sera marshaled what composure she could and replied, "Then it's undoubtedly for the best that the girls will not be under your daily influence."

"And they're going to be that much better off being under yours?" he challenged, grinning and tilting his head to the side in the same way that Beatrice did when intrigued by some new discovery.

And in his gesture, small though it was, she made several important discoveries. The first was that beneath the rakish persona of Carden Reeves lay an unaffected man who possessed both unbridled curiosity and a sense of humor. The glimpse of the real man led instantly to the second realization: she found him attractive in a way she'd never thought of a man before. It was also impossible to remain angry at him. *That* revelation thoroughly flustered her. It frightened her as well. The boyish Carden Reeves posed a very real danger to her good sense and what little remained of her pride and virtue.

"If you feel that I'd be an inappropriate influence on your nieces, your lordship," she offered, her heart racing, "please feel free to hire a more qualified person. I'll gladly remain until you can do so, of course."

"The country house is under renovation," he said, completely ignoring her attempt to escape. He made a sweeping gesture toward the drawing on the easel in the corner. "A rather extensive one, I'm afraid. Percival started it just weeks before he did the facer into his breakfast. It'll be largely uninhabitable until the end of the season."

Sera could see distinct advantages to being well distant from the girls' uncle. Temptation out of sight was generally well out of mind. "So we're to go where in the meantime? Have you a second country home?"

He shook his head. "No, sorry. For the short term, you'll remain here. I'll make what accommodations are necessary to keep my nieces' naïveté intact."

"Thank you," she replied tightly, wondering just how long the London season was and how deeply his self-discipline ran.

One corner of his mouth quirked up and a spark of devilment brightened his blue-gray eyes. "That was very gracious."

"I'm trying."

"Yes, you are," he laughingly teased. "Very trying, indeed."

Her heart was thundering against her breast again and her only coherent thought was that she needed to get away from him before she did or said something that would embarrass her for the rest of her life. "Is our conversation concluded, your lordship?"

"Not quite." He returned to his desk and half-sat on the corner, adding, "There are several matters I've yet to address."

Good Lord. How was it that having seen a glimpse of the real Carden Reeves made the arrogant side of him more tolerable? She fell back on the strategy that had served her well on the front steps. "And these matters are?"

"First, my nieces look like they've come off the streets of Cheapside. I expect you to see that they're properly attired before the week is out. Don't concern yourself with the expense of seeing it done. I can well afford it."

Sera nodded her acceptance of the task. "Secondly?"

"I meant what I said about not wanting to be an earl,"
he went on earnestly. "There are incredible restrictions and
unpleasant realities that go with the title and I intend to
avoid them at all costs. Should anyone ask you about Arthur, I expect you to maintain that his return to England
is imminent."

"That would be a lie," Sera protested.

"Not necessarily." He cocked a brow and crossed his
arms over his chest. "But even if it is, you're to maintain
it. I'm a third son and intend to stay one for as long as I
possibly can. You are *not* to address me as 'your lordship,'
either in public or private. Is that clear?"

"Quite," she all but snapped, not liking one whit the
position in which he'd placed her.

"Good."

"Is there a third point on which you wish me to be
equally clear?"

He pursed his lips and squinted toward the closed doors
of the study. "I don't want to trip over girlish things as I
walk through my home," he said after a moment. "Make
sure that they confine their belongings to their floor of the
house."

So imperious, so selfish. "Are they to be physically
restricted to the schoolroom and their bedchambers?"

Carden chuckled and winked at her. "There's that tart
tongue again, Mrs. Treadwell."

"My apologies, Mr. Reeves."

She hadn't been any more sincere in this apology than
she had in the one she'd offered before. A most interesting
woman, this Mrs. Treadwell. On the surface of things, she
held to social expectations, but, beneath all the polite niceties, she didn't honor the rules any more than he did. A
woman after his own heart. He was going to enjoy having

her around just for the breath of fresh feminine air she provided.

"I expect my nieces to generally conduct themselves as do other young ladies of their social class," Carden replied, deliberately skirting her query. "I'll leave Sawyer to inform you of the daily household schedule. I'll plan to dine in on a fairly regular basis for the duration of your stay. In the interest of creating a sense of family for them, they'll dine with me. Please have my nieces dress appropriately for the evening meal."

"Of course."

"You'll be expected to join us, as well," Carden went on, working to contain his smile, "so see that you have suitable attire for the occasion. At my expense, of course." She hesitated and he could practically hear the mental wheels whirling in her brain.

"Thank you," she said stiffly.

He tilted his head and grinned. "That was painful for you to say, wasn't it?"

If her heart hadn't been skittering all over her chest, she might have acted on the urge to slap him across his very handsome cheek. Instead, she drew her shoulders back, lifted her chin, and fixed her gaze on a point just over his incredibly wide shoulder. "I've never been in employ, Mr. Reeves. I'm not at all comfortable with it."

"You'll adjust in time."

"I doubt that very much," she retorted icily.

He shrugged. "If you're truly uncomfortable with the notion, perhaps we could negotiate an exchange of sorts. A service for a service."

"Perhaps," Sera repeated dubiously. She could well imagine just what services he had in mind. As humiliating as it was being in employ, it was a condition far more honorable than being a decidedly temporary mistress. She took a deliberate step back, asking, "Are we concluded?"

"I believe so."

"Then I'll return to your nieces and the affable Mr. Terrell," she declared, turning and starting for the doors.

The handle was in her hand, escape just a mere second away, when he called out, "Oh, there is one more thing."

She paused, waiting, but when he said nothing further, she drew a deep breath and turned back to face him. "And that would be?"

His smile was devilish again. "Introductions may be necessary from time to time. Do you have a Christian name?"

"Yes."

Carden laughed outright. Damn if she didn't give as good as she got. "What is it?"

"Seraphina."

"For the angels?" he asked, his grin so wide his face actually hurt.

The color was flooding her cheeks again when she opened the door and stepped out of the room saying simply, "My parents had illusions."

"I don't," he whispered as he watched her pull the door closed behind her. "Seraphina Treadwell." He liked the sound of it; it rolled off his tongue very nicely. He liked the woman who bore the name, too. She was so delightfully different from all the other women in his world. No coy eyelash-batting. No miss-ish airs. No obedient subservience. No pretending that she was physically unaware of him. Seraphina Treadwell challenged his mind and made his blood race. Oh, yes, he was definitely going to enjoy having her under his roof for a time.

Pushing himself off his desk, he crossed to the sideboard and poured himself a brandy. Lifting his glass toward the doors, he said softly, "To the seduction of exotic angels."

CHAPTER 4

Sera stood at the window of her room and listened. While all three of them had rendered dramatic protests over retiring for an afternoon nap, the girls had nevertheless gone to their nicely appointed room—where they'd managed to resist all of two minutes before slipping off into their dreams. Alone in the silence, Seraphina looked out over the gloomy outlines of London's rooftops and assured herself that she'd made the right decision, the only one she could have made. It didn't matter that London was dreary, damp, and bone-numbingly cold. Seeing the sun and blue skies wasn't significant among her concerns. Being comfortably warm wasn't nearly as important as making the girls' future secure. She could light a fire in the hearth if she wanted.

And she could leave London, too. Eventually. Sera slowly shook her head. To think that, like all far-flung Britons, she'd hoped to come here someday, to make what amounted to a holy pilgrimage to the center of the British Empire. Now that she had accomplished the quest, she couldn't help but think that the dream was ever so much nicer than the reality. England certainly was an interesting place to visit, but, from what she could tell to this point, it didn't hold much promise of ever feeling like home.

Not that she truly had one of those, she reminded herself. Her parents' house in Jamaica had been taken for
unpaid taxes. The tent that had housed them in Belize had
long since rotted away. What Gerald had considered a
suitable dwelling had no doubt collapsed during the first
heavy rain of the past winter. It had been on the verge of
doing so for the last two years. Very much like their marriage.

Sera sighed and managed a smile of sorts. The very
best part of being in London was that it would be the last
place on earth Gerald would think to look for her. Her
smile faded and she crossed her arms over her midriff to
ward off a deepening chill. Gerald was dead. She was free
of him, free of the humiliation and the poverty. God had
taken pity on her, rewarded her for having endured. Gerald
Treadwell and the misery of an arranged, loveless marriage were in the past. Never again would she willingly
travel down that path.

Which, she suspected, Carden Reeves knew instinctively. Her mother had always maintained that men had a
sixth sense when it came to assessing the prospects for
casual seduction, that they could tell by merely looking
which women were in the marriage market and which
viewed matrimony as nothing more than human bondage.
The latter—strictly from their point of view, of course—
made for much safer liaisons. From the female point of
view . . . Carden Reeves was clearly the kind of man her
mother had admonished her to avoid at all costs.

Sera smiled weakly. Her mother hadn't mentioned how
flattering the attention of such a man could be. Or how
exciting. The assumption that the strength of her moral
fiber would prevent her from being dazzled appeared, at
the moment, to be not only too optimistic, but also a bit
naïve. Thank heavens for the power of good judgment and
common sense; they were her best defenses against weakness and temptation.

She'd once been weak and surrendered to the temptation of what had been offered as a certain future. She'd learned her lessons well—albeit the hard way. Her life had begun anew the moment she'd led the girls up the gangplank and set sail for England. Today and all of her tomorrows were hers to make of as she willed. She could and would make her life a happy and fulfilling one. Sera rubbed her hands briskly over her upper arms, turned away from the window, and quietly added, "Or freeze in the attempt."

The fire was burning brightly and, best of all, providing a lovely sheet of warmth when someone knocked on her door. Seraphina frowned at the panel and regretfully abandoned her seat on the hearth. The chill returned midway across the room and was already settling back into her marrow by the time she opened the door.

A tall, white-haired man stood at stiff attention on the other side. His arms at his side, his gloved fingers curled slightly back into his palms, he looked over her head, cleared his throat softly, and said, "Good afternoon, Mrs. Treadwell. I am Sawyer."

Ah, yes, the man whom Carden Reeves had said was going to inform her of the daily household schedule. "Good afternoon, sir."

"Mr. Reeves requests your presence in the parlor to meet the new housekeeper."

There had been no servants in her childhood and she wasn't quite sure how one was supposed to speak to a butler. Hoping that she wasn't botching things too badly, she replied, "Please tell Mr. Reeves that I will be along very shortly. And thank you, Sawyer."

"Very good." His gaze dropped just long enough for her to note that he had dark brown eyes that were clear and quick like those of a bird. Once again he looked over

her head and cleared his throat. "And may I extend my
welcome to Haven House. If there is anything I can do to
be of service to you, please do not hesitate to ask."

Haven House? If ever there was an aptly named
place . . . "Thank you."

"Dinner is served promptly at seven. Will you and Mr.
Reeves's nieces be dining downstairs this evening? Or
would you prefer to have your meal served in the schoolroom?"

Carden Reeves had issued a command and she wasn't
in a position to disobey. "We'll dine downstairs, Sawyer."

"I will inform Cook." He bowed, again met her gaze
only momentarily, saying, "Madam," and turned and
marched away.

Sera quietly closed the door, listened for sounds of the
girls stirring, and, hearing only the popping warmth of the
fire, sighed and resigned herself to following in Sawyer's
dignified wake.

She found Carden Reeves precisely where Sawyer had
said she would. He was standing in front of the unlit
hearth in the parlor, his arm lying causally along the mantel, the very picture of wealth and ease.

He straightened at the sight of her and smiled broadly.
"Ah, Seraphina, do come in."

Seraphina? She barely had time to mentally register the
familiarity. As he spoke, a rather large mass of black rose
from the settee and turned toward her. The woman was of
middling height, but with wide shoulders and a bosom that
filled the bodice of her black gabardine dress all the way
to the waist. She had a pleasant smile that reached to her
soft brown eyes and waves of wiry gray hair that peeked
out from beneath the edge of her black straw hat. A resilient woman in mourning, Sera decided as she returned
the smile.

"Allow me to introduce the new housekeeper," Carden began. "Seraphina, this is Mrs. Blaylock. She comes with impeccable references and considerable experience. Mrs. Blaylock, may I present Mrs. Seraphina Treadwell, late of Belize, and the companion of my young nieces."

Mrs. Blaylock dropped a brief curtsy. "It's a pleasure, madam."

Again Sera regretted the lack of servants in her earlier life. Mrs. Blaylock, however, didn't seem to be as formal as Sawyer. Trusting her to overlook any social gaffes, Sera replied, "The pleasure is mine, Mrs. Blaylock. Welcome to the household."

Carden didn't give either of them a chance to exchange additional pleasantries. "Mrs. Blaylock will be bringing her daughter, Anne, with her to serve as the upstairs maid. I've instructed her to hire within the week a second girl to serve the downstairs. Do you have any preferences for the type of young woman she selects?"

As though she knew anything at all about such matters, Sera silently scoffed. Not that she was willing to publicly admit her ignorance. It was for precisely these kinds of occasions that people had invented good manners. She met his gaze and confidently replied, "I trust that Mrs. Blaylock well knows the requirements of the job and is perfectly capable of hiring someone who will perform their duties to the satisfaction of all."

His smile said he recognized her effort for the evasion that it was. His wink was fleeting but congratulatory nonetheless.

"Mrs. Blaylock," he said, motioning broadly toward the parlor doors and the foyer beyond, "I will see you, your daughter, and your respective belongings tomorrow morning, then?"

Taking her cue, the new housekeeper bobbed another curtsy, saying, "Very good, sir. And thank you, sir." She had taken only two steps toward her exit when Sawyer magically appeared in the foyer, her cloak draped over his left arm.

Sera was watching the two of them move toward the front door when Carden Reeves quietly asked, "Are you not happy with her, Seraphina?"

"She seems to be a nice woman," Sera replied coolly, slowly squaring up to him. "If you say her references are excellent, I'll take your word on it."

"Then why the look of displeasure?"

She took a fortifying breath. "I don't recall having granted you permission to address me by my Christian name."

"You didn't." He grinned. "Seraphina."

"Mr. Reeves—"

"Carden."

Sera sighed and forced a smile. Firmly, pointedly, she began again. "Mr. Reeves—"

"Car-den."

"I am not your nieces' companion," she countered, temporarily abandoning her first effort for a new one. "I am their governess. As I recall, we came to that agreement less than three hours ago."

"Yes," he agreed, nodding and moving slowly closer, "but you expressed some discomfort over the status of employee and I've been giving the matter some thought with the idea of how to make you feel better about it all. I think that 'companion' works rather nicely, don't you?"

"Why are you the least little bit concerned over my feelings on the matter?" she asked warily, suddenly feeling too warm.

"I would prefer that you be happy and comfortable."

Resisting the urge to tug at her collar, she took a step back, asking, "Why would you care?"

He leaned a hip against the table behind the settee and crossed his arms over his chest. His smile was bright. And roguishly inviting. "Are you always so ungrateful?"

"I'm not ungrateful," she corrected, her heart racing at an embarrassing rate. "I'm suspicious."

"All right, then," he said, chuckling. "Are you always so suspicious?"

"Yes, in point of fact, I am." *And especially of handsome men who go out of their way to be charming.*

He tilted his head to the side in that boyish way of his. "Why?"

A direct question required an equally direct answer. "It has been my experience that men do not do things for others—especially women—out of the kindness of their hearts," she supplied honestly. "They are, instead, generally motivated by hopes of being rewarded in one way or another."

"You haven't known very many gentlemen in your life, have you?"

Seraphina considered the man in front of her and laughingly replied, "I've always found gentlemen to be the worst of the lot. Their refined manners tend to serve as both an excellent disguise and an effective distraction."

"Wolves in sheep's clothing."

"A most accurate description, Mr. Reeves."

"Carden," he instantly amended. His eyes sparkled and his smile broadened yet another dazzling degree. "And just what reward do you think I might be hoping to get from you?"

"I can't say." Or rather she wouldn't, she silently added. Ladies didn't discuss such matters with men. Ever.

"You don't know me well enough?"

"That's a fair statement," she allowed, relieved that he'd been mannered enough to afford her the avenue of evasion.

He nodded, studied the carpet at her feet for a long moment, and then lifted his gaze to meet hers. His smile still bright and broad, he straightened, saying, "Since we're to be existing under the same roof for the immediate future, it would probably be in the best interests of harmony for us to become better acquainted, would it not?"

Her heart skittered and her mind raced. Better acquainted? Her every instinct said that even the least bit of familiarity was a dangerous thing where Carden Reeves was concerned. The man didn't strike her as the sort to have female acquaintances. In fact, were she pressed to wager, she'd hazard that the women in his life could be divided into two broad categories: paramours of his past and those of his future. Even Mrs. Blaylock had cause for concern. Heaven help her daughter, Anne.

"And then there are the girls to consider, as well," he went on. "We must work together in order to see that their needs are met in a timely and proper manner. To my thinking, good communication and a full understanding of each other would be requirements of achieving that end. Don't you agree?"

It was a transparent ploy, using her devotion to his nieces to achieve his own ends. It was just the sort of thing she should have expected of a dedicated rake. "I recognize manipulation when I see it, Mr. Reeves," she said. "And I find—"

"Carden," he corrected yet again, the brilliance of his smile undampened by her rebuke. "And since you can see through me so clearly, I trust that you'll be able to adequately protect yourself. Would you care for a tour of the public rooms of the house? There are several of them which I'm sure you'll want to use in the course of the girls' education."

The man simply didn't stop. Like a hurricane, he held to his course, relentlessly plowing his way through all attempts to deter him. Battling him on every little point had proven to be not only exhausting, but also fruitless. Better that she conserve her strength for the contests that truly mattered. "A brief tour would be fine," she said, relenting.

"When would you like to undertake it? After dinner, perhaps?"

He presented his arm. "Why delay? There's no time like the present."

Good manners lay in tucking her arm around his and walking at his side. Good sense lay in ignoring his gesture and following at least a half-dozen paces to the rear—well out of arm's reach. What would her mother have advised her to do? Sera wondered. Neither, she realized. Maria Magdalena Miller would have reminded her daughter that she was in this predicament because she hadn't remained in Belize to stoically await the emergence of her husband from the jungle. A good wife would have never set out on her own course. If she now found herself in a difficult situation, then it was of her own making and thus fully deserved.

Carden watched the emotions play across her features. Surprise, wariness, and then confusion. And now . . . Anger, judging by the set of her jaw and the defiant light blazing in the depths of her eyes. He braced himself, knowing that while he hadn't overtly pressed the bounds of propriety, he'd definitely given them a solidly oblique push. Seraphina Treadwell would be perfectly within rights to pin back his ears.

To his everlasting surprise, she stepped close and slipped her arm around his, resting her hand genteelly on his forearm. The color in her cheeks, high since the moment she'd come into the room, was deepening by the second. Concerned that she might reconsider her acceptance and withdraw if he gave her so much as half a chance, he immediately moved out of the room with her.

They'd barely stepped into the foyer when she spoke. "May I ask you a question?"

"Certainly."

"Do you squire every female guest about the public rooms of your home?"

Carden grinned. "Only those who will be staying a while." He turned his head so that he could see her face as he added, "You're a member of a very select group. In fact, you're the only member."

"How fortunate I am."

Not that she actually thought so, he knew. There was a tension to her, a stiffness to the way she moved and held herself. He could feel it radiating out of her hand and into his arm. It was her good fortune that he was very skilled at melting ladies' tensions. "It's not every day that a man acquires a beautiful houseguest from Belize."

"I'm originally from Jamaica," she clarified, ignoring the compliment. "My father undertook a research project in Belize and wanted Mother and I to join him."

He knew he was being guided away from the truly personal, but since her past was something about which he was curious anyway, he obediently asked, "What sort of research?"

"He was a botanist," she supplied, seeming to relax a bit. "Mother was largely disinterested in his work and so I—being too young to resist—was pressed into being his assistant."

Carden gestured as they passed a set of open doors. "As you no doubt recall, this is my study. And your late husband . . . Was he a botanist, as well?"

"No," she answered and then hesitated. After seeming to carefully decide on her words, she added, "He was something of an adventurer wrapped in a business suit."

Ah, no great love lost. Just to be absolutely sure, though, he casually pressed, "I gather from your tone that the marriage wasn't an altogether happy one."

"From what I've seen, few arranged marriages are," she countered noncommittally as he led her into the library. Or, more accurately, what was supposed to be a library.

Drawing her arm from his, she stepped away to peruse the meager contents of the mahogany shelves. Without looking at him she said, "It's an interesting collection, Mr. Reeves."

"Carden."

She turned her head and met his gaze. "I'm aware of that. I simply choose to ignore it."

If she could choose to ignore an issue, then so could he. "As libraries go, mine is underwhelming. My friend Barrett has described it as being decidedly heavy on furniture and lean on books. You'll meet Barrett at dinner this evening."

The look she shot him just before she turned back to the shelves said she knew he was playing a game of tit for tat. It also promised that she wouldn't abandon her commitment to formality. He watched as she trailed a fingertip over the leather spines of his collection. She had truly beautiful hands, delicate and graceful. God, what he wouldn't give to have her draw such a line over his ribs and down the length of his torso. The back of the sofa was high. He could stand behind her, slip his arms around her waist, and nibble at her delectable nape until she let him draw her to the sofa and lay her down. Assuming they could be reasonably quiet about it, no one passing by would even know they were there. Someday . . .

How soon? he wondered. How long would it take to melt her frosty, formal defenses? Not that time really mattered to him. He had enough experience with women to know that Seraphina Treadwell would be well worth whatever wait he had to endure.

Still, betting was an enjoyable pastime and setting himself the challenge of meeting a deadline would make the seduction even more exciting. A week. Yes, he'd set his goal at one week. By Thursday next, she'd be in his bed. Happily and contentedly naked, her dark hair fanned—

"It would appear," she said, shattering his fantasy, "that the vast majority of your books relate to mathematics and engineering of one sort or another."

"Yes." He swallowed hard and stuffed his hands into his trouser pockets, casually blousing the drape of his jacket. More interested in distracting than edifying her, he quickly added, "Those are my primary areas of academic interest. I'm an architect."

"I surmised that earlier today," she said, nodding and offering him a tentative smile. "I saw the drawing on the easel in your study and the models on the shelves behind your desk. I noted that you had some bridges as well as houses."

"I was an engineer in Her Majesty's Army for a time," he supplied with a dismissive shrug. "I'm assuming that you brought with you those books Arthur owned?"

"Yes. And my father's collection, as well." She gave him another of her faint, hesitant smiles. He was struggling against the impulse to wrap her in his arms when she continued. "Neither is particularly large, of course. Quality books are something of a rarity in the farther corners of the empire. Arthur's library, in following his interests, centers around ancient history. I hope you'll be willing to find room in here for it?"

"Of course," he answered, deciding he'd best move them along before temptation got the better of him. Presenting his arm again, he offered, "And obviously there's room to store your father's, as well. Presuming that your father's titles follow in his interests, it will round out the library quite nicely, won't it?"

She closed the distance she'd put between them earlier, saying, "There should be a sufficiently broad spectrum that the girls won't soon outgrow it."

It pleased him that she didn't hesitate to slip her arm around his this time. It was a small step, but it was in a forward direction. "Have my nieces developed any pronounced intellectual interests as yet?" he asked, leading her out of the library and toward their next destination.

"Beatrice definitely follows in her father's footsteps and

can ably discuss both the ancient Egyptian and Sumerian cultures," she explained, her voice suddenly more animated than he'd ever heard it. "Camille, so far, seems to be interested only in bugs and small—preferably furry—animals. You'll be pleased to know that Amanda, like yourself, enjoys mathematics and the physical sciences."

"Well, if nothing else, it should make for interesting dinner conversation," he laughingly observed, drawing her through the breakfast room. "And what are your interests, Seraphina?"

"I draw and paint some."

Ah, so very mundane. Every female over the age of twelve slapped thick layers of oil paint onto canvases and proudly called them landscapes. He'd truly expected Sera to enjoy diversions that were a bit more unconventional. "Perhaps you would show me some of your work," he suggested gallantly. As always. Women liked to have their talents praised. The honesty of it seemed to matter very little to them.

"If you'd like."

She had the most interesting ability to provide the expected, polite reply and yet—with the very same words—fully convey her true thoughts. He didn't have the slightest doubt that she'd willingly share her artwork with him when—and only when—hell turned to ice. The why of her attitude intrigued him. Did she, unlike most women, know that she lacked talent? he wondered as he opened a door and withdrew his arm.

Stepping aside to allow her to precede him, he considered yet another possibility. Her reluctance might come from the fact that her subjects were the sort that ladies didn't view in the company of gentlemen. Aiden's mother was an artist whose work had created something of a minor scandal. It could well be that Seraphina's work wasn't nearly as stodgy and banal as he'd presumed.

"Oh, dear."

For the second time in less than ten minutes, Carden found himself abruptly pulled from a pleasant fantasy. He blinked to bring reality into clearer focus. Sera was moving slowly down the center walkway of his conservatory, reaching out to gently touch the crisp, brown leaves that lined the path. It had all looked considerably greener the last time he'd been in here. Which, he realized, had been the day he'd taken possession of the house.

Sera, examining one particularly pathetic-looking specimen, made a whimpering sound that prompted him to explain, "The gardener remained in the employ of the former owners and departed when they did. I'm afraid that it's been somewhat neglected for the past few months."

With a sigh, she let her hands fall to her sides. Turning a slow circle, her gaze passing over the whole of the disaster, she said, "You have a true gift for understatement, Mr. Reeves."

"Carden. Hiring a new gardener is next on my list of tasks," he hurried to assure her. "You seem to have some familiarity with conservatories . . . Are there any particular qualifications for which I should be looking?"

"An ability to work miracles would be nice," she quipped, pulling a dead leaf from a whole pot of them. She held it up for him to see, saying, "This was a very rare specimen, you know."

Actually, he didn't. But he clearly understood that she considered the state of his conservatory to be indefensible. And him, for allowing it to happen, a criminal. A callously indifferent, cold-blooded plant killer.

"Maybe a bit of water would bring it back?" he asked, hoping to redeem himself.

"That along with some heat, some sunshine, a good bit of humus-rich soil, and a healthy seed." Shaking her head, she tossed the leaf aside and resumed her general survey of the greenhouse.

"So in other words, one must simply start over."

"Yes," she agreed, lifting the hem of her skirts and setting off for the far corner. "You are, however," she called over her shoulder as she went, "most fortunate in that I happen to have brought with me a good many of those particular seeds."

He went after her, intrigued by the sudden change in her manner. If he hadn't seen it happen with his own eyes, he wouldn't have believed how instantly the coolly reserved woman had been transformed into a . . . Well, a forest nymph.

By the time he caught up with her, she was at the gardening bench, busily—and apparently quite happily—sorting through a rather abused-looking collection of tools and pots.

"I imagine that, as a botanist," he ventured, "your father made a collection of seeds and such things."

"An extensive collection," she said, without looking away from her task. "Were I so inclined, I could make a very profitable business out of supplying private conservatories throughout the whole of England."

"You've given the matter some thought?" he asked, incredulous.

She stopped her work and met his gaze squarely. "Yes. I was prepared to be dismissed after delivering the girls into your care. As it happens, over the years I've developed something of a fondness for eating on a regular basis. And I prefer to be independent if at all possible. Being at the mercy of another's good humor and whim is neither an enjoyable nor a secure state."

"And yet you've agreed to stay with my nieces, to be in my employ," he observed, his curiosity stirred. "Why?"

She shrugged and resumed her inventory. "I can pursue my own aspirations at any time. For now, caring for the girls is far more important. It would be selfish to abandon them when they so desperately need the comfort of the familiar."

"And when they no longer need the familiar, you'll leave them?"

"I'll always be there for them should they need me, Mr. Reeves. We've been through a great deal together. As they say, our bonds have been forged in the fires of adversity. There will come a time when my daily presence in their lives won't be necessary, but even then they'll know how and where to find me should they need to."

"You're a most practical woman."

She nodded. "By necessity, Mr. Reeves."

Slowly, pointedly, he said, "My name is Carden."

With a heavy sigh, she laid aside a rusty little shovel and turned to him. "In addition to being practical, Mr. Reeves, I am also blunt. And bluntly speaking, I won't address you by your Christian name because you strike me as the kind of man who, once he's successfully wedged his foot in the door, promptly pushes the rest of himself through it."

He leaned his hip against the edge of the table, crossed his arms over his chest and grinned. "That was your idea of blunt?"

Her hands went to her hips and her chin came up. So did the color in her cheeks. "To call you by your Christian name would remove barriers to intimacy that I prefer to leave in place."

"Why?"

"I'm a married woman."

Damn, but he liked her spirit. "As I recall, you're a widow."

"Be that as it may, I—"

"Widows aren't held to the same social standards as wives."

"Be *that* as it may, I am not in the habit of entering into temporary romantic liaisons."

He looked off into the distance as though he were considering a monastic life of his own. After a long moment he drawled, "Define temporary."

"Any time less than eternity."

He cocked a brow and was about to remind her that less than forever could be a good thing—her marriage being a fairly obvious case in point—when he heard the unmistakable sound of a polite intrusion. Sera's gaze darted past him and to the left, suggesting that Sawyer was stepping from amidst the dead plants in that general direction.

"Yes, Sawyer?" he asked on a sigh, not bothering to look over his shoulder.

"The carter has arrived with the belongings of Mrs. Treadwell and the young ladies, sir."

"Thank you, Sawyer," Sera said, brushing her hands clean over the table. "I'll attend to it immediately." She barely paused long enough to say, "Thank you for the tour, Mr. Reeves. It was most enlightening," before she pulled her skirts aside and strode away.

"Yes, it was, wasn't it?" he called after her, smiling, watching the taunting sway of fabric. In a fashionable dress, she'd turn male heads everywhere she went. He was going to have to make a point of confining her to the house for the next few weeks or so.

"Sir?"

"Yes, Sawyer?" he asked, distracted.

"Lady Lansdown is in the parlor."

His stomach plummeted to the soles of his feet. "Honoria? Honoria is here?"

"I believe that is what I said, sir."

Carden swore and raked his fingers through his hair as his mind staggered through a maze of thoroughly unpleasant possibilities. "You didn't tell her about Arthur, did you?"

"Of course not, sir," Sawyer replied, utterly unruffled by the crisis. "Your instructions were most specific."

God help him if Honoria discovered the truth. She couldn't keep a secret to save her soul. Once she knew something, all of England did within the hour.

"Shall I have Cook prepare for another dinner guest, sir?"

Oh, God. Dinner with Honoria. And Seraphina and the girls. Together. Carden swallowed and willed himself to take a breath, to accept his circumstances with dignity. "I don't see any polite way to avoid inviting her to stay. Do you?"

"Very good, sir. I'll attend to it right away."

Carden nodded, silently dismissing his man. Why the hell had Honoria come back to London? And chosen today of all days to call on him? Dinner was going to be a nightmare. If one of the girls offered so much as a single unguarded word . . . "I'm buggered," Carden groaned. "Buggered."

From the distance he heard Sawyer dryly reply, "Merely wishful thinking, sir."

CHAPTER 5

By the time the carters were through with their hauling, huffing, puffing, and swearing, it had been four o'clock and the schoolroom looked like a hundred Christmases and birthdays had dropped through the roof all at once. For the girls it had been a joyous celebration of arrival. A reunion of sorts. For her . . . Nothing seemed to be where she remembered packing it. Everything needed to be opened and sorted and placed. And the instant the mantel clock had chimed six, she'd known that it had been a mistake to say they'd dine downstairs. But done was done and all she could do now was thread her way through the maze and manage the chaos so she and her charges would be ready to go in time.

And it really wasn't going very well, Seraphina silently admitted as Camille turned her head—yet again—to see what her sisters were doing on the other side of the room. Fine auburn tendrils slipped through Sera's fingers. "Please, Camille," she pleaded in desperation. "Hold still and allow me to get this bow situated in the center of your head."

Camille whipped around to meet her gaze in the dressing mirror. Her grin was wide and too full of excitement to hold even the barest hint of apology.

"I can't find my crinoline!" Amanda cried, causing Camille to instantly turn.

As Camille's baby-fine hair slipped away, Sera stifled an exasperated sigh and asked with all the patience she could muster, "Have you looked in your trunk?"

"Yes. I've looked everywhere and it's gone. Gone!"

"Well, look again," she countered. "I'm sure it's there somewhere. Did you lift anything to look toward the bottom of the trunk?"

"No."

"Do you think that might be a strategy worth employing?"

Amanda moaned and muttered but bent over to do as suggested. Camille's gaze came back to the mirror just as Beatrice bounded over a crate and came to a breathless halt beside them.

"There's a hole in the heel," she announced, lifting her stocking-encased arm for Sera to see her fingers protruding—and wildly wiggling—from a hole precisely where she'd said it was.

"Well, for heaven's sake, don't make it any larger than it already is."

"It's my best pair."

"It's your only pair," Sera corrected absently, trying to gather the strands of Camille's wayward locks back into hand. "Please fetch my sewing basket and I'll darn it as soon as I've finished with your sister's hair."

"And after you've found my crinoline."

"Keep looking, Amanda. Camille, *please* sit still."

"I could simply go without stockings this evening," Beatrice suggested, making a closer examination of the rend.

"You simply could not. Now please stop picking at the threads and get the sewing basket as I asked."

"Or," she said, backing up slightly and turning sideways, "I could just wear one and walk like this so no one would notice I didn't have two." She stepped toward Sera in slow, deliberate profile. Camille considered her sister with knitted brows and pursed lips.

"They'd think you were either daft or deformed," Amanda declared, her hands on her waist, her search abandoned. "Don't you dare embarrass us."

"Have you found your crinoline yet?" Sera asked, giving up hope for perfection and whipping the ribbon around what hair she still managed to hold.

"No."

"Then I suggest that you've a better use for your time and attention than insulting your sister." The bow she quickly pulled into existence wasn't exactly centered, but it was fairly close and somewhat correctly shaped. It would have to do. Perhaps the dining room light would be fashionably dim.

She was hastily smoothing the worn lace on the shoulders of Camille's dress when there came a knock on the door. A quick glance at the mantel clock suggested that Sawyer's timepiece ran ahead of hers. Being late for dinner their first night. It certainly wasn't the way she'd have preferred to start things off.

"Get the sewing basket and prepare the needle and thread for me," she instructed, trying to brush the worst of the wrinkles from her freshly unpacked skirt as she moved to answer the summons. Over her shoulder she added, "You have two minutes to find your crinoline and get into it. And Camille, do *not* fidget with that bow. Just sit there and don't move."

She flung open the door with far more speed and force than she'd intended. The eyebrow that shot up on the other side wasn't Sawyer's, though, it was Carden Reeves's. Who, in the soft light of the hallway, looked positively dashing in his dark, well-tailored suit. And even more devilishly handsome than he had that afternoon.

Even as she inwardly winced at the thought of her

badly wrinkled skirt, he smiled and said, "Good evening, Seraphina."

"Mr. Reeves."

His smile instantly evaporated and he heaved a small sigh. "For the moment, I'll set the matter of names aside. I've come here for two reasons, the second of which is to escort you and my nieces down to dinner."

"Thank you. And the primary reason for your appearance at our door?"

"I've come to beg. Grovel if I must." She arched a brow in silent question which succeeded in prompting him to add, "It's rather complicated."

"I'll try to follow along as you explain," Sera countered, stepping into the hall and pulling the door closed quietly behind her.

He nodded, clasped his hands behind his back, and looked at the wall beyond her shoulder. "Percival's widow, Honoria, is dining with us this evening."

"How lovely," she observed, knowing there had to be more even as she fought the urge to reach up and adjust the folds of his silk stock. "It will be refreshing to have an adult conversation with another female. It's been ages. I promise to mind my manners." *And my hands*, she silently added.

"It's not you I'm worried about."

"Is Honoria bad-mannered?"

His gaze slid over to meet hers. "Well . . ."

"I find it hard to believe that the widow of a peer makes her way roughshod through social occasions."

"That's not it at all. Honoria's a sweet darling," he quickly offered. "It's just that she doesn't have the slightest inkling of why anyone would want to maintain a secret."

"Ah, the matter of Arthur and his demise," Seraphina rejoined, her blood heating with anger. "It was extremely difficult for the girls to accept their parents' death and to replant so much as a seed of hope in their hearts would be horribly cruel. I won't do it to them."

"I've decided—"

"And I won't allow you to do it, either," she interrupted. "You will have to accept your fate. Hopefully with some small degree of grace and dignity."

He took her measure for several moments. "Do you have any idea of what's at stake?"

"A seat in the House of Lords?"

"And do you know what comes with that seat?" he shot back.

Her patience had been worn in surviving, frayed in traveling halfway across the world, and tattered in dealing with the mounds of baggage that had been unceremoniously dropped at her feet. She had three girls to get ready for a dinner with their long-lost aunt and uncle, and Carden Reeves was whining about the burdens of being a peer?

"We've had this conversation before," she replied, deciding that being fired might well be the best thing that could ever happen to her. Lord knew it would considerably reduce Carden Reeves's chances of being bludgeoned to death with the nearest heavy object. "As I recall, being elevated to the peerage provides one with a title, land, wealth, power, and a considerable improvement in social standing."

"Hopefully," he countered, clearly just as willing to do battle, "you'll also remember that I mentioned that all of that came with expectations that I would prefer to avoid."

"I do. You did not, however, detail for me those ever-so-hideous standards."

"Do you have a lifetime to listen?"

She heard the cauldron of frustration bubbling beneath the surface of his taunt and something inside her suggested that perhaps she needed to listen more and think a bit less. She lifted her chin, took a steadying breath, and with all the gentleness she could muster, said, "I'm assuming that dinner won't be served until you choose to arrive in the dining room. If it's midnight, then it's midnight. You are, after all, the master of this house. Take what time you require for an explanation. I'm willing to listen with as open a mind as is humanly possible."

Again he considered her. And for the first time since they'd met, she had a sense of his appraisal taking in the whole of who she was, not just her physical attributes and the potential they offered for his enjoyment. It was something of a forward step, a most surprising one, and she was grateful for it.

"Have you ever known any upper-class gentlemen, Seraphina?" he asked quietly.

His voice was a caress and her resolve sighed and softened at its touch. "Not in a personal sense," she replied, smiling up at him. "From time to time, some would visit friends or relations in Jamaica. Everyone was generally aware of their presence."

"What did those gentlemen do with their days while in Jamaica?"

"They dined, rode horses, and strolled."

"And what did they do with their nights?"

"Publicly, they played cards, drank, dined, and smoked. I wouldn't venture to guess as to their private activities."

A roguish smile tugged at the corner of his mouth but he brought it under control to nod and ask, "What do you suppose they do with their days and nights when they're not in Jamaica? When, say, they're in London?"

"I have no idea. Tend to their businesses?"

He shook his head slowly, his gaze holding hers. "They dine, ride horses, gamble, drink, stroll, and smoke. Because upper-class gentlemen—and especially peers of the realm—do not have businesses. Only the common classes engage in trade. Only the great disgustingly grubby masses need to do something with their days to produce money."

"And the upper classes send their servants out to pluck it off the trees of their estates?" she countered skeptically. "I wish my father had found some of those. It would be very nice to own an orchard of them."

"Yes. I suppose it would." He shrugged and a soul-deep kind of sadness edged his voice when he added, "Perhaps."

"I'm sorry that I don't know about these things," Sera offered sincerely. "Most of my father's friends were businessmen and saw nothing wrong with the making of money. Not that my father was all that conscientious about doing so, you understand. His focus was his research and nothing else mattered as much to him."

His smile was thin. "And to the upper class nothing matters as much as the illusion that one has so much money that one need never think about making it or the consequences of spending it."

"How is that possible?" she asked, both repelled and fascinated by the very notion of such a world. "Given the realities of living, I mean. How do they put food on the table and keep the roofs over their heads from leaking? Surely they have to have money."

"Not necessarily."

"They live on the goodness of others? On charity?"

"The only truly acceptable way for a peer to obtain money is through the collection of rent from his tenant farmers. And he would never take the cash in his own hand or rap his knuckles on a farmhouse door. He has a manager do that for him."

"Several of my father's friends were landlords," Sera mused aloud, intrigued by the puzzle he'd presented her. "There was no shame in it. In fact, owning the right properties was considered to be a sign of one's true genius. Why is living off rent monies something you would want to avoid?"

"It's often a very meager income. Bad weather. Crop

failures. And as industries rise, more and more of the young are abandoning farming to take up trade work in the cities for regular wages. Most peers lie awake at night counting tenant farmers, not sheep. On the other hand, I happen to make a very good living as an architect."

"You would have to stop being an architect to become a peer?"

"Of course not. I have talents. I'd be expected to contribute them to charitable causes."

"But you couldn't accept money for it?"

"I could, but I'd be roundly censured for it. In the minds of the upper class, it's far better to be idle, bored, and secretly poor than productive, happy, and genuinely wealthy."

"I see," Sera whispered, thinking that it was the most twisted logic she'd ever encountered. To live your life, day in and day out, desperately maintaining an illusion that made you utterly miserable . . . What a sad waste of a person's time on earth. Why bother to rise every morning?

"Wanting to be productive, happy, and wealthy is inexcusably shallow of me," he said softly. "I know that, but there it is. I'm a selfish man."

No, it wasn't selfish. She could understand how he felt that way, wanted more to his life than illusions. Didn't she want the same basic things for herself? It wasn't fair to deny a person a chance for a pleasant life simply because they'd been born to a social class whose foolishness all but made it impossible.

"And then there are the mamas."

Sera blinked at him, struggling to come from the mental maze she'd been wandering. "I beg your pardon?"

He stuffed his hands into his trouser pockets and nodded. "The upper-class women who are determined to see their darling daughters married—no matter the obstacles— to a peer."

"Even to an impoverished peer?"

"Wealth doesn't count as much as prestige."

"Prestige doesn't fill one's dinner plate," Sera countered.

"True," he quickly agreed, "but the social whirl of a peer involves a good many dinner parties. She can stuff her reticule when no one's looking."

"You're being facetious."

"You'd be shocked," he replied, grinning. He sobered slowly and then quietly said, "I've always been a third son, Seraphina. No one's ever cared how I made my way in the world as long as I wasn't imprisoned for it or I didn't get too dirty in the process. No one has ever tripped me on a public walkway so they could introduce me to their desperate daughter."

"But now you're an only son."

"And suddenly how I make my living is an appropriate subject for public comment. Who I eventually marry . . ." He shook his head and sighed. "Pigs at county fairs are sold with more dignity and less social commentary."

It was one thing, she knew, to gracefully accept one's circumstances, but it was entirely another to resign oneself to wallowing in them for all eternity. Had she done that, she'd still be in Belize, waiting to starve to death. "And you can't be a peer who grasps his own fate and goes his own way?" she suggested, thinking that if ever there was a man capable of making his own rules, it was Carden Reeves.

"Peers don't go their own way, Seraphina," he explained with what appeared to be a great deal of patience. "They live, breathe, procreate, and die by very specific and rigid social expectations."

"And the empire would immediately collapse if they deviated?"

"Their personal existences would," he assured her. "They'd be vilified and ostracized. It would be an extremely difficult, lonely way to live. No woman in her right mind would willingly marry him."

"Considering your commitment to bachelorhood," she quipped, "the latter would be a rather positive consequence of the whole thing, wouldn't it?"

His grin was instant and broad, brightening his eyes and—for some strange, unknown reason—lightening her heart. "Peers are expected to produce legitimate heirs. To not do so is terribly unpatriotic. I'm obligated to give it my best for Queen and country."

She laughed softly, liking the easy banter between them, enjoying his irreverent sense of humor and the way he made her pulse sing. This Carden Reeves was ever so much more comfortable to be with than the smoothly polished parlor predator.

"Can you see why," he asked softly, "it's so important to me that everyone believes Arthur will return?"

"Yes. I can," Sera admitted. With genuine regret she added, "Unfortunately, though, Arthur isn't going to return. The best you can hope for is to delay the inevitable. And I simply don't see the point in doing that."

"I'm not sure that I do, either," he confided with a shrug. "But I know that I feel a desperate need to do so. All I'm asking for is time. Time to find something of a solution that allows me to live my life the way I want to live it."

"From all that you've told me," she offered gently, "I think that you might as well cry for the moon."

"But you will let me cry for as long as I can stand the self-pity?" he asked hopefully. His eyes sparkled again. "I'm fairly sure I'll come around eventually."

Not that he would have any choice about it, she knew. But she had a choice and it was to be kind and understanding of another's fragile, dying dreams. "I won't ask the girls to craft a fantasy about their father," she declared gently, again resisting the urge to fiddle with his silken neckwear. "But I will make every effort to change the subject should his fate or whereabouts arise in the course of conversation. It's the best that I can do and live with my conscience."

"It's a perfect compromise," he said, bowing briefly at the waist. "And I appreciate your willingness to make it. You certainly didn't have to."

Seraphina disagreed, but didn't say so. No man wanted to know that he was pitied by a woman.

"Are you ready to go down for dinner?"

Dinner. Sera glanced down at her skirt and resigned herself to offering apologies if necessary. "I am," she replied. "The girls, however, could well be another matter entirely," she added, turning away from him to knock quietly on the door as she turned the knob.

"Ladies?" she called, poking her head through the door to be sure they were sufficiently clothed to be seen by a male. "Your Uncle Carden is here to escort us to dinner. Are you ready?"

They were all three standing together beside the dressing table. Judging by the frozen poses, guilty expressions, and the too-quick nods, Sera guessed that she'd interrupted yet another of their regular sisterly contests. Whether this one had been of wills or temperaments, it seemed to have been suspended for the moment. Thankfully, they'd managed to make themselves fully presentable before they'd succumbed to their combative tendencies. Sera pushed the door fully open and motioned for her charges to join them in the hall.

"Good God," Carden Reeves whispered from behind her as they sorted—with the usual jostling and elbowing— themselves in their customary order.

She glanced over her shoulder to see him appraising the girls' clothing from shoulder to hem. "They're growing," she explained. "And there hasn't been any money for new clothing. We've made do by letting out or taking up seams and hems as necessity dictated. Keeping them in shoes that fit their feet has been the greatest of the challenges. Try as I might, I can't make shoes."

"You actually tried?"

His amusement was obvious. She thought she heard a bit of respect and perhaps even a smidgen of awe, too. Pleased, she smiled up at him as she stepped back to allow the girls to move through the doorway. "Of course. Had I been successful, it would have been an accomplishment I could have bragged about for the rest of my life. Can you make shoes?"

"I have absolutely no idea," he laughingly admitted.

It was the most inexplicable impulse that had ever struck her. One moment she'd been standing there, mindful only of providing an explanation for the girls being pathetically dressed, and in the next she was thinking that it would be perfectly right and wonderful to step forward and kiss Carden Reeves. Good God, what had happened? And why was the impulse not fading?

Her heart, instantly jolted, was racing, making it difficult to breathe and sending a wave of heat fanning across her cheeks. At the edge of her awareness she saw the girls pass between her and . . . Their uncle *knew* what she was thinking, feeling. His eyes were bright with appreciation and his smile was ever so soft and inviting. *Go ahead, Sera,* it said wordlessly, *kiss me. I'll kiss you back. You'll enjoy it.*

Yes, I would. And so would you.

He slowly cocked a brow, stopping Sera's heart and painfully catching what little breath she had left in her lungs.

"Miss Sera?"

She tore her gaze from Carden Reeves's and weakly but gratefully smiled down at Beatrice. "Yes, dear?"

"I pulled my stocking down so that the hole doesn't show."

Her heart was beating again and she was able to draw a full, calming breath. "Very good thinking, Bea. I'll darn it after dinner."

"You'll go to the dressmaker's first thing tomorrow morning. All of you."

Imperious. So blessedly, typically Carden Reeves, lord of his manor and all that he surveyed. "As you wish, Mr. Reeves," Seraphina replied, utterly relieved to have been returned to the safety of ordinary ground.

"Carden. And I'll accompany you there."

"You're familiar with the particulars of selecting ladies' wardrobes?" she asked, willingly playing her part in the charade.

His eyes sparkled devilishly. "Actually, I'm quite good at it."

"I should have guessed."

She took his offered arm without thinking, only in doing so realizing that touching him had become something not only comfortable to do, but enjoyable. Considering that she'd been in this house less than half a day . . . Part of her was fascinated by the speed and ease with which she was allowing the distance between them to close. Another part of her was shamed by what that implied about the strength of her moral fiber.

What, precisely, she wanted to do about it was difficult to decide, though. Especially as they made their way down the hall toward the stairs. The warmth of him next to her, the slight, easy friction of their bodies as they moved together, the woodsy scent of his shaving cologne, the sense of being sheltered and protected . . . It had been a very long time since she'd been this physically close to a man. And even then it had never been an experience as thoroughly pleasant as this. Yes, being with Carden Reeves wasn't at all like being with Gerald Treadwell.

Physically, there was no point in denying that he was wondrously exciting.

Emotionally . . . She slid a glance over at him and caught the inside of her lower lip between her teeth. Carden Reeves was a man who specialized in casually shattering illusions and breaking hearts. In that respect, he was just like Gerald had been.

Forewarned is forearmed, she told herself as they made their way down the stairs, the girls following behind them like little ducks.

CHAPTER 6

There was something about Honoria . . . Seraphina stood beside the blazing hearth, trying to get warm as she considered the tiny woman holding court from her place on the parlor settee. She couldn't recall exactly how Carden had described his sister-in-law, but she knew that she'd been left with the impression that Honoria Reeves was something of a good-natured bit of feminine fluff.

On the surface of things, it seemed a fairly accurate depiction. Honoria was silver haired, very small boned and so short that in another year or two Amanda would tower over her. And Honoria was indeed very kindly engaging her nieces in spirited conversation, inquiring after their interests and talents and promising to share with them every wonder to be had in all of the British Isles. The girls were, while not physically wrapped around her fingers, completely hers as they sat at her feet and looked up at her in rapt, openmouthed attention. Honoria was obviously enjoying herself. So were the girls.

And yet . . . Seraphina had the strongest, strangest feeling that Honoria was far more substantive than she appeared. Why she felt that way, she couldn't fathom, though. Neither could she explain to herself why she felt slightly menaced by it. Carden had brought them all into the room and handled the introductions in what had seemed to be perfect accordance with upper-class social protocol. At least as she understood upper-class protocol. They'd definitely been interminable and very formal. Honoria had smiled when she was supposed to. She'd smiled when it was her turn. They had both exchanged the customary, expected greetings without the slightest stumble or falter. And then Honoria had turned her attention to her nieces and become the epitome of the elderly, doting aunt.

The woman had done absolutely nothing to account for the wariness that swirled around in Sera's stomach like a school of mullet. Absolutely nothing. And yet the feeling wouldn't go away. Carden stood on the other side of the hearth, his hands in his trouser pockets, watching Honoria and the girls. He seemed a bit tense, his smile just a little too controlled, but she couldn't attribute it to anything other than his concern that the girls might tell Honoria that they were orphans.

Puzzle it from all directions as she might, Seraphina still couldn't understand why she was reacting to the older woman the way she was. It was most odd. And because it was inexplicable, it was disconcerting. She kept her distance, quietly watching, hoping to come to some sort of understanding—no matter how vague.

The bell rang at the front of the house. The last notes were still reverberating as Sera saw Sawyer pass across the open door of the parlor on his way to answer it.

"The last of our dinner party has arrived," Carden said softly as he walked past her. "It'll get livelier from here. I promise."

She didn't have a chance to respond. She watched him stride out into the foyer and greet the two men Sawyer was divesting of canes, hats, scarves, gloves, and coats. One man she instantly recognized as Aiden Terrell. The other she presumed to be the friend who held Carden's library in such disdain.

Barrett, she recalled. He was slightly taller than Aiden, coming closer to matching Carden in that respect and in age. The three of them together were an impressive assembly of male physique. They all had broad shoulders, narrow hips, and long legs. And they were all breathtakingly, classically handsome.

Carden and Barrett looked quite similar in coloring: dark haired and dark eyed. Barrett didn't have the distinguished strands of silver at his temples that Carden did, though. His misfortune, Sera thought with a small smile. Other than that, they could have been easily mistaken for brothers.

Aiden on the other hand . . . As people were wont to do, they would likely assume that Carden and Barrett favored their father while John Aiden was the male image of their mother. Sera smiled. Or perhaps the rogue Irish cousin sent to be tutored in the British Way. There was something a bit unbridled about Aiden Terrell. In all likelihood it was a consequence of his youth, but she liked him for it and was glad that he'd come to dinner. He was easy to talk to and could so ably charm and entertain the girls.

Which, now that she thought about it, explained why he seemed to fit so well with Carden and Barrett despite the age and appearance differences. Charming females was charming females. Age didn't really matter. The three men advancing into the parlor were all clearly cut from the same fine bolt of masculine cloth. What Aiden was learning at the knees of Carden Reeves . . .

And from his friend Barrett, Sera mentally amended as the man met her gaze. His regard wasn't bold, but it was open and honest and quietly appreciative of what he saw. Clearly, he was an experienced rake, too. The smile he gave her in acknowledgment was eloquent, wordlessly telling her that he was a man who abided by well-defined rules and that for the time being, where she was concerned, he was willing to be the second of Carden Reeves. But should Carden choose to remove himself . . .

As direct as it was, his manner wasn't the least bit threatening. Quite to the contrary, she decided, after a moment's reflection. Something about him suggested that he would be a most respectful, considerate champion should she ever need one. Rather like the older brother she had often fantasized about having when she'd been a little girl.

"Honoria," she heard Carden say, "may I present my friends, Mr. Barrett Stanbridge and Mr. John Aiden Terrell. Gentlemen, my late brother's wife, Honoria Reeves, the Lady Lansdown."

"A very real pleasure, madam," Barrett said, bowing over Honoria's hand. She lowered her chin in silent, regal response.

Aiden immediately stepped into Barrett's place and also bent down, saying, "It's an honor to make your acquaintance, Lady Lansdown." Again Honoria played the Queen.

And then the three men turned to her. "Seraphina," Carden began, his manner considerably easier than it had been when addressing his sister-in-law, "you of course met Aiden earlier today."

"It stands as one of the best parts of my day," she replied, extending her hand for him to take. "I'm glad you could join us for dinner, Mr. Terrell."

"Wouldn't have missed it for the world," he countered. "And please call me Aiden."

She nodded her acceptance of the request even as Carden frowned and continued with the introductions. "And this is Mr. Barrett Stanbridge, formerly of Her Majesty's Royal Engineers and now an aspiring private investigator. Barrett, I present Seraphina Treadwell, my nieces' companion."

His smile was warm and genuine. Friendly. "A distinct pleasure, madam."

"Which is all mine, sir," Sera dutifully replied. She intended to also thank him for joining them for dinner, but didn't get a chance.

Carden took his friend by the elbow and physically drew him away, saying, "Aiden's already met the girls. Let me introduce you to them, Barrett."

The process continued and they all politely waited through it. Halfway along, Sawyer arrived with a tray of various drinks and silently made the rounds of the room. And when the civilities were at long last concluded, Honoria sat regally on the settee, the girls sat at her feet, and the rest of them stood along the edges of the room holding their glasses and waiting for someone to say something conversational. It was Honoria who sailed mercifully, if imperiously, into the breach.

"I detect a slight foreign sound to your English, Mr. Terrell."

"I'm from St. Kitts. In the Caribbean."

"Oh? And what brings you to London?"

"My family owns a shipping line. I'm in England to take delivery of an overdue ship out of the yards at Bristol. But since there's nothing for me to do there, I'm twiddling my thumbs in London while I wait."

"And how did you make the acquaintance of Carden?"

The tone and pacing of Honoria's questions struck Sera as being a bit inquisitional but Aiden didn't seem to mind. Ever affable, he answered, "We met at his club, where, every night for a full two weeks, he routinely plastered me at cards. We eventually reached a point where my friendship was the only thing I had left to offer him."

Carden chuckled. "Which is turning out to be one of my more interesting winnings in the last year."

Honoria shot him a disapproving look—whether for the gambling or for having interrupted her interrogation, Sera couldn't say.

"And you, Mr. Stanbridge?" Honoria went on, very deliberately putting a smile on her face and turning her attention to Carden's other friend. "How did you meet my brother-in-law?"

"We were garrisoned together in the Transvaal for almost three years."

Honoria frowned momentarily and then brightened. "Didn't I hear somewhere that Lord Wickerly's third son is also garrisoned there?"

"It's his fourth son, Harry," Carden corrected coolly.

Barrett nodded. "And Harry is a blight on humanity."

"Then that particular apple didn't fall far from the tree," Honoria observed breezily. "His mother is a saint, you know. Endures her husband in absolute silence. I don't know how she does it."

"It's a shame she didn't raise her voice just once," Barrett quipped, a noticeably sharp edge to his voice. "She might have spared the world Harry. It would definitely be a better place without him."

Honoria blinked and found another smile. "What was it that you did for Her Majesty in the Transvaal, Mr. Stanbridge?"

"Primarily we built railroads. Carden's a trestle wizard, you know."

"Really."

Sera silently, instinctively bristled. Engineering certainly wasn't her forte but if one specialist claimed that another was brilliant at it, far be it from her to question the assertion. But the fact that Honoria felt free to do so bothered her and deepened her sense of wariness. It seemed to bother Carden, as well. His polite smile was brittle as he stared at the curtains behind his sister-in-law's shoulder.

"There was no span too big," Barrett explained. "No sand too shifting, no rock too hard to deter the bridges of Captain Carden Reeves."

"No river was too deep or too fast, either," Aiden tossed in brightly. "No natives too hostile."

Honoria arched a silver brow. "You were also in the Transvaal, Mr. Terrell?"

"No," he admitted, grinning from ear to ear, "but I've heard the stories at least a thousand times. There are moments when I certainly feel as though I'd been there."

Barrett made a snorting sound around his smile. "Every day was a challenge of one sort or another. But we got them built and built correctly. They'll last into the next century and well beyond."

"It sounds as though you were not only very good at it, but also enjoyed the work. Why did you choose to abandon it?"

Cocking a brow, Barrett asked, "Didn't I mention that Harry is a pox on all of mankind?"

Carden cleared his throat and pointedly met Honoria's gaze. "Let's say that a conflict of interest developed and leave it at that, shall we?"

"It must have been a significant one."

Again Barrett snorted. "You don't know the half of it."

"And shouldn't," Carden declared crisply, finishing off his drink and setting the empty glass on the side table. He glanced toward the doorway and then stepped toward the settee. No trace of his earlier irritation remained as he smiled down at the elderly woman, offered his arm, and said, "Sawyer is about to announce dinner. Honoria, if you'd do me the honor."

Barrett Stanbridge was at Sera's side in the next instant. "May I?"

She took his offered arm. "Thank you, Mr. Stanbridge."

"Formality has a way of impeding the development of friendships. I'd prefer if you'd call me Barrett. And Seraphina is such a beautiful name it would be a shame to be denied the privilege of saying it."

She'd known the request was coming and acceded with

a nod. She didn't miss the quick look Carden threw over his shoulder at her and knew that there was going to be a reckoning with him over the issue the next time they found themselves alone.

How she'd feel about it at that point she couldn't be certain. There was something to be said for maintaining the bounds of their employer–employee relationship. It was by far the safest course. She did have to admit, though, that something had decidedly shifted between them as they'd stood together in the upstairs hallway. Had the girls not been there, the entire matter might already be a moot one. Whether it was proper or not—or even wise—thinking about kissing a man generally moved a relationship to a first-name basis.

"And if you wouldn't mind too terribly sharing me, Seraphina," she heard Barrett say. Abandoning her musing, she smiled appreciatively as he extended his other arm. "Miss Amanda, if you would do me the distinct honor?"

"Thank you, sir."

"Ha! Fools!" Aiden chuckled, extending his crooked arms to Beatrice and Camille. "They've left the prettiest two of the bunch for me to escort. Shall we, ladies?"

Seraphina allowed Barrett to escort her into the dining room, listening to the girls chattering and laughing as Aiden brought them along behind, and knowing with absolute certainty that bringing them to England had been the right thing to do.

Carden might well have delayed hiring a housekeeping staff, but he hadn't compromised the part of his lifestyle that came from the kitchen. It was the grandest, most decadently delicious meal she'd had in a very, very long time. The girls had never in their relatively short lives seen such a feast at all and their eyes had grown larger with every course that had appeared. They'd made do with so little for so long in Belize. And the food aboard ship had barely been edible most days. Now, watching them struggle to practice the good manners of restraint in the face of such a bounty . . .

"Beatrice," Carden said, interrupting Sera's observations, "you look like a young lady who would like another helping of potatoes. And maybe another slice of roast to go with it, too. Monroe, if you would, please."

The foot man smiled and silently moved forward with the platter of meat, holding it as Beatrice carefully selected a dainty piece.

"Take another, Bea," Carden pressed, smiling at her around the rim of his wine glass. "A big one. No one leaves my table hungry. Food's meant to be eaten and enjoyed. Monroe, please see that Miss Amanda and Camille have additional portions of everything, as well. Seraphina?"

"Thank you, but I couldn't possibly eat another bite. My sincerest compliments to your cook, Mr. Reeves. Everything was heavenly."

Barrett lifted his glass. "And compliments to you, Carden—yet again—for having the foresight to bring Cook and Monroe with us out of the Transvaal. A stroke of pure genius."

"No, it was pure selfishness and you know it."

Honoria looked between the two of them, blinking. "You absconded with soldiers from Her Majesty's Army?"

"I didn't kidnap them, Honoria," Carden laughingly explained. "Their enlistments were up and I offered them passage home, steady employment, and the deep and everlasting appreciation of myself and my friends."

"And your family," Amanda added happily, taking another helping of the offered roast.

"Yes," Carden amended, lifting his glass in his niece's direction, "and that of my family."

"Amanda, my sweeting," Honoria said crisply, her tone instantly snapping Amanda's gaze to hers. "A small but important point of manners. Children, when invited to the table to dine with their elders, are not to speak unless directly spoken to."

Amanda was crushed, but valiant in her effort to conceal it. She nodded and smiled tightly even as she silently replaced the empty meat tongs on the tray Monroe held at her side. Honoria dipped her chin in acceptance and then smiled as she resumed pushing the food around on her own plate. Amanda stared glumly at her roast. Beatrice squirmed and Camille looked at Sera, wordlessly pleading for an explanation. Sera counted to five before she felt she had sufficient control of her anger.

"It's all right, Amanda," Sera said breezily, drawing everyone's attention her way. "No one is going to die at a small lapse in manners. We have much to learn about living in this new world and it will take some time. We're all going to make mistakes in the process. What's important is that we profit from them in the end."

Honoria blinked several times. "Are you saying that children speaking freely at the table is customary in Belize?"

The question had been asked on an incredulous note and yet . . . there was something of a challenge in it, too. Sera could feel it even though she couldn't say where in the words or what—precisely—it was. She knew with absolute certainty, however, that she didn't like it and that she couldn't afford to pretend it wasn't there. The girls were so very vulnerable now and needed her to stand up for them.

"Yes, Lady Lansdown, in the Reeveses' home, the girls are allowed to speak freely," she answered. "But their home is unusual. Theirs is one of the very few in Belize that actually has a table."

There was a flash of steel in Honoria's hazel eyes and then it was gone. What replaced it, Sera couldn't tell. The rapid blinking served to mask it remarkably well. "I had already concluded that the standards in general must be very different there," Honoria said, her manner light and conversational. "Otherwise there is simply no explanation for Arthur's having sent his daughters home with such wardrobes. I've never in my life seen such pitifully attired children."

Heat flooded Sera's cheeks. She clenched her teeth, knowing that if she retorted in anger, she'd only make matters worse. Honoria, despite her outward appearance and manner—and Carden Reeves's assurances—was no harmless bit of feminine fluff.

"You haven't been out of Mayfair recently, have you, Honoria?" Carden asked coolly.

Honoria blinked some more and in the lull Sera stepped in to make explanations for the sake of the girls' feelings.

"It was an unavoidable situation, the specifics of which I won't bore you, Lady Lansdown. But rest assured that Mr. Reeves is taking us to the dressmaker's tomorrow. He intends for the girls to have entirely new wardrobes as soon as is humanly possible."

"Oh really, Carden," Honoria gushed, waving her hand dismissively. "What would you know of selecting proper clothing for young ladies?"

"And just how is it that you would know more?" he countered.

"I was once a little girl myself. And although small details tend to slip my mind these days, my memories of childhood are quite intact and available for recall. As I'm sure you have much more productive ways in which to spend your time, I shall accompany Seraphina and the girls to the dressmaker's tomorrow."

Sera's heart sank into her stomach. An entire day with Honoria, always watching for barbs, deflecting criticisms, having to ever be on their very best behavior . . .

"I think Miss Camille should choose in the pinks, don't you, Seraphina?"

There had to be a way out of this. But until she found it, Sera didn't see any choice but to appear to be politely amenable. "Pink is always a good color for her. The darker shades being the best."

"I agree. And light blues for Miss Beatrice. For Miss Amanda . . . I see the palest, springiest greens."

And never mind what the girls see or want for themselves, Sera angrily added.

"And what do you see for Seraphina?" Carden asked from his seat at the end of the table.

"Jewel tones, I should think," Honoria supplied, squinting at her. "Very deep and rich colors. She would be simply stunning in jades and sapphires."

Carden slowly shook his head. Softly, he smiled and said, "Rubies."

Barrett Stanbridge leaned forward in his chair to meet her gaze and say, "I think she's quite stunning just as she is at present."

"Hardly," Sera protested, "but thank you nonetheless, Barrett. You're most gallant." She turned to Honoria, determined to establish herself as an independent mind. "As for the matter of my wardrobe, I really don't think a new one is all that necessary. What I have—"

"Nonsense, my dear," Honoria declared with another wave of her hand. "Carden can well afford it and every woman should, at least once in her life, have a wardrobe befitting her beauty."

"Very true," he concurred. "All of it. And I insist on seeing that you have one."

Seraphina opened her mouth to protest but Camille chose that moment to reach over and tug on her Uncle

Carden's coat sleeve. He grinned and looked down at her. "Yes, Camille? What is it?"

"Uncle Carden, would be it all right if Mrs. Miller has a new dress, too?"

One corner of his mouth quirked up. "And who is Mrs. Miller?"

"Her doll," Amanda supplied with a quick but openly defiant glance at Honoria. "Mrs. Miller, Miss Sera's mama, gave her to me a long time ago. When I outgrew such things, I gave her to Beatrice."

"And I gave her to Camille," Beatrice added. "She has a china face and hands."

"And jet-black hair," Amanda contributed. "Just like Miss Sera's mama had. That's why I named her as I did."

Camille nodded earnestly and in childish awe whispered, "She's very beautiful, Uncle Carden."

Sera watched, her heart melting, as Carden Reeves grinned at his youngest niece, chucked her chin, and said, "It certainly sounds as though she is, Camille. Of course Mrs. Miller can have a new wardrobe, too. Perhaps we could get her dresses to match your own. Would you like that?"

"That would be lovely, Uncle Carden. Thank you."

"It will be my pleasure, Camille. Just remember to take Mrs. Miller with you tomorrow. They'll need to take her measurements when they take yours."

Camille nodded, adoration brimming in her dark eyes. And Sera watched as Carden Reeves drank from the well and let her take his heart prisoner. Smiling, Seraphina eased back into her chair, happier than she could ever remember being. Everything was going to be fine. Carden was well on his way to being the perfect uncle, the perfect hero. She couldn't have asked for more.

"We've never been to a dressmaker's before," Beatrice blurted.

"Never?" Honoria repeated, clearly stunned.

Amanda nodded. "Mama always made—"

"Oh, dear," Sera gasped, bolting forward in her chair, all too aware of where the sudden turn in conversation could take them. Any reference to their parents in the past tense would invite another of Honoria's rapid-fire inquisitions.

"I had no idea it was so late," Sera quickly went on, tucking her napkin beneath the edge of her plate. "My darlings, I'm afraid we must put an end to our day. If we don't retire in the next few moments, we'll be too exhausted to properly enjoy our adventure tomorrow." She smiled and glanced around the table even as she began to rise. "If you all will accept our thanks for the excellent meal and the pleasant company, we will bid you a good evening."

All three of the men politely bolted to their feet with murmured acceptances but it was Barrett Stanbridge who stepped to the back of her seat to assist her. John Aiden moved to assist Beatrice, and since Camille vaulted out of the chair on her own, Carden was left to help Amanda.

"I won't accept," Honoria said flatly, firmly.

Carden froze and stared down at his sister-in-law. "I beg your pardon?"

"And with whom will I have after-dinner conversation and sherry if Seraphina retires with our delightful nieces?" Honoria asked imperiously. "Am I supposed to remain with you gentlemen for port and cigars?"

Sera's stomach turned to lead. There was no polite way out of it; she had to stay. And she would have to formally atone for what had been a significant social gaffe. But humbling herself was all the sacrifice she was willing to make for social protocol and Honoria Reeves.

"My sincere apologies for not having thought of that, Lady Lansdown," she said softly, easing herself back into her chair. "Of course I'll remain with you. But I must insist that the girls retire. Amanda is perfectly capable of seeing herself and her sisters tucked in for the night. She's very grown-up."

Amanda momentarily sagged with obvious relief and then predictably stiffened her back and squared her shoulders.

"What about my stocking?" Beatrice whispered. "I'll need to wear it tomorrow."

"I'll darn it before I retire for the night," Sera promised.

"I'll see to it, Miss Sera," Amanda offered, taking Camille's hand in hers. "I'm very good with a needle."

"You are, indeed. And sewing is only one of your many talents. Thank you, Amanda."

Amanda beamed and Carden Reeves nodded, his smile appreciative. The girls then said their good-nights, graciously accepted the offered wishes for pleasant dreams, and departed. And when they were gone, Sera reached for her wine glass, knowing from Honoria's arched brow that she was going to need the fortification.

CHAPTER 7

Seraphina had a vague sense of moving her feet but that was all the conscious effort she could contribute to moving into the parlor with Honoria. She was so very tired and the wine, rather than strengthening her, had instead wrapped her in a wonderfully comfortable warmth that invited her to sit down, close her eyes, and drift off into dreamless sleep. And motionless sleep, she realized with a faint smile. It had been months since the bed under her hadn't rocked on the waves.

Honoria settled herself on the settee and folded her hands in her lap with an expectant air. Sera paused in the center of the room, her mind stumbling along the course of trying to guess what the woman wanted.

"Sherry, dear."

"Thank you, Lady Lansdown," Sera replied with a small shake of her head. The motion did little to revitalize her but it did provide a momentary clarity that allowed her to cross to the sideboard and pour them both a small glass of sweet sherry.

Honoria accepted hers, saying breezily, "You really mustn't make a habit of complimenting children excessively, Seraphina. It's not good for them to think too highly of themselves. It makes it difficult to manage them."

She was too tired to put up a truly spirited defense, too tired to work at evading a conflict. "I happen to think otherwise, Lady Lansdown," Sera countered quietly, settling into the opposite settee. "Children deserve to be praised for what they can do right and well. I believe recognition and respect serves to inspire them to not only do better, but to be better people."

"Oh? And do Arthur and Mary subscribe to the same views of childrearing?"

Of course they had. They'd been the ones to impart them to her. "Do you think they would have entrusted me with their children if they didn't?"

"Actually," Honoria replied, pausing to sip her drink, "despite Carden's explanations, I think Arthur and Mary are dead."

Sera caught her glass just in time. Her heart in her throat and racing, she arched a brow in what she hoped was a nonchalant fashion and said, "I beg your pardon?"

"Despite your decidedly liberal views," Honoria said, examining the color of her sherry in the firelight, "I'm certain that you're reasonably capable of caring for my nieces, Sera. You have, after all, safely brought them home from halfway around the world. But unless Arthur has changed a great deal in the twelve years since I last saw him, it just isn't in his character to let another be responsible for the care of his prized possessions if he were able to do so himself. The only logical conclusion to be drawn is that Arthur didn't bring his children home himself because he cannot. And the only reason sufficiently dire to prevent him from doing so would be death."

Sera said nothing and Honoria met her gaze squarely.

"And their mother must have passed on, as well," the woman continued. "Arthur married after I last saw him and so I never met Mary. However, knowing Arthur as I did, I can be quite certain that she was possessed of qualities very much like his own. The same reasoning applies.

If she didn't accompany her daughters home to England, then she must have also died."

The woman's logic was flawless and astute. There was no attacking it in any equally reasonable way. Neither was it possible to simply dismiss it out of hand or to admit the truth of it. Sera saw only one real choice. "Mr. Reeves has asked me to say nothing about this matter."

"Oh, do let me guess," Honoria snapped. "Carden doesn't want anyone to know that Arthur has died so that he won't have to bear the crippling weight of being a peer."

That was the essence of it, Sera knew. Carden Reeves had very legitimate reasons for being selfish but in the end . . .

"I've known Carden since he was a boy," Honoria declared, obviously not needing Sera to confirm her suspicions. "And allow me to share with you the essential core of his hope to evade his responsibility. Carden does not want to grow up. He never has. He wants to play at whatever amuses him at the moment. Four years ago, it was being an officer in Her Majesty's Corps of Engineers. Apparently that didn't quite develop the way he envisioned.

"I don't know the specific circumstances for his having resigned his commission, but I suspect that, as usual, it had something to do with the expectations being more than he was willing to meet. For the last year—since his return from the Transvaal—he's been dabbling at being an architect when he wasn't preoccupied with chasing pretty skirts all over town day in and day out. The latter, it would appear, is his one and only truly consistent interest."

Sera waited to see if the woman was simply pausing for a breath. When the silence stretched out to the point of becoming noticeable, she ventured, "You're painting a not very attractive picture of your brother-in-law."

"Carden is a very intelligent and generous man, Sera.

Considering the kind of woman his mother was and the appalling lack of supervision he had as a child, he's turned out to be a far better man than anyone honestly expected. But having said that, I'd be remiss in not warning you about his less than sterling qualities. He's far too handsome for his own good and he can charm anyone if he sets his mind to it. Just be certain that you don't allow yourself to blindly fall under his spell."

She knew about Carden Reeves's tendencies. She had, in fact, surmised him to be a rake the moment he'd opened the door to her that morning. It rankled her pride that Honoria Reeves thought her too thick to have done so on her own. "I appreciate the concern that prompts you to warn me, Lady Lansdown," Sera replied politely, "but I don't think that Mr. Reeves has any intention of charming me."

"Oh, he fully intends to seduce you. Of that I'm certain," Honoria instantly, confidently countered. She laughed and quickly added, "Don't look so put off, Seraphina. I'm old enough that I don't have to dance around delicate topics anymore. I've also seen enough in my years that biting my tongue seems selfish in the extreme.

"Carden has excellent taste in women even if he isn't at all exclusive with his favors. I can see the appraisal in his eyes whenever he looks at you. He's never been particularly good at hiding his thoughts, you know. As transparent as window glass. He finds you exceedingly attractive and has decided to make you his next grand conquest."

She'd surmised much of that on her own, as well, but was acutely uncomfortable with discussing such a very personal matter with someone who was virtually a stranger. A stranger with a quick and apparently acid tongue. Sera took a sip of her sherry and thought to put an end to the subject. "Well, I can assure you that I have no intention of being seduced, Lady Lansdown. I am, legally, a married woman."

Honoria rocked back slightly. "Oh? No one mentioned this earlier this evening. I distinctly recall that Carden introduced you as *Miss.* And where is Mr. Treadwell, if I might ask?"

"Yes, I noted the change Mr. Reeves made in my marital status at the time of introductions, but didn't see a naturally appropriate place to make the correction. My apologies for allowing you to labor under the false impression." *Not that my status is truly any of your concern or business,* Sera tartly, silently added. "And Mr. Treadwell was the guide for Arthur and Mary on their last expedition. He hasn't returned."

"So Arthur and Mary are dead, aren't they?" Honoria pressed. "Along with your husband."

"I would prefer not to discuss it, if you don't mind," Sera announced firmly, politely, rising from the settee and moving to the sideboard. "Would you care for more sherry? I'd be glad to refresh your glass."

"No, thank you. I'm fine. I don't much care for sherry, actually. Have you ever had an affair, Seraphina?"

"What? Of course not!"

"In the absence of your experience in this realm, let me share mine with you. Men are irresistibly drawn to lonely married women. First, there's the attractiveness of committing a sin—what with infidelity being the major transgression it's generally regarded to be. And then there's the likelihood of being caught in the affair itself. Danger always intensifies desire. Last, but certainly not least in their considerations, is the fact that one can't be forced to marry a woman who already has a husband. Thus, married women are the male's preferred choice for lovers. Danger, desire, risk—and all with no lasting consequences they have to bear."

What was one supposed to say in such situations? It

stood as the single most starkly frank presentation of such matters Sera had ever heard. And despite her shock at the bluntness of it all, she did have to admit that Honoria's logic was—as seemed usual—flawlessly sharp.

"You are not only a lonely married woman, Seraphina, you're also very beautiful and quite at hand. Carden can't resist the combination. Not that it's ever occurred to him to make the effort, mind you."

She was really much too tired to deal effectively with all of this. "I'm very capable of fending off his attentions," she asserted simply. "You're concerning yourself needlessly."

"Carden is nothing if not determined and persistent."

"I believe I possess similar strengths of character."

"I have no doubt that you do, my dear," Honoria replied. "Of course one must ask oneself if it's a wise decision to be so strong and virtuous. Despite his best efforts to evade his responsibilities, there will come a time when Carden has no choice but to accept them. When that day arrives—and arrive it will and sooner than he thinks—Carden Reeves will be the seventh Earl of Lansdown. Earls are always a valuable prize worth capturing. The queue will be a long one. An intelligent woman would try to place herself to the front of it."

Sera knitted her brows, disconcerted by the unexpected turn in the woman's thinking and wondering if perhaps she'd misunderstood. Hadn't they just been speaking of the wisdom in evading Carden's attentions? "Are you saying that I should let Carden seduce me in the hope of someday being asked to marry him?" she asked, unable to keep the incredulity from her voice.

"Your husband is presumed dead," Honoria observed with a shrug. "I'm sure the Queen's courts would clear that unfortunate little obstacle out of your bridal path."

Resisting the urge to rub the dull ache blooming between her brows, Sera shook her head and summoned patience. "I'm hardly the type of woman that a peer would marry. My father was a scientist of sorts, my mother the daughter of a Spanish ship's captain. I come from a family of neither wealth nor consequence."

"Some women wouldn't let such a little detail prevent them from achieving a grand social coup," Honoria countered, thoroughly undeterred. "I can't tell you how many females I know who claim lineages whose authenticity can only be described as dubious at best."

"I have absolutely no desire whatsoever to marry again, Lady Lansdown. Once was more than enough for me."

"A lonely, *unhappily* married woman. Your appeal just soared another full ten degrees," she declared with a majestic wave of her hand. "If you truly intend to resist Carden's advances, you'd best keep that bit of information carefully tucked away. Not that he'd be incapable of ferreting it out anyway. The only time men seem able to read female minds with any clarity is when it comes to seducing them. Once that's accomplished, however, they become as thick as planks. I honestly think there should be some scientific study as to how that happens, don't you?"

"It would no doubt prove interesting." And interesting was what her next conversation with Carden Reeves would be, as well. If the man honestly thought his sister-in-law was nothing more than a sweet little gossip monger, then he really needed to have the blinders removed. Preferably by considerable force. She'd be more than happy to oblige him.

"So tell me about yourself, your family, Seraphina. You said your father was a scientist of sorts."

Recalling the paces through which Honoria had put John Aiden earlier in the evening, Sera steadied herself for the onslaught and replied, "He was a botanist who specialized in tropical species. He thought to someday publish his work but died before he could see it done."

"And your mother?"

"Unlike Lady Wickerly, she didn't endure in silence. My father always maintained that it was her Spanish blood that made her tongue as sharp and quick as it was."

"Their union wasn't a happy one, then."

It would have been easiest to agree and leave it at that. But she couldn't. Not in good conscience. Her parents' relationship had been a complex but generally companionable one. "My mother wanted to escape life on the sea. My father needed someone to manage the dreary day-to-day details of his life. Their relationship was more practical and businesslike than romantic. And since neither entered the marriage with illusions of it ever being more than that, they were actually quite content with their circumstances and each other."

Honoria didn't so much as pause to digest what she'd been told, much less offer a positive comment on it. "And your late husband . . . how did you meet?"

"He made a public pretense of being a business associate of my father's," she dutifully, sketchily supplied. "In actuality, he exchanged empty promises for meals and lodging."

"And for you."

She'd never looked at it quite that way, but there was a kernel of truth in Honoria's observation. "In the final analysis, yes, he did," she admitted, not liking at all what it implied about her ability to make intelligent judgments.

Honoria said something else—on what subject Sera had no idea and didn't really much care. Carden and his friends were in the foyer and coming toward the parlor, their glasses in hand. She was about to be rescued and she would be eternally grateful to whichever of them had been the one to think she might need it. With any luck at all, the longest day of her life might soon come to a solitary and silent close.

• • •

If Seraphina hadn't been so obviously miserable just a moment before, Carden might have smiled at the look of utter relief that came over her beautiful face as he approached the parlor doors. Still, it did a man good to know that his presence was welcomed and appreciated. It made engaging in parlor talk an almost worthwhile torture.

"Carden," Honoria said a bit too sharply, turning to follow Sera's line of sight. If her tone hadn't adequately conveyed her annoyance at having them join them, her frown most certainly did. "Don't tell me that the three of you have had your fill of port and smoke already."

He ignored her disapproval. "We discovered the pleasures of both to be sorely lacking in the absence of sparkling feminine conversation."

"That," Barrett added, "and we're rather hoping to find that you've solved all the problems of the empire while we've been gone."

"We were making our way in that direction," Honoria countered with a tight, obviously false smile. "A pity that you didn't have a bit more patience. We've been discussing tomorrow's proposed foray to the dressmaker."

Sera started. Only slightly and she recovered quickly, but the reaction was sufficient to tell him that Honoria was about to try to lead him down a primrose path. He always figured it out sooner or later, but it was nice to know at the outset for a change. Bless Seraphina and her innate honesty.

"Considering the size of the order, Carden, I don't think it would be at all inappropriate to ask the dressmaker to come to Seraphina and the girls. Why should they bundle themselves in and out of carriages and through town so that Mr. Gauthier can make a handsome profit?"

"Gauthier?" he repeated, watching Seraphina out of the

corner of his eye. He'd guess she'd never heard the name before, either.

"My dressmaker, Carden. He's newly arrived from the Continent and already the toast of London. Surely you don't intend for our nieces and Sera to be clothed by a second-rate seamstress, do you?"

"Of course not," he said, deliberately reminding himself that Honoria didn't mean to insult nearly as often as she did. "If you want to send for the great Gauthier, then by all means send for him."

"Thank you for being agreeable."

His sister-in-law turned her attention fully to Sera— who visibly squared her shoulders as Honoria drew breath. "Would the day after tomorrow be soon enough, Seraphina? I know the girls are in desperate need, but the initial meeting with a dressmaker is always an exhausting ordeal and I'm afraid that conferring with Mr. Gauthier in addition to moving might be just a bit much for them to manage well in a single day."

Sera's brows came together for a split second. In the next, she touched her tongue to her lower lip. It was enough to tell him that this was the very first she'd heard of the notion.

"Moving?" he asked casually. "Who's moving?"

Honoria's shoulders sagged dramatically. She added to her performance by looking at him and then rolling her eyes and sighing. "Why, Seraphina and the girls, of course. They can't possibly stay here with you. An unmarried man keeping an unmarried woman under his roof? Really, Carden. You know the tawdry kind of speculation that would invite."

The look Sera shot him was one of almost panic. He might have thought she was truly concerned about scandal had she not immediately glanced toward Honoria and suppressed a tiny shudder. Lord knew he could understand how she felt.

"Seraphina is our nieces' companion," he explained kindly, but firmly. "A full and good step up from being an employee but hardly an elevation to the pedestal of being a mistress. The distinction is clear and I'm sure everyone will be able to make it without undue fuss. There's absolutely no need to uproot Sera and the girls and cart them across town to live with you."

"Seraphina, my dear," Honoria pressed. "In light of our—"

"I understand your concerns, Lady Lansdown," Sera interrupted, her smile so tight it made Carden's face ache. "And I most certainly appreciate them. But truth be told, the girls and I have just today concluded a very long, very draining journey. We've barely begun to unpack and settle in. But begun we have and the very idea of putting our things back into our trunks and setting forth again . . ."

She slowly shook her head. "The distance doesn't matter. Even were it a matter of a few feet down a public walkway, I think I'd rather let you pick up that spyglass from the end table and beat me about the head and shoulders with it."

"Please think of your reputation, my dear."

"Whatever Mr. Reeves chooses to call me," Sera answered, "I am, in essence an employee. I'm no different than Mrs. Blaylock, the new housekeeper, or her daughter, Anne. If society chooses to speculate as to the possibility of untoward goings-on in his household, then it really should find a more productive use for its time. I refuse to exhaust myself and the girls because those in society are bored with their own lives."

"Bravo, Seraphina!" Aiden cheered, clapping. "Bravo!"

Barrett lifted his port glass in salute. "Exceedingly well said."

Yes, Carden had to agree, Seraphina Treadwell was truly magnificent. Honoria had finally met her match in the grand feminine contest of wills. And he'd seen it with his own eyes. He'd have to buy her a suitably wonderful present to thank her for the rare gift she'd just given him.

"In the belief that one should always retire while holding the high note," Sera went on, "I do believe that I shall ask you all to excuse me. While it has been a most enjoyable evening, it's come at the end of an arduous day."

"Of course, Sera," Carden said, aware of the fragile edge that had suddenly come to her voice. "My sincerest apologies for having contributed to the length of it. Sleep well and soundly."

"Thank you," she replied, her smile truly relieved as she set aside her full sherry glass. "I believe I shall."

Honoria, as always never content to let someone else have the last word on anything, nodded and said, "Not to worry yourself concerning Mr. Gauthier, Seraphina. I shall take care of it all and make myself available to assist you in any manner necessary."

Sera was gracious in her exhaustion and her victory. "Thank you, Lady Lansdown. It's most kind of you. I'm sure I'll need all the help anyone would care to give. Your nieces and I are here at your convenience."

Her gaze touched his for a long moment in which he could have sworn he heard her offer her heartfelt thanks and then it was gone, touching the gazes of Barrett and John Aiden briefly as she softly said, "Gentlemen, good evening."

There was nothing the least bit disrespectful in his friends' regard as they watched her leave. If anything they looked like besotted fools. It occurred to him that—given their obvious approval—he should feel a certain sense of masculine pride for having such an incredible woman living under his roof. And yet that wasn't what he was feeling at all. It was a gnawing sensation, deep in the center of his chest, and he found it decidedly irritating.

"Carden, if you would be so kind as to have Sawyer inform my driver that I am ready to go home."

"Of course, Honoria," he said, bowing briefly, grateful that she'd offered a distraction. "I'll leave Aiden and Barrett to entertain you for the moment. Please don't marry them off while I'm gone. They're my only friends."

Barrett and Aiden laughed—were still laughing as he walked out of the parlor. But he'd seen the look in Honoria's eyes and knew they wouldn't be laughing long. He grinned. *That* would take their minds off Seraphina Treadwell.

CHAPTER 8

Seraphina glanced up through the roof of the greenhouse, smiling at the sun. Lord only knew how long it would last but she intended to enjoy every instant of it that she could. Life sometimes took unexpected turns that worked out in the most wonderfully convenient ways. She owed a morning of time to paint to the fact nothing around her had gone according to her well-made and carefully laid out plans.

Sawyer had brought breakfast to the schoolroom, informing her in the process that Carden had gone out to take care of some pressing professional concerns. He didn't know when he'd be back and she gathered from Sawyer's manner that they should all hope that it would be a good long while. His absence had been something of a fly in the soup of her plans, but Sera had been grateful to postpone the less than pleasant prospect of having to tell Carden Reeves that Honoria was on to his game.

Mrs. Blaylock and Anne had arrived shortly after that, tossed their few belongings into their quarters, and then set about earning their keep with a steely-eyed, polishing-cloth vengeance. It was patently obvious that nothing was going to stand in Mrs. Blaylock's way of fully imposing a new household order by sundown. No room was ig-

nored, no surface untouched. Deciding to take herself and
the girls to the seclusion of the greenhouse had been more
an act of self-preservation than mere courtesy.

She'd still been organizing their supplies for the retreat
when the front bell had begun ringing. The first had been
a messenger from Mr. Gauthier. He'd been informed of a
desperate fashion need, was honored to be considered the
only man in Christendom able to perform the rescue, and
would be there as soon as was humanly possible. She was
to be brave until then. She'd laughed outright, jumped in
front of Mrs. Blaylock just long enough to tell the housekeeper of the courtier's impending arrival, and then
vaulted clear of the dervish she'd set off.

The second bell had been rung by Honoria's footman
who had handed Sawyer a quickly scribbled note of regret
and dashed away. Sera smiled, remembering how she'd
still been thanking the gods for the merciful reprieve when
the bell had rung a third time and Sawyer had admitted a
grinning Barrett Stanbridge.

The bell was ringing—and Sawyer was answering—
yet again when Barrett had gallantly offered to carry their
easels and paint boxes to the greenhouse for them. She'd
graciously allowed him to do so, and as she carried her
portfolio herself, they'd all set off for the rear of the house
in a happy, laughing entourage that to her mind greatly
resembled a group of picnickers. The thought had still
been with her when she'd caught a glimpse of Monroe in
the butler's pantry and she'd paused to ask him if it might
be possible to have lunch brought to them in a basket.
He'd been agreeable and she'd left the ringing doorbell
and the household chaos behind.

Helpful though Barrett genuinely tried to be, he'd
proven himself to be largely worthless in getting the easels
set to the best advantage of the sunlight and so she'd eventually sent him off to subtly oversee the girls as they ex-
plored the conservatory while she took care of the

placements herself. Of course, she admitted, looking around herself now, there wasn't a specimen in the whole of the greenhouse that was worthy of being painted.

It boggled her mind to think that Carden Reeves had allowed it all to come to the sad state it had, that he hadn't considered the employment of a gardener to be as essential as that of a butler, a cook, and a footman. Or of a housekeeping staff, for that matter. His priorities were so typically male.

But then, she admitted in the spirit of fairness, she saw plants differently than most people did. They were her life, the center around which every other facet of her waking hours had always revolved.

Undistracted this time by Carden's presence, Seraphina took the opportunity to carefully study the greenhouse. She appreciated the structure of it, noting the solid construction and the well-designed areas for specialized cultivation. With time and effort, it would be a magical place to spend the mornings. And in the coming winter, it would be a haven for the cold-numbed senses. Assuming, of course, that she and the girls were still here then. Carden Reeves had, after all, announced his intention to send them off to the country house as soon as the renovations were completed and it was habitable.

Of course that had been yesterday when he'd thought sending them away could actually keep Arthur's fate— and his own—a secret. He might have been able to cling to the illusion into today had Honoria not descended on them for dinner last night. Now . . .

Sera chuckled and shook her head as she set about arranging the small grouping of well-cushioned rattan furniture that had been haphazardly left about beneath a nearby arrangement of huge but sickly looking potted palms. There was a nice little, low table that would be perfect for serving when Monroe brought their lunch basket. Around it, she placed the four armchairs and used their individual footrests as side tables for the beverages that would no doubt accompany their meal.

The chaise longue—a long and decadently comfortable-looking piece of wicker artistry—didn't fit into the grouping with any sort of natural ease and so she dragged it slightly off to the side and took a few moments to create what she could of a miniature world for it to anchor. Surrounded by a wide variety of brightly glazed pots containing some straggling bits of determined green and with her easel angled just so, she decided that it was all surprisingly cozy despite the quickness of the effort and the lack of decent botanical accents. Nodding with satisfaction, she brought her supplies and portfolio into her little island and then prepared a collection of empty pots and interestingly dried plant materials for the girls to use as a subject.

Watercolors, she decided as she considered the various mediums they could explore that day. The thought gave her sudden pause. Water. Everything so desperately needed a long, healthy drink of water. There had been a lovely if slightly dented watering can under the bench she'd worked at a bit yesterday. There had been a stack of buckets, too, if she remembered correctly. Somewhere, likely tucked discreetly behind a bank of dead plants, there had to be a water pump. And just as there had to be a pump, there had to be a coal stove. If she could get Barrett to find it, light it, coax just a bit of heat out of it . . .

It certainly wasn't how she'd planned to spend her day when she'd risen that morning, but she knew that nothing else would give her even half the satisfaction. And it had been a very, very long time since she'd felt such high excitement about any course of action. There was definitely something to be said for that.

"Girls!" she called, happily gathering her skirts and setting out to find them. "I have an idea!"

• • •

Lady Caruthers might very well be a lady, but she had the sense of a goose. A *stuffed and roasted* goose. "Go look at Lady Godwin's conservatory," Carden sniped, slamming the front door closed behind himself.

His butler stood beside the foyer table as though waiting for him. "Good afternoon, sir."

"Well, against my pride and better judgment, I've spent the morning doing just that, Sawyer," he barked. "And from what I've seen, it looks to me like Lady Caruthers wants a conservatory half the size of a single rail car and she wants it built out of slivers of tin and dried-up old twigs. I won't do it. Not for all the tea in India or all the diamonds in the Transvaal. Lady Caruthers can damn well find herself another architect."

"Very good, sir," Sawyer replied. He picked up the silver tray from the foyer table—laden with a precarious stack of envelopes—and held it out to him, asking, "Will you be having luncheon in the conservatory with the others?"

"What's all this?" Carden asked, taking the correspondence before it could cascade to the floor at his feet.

"They have been arriving in a constant stream all morning, sir. If you'd care to stand there for five minutes, you can easily acquire another two. I see the carriages pulling up."

Carden glanced over his shoulder, seeing through the sidelights that Sawyer was—as always—correct. Two carriages were indeed parking in front of his house. He looked down at the envelopes, noting the fine stationery, the elegant penmanships. And he *knew*. He tore one open and pulled the card from inside in a desperate attempt to prove himself wrong. He wasn't.

"Where is Seraphina?"

"In the conservatory," Sawyer supplied. "With your

nieces and Mr. Stanbridge, sir. Monroe took them a basket lunch a short while ago."

His already racing pulse shot a sizzling jolt through his veins. "What's Barrett doing here?"

"I have no idea, sir." Sawyer met his gaze and cocked a white brow. "Was I to have asked before I admitted him?"

"No," he snarled, heading off, the envelopes gripped tightly in his hand, and feeling a strange, rather ill-defined but decidedly unsettling mixture of emotions. There was certainly a healthy dose of anger in it all; he'd been working up that one all morning. First with the nameless nincompoop who had thought to build a conservatory and hold himself up as an engineer. And then Lady Caruthers who thought he should surrender all concerns about competency in exchange for her pounds and shillings. And now Seraphina Treadwell, Honoria, and Barrett seemed to be trying to elbow their way past each other to make the top of his resentment list. They might just have to share it, he decided, as he stormed toward the rear of the house. He couldn't decide with which of them he was more angry.

Carden yanked open the conservatory door, took a single long stride in, blindly shoved the door closed behind him, and stopped dead in his tracks.

There, right in front of him, semi-reposed on a chaise in a soft pool of light was Seraphina. She looked over her shoulder at him and smiled. And in that small, very feminine gesture, his senses flooded. The air wrapped around him, warm and thick and moist, smelling profoundly alive and dancing through the shafts of sunlight, bathing Seraphina's golden curls and creamy skin, brightening her breathtakingly blue eyes.

Eden. And Eve. The easel, the half-done watercolor, the small plate on the cushion with bread and cheese. Seraphina, somehow looking both serene and vibrant. If ever there was an angel of sweet come-hither. . . His knees slowly weakened.

"Ah, just in time for lunch."

So delectable. For dinner, too.

"Card?"

The cocoon of his fantasies pierced by the sharp edge of reality, Carden started, realizing too late that he and Seraphina weren't alone, that Barrett sat in a wicker throne off to the side, a witness to his momentary loss of calculated control. The embarrassment of bruised pride sparked his anger anew. Thank God the girls were—judging by the sounds—somewhere in the back of the greenhouse and hadn't seen him make a drooling fool of himself.

"Do you know what these are?" he demanded, striding toward Sera, practically shaking the stack of envelopes at her.

She arched a delicate brow and took them from him, her gaze searching his warily. He took up a broad stance, folded his arms across his chest, and glared down at her, silently commanding her to look and then explain as best she could. With a sigh, she obeyed, reading the one he'd already opened and simply shuffling through the rest.

"They're invitations," she said evenly, handing them back to him. "You're supposed to reply to them in some manner approximating gracious."

No immediate explanation. No instant apology. This wasn't proceeding as he thought it rightly should. "Do you have any notion as to why my foyer table is being littered with them even as we speak?"

"Well," she answered blithely, "it certainly can't be because people want to revel in your sparkling good humor."

His pulse was hammering in his temples, but not loud enough to obliterate the sound of Barrett chuckling. Carden turned, glared at his friend—who had the sense to at least cover his grin with his hand—and began to pace.

"These are being delivered by the wagonload," he growled, "because the word has gone forth. Carden Reeves is the new earl! Polish the plate and queue up the daughters!"

"I didn't say a word to Honoria. I fully honored our agreement," Sera asserted, apparently unruffled by his agitation. "She deduced it all on her own. And in all likelihood long before I ever came down the stairs to meet her last night. But if you want to climb to the rooftop and proclaim Arthur to be alive and well in Belize, go right ahead. For a while, it would be your word against Honoria's."

He thought about it, pictured himself on the roof. In his club. On public walkways. He stopped pacing. "That would be pathetic."

"Yes, it would."

He could have done without her quick and easy agreement. It was salt on the battered heap of what had been his hopes for a relatively normal, private life. It was especially embittering to realize that he hadn't been allowed the time to even consider how he might go about accomplishing it.

Not that any of it was Seraphina's fault, he knew. And that was the oddest thing. Part of him wanted to be angry—truly, ragingly, wildly angry—about the unfairness of it all. But he couldn't seem to muster so much as a sliver of the passion necessary for such a display. The notion of lying down on the chaise with Sera was another matter entirely, though. *That* he could do wholeheartedly and quite passionately.

"What's this?" he asked, suddenly aware of Barrett standing beside him, an envelope in his own hand.

"Oh, guess," Barrett drawled as he surrendered it. "Make it fun."

Carden slipped his finger beneath the flap, popped it open, and extracted the formally printed invitation tucked inside. A handwritten note had been hastily scribbled across the bottom. "Your mother, too?" he asked, meeting Barrett's gaze.

"Everyone knows, Carden," his friend said with a chagrined smile. "Mother received two notes from friends about your elevation before breakfast was half over. Please tell me you'll be there. I really don't want her to be disappointed. She thinks she has a good chance of pulling off the greatest social coup of the season."

Barrett's mother was a wonderful woman, kind and gentle, the perfect hostess. He'd been a guest at her table many a time and always when she'd nothing to gain socially from inviting him. To his thinking, if ever there was a person who deserved to achieve a coup, it was Melanie Stanbridge. And if he was going to hand out coups, then he was going to take the opportunity to make one for himself, as well.

"All right," he said, his course quickly but clearly charted. "I'll go. But it's the only invitation I'm accepting. The *only* one."

"Mother will be over the moon," Barrett offered, obviously relieved and grateful. "Thank you, Card."

"I'll send the formal reply, of course, but when you tell her it's coming, also tell her not to trouble herself with finding a dinner companion for me. I'll be bringing my own."

"Oh?" Barrett asked even as his gaze slipped past Carden and in the direction of the chaise.

Carden chose to ignore him and turned to Seraphina with a smile, warmed by the plans he had for her social debut. The timing was perfect—if he could get everything else to fall into place around it. "What have you heard from the great Gauthier?" he asked crisply, the gears of his brain clicking furiously.

"He sent word that he'll be here at two. Today."

"I thought Honoria was arranging for him to call to-morrow."

"Apparently he's willing to scurry to attend the nieces of the new Earl of Lansdown."

That was a double-edged sword, but he'd live with it. "And Honoria?"

Sera either didn't make the slightest effort to hide her relief or it was simply too great to be contained; he couldn't tell which. "She sent her apologies just a while ago. She stumbled across a love poem Percival wrote her and she's prostrate with a new wave of grief."

"Percival never wrote a poem in his life," Carden declared with a derisive snort. "Limericks, yes. Horribly obscene ones. But never a poem. Honoria's hiding from me."

"Well," she observed, quiet laughter in the gaze she turned up at him, "I can't say that I blame her."

He had to give Sera that one. He had been a bad-tempered bear when he'd come in. But now . . . He'd be damned delightful company if only Barrett would toddle off to tell his mother the good news. Irritated that his friend wasn't making the slightest effort to be clairvoyant, Carden clenched his teeth and deliberately turned his thoughts in another direction.

"No, now that I think about it, Honoria's not hiding," he said. "At this very moment, she's in her carriage, clinging to the straps as her driver careens through town on two wheels so that she can spread the word as far and fast as she can. I warned you about her, Sera."

"Oh, yes, I remember that," she instantly scoffed. "You told me she was sweet and couldn't keep secrets. You made her sound like a darling, well-intentioned, little old gossip. Ha! Honoria may be somewhat aged and tiny, but make no mistake about it, Carden Reeves, your sister-in-law is nothing short of a social shark."

"A shark?" he repeated, rocking back on his heels,

stunned by Sera's unexpectedly strong opinion. "Don't you think that's just a bit over the top?"

She arched a brow. "No, I don't. When it comes to manipulation, she puts Machiavelli to shame."

"Well, yes," he conceded, deciding that he liked Sera's feathers a bit ruffled. All passion was linked and one kind quite often led to another. How, precisely, Sera's emotions were strung together remained to be seen. "But Honoria's harmless and ineffectual in the end," he said, carefully watching the light in Sera's eyes. "Isn't that what women are all about?"

Apparently not Seraphina Treadwell, he instantly noted. No one would ever walk over her and not have a bruise to show for it.

"Are you suggesting that all women are manipulative?" she asked ever so calmly, curling her side into the back of the chaise so that she could better look up at him. "Or are you saying that they're harmlessly ineffectual at it?"

"Be careful how you answer that, Card," Barrett laughingly said as he beat a retreat toward his wicker chair under the potted palms.

"Don't you have a crime you should be working to solve?" Carden called after him, hoping that he'd take the hint and use it as an excuse.

"Not at the moment."

Damn, Barrett could be a pain when he wanted. "Perhaps you ought to be out looking for one."

Barrett dropped unceremoniously into the chair, propped his feet up on the little table with the food basket, and grinned. "I think there's a very good chance a crime might be committed right here. Of course, male stupidity isn't criminal. Just embarrassingly common. And if Seraphina kills you for it, it could be considered an entirely justifiable homicide. Either way, there isn't going to be much for me to investigate. It does, however, promise to be highly entertaining in other respects. Do go on, Carden. You were insulting the female mind."

Yes, he had been, actually. And to his overall discredit, deliberately. Being around Sera tended to make mush of his better judgment and shred his sense of self-restraint.

Before he could turn back to her and offer something along the lines of an apology, Seraphina glided past him, asking, "Would you care for something to eat? There's plenty left and it couldn't help but improve your general disposition."

"At the very least," Barrett contributed, sitting forward and flipping the cloth cover off the basket for Sera, "eating would prevent you from putting your foot in your mouth again."

Seraphina began to assemble a plate of food as his friend sat back in his chair again and asked, "Just out of morbid curiosity, what have you been doing this morning to have your attitude so thoroughly soured?"

There was something too comfortably domestic about the way Barrett and Seraphina shared the space around the little table. He didn't like it. "I went to look at Lady Godwin's conservatory," Carden supplied, making his way to the chair next to Barrett's. "Lady Caruthers suggested that I do that so I'll know what she wants and can get the next set of drawings . . ." He clenched his teeth and forced himself to finish. *"Right."*

"And?" Sera gently pressed without looking at him.

"Lady Godwin's conservatory was built a good fifty years ago and mostly out of wax and spit. I'm surprised it's still standing." He paused a moment, remembering, and then added, "But considering my disgusted departure and the way I slammed the door behind me, it may well not be now."

Sera handed him a large white linen napkin and a plate generously filled with meats, cheeses, and fruit. "Thank you," he said, noting the little smile playing at the corners of her mouth and regretting again his having baited her. "You haven't poisoned it, have you?"

"No," she answered, settling into the chair opposite him. "Your poisonous plants were among the first to die from the neglect."

He was pondering whether or not she'd honestly given the notion serious consideration when she asked, "Was there anything at all to like about the Godwin conservatory? Was the ventilation adequate? Was the lighting good, the heat even?"

"I couldn't tell beyond it being stifling. There was barely room to walk into it. I had to all but back up to get out. What I know about it structurally is what I was able to discern from walking around the crumbling exterior of it."

"Ah, that's it, then," she said softly, almost as though to herself.

"What's it?"

She studied him and he could see her choosing not only her words, but a path of some sort. "Lady Caruthers isn't at all interested in the structure itself," she finally ventured. "What she wants is a jungle."

"To have a jungle in London," Carden countered, "one has to grow it inside a rather large glass box."

"Agreed. But while *you* care about what the box looks like, Lady Caruthers cares only about what's inside it."

He was about to point out that what was inside depended in large measure on what was built around it when she continued. "You said that she wanted the next set of plans done right. What did the first set look like? In a general sense."

"They're plans," he said simply. She arched a brow, silently informing him that it wasn't nearly as simple as he thought. "Standard engineering drawings," he clarified. "An idiot could take them and build the structure as long as he could read and competently use a measure."

"Did you present her with any drawings of how the structure would look when it was lushly, extravagantly stocked with plants?"

"I'm an engineer, not a gardener. How she fills it up is neither my concern nor my responsibility."

"He has a point," Barrett offered in his defense, reaching for an apple and a knife.

"That can only be maintained," Sera instantly contended, "out of sheer stubbornness and at the price of having his plans rejected."

"Well, I can live without building Lady Caruthers a conservatory," Carden pointed out a bit more testily than he'd intended. "Her rejection isn't going to give me any sleepless nights or have us living on the street."

"Yes, but if you were to give her pretty pictures with lots of green and wild splashes of bright colors, she'd be happy as a lark and would let you build whatever your heart desires. Your pride and reputation needn't be bruised."

It occurred to him that he should be bothered by Sera's ability to see through him so easily, but he wasn't. He was too interested in the way her mind worked. "You're quite confident of that, aren't you?"

"Yes, I am."

"Why?"

"The last few months we were in Belize," she explained, "what money we had came from the art I was able to sell to the locals and to the travelers that passed through from time to time. The men always preferred the subjects realistically portrayed down to the smallest detail. The women, on the other hand, wanted me to capture their dreams and, in that way, make them real. Effectively making that distinction between what I offered the two types of patrons determined whether or not we ate."

He couldn't imagine living like that; hand to mouth, moment to moment, dependent on hawking something of yourself to complete strangers. And yet, to hear Seraphina tell of it, it had been a perfectly manageable state of affairs, a business like any other. It really was a most amazing perspective.

"So Lady Caruthers wants Carden to design her *dream* conservatory."

"Yes," she answered, nodding. "And her vision is of the exotic treasures inside the box, *not* the box itself."

"I'm not an artist, either," Carden felt obliged to point out. "I'm an architect. I specialize in boxes."

"Well," Barrett drawled as he cut himself another slice of apple, "how very fortunate you are that you happen to have an artist in residence."

Did he honestly care about Lady Caruthers's damned floral dream? Not really, he had to admit. But there was his pride to consider. He'd never in his life had a proposal rejected. And then there were the benefits to working professionally with Seraphina. Which weren't altogether professional in their potential.

"I'll pay you for your services, of course," he offered, his pulse racing. "Assuming that you're inclined to do the drawings."

Her smile was soft and so in contrast to the mischievous sparkle in her eyes. "I wouldn't have broached the subject had I not been willing from the outset to offer my talents to the cause. And while pay isn't necessary, additional art supplies will be. Mine have become embarrassingly depleted."

It was a vague feeling, one he couldn't quite grasp, much less define . . .

"You know, Card, I have the distinct impression that you've been effectively, artfully manipulated. And by—wonder of wonders—a female."

That was it. He'd all but been taken by the hand and led along. And he'd gone without so much as an inkling of what was happening in the larger scheme of things. And damn Barrett for seeing and understanding it before he had. This wasn't how things usually went. What was wrong with him? And why the hell wasn't he angry with Seraphina for having played him like the proverbial fiddle? His conscience quietly suggested that perhaps it was because he knew that he'd deserved it.

"When are you scheduled to present Lady Caruthers with a revised plan?" Sera asked, gracefully moving past his embarrassment.

"Tuesday, next," he supplied, deciding that the smartest thing to do was focus his present attention on future possibilities. "You'll need to see my existing plans so that you can incorporate some of the structural features into the drawings, won't you?"

"Yes, although you may well have to explain to me what it is I'm looking at. I'm an artist, not an engineer."

She was a good winner, gracious and not inclined to gloat. That made her a better person than almost everyone he knew. Including himself. She was also insightful, genteel, and loin-hardeningly beautiful . . . Yes, there was no denying it, Seraphina Treadwell came damn close to being feminine perfection. The only thing that kept her from actually achieving it was the sense of formality and distance she kept between them. To have her melt at his touch . . . And he'd decided that he could be patient about easing past those barriers and seducing her? What had he been thinking?

Whatever answer his conscience might have offered this time was precluded by the sound of Sawyer clearing his throat in the near distance. "Mr. Gauthier has arrived."

"I didn't hear any trumpets," Carden quipped.

"I'm surprised, sir."

"Thank you, Sawyer. We'll be along directly," Sera promised, starting to rise from her seat.

He and Barrett both vaulted to their feet, but he was the first to extend his hand and Barrett was left to deal with packing up the remnants of the lunch basket.

"Ladies!" Sera called toward the rear of the greenhouse as he tucked her arm around his. "It's time to go! Please put things back in their places and come along!"

In the distance there were flashes of skirts as his nieces hurried to obey. As Barrett hefted up the basket, Carden smiled down at the woman at his side. "I like what you've done with the conservatory this morning," he said. "It feels very different than it did just yesterday. Much more alive." *He* felt more alive, too, but decided that saying so would be entirely too soppy.

"I'm glad you approve," she replied happily. "The girls and I will be coming here frequently. I hope you'll join us as often as you can so that you can watch the progress with us."

He'd prefer to be with her alone here. He had plans for that chaise. But time with Sera was time with Sera and, for now, he'd take it however he could get it. And to imagine that just over twenty-four hours ago he hadn't known she existed. At least Fate had been kind enough to send grim news with a gorgeous messenger. He had to be thankful for that.

All three of the girls bounded up, breathless and buoyant.

"Is Aunt Honoria here after all?" Beatrice asked, tugging her stockings up.

"No, darling, she isn't," Sera supplied. "We'll have to muddle through on our own and hope for the best."

Amanda whirled on him, her eyes bright. "If Aunt Honoria isn't here to help us choose new dresses, must I have the palest, springiest greens anyway?"

She was asking him? He couldn't fathom why, but he was willing to find out. "You don't want green?"

"I'd prefer to have bright red."

"No," he declared, seeing where Amanda had hoped to go. He might be a bachelor, but he wasn't about to allow his nieces to become the kind of women with whom he ever so casually socialized. "Young ladies do not wear red. Of any hue. They wear pastels in the spring and summer and muted shades in the fall and winter. You may have a red dress when—and *only* when—your husband buys it for you."

Amanda wasn't happy with the pronouncement and she stomped off, following her sisters and Barrett toward the door. Carden watched her go, thinking that in a few years she was going to be a handful. They weren't going to be able to let her out of their sight for more than ten seconds at a time. And he suspected that there would be occasions when ten seconds would be eight seconds too many.

"You do know something about choosing female wardrobes," Sera said softly, calling him from his musing. He'd looked down to meet her gaze before she added, "I'm most impressed, Carden."

His heart soared ridiculously into his throat. "I'm a male," he managed to say around it. "I pay very close attention to details." He paused to swallow. "Seraphina."

"And thank you for the paternal response to Amanda's attempt to grow up too quickly. It was perfect."

"Sometimes I actually get things right," he admitted with a shrug.

"Yes, you do," she said, drawing her arm from his and stepping back with a bright smile. "Now, if you will please excuse me, I have no intention whatsoever of allowing you to make even the slightest attempt to do right by *my* wardrobe selections."

"You don't trust my taste?" he asked, hoping to keep her engaged in conversation.

"Somehow," she laughingly replied, turning away, "I doubt very much that you have any experience at choosing clothing suitable for a proper governess."

She was right, of course. Not that he was going to let her idea of proper stand in his way. He'd bide his time here for a little while and then speak alone with the illustrious Mr. Gauthier. As two men who no doubt shared an appreciation for the female form, they'd be of like minds when it came to clothing Seraphina's.

Stuffing his hands in his pockets, Carden wandered over to Sera's easel. Clearly she wasn't painting anything real. Nothing in his conservatory looked that alive and healthy. In fact . . . Yes, it certainly looked as though Sera were making a reasonable attempt to emulate the style of botanical prints that had taken the empire by storm. Every woman who considered herself fashionable had flower pictures nailed to every wall in her home. Colonel Collier's wife had even put the damned things up in the officers' mess. Barrett's mother was an avid collector of them, too. He'd bought her three of them for Christmas last year.

Carden shook his head. Sera wasn't a bad artist. Technically, he couldn't fault her on any point. Her sense of proportion and perspective were excellent and her work was generally quite appealing to look at. He didn't have a doubt as to her ability to paint pictures that Lady Caruthers would love. But he really had hoped that she was more the daring, risk-taking type.

Maybe with time and encouragement, he told himself as he turned and set off to find Mr. Gauthier.

CHAPTER 9

Carden heard them coming down the stairs; girls seemed to be always chattering about something. He cast a quick glance toward the crates that had been stacked against the library wall since their arrival and hoped that today would be the day he would finally be in the right place at the right time. He'd seen more of Mrs. Blaylock in the last couple of days than he had Seraphina.

Just in case his miserable luck was about to change for the better, he flipped open the drawings he'd placed on the central table and struck a studious pose. From the corner of his eye he saw a flash of ruffle in the doorway. There was a God and He was good.

"Good morning, Uncle Carden," Beatrice called out as they trooped into the room with Sera, like a good shepherd, trailing behind. "We have come to put away the books."

"Well, hello, ladies. And how are you today?"

"We're fine," Amanda answered for them. "Thank you for asking. And yourself?"

"Never better."

Sera crossed the threshold and stopped, casting a glance at the table before meeting his gaze and asking, "Are we interrupting? We can come back later."

"Not at all," he hastily assured her. "I was just looking at the Caruthers plans."

The ploy produced precisely the reaction he'd intended. Sera started and then stepped forward, saying, "Would now be a good time to share them with me? The girls are quite capable of putting the books on the shelves without my assistance."

"If you'd like," he replied with all the nonchalance he could muster. "That would be fine with me."

Camille dashed up to all but bounce in front of him. "Mr. Gauthier is bringing some of our new clothes today, Uncle Carden."

He knew that already and he had a plan for it, too. "Oh, he is? Tell you what," he said, bending slightly to bring his gaze more even with that of his youngest niece. "When he does, why don't you all put on your new walking dresses and we'll go for a stroll in the park to show them off? Would you like that?"

Camille's eyes widened to the size of saucers. "With our parasols!" she gasped. In the next second she was gone, bounding toward her sisters—who were just as wide-eyed, but trying very hard to be more mature about it all.

"The library must be in order before we do anything else, ladies," Sera announced, coming to stand beside him. "We've allowed the clutter to sit for too long already. Mrs. Blaylock has been tolerant for the better part of four days, but I don't think it's wise—or very nice—to test her limits any further.

"And be mindful of bugs," she added. "Remember that they survive just as well on paper as they do on decaying trees. Don't put your hands anywhere you aren't looking."

Three heads bobbed in unison even as the bodies they were attached to whirled about and set to work—amid a constant stream of comment. Beside him, Sera smiled at them, and it took every measure of his self-restraint not to reach up and trace the curve of her cheek.

Sera forced herself to swallow and breathe. Never in all her life had she been so acutely aware of a man's appraisal. It slid over her slowly, caressingly, warming her skin in the most incredible, wondrous way. There was no denying—at least to herself—that she liked the sensation. Of course, the attention of a handsome man was always flattering. A fact of which Carden Reeves was no doubt very much aware, she reminded herself sternly. It wouldn't do to let him know how deeply and pleasantly his consideration affected her.

And it most certainly wouldn't do to ever let him know that she'd found herself missing his company during the last several days. She'd sufficiently embarrassed herself with how frequently she'd looked over her shoulder, hoping to find him standing there. She'd die of mortification if he ever found out.

"Are you about settled in?"

"Yes, finally," she replied, pleased with the evenness of her voice. "With the exception of the miscellany to be organized in the greenhouse, this is the last of it. I can't believe how long it's taken us to unpack and properly put things away. I distinctly recall that it took me only a single day to crate everything up."

"Have you discovered anything damaged and needing to be replaced?"

Good Lord, even his words were caressing. Hoping that he couldn't hear the frantic beating of her heart, she breezily replied, "Nothing beyond clothing the girls outgrew while we were en route. And, thanks to your generosity, that need has already been addressed. They are so excited, Carden."

His eyes brightened at her casual use of his name and she felt some measure of control mercifully returning. Until he cocked a dark brow and gave her one of his quirked grins. Heaven help her, when he looked at her like that all she could think about was melting into his arms.

"No pouting over the lack of a bright red dress?"

It took all the self-discipline she could muster, but Sera put away the wanton mental images and blithely replied, "Mr. Gauthier would do well in Her Majesty's diplomatic corps. He easily placated her with a rosy pink in silk faille."

"Speaking of placating," he countered, slowly turning with a broad gesture toward the large sheets of paper spread out on the table. "Lady Caruthers's conservatory plans."

Sera stepped up to peruse them, grateful for the distraction. It lasted mere seconds, until Carden stepped up beside her, placed his hands on the table, and leaned forward to look at something in them that had apparently caught his interest. Just as she'd been so vitally aware of his appraisal only moments ago, so she was now of his physical presence. His cologne was spicy and woodsy, deliciously exotic. His shoulders, so close that she could feel the warmth of them . . . They were not only broad, but thick. Were she so bold as to try, she doubted that both of her hands would be big enough to encircle his upper arm. And his hands . . . Large and yet gracefully constructed, they looked to have the deliberate but sensitive strength common among sculptors.

From the deepest recesses of her brain came a fleeting whisper bearing a profound and certain truth. Whatever Carden Reeves touched with his hands, he understood to its essence, claimed to its core. And she ached for the wanting of being possessed so completely, so wholly and reverently.

But not temporarily, she added over the wild hammering of her traitorous, foolhardy heart. Aghast at her careening sensibilities, she took a steadying breath, deliberately focused her vision on the lines and spaces in front of her, and firmly closed the door on her troublesome emotions.

"It's a stunning structure," she said after a moment, genuinely impressed. "Lady Caruthers is blind for not seeing it in the drawings just as they are."

"Thank you."

How two simple, softly spoken words could ignite the temptation to reach out and touch . . . "I especially like your use of the repeating arches in the side walls," Sera added quickly, trying to keep her thoughts focused and her hands where they belonged. "It adds so much to the sense of height and space while, at the same time, establishing a timeless elegance. It's all very graceful and light. Just as a conservatory should be."

She straightened and stepped back, her hands primly at her sides. "You're a very good architect, Carden Reeves."

He shrugged and looked down at the drawings. "It's nothing more than trestle engineering using slightly less substantial materials and on a much smaller scale."

"Lady Caruthers isn't worthy of your talent."

He tilted his head to meet her gaze. His smile, the twinkle in his eyes, was devilish. "You're probably right. Which means I'll truly enjoy charging her an outrageous sum."

The spark was instant. It bloomed just as quickly, revealing the truths within it. He was the most roguishly handsome man she'd ever met. She admired his spirit and enjoyed his irreverence. And all of it went into why she was drawn to him in a most provocative way.

What to do about it? she wondered, searching his sobering gaze. Pretending to be unaffected was out of the question. Carden Reeves could well recognize the signs of feminine fascination. To claim she wasn't would be laughable.

But to surrender to temptation? No. Pride, self-respect, and wisdom wouldn't let her do that, either. On the other side of an affair lay the certain humiliation of rejection. He wouldn't set her aside unkindly, she knew. Carden Reeves wasn't a callous man. He was simply the kind of man who didn't believe in forever. And whether it was rational or not, there was disgrace and shame in not being woman enough to change him.

He could see it in her eyes; she would eventually be his. The usual thrill of impending victory came with the realization, but it came wrapped in an emotion that he couldn't quite identify. It was solemn—not in a heavy, grieving sort of way, though. No, it definitely wasn't a sad feeling at all. Whatever it was, it intensified his hunger most remarkably. If the girls weren't there, he'd take her in his arms and kiss her into sweet oblivion. She'd let him; she was every bit as aware of the connection between them as he was.

From the doorway came the usual throaty trumpet heralding Sawyer's arrival.

"Let me guess," Carden said, his gaze still locked with hers. "Mr. Gauthier is here with a mountain of boxes."

"And a supporting cast of hundreds, sir."

The girls squealed in unison and bolted for the door in a flurry of petticoats, auburn curls, and streaming ribbons. Sera blinked, breaking the bond, and whirled about. Over their girlish squeals and exclamations, she called, "Slow down! Ladies do not run!"

They didn't so much as pause, forcing Sawyer to jump out of their path or risk being trampled. Carden laughed outright as, in the very next instant, Seraphina hiked her hems and took off after them. God, he loved how she could be so prim and proper one moment and so freely herself in the next.

"Is anything injured except dignity, Sawyer?"

"Mercifully no, sir."

"Good. Would you please have the coach readied.

We'll be going to the park for a fashion debut. The girls will be down as soon as they've changed."

"Thank you for the warning, sir."

Carden smiled and headed to the sideboard to pour himself a brandy. He splashed a small amount into the snifter and glanced at the clock. Ten minutes at the most, he decided. Once Sera discovered what he'd done . . . He grinned and filled his glass to the rim.

The girls having been gently admonished for their having almost killed Sawyer and then put into the capable hands of the dressmaker's assistants, Seraphina made her way to her room to see what the courtier had managed to complete of her wardrobe in the last several days. Most of it, she expected, since she'd chosen relatively simple designs and serviceable fabrics.

She froze just inside the room. Mr. Gauthier stood between the side of her bed and the armoire. Open boxes and tissue littered the coverlet. In a vague way, she noted that three of the dresses she'd ordered had been draped over the edge of the bed. It was the one the courtier was placing on a satin-covered, padded hanger that stunned her—a vibrant amethyst silk with jewel-encrusted cascades of dyed-to-match ribbon flowers at the shoulders. Or what shoulders there were. There certainly wasn't any décolletage to speak of. The whole of the full-skirted marvel hung from the hanger by two tiny ribbons.

"Mr. Gauthier?"

He looked up from his task and beamed. "Yes, madam?"

She took a deep breath and forced herself to smile. "That's a beautiful gown, but it's not mine."

"Yes, madam, it is," he declared, then promptly turned and hung it in the armoire.

"No, Mr. Gauthier," she pressed. "I would definitely

remember ordering such an extravagant dress. It's not mine."

"Lord Lansdown ordered for you, madam," he said, popping the lid off another box. Tissue went sailing as he added, "I believe he meant for it to be a surprise."

"Well, it certainly is," she admitted, her hand pressed to her midriff in the hope of settling the butterflies that had taken wing in her stomach. Why had Carden—

"I hope you're as pleased with the others."

"Others?" she repeated on a strangled breath. "There are more?"

"Oh yes, madam. I have brought five today. Another three are yet to be completed."

Eight? Eight dresses? "Are they all so . . . so . . ."

"Exquisite?" He didn't wait for her to squeak out a response. From the box he lifted a loosely folded bundle of ivory sateen and then, with a well-practiced flick of his wrists, unfurled it for her inspection. If not for the gold and ivory ribbon flowers there wouldn't have been a décolletage at all on this one. A garland of them was all that passed for sleeves. Another garland of them edged the gauze overskirt—which was sprinkled with little clusters of golden balls and seed pearls.

"Of course they are exquisite, madam. Lord Lansdown has both excellent taste and an eye for beauty."

She wanted to cry. She nodded in agreement instead and asked, "And the next gown, Mr. Gauthier?"

He laid the bit of heaven aside and flung open another box. From the clouds of tissue he produced a creation in thalo green faille. Bright and yet rich and deep, the décolletage was yet again daringly low. This one had been liberally covered with swirling lines of glittering crystals. Ropes of them were fashioned into narrow, draping sleeves. The whole of it reminded her of the calm, sun-struck waters that lay between the reef and the shore.

"The beads are Austrian crystal. Are they not spectacular?"

"I've never seen anything so beautiful," she admitted, pressing her hands tighter against her stomach.

"Thank you, madam. And the third . . ."

Another box, more tissue, a flourish . . . This one was ultramarine silk damask. Strong and intensely cool, it whispered of midnight gardens and starlit skies, of champagne and long, languid kisses. Its décolletage edge was softly folded bands of matching satin that also served as the sleeves. It was unadorned except for the glittering diamond brooch set in what would no doubt be the center of her very apparent cleavage.

"Oh my," she whispered, her knees weakening. Why was Carden doing this? "And the last?" she asked, almost desperate to have the display ended so that she could breathe and think coherently again.

"Lord Lansdown was most specific about this one, madam," the couturier declared, flinging aside tissue, his grin practically splitting his face. "It was the first he selected," he said, moving to block her view of the dress as it came out of the box. Sera swallowed down the rising swirl of butterflies. He flicked, flourished, and turned in one smooth motion.

It . . . It was . . . "Crimson?" she gasped. A waterfall of tiny, sparkling crimson crystals. On polished crimson satin.

"Is it not sumptuous?"

The décolletage was typically low and heavily encrusted. A fringe of crystal strands served for sleeves. "I'm absolutely speechless."

"High praise, indeed. Thank you, madam."

She had to say something polite. Clearly the couturier was proud of his work—and justifiably so. It wasn't his fault that she had absolutely no use for dresses of this quality. Carden, on the other hand, knew that perfectly well. And she knew precisely what he hoped to reap from her breathless, awed gratitude. The rake!

"Mr. Gauthier," Sera began with a deep, steadying breath and a smile, "you have outdone yourself. I can only imagine what the other three gowns will be like."

"I am afraid that you have no choice but to imagine, madam," he countered apologetically. "Lord Lansdown has instructed me to say nothing of them in any specific terms."

One of them would no doubt be of utterly transparent gauze. "If you would please excuse me, Mr. Gauthier," she said, smiling painfully as she backed out of the room. "I really need to thank Lord Lansdown for his generosity."

"Of course, madam. I will see to the storage of your items."

She thanked him, but it was a mere courtesy she threw over her shoulder as she turned and headed for the stairs. Carden Reeves had gone too far. If he thought she was going to swoon into his arms . . .

One look at her as she sailed toward the library door was all he needed. Oh, she was determined. And lusciously, deliciously angry. He took another sip of his brandy, propped a hip against the corner of the table, and with a racing heart, watched her come at him.

She met his gaze at the threshold and held it as she advanced without pause, saying, "Carden, a word with you, please."

"Just one?"

"Several, actually," she declared as she came to skirt-swaying halt just in front of him.

He cocked a brow. "Shall I keep count?"

"No." Her hands went to her narrow waist and her eyes sparkled like sapphires in firelight. His pulse tripped and then surged. "They are beautiful dresses. The most extravagant, decadently beautiful things I have ever seen."

"You're welcome."

Her chin came up. "I cannot accept them, Carden."

"Why not?"

"I have absolutely no use for them whatsoever," she replied, her accent thickening. "I have nowhere to go where they would be appropriate attire. And as expensive as they no doubt are, it would be criminal to leave them to rot on their hangers in the armoire. I simply cannot in good conscience accept them."

"Melanie Stanbridge's dinner party is Saturday night," he countered. "I was hoping you'd wear the red gown."

Sera's heart skipped a beat. God help her, she didn't want to assume, to read more into his words than he intended, but . . . Hadn't he—more or less—asked her to attend a social affair with him? Memories flooded her. The palatial houses of Jamaica, the candlelight and music drifting out the doors and into the gardens where a little girl sat in the shadows, watching and dreaming. It had seemed such a glorious way to spend the evening then. And even now the small part of her that was still a child thrilled to the prospect of being invited inside to dine and dance in splendor. The part of her that wasn't a child, however, clearly saw the potential for social disaster and cringed. Better, Sera decided, that she hold tight the sweetness of the dreams than let them be destroyed in trying to make them real.

She gathered herself, determined to preserve her dignity. "You've said nothing of this to me."

"I know," he admitted with a casual shrug and half-heartedly apologetic smile. "It would have rather spoiled the surprise, don't you think?"

"I don't like surprises."

"So I gather." He tilted his head to the side in his boyish way. "Why?"

"Because," she replied, her resolve faltering, "it generally puts one on very shaky ground and not all that certain as to where and how to step to avoid a catastrophe."

"Melanie Stanbridge is the consummate hostess," Carden assured her, knowing that this wasn't Sera's concern at all. Seraphina Treadwell had the grace and balance of a cat. "You won't have to worry about making a misstep. She won't let you."

"I . . . I can't." She squared her shoulders. "I'm sorry."

If she thought a simple refusal was going to undo his plans . . . "It's too late to beg off. It would utterly destroy Mrs. Stanbridge's seating arrangements." He smiled and tsked. "I'm afraid you'll just have to sail through it at my side. And in your new red dinner dress."

She swallowed, took a deep breath, and squared her shoulders. "Peers do not escort governesses to social functions. I might well be from the backwater of the empire, but I know that it's just not done, Carden."

Ah, now they were to what really bothered her. "This is a dinner party among friends," he assured her. "It's not high society."

"I am not a friend, Carden," she said firmly. "I am your employee."

And to what most needed to be clarified between them. He set aside his brandy glass and stood. Meeting her gaze, he quietly gave her the absolute truth. "You are the most exotically beautiful woman in all of London. And I want to be seen with you on my arm."

Her breasts rose and fell and his heart twisted at the disbelief that clouded the fire in her eyes. It was a long moment before she took a half-step back and declared, "You simply want to use me as a shield. You want to keep the mamas at bay."

"Not true, Seraphina," he replied, letting her put the space she needed between them. "The mamas won't be the least bit deterred. They'll just have their daughters affect an accent and sit out in the sun trying to brown their skin to the luscious hue of yours. Only they won't brown, they'll burn. And they won't have delightful accents, either. All they'll manage to do is lisp and spit. Try as they might, they will never be able to hold a candle to you."

She was lost, not knowing what to say, what to think; he could see it in her eyes. It bothered him that she didn't know how to respond to sincere compliments, that no one had ever treated her as the marvelous, rare jewel she was. He was going to change that.

"I've decided to take your advice, Seraphina," he said, easing back down on the corner of the table. "If I'm going to be a peer—and mind you, I haven't publicly acknowledged so much as the possibility yet—then I'm going to be a peer who goes my own way. If I want to escort my nieces' governess out for an evening, then I will."

"And what will people say about me?" she asked, trying to sound self-assured.

"That you're stunningly beautiful, naturally gracious, and incredibly intelligent," he supplied gently, ignoring the point she was obliquely trying to make.

Her chin came up. "No, they'll think that I'm the mistress of Carden Reeves."

There had never been a mistress in his life, but he knew that confiding that fact wouldn't reassure her the least little bit. "One dinner, in the home of friends, is not going to be the destruction of your reputation, Sera. I promise."

"One dinner?" she parroted, her hands going back to her waist. "Then why, I must ask, do I have five ball gowns upstairs and—according to Mr. Gauthier—three more yet to be finished and delivered?"

"Barrett and Aiden receive social invitations, too, you know. You wouldn't want to wear the same dress out time and time again. People *would* talk about that."

Sera stared at him in disbelief. And, she had to admit, with an embarrassingly deep sense of disappointment. What a fool she'd been, even if for a few private moments, to think that Carden Reeves considered her special enough to keep for himself. The power of flattery, the girlish hopes of a woman who had always wanted to be more than she was. Anger flickered and she seized it as armor.

"You've ordered gowns for me on the presumption that they . . . that they . . ." Good Lord, her experience was so removed from this world that she didn't even know the proper words to use.

"Yes. They're not blind. And they certainly aren't monks."

"And you've *presumed* that I would accept their invitations?"

Carden's stomach curiously clenched at the possibility. "Actually, I hope you don't, but I'm willing to try to be gracious about it if you do."

"I am here as your nieces' governess," she declared, her accent again deepening, the fire in her eyes sparkling in the most alluring way. "I did not come to London to dance and dine and live the life of a princess."

"Well, I'm sorry, Sera," he countered, crossing his arms over his chest, "but you're in for another surprise or two. Beautiful women are noticed everywhere and especially in London during the season. You are going to be invited out. And before everyone decamps to their country homes, a good dozen besotted men will have fallen to their knees and begged you to marry them."

The anger was gone, again replaced by the confusion that wrenched him to the center of his soul. "Honestly, Sera. God's truth. You'll have your choice of London."

A spark returned to her eyes and color flooded her cheeks. "How utterly ridiculous," she said, turning away.

He came off the table to gently catch her arm and stay her. She looked over her shoulder at him, her brow arched in silent question. "Sera," he said softly, "there's nothing wrong with being treated like a princess. Put on your pretty dresses and enjoy life. It will do you good."

"And what will it do for you, Carden?"

Free me from guilt. Stunned and troubled by the unexpected intrusion of his conscience, Carden released his hold and summoned his most roguish smile. "As a lady, you probably don't want to know."

Any other woman would have gasped or huffed at the innuendo and fled. But not Seraphina Treadwell. No, not Sera. She slowly turned to stand squarely in front of him, so close that her hems covered his feet and she had to tilt her head back to meet his gaze. "You're right, I probably don't want to know, but I should anyway. What will you gain from my playing the princess, Carden Reeves? Why are you willing to spend outrageous sums of money on lavish gowns for me?"

It was a stunningly direct question; the answer to which should have been very clear and simple. Only it wasn't. Yes, he wanted to bed her; he'd wanted that from the moment he'd opened the door and found her on his doorstep. He'd selected her gowns with seduction in mind, with the notion that if she felt beautiful she'd also feel desirous and he would reap the heady reward. He'd played the game a thousand times before. It was an uncomplicated matter of give-and-take.

And yet as he looked down into her searching blue eyes he couldn't deny that he felt more than pure desire. Another—edgy and undefinable—kind of want was worming its way into him. He could vaguely sense a substance to it, knew that it made him feel restless and harassed. Knowing what would satisfy the hunger, however, eluded him.

What he did know, he silently growled, angry with himself and his indecisiveness, was that dwelling on it complicated the hell out of being with her. Unnecessarily so. Sera was no sheltered virgin; she was a widow and knew about the natural desires of men and women. And because of that he had absolutely no reason to feel even the slightest twinge of guilt for encouraging her to act on instincts as old as time. She'd asked a blunt question, very deliberately putting them at a crossroads. He wasn't inclined to back away from making a choice of paths, but he was gentleman enough to allow her the chance to do so. Only a cad found satisfaction in seducing an unwilling or unwitting woman.

"My motives," he drawled, "aren't terribly complex. The question, Seraphina, is how honest you want me to be about them."

He'd handed her Pandora's box and dared her to open the lid. She knew what would happen if she surrendered to temptation, just as she knew what would happen if she clung to propriety. The fear of uncertainty begged her to choose the familiar comfort and safety offered in the latter. All she had to do was declare his intentions disgustingly clear and retire to the schoolroom with regal disdain. And then spend the rest of her life wondering what treasures she might have found had she been brave enough to accept his challenge.

"I think it would be best," she replied over the frantic pounding of her heart, "if you were to be completely, brutally honest."

His pulse shot like lightning through his veins even as the air froze painfully deep in his lungs. "Never brutal, Seraphina. Never," he whispered, gently placing his hands on her shoulders and lowering his head to brush his lips over hers. She trembled at the prelude but didn't back away and so he slipped his arms around her, drawing her closer, possessing her more fully.

She had never been kissed like this, so slowly, lingeringly, and with a kind of reverence that made her ache, body and soul, with wanting. Her hands went to his waist to steady herself, and when he trailed the tip of his tongue over her lips, she parted them, moaning with pleasure as he laid slow, tender claim to the whole of her mouth. Reveling in the smoky sweet taste of him, she leaned into his strength and warmth, surrendering to the temptation to touch her own tongue to his.

He groaned and tightened his arms around her even as he slowly drew back and broke their kiss. "Sera," he whispered, feathering quick, breathless kisses to the corners of her mouth. "I want you, Sera." He caught her lower lip between his and languidly stroked it with the tip of his tongue.

And she wanted him. With every thrumming fiber of her being and as she'd never thought it possible to want a man. She couldn't breathe, couldn't think beyond the pulsing heat that was consuming her.

"Oh, God," he murmured, his breathing just as ragged as her own as he released her lip and straightened. She opened her eyes to meet his gaze and silently plead for more.

His sigh was regretful as he eased his hold on her and set her squarely on her feet. Smiling painfully, he said, "The girls are coming down the stairs. You'd best be getting dressed for our outing. We don't want to keep them waiting."

Reality crept back into her awareness by lethargic degrees. He had the softest, most inviting eyes. She could get lost in them so easily. And his voice was like the most expensive velvet; soft and rich and caressingly warm. The girls . . . She started, suddenly fully aware of where she was, what she'd been doing, and that if she didn't move she was going to be caught in a most compromising situation. The girls were far too young to understand any explanation either one of them could give.

Her pulse skittering, she stepped back and instinctively reached to check her hairpins.

"I'll remove those for you later, Sera."

The image was instant and full, moonlit and erotic. Unable to breathe again and hearing the girls in the hall, she did the only thing she could. She gathered her skirts in hand, turned her back on temptation incarnate, and fled.

Carden expelled a long, hard breath as she disappeared around the corner and then reached for his brandy glass. He drained it and waited for the heat to burn away the blinding haze of desire, desperately hoping that it would be under control by the time his nieces bounded into the room. Especially Amanda. She was old enough to be aware of tensions that her sisters would miss completely. And still too young to know not to ask embarrassing questions about them.

To his dismay, the girls came into the room before the proof of his desire had completely subsided. There was nothing else to do but stuff his hands in his trouser pockets, pretend a great interest in the new books on the library shelves, and wonder what time they retired for the night.

Sera smoothed the front of her new walking dress and considered her reflection in the mirror with a heavy sigh. She'd always known that she was pretty; she would have had to have been blind not to notice the looks men had always given her in passing. But passing was all it had ever been. Her parents hadn't considered her appearance to be of any positive consequence whatsoever. Talent and intelligence, they'd always said, would serve her better and longer in life than a perky nose and creamy skin. Beauty did not make for a fulfilling life or make a noteworthy contribution to the welfare or knowledge of mankind.

In that belief, they'd seen to it that she was too busy to be courted by what they considered to be shallow men in search of nothing more than a conquest or a social adornment. They had protected her as they thought best. And in the end, they had approved of Gerald Treadwell largely because he approved of her work and believed it to be valuable.

She smiled ruefully, remembering. Gerald had never once complimented her on how she looked or who she was as a person. What appreciation he had ever expressed had been for the money that might someday come from her painting. If she practiced, if she could somehow improve her techniques. Like her parents, he had seen her value strictly in terms of what she could do and how it could contribute to his own goals and aspirations.

Carden, though . . . Sera swallowed down her heart and faced the truth squarely. Carden Reeves saw only her beauty and wanted only her body. Her parents wouldn't have approved of him at all. And for the first time in her life she understood why they had raised her as they had. Beneath the heady intoxication of Carden's adoration, beyond the thrill of his tender kisses, there was nothing but an aching emptiness that he would never see, could never fill. In his own way, he was every bit as blind as Gerald had been.

But he was ever so much better at kissing. Infinitely better. He was bone-meltingly, common-sense-shatteringly *good*. And, heaven help her, she truly liked feeling the way she did in his arms. Could she lie with a man knowing that it was only for the pleasure there might be in doing so? Was being a wanton once in her life—for just a short while— such a horribly unforgivable thing? If she could be sure that no one would ever know . . .

CHAPTER 10

Hoops. And sticks. He'd never suspected that Sawyer had a mean streak until the man had handed the damned things into the carriage and suggested that the girls might enjoy trampling unwary pedestrians in the park. Where the hell the iron circles had come from was a mystery. But Lord knew that between the rolling hoops, the hooped crinolines, and the yards and yards of flounced fabric, the carriage had the definite feel of an overpacked sardine tin. Matters would have been a bit more endurable if the three littlest sardines hadn't insisted on wiggling and bouncing all over the seats. He winced and clenched his teeth as Camille kicked his shin for the fifth time.

A second carriage, one reserved strictly for the transport of the girls, was going to be a necessity within a very short while. They were growing and that meant that their hoops and skirts were only going to get bigger. If he didn't get them their own carriage, his driver would open the door one day, hand the girls out, and then find him crumpled in the cushions, suffocated and kicked to death.

Not that he was opposed to sharing his coach, of course. He smiled at Sera who sat opposite him in the forward-facing seat. Riding alone with Seraphina would be a most wonderful way to pass any journey. The longer

it went, the better. Especially at night, over slightly bumpy
roads. And most definitely without a child on either side
of him and one beside her. Yes, the girls would have their
own carriage by next week, he decided as they rolled to
a stop above the Hyde Park fountains. He'd play the doting uncle, the girls would feel exceedingly grown-up, and
Sera would protest until he kissed her into a breathless
appreciation for privacy on wheels.

As plans went, it was a positively brilliant one, he admitted, tucking his walking stick under his arm and leaning across Beatrice to open the door. He let himself out
and then turned back, meeting Sera's gaze and offering
his hand. She emerged to stand beside him, smiling
sweetly and looking absolutely virginal in her prim, dusty
blue walking dress and her lace-trimmed bonnet. Knowing
how she tasted, how she felt pressed against him, her arms
around him, remembering her little moans of pleasure . . .
The contrast between reality and appearance was delightfully evocative.

It occurred to him, as he turned away to assist his
nieces from the carriage, that every man dreamed of
knowing a Seraphina Treadwell in the course of their
lives. The vast majority never did and existed on the fantasy alone. Only a very few ever got the chance to even
meet a woman like her. The man who was actually allowed to strip away the prim and proper façade and take
the lioness to his bed . . . That lucky bastard died one
happy, supremely enviable man.

Bless Fate for choosing him, Carden concluded with a
grin, closing the door behind Camille and turning away
from the carriage. The girls, hoops and sticks in hand,
stood before Sera who was considering them with an
arched brow.

"You will be mindful of others and control your
hoops," she said, her gaze passing over each of them in

turn. "And you will remain where your Uncle Carden and I can see you at all times. Is that clear?"

They nodded in unison, their curls bobbing.

"Then you may go," Sera finished, clearly fighting a smile. She tilted back her head and laughed outright as they squealed and bolted for green grass.

God, what he wouldn't give to be back in the library alone with her. Hell, alone anywhere would do; he wasn't inclined to be choosy at the moment. Fate might have blessed him, but she certainly wasn't above challenging his patience along the way. It took considerable effort, but he managed to find some. He smiled and offered Seraphina his arm.

"Thank you, but no," she said sweetly, turning to see where the girls had gone.

Stunned by the rebuff, he quickly stepped to her side. "Why ever not?"

"Because I'm the governess and you are my employer," she replied, starting down the path that ran along the Long Water.

"Are we back to that?" he asked, falling in beside her. "I thought we'd cleared that particular hurdle rather permanently."

"There's a great deal of difference between private and public behavior. Would you like your nieces walking on the arm of any man who offered one? Without a concern for the consequences of it? We must set a good example for them."

"Serving as a good example is highly overrated," he countered, irritated by the physical distance she'd put between them. "I believe in letting someone else do it whenever possible."

"Then it's a very good thing that you intend to send us to the country house as soon as the renovations are done. When do you think that will be?"

He'd completely forgotten about having threatened to

do that. In hindsight, it had been an incredible bit of short-sighted stupidity. "The end of the season. Assuming that no major problems develop," he answered. "But I distinctly recall you saying that you were opposed to the girls' going to the country, of their being denied the nurturing circle of family. Although now, from the sound of your voice . . . Have your feelings on the matter changed?"

"I can see certain advantages in being removed from London."

He couldn't. Not anymore. His stomach actually clenched at the possibility. "For the girls or for you?"

"For all of us. Including you."

"Oh?" he asked casually, hoping that she couldn't hear his heart thundering. "How would it be to my advantage to have you gone?"

"You'd be free to live as a carefree bachelor again," she replied, sliding a glance his way. A tiny smile flirted at the corners of her mouth. "If we were gone, you'd be able to walk about the house in your dressing gown at noon and kiss women in your library without worrying about being interrupted."

Grinning, he eased closer and, careful to keep his voice low and their exchange private, said, "Avoiding interruptions is a matter of careful planning and good timing. Would you care to meet me back in the library at midnight and let me prove it?"

She tilted her head and met his gaze. "Not tonight. Perhaps another." He was still trying to catch his breath when she arched a delicate brow and added, "If the invitation is a standing one, of course."

His knees threatening to give way, he desperately mustered both the resolve to keep moving and the voice to ask, "You're tempted? Seriously?"

She nodded, but didn't look at him. "I'm wrestling with the decidedly uncomfortable notion that to succumb to curiosity would forever brand me a woman of loose virtue.

I do believe that I'd prefer to avoid that reputation if at all possible."

"Understandably," he countered, wondering why the hell they couldn't have had this conversation in the privacy of Haven House where he could actually *do* something about moving her off the button. He couldn't very well kiss her senseless on a public walkway. "Would it help you decide if I assured you that I'm a man of considerable discretion?"

She chuckled dryly. "I'm afraid that it's of no help at all. Rakes offer such assurances as a matter of course, Carden."

"And just how many rakes have you known?"

"Aside from you, one. But he provided me with a most thorough education during our blessedly brief marriage."

A woman uttering the word "marriage" always made him nervous. He knew too many men who had wandered into seemingly innocuous conversations and found themselves standing, completely poleaxed, at the altar. In instinctive self-defense, he observed, "Rakes make especially bad husbands."

"I couldn't agree with you more."

"We make very attentive lovers, though."

She arched a brow and laughingly retorted, "So you claim. Unfortunately, that wasn't my experience at all."

"Well," he replied, leaning close again, "I think you owe it to rakes the world over to give me the chance to redeem our reputation."

She laughed outright, tilting her head back and gazing up at him in a way that all but shredded his commitment to public decorum. God, he wanted to kiss her; long and hard. To kiss her until she breathlessly begged him to take her home and to his bed.

And given that aim, it was best to be absolutely clear on the long-range expectations of the romantic aspects of their relationship. And now, before they took one more

step in that direction. "I gather that marrying isn't something you're anxious to do again very soon," he posed as
he tipped his hat to acknowledge a couple passing by, the
man a member of his club, the woman—most surprisingly—his wife.

"I might consider it. It would depend largely on the
qualities of the man. Another rake is out of the question,
though," Sera answered lightly, fully aware that the
stranger had looked over his shoulder to watch her a while
longer. And that Carden had glanced over his, as well.
With a truly menacing scowl.

"And you, Carden?" she asked, calling his attention
back to her and their negotiation of terms. "Under what
conditions would you consider marriage?"

"The threat of a slow and painful death." He laughed
softly, and from the corner of her eye, she saw him shrug.
"Maybe. I'd have to ask for some time to think about it."

And she didn't have the slightest doubt as to what he'd
decide in the end. Carden Reeves was the kind of man
who made love and walked away with equal amounts of
passion. No woman on earth would ever be lover enough
to hold his interest for longer than a single night. To hope
for more, for longer . . .

A knot formed high in her throat and with it came a
surging sense of melancholy. She instantly and silently
chastised herself for the sentimentality. Carden hadn't told
her anything that she hadn't already known. To so much
as think that he'd become a different person in order to
bed her was ludicrous. He was handsome, charming, roguishly daring. He wasn't the stuff of which good husbands
were made. That being an utter certainty, the question remaining to be answered was whether she possessed the
qualities of a most temporary lover. Despite her misgiv-
ings, she had to admit that there was something excep-
tionally compelling about the notion of lying with a man
without having to surrender the whole of your life for one

night's experience. The freedom to exercise that kind of choice ... If only she'd had these kinds of notions and feelings when Gerald had been part of her life. One night would have been all he had ever had of it. And not a full night at that.

A night with Carden Reeves, though ... That was a very different prospect altogether.

She glanced over at him, noting the chiseled planes of his face, remembering the intoxicating power of his kisses, the hard warmth of his body, the delicious way he made her feel. How long, precisely, was a night? And was one required to waste any of it sleeping? Did you bow and curtsy in the morning, thank each other, and then pretend nothing had happened? There were so very many things she didn't know about the world Carden wanted to share with her.

"Look, Sera. There's Honoria."

She returned to the reality of Hyde Park with a start and an almost audible thump. Straight ahead of her, bearing down on them with clear purpose, was indeed the tiny hurricane named Lady Lansdown. "And it's too late to run. She's seen us," Sera muttered darkly. "Dammit."

"Seraphina Treadwell!" he admonished, a grin splitting his face. "I'm appalled."

"Well, Honoria will make you forget all about my language," she countered through a tight, false smile. "And I give her less than two minutes in which to do it."

"Oh, I'm sure that it won't take her that long."

"Seraphina! You look marvelous!" Honoria exclaimed when she was within earshot. She raised her hand and twirled her index finger. "Turn around for me and let me see."

Sera obediently, if reluctantly, played the marionette while Honoria clapped her hands and went on, saying, "Isn't Mr. Gauthier simply a wizard with cloth and thread? Aren't you ever so glad I sent him to you? Carden, you're looking positively respectable this afternoon. Dare I say even paternal?"

Sera stopped turning and waited for the world to do the same. From beside her, she heard Carden drawl, "Yes, she does. Gauthier's a genius. Yes, she is. Thank you. No, you may not. And fair warning, Honoria, I may strangle you in the next moment or two."

Sera fought a smile as Honoria pressed a wrinkled hand to her heart and tried to look surprised and innocent.

"Whatever for, Carden? What have I done?"

He leaned forward and kept his voice low. The volume did nothing to lessen the force of his obvious displeasure. "You bloody well know what for and what you've done, Honoria. What aspect of 'Arthur is still alive' did you fail to grasp? Was there something lacking in the explanation?"

She drew herself up, sniffed once, said, "Credibility," and then pointedly turned away from him.

As though not one bit of unpleasantness had just passed, she smiled, took Sera's hands in hers, and breezily said, "I just left my stationer's and happened to meet that nice Mr. Terrell on the street outside. We had a delightful conversation during which he confided that he had felt obliged—some time ago and for some reason or another which I forget—to accept an invitation to the Martin-Holloways' dinner party this week."

The fact that Honoria had paused for longer than necessary to take a breath seemed to suggest that she was expected to say something. Sera swallowed and politely offered, "I'm sure he'll have a lovely evening."

Honoria beamed and practically squeezed the blood from her hands. "He wasn't as certain about the prospect so I suggested that he ask you to attend with him. The mere idea considerably brightened his mood. You did order some suitable evening gowns from Mr. Gauthier, didn't you, dear?"

"She did," Carden growled before Sera could sufficiently emerge from her shock to answer. Honoria was arranging her social life? Pairing her with one of Carden's friends? Good God.

"Wonderful," Honoria declared, again squeezing her hands. "How perfect. I should think that Mr. Terrell will be calling on you sometime today to beg the favor of your company that evening. He was concerned about the shortness of the notice, but I assured him that you would understand and forgive the lapse just this once."

Then, without warning, she released Sera's hands, took a step back, and made a rather limited attempt to glance around her while asking, "And where are my darling nieces? Surely you didn't come strolling without them. That would be too scandalous even for Carden."

A rather ominous sound came from low in Carden's throat and Sera hastily turned toward the grass between the river and the path saying, "They're . . ."

The girls weren't where she had last seen them. She looked a bit farther up the bank and then back along the way they had come. A bubble of panic was building in the center of her chest as she quickly looked along the park side of the path. "Carden, where are they?" she cried softly, turning back to scan the riverbank again. "Do you see them?"

"You have lost the children?" Honoria asked incredulously.

"They were rolling their hoops over this way as you arrived," Carden offered in her defense. "They couldn't have gone far."

But apparently they had and she couldn't see them anywhere. "Oh, Carden. How could I have been so irresponsible? What if they've fallen into the river?"

"All three at once and without a hue and cry that would wake the dead?" he posed, also scanning the bank and the lines of people strolling along the path beside it. "No, they haven't fallen in the river. Even if they had, someone would have seen them and hauled them out. Don't worry, Sera, they're here somewhere. We'll find them." He took her by the elbow and with a curt bow to his sister-in-law, said, "If you'll excuse us, Honoria."

They were already moving past her when she replied, "I shall have my driver take me down and around the Serpentine to look for them. I'll return shortly."

His hand cupped around her arm, Carden could feel Sera's trembling. Fear rippled through her voice as she asked, "What if someone has taken them?"

"Why would anyone want to do that?" he countered, hoping she'd be soothed by his relative calm and rational approach.

"I don't know. For ransom. To do unspeakable things to them. The world is full of crazy people, Carden. Haven't you noticed?"

Yes, he had, but admitting it wasn't going to make her feel any better in the short term. He continued to make their way up the walk, his gaze darting among the passersby in search of three smaller ones who looked confused and lost.

"The general lunatics confine themselves to Speakers Corner on the other side of the park," he offered Sera by way of reassurance as they went. "The truly dangerous ones are locked up in Bedlam. No one's taken the girls, Sera." When they found the girls he was going to lock *them* up. And he wasn't going to let them out until their husbands came to beg for them.

Sera stopped without warning and turned to look back. The haunted, anguished look in her eyes tore at his heart. He'd often heard the fathers who belonged to his club threaten to kill their children and he'd always considered it an appalling thing to say, a hallmark of a man who lacked reasonable self-control. But now he understood them and just how they could be driven to the brink of sanity.

Still holding on to Sera's arm, he strained up on his toes and stretched his neck to see as far as he could. There were people on the bridge, others walking down the paths on either side of the river, a few picnicking with hampers along the banks on the far side and— He heaved a sigh of relief and pulled Sera around, slipped an arm around her shoulder, and leaned close so that she could sight along his extended arm.

"Look, Sera!" he commanded. "Up by the bridge, just this side of it, a bit off the path. Do you see them? They're standing together. All three of them and they appear to be perfectly fine."

"Thank heavens," she whispered, sagging into him before apparently remembering where they were. She instantly straightened and stepped from his embrace to gather her skirts in hand and set off in the direction of the bridge.

"Of course," Carden said, as he strode at her side, his gaze fixed on his errant nieces, "they're not going to be perfectly fine for very much longer. Whatever it is that's enthralling them isn't excuse enough for frightening you. They were told very clearly not to wander off."

"I certainly expected Amanda to have better sense and to take care of . . . Carden? What is that man on the bridge doing?"

He looked up from the girls to see a rag-dressed man holding a burlap bag over the edge of the bridge. A large, reddish dog was beside him, paws on the railing, frantically barking at the sack. As he watched, the man shoved the dog aside and released his hold on the sack. Sera faltered and choked on a cry.

"Jesus Christ."

The bag hit the water with a splash even as Sera, hems

held high, dashed toward the horrific scene yelling, "Amanda! No! Don't!"

Carden looked past her just in time to see Amanda knife into the surface of the water, her hooped crinoline and skirts a huge bell billowing behind her. It was only a matter of time before they flipped up over her head. And once they did . . . His heart rammed high in his throat, he took off running, precious seconds clicking away in his head.

Sera fought back tears and burgeoning panic. With every step she took, her dress grew heavier, her corset tighter. She couldn't draw breath deep enough or fast enough and the world was going gray around the edges. Reality came in fractured snippets; the smooth surface of water where Amanda had disappeared, the girls' abandoned hoops in the grass, the sound of Beatrice and Camille screaming, a dog barking, uneven ground beneath her feet. Carden.

Carden was there, ahead of her, on the bank, flinging aside his walking stick, his boots, his coat. Then he arced out over the water and was gone. Her heart hammering against her breast, her pulse thundering in her ears, Sera reached the bank and stopped, greedily dragging all the air she could into her burning lungs and willing the tendrils of fog from her vision. She had to find Beatrice and Camille, had to be ready to help Carden bring Amanda out of the river and onto the bank.

"Miss Sera!"

She whirled toward the sound of Beatrice's voice, grateful to hear it as strong and confident as always, even more grateful to see the child and her younger sister— both apparently unharmed—being dragged toward her by a huge red dog tied to one end of a rope Beatrice held in her hand.

She'd barely managed to take a single, mercifully steadying breath when both girls looked out into the river.

Sera spun about and then nearly collapsed in relief. Two dark heads had broken the surface of the water. Carden immediately brought his arm up, the sack clutched tight in his fist, then turned on his side and struck out for the bank. Amanda, unburdened by anything—including, apparently, the lower half of her dress—yelled for him to hurry and then followed, her strokes the sure and strong ones of a child who had grown up at the water's edge.

Dropping down on the bank, Sera leaned out as far as she could and took the bag the instant it was within reach. Turning, she placed it on the grass and frantically struggled to untie the swollen cord binding it closed.

"Get the puppies out of the sack!" Amanda cried as Carden shoved her up onto the bank. "Hurry! They're drowning!"

Tiny, weak yips came from inside and the dog tore free of her young handler, rushing forward to nuzzle the sack and pound Sera with its tail. "Beatrice," she called, desperately trying to hold on to the loosened knot while pushing the dog out her way, "come get her. She's not helping. Carden, are you all right?"

Water streaming down his face, he nodded crisply, climbed up onto the bank beside her, and instantly produced a short sword from the back of his waistband. "Let me at the sack, Sera."

She obeyed and watched, wide-eyed, as he seized the top of the bag with one hand, drew it taut, and then lopped it off with a single swipe of the blade.

As Sera and Amanda began the grisly task of sorting the living from the dead, Carden tossed the top away and sat back, sucking deep breaths and knowing just how damn lucky he was. If he hadn't been drawn into that little shop in Natal that morning . . . If he hadn't been intrigued enough with the secret sword to pay a king's ransom for it . . .

"This one's moving and breathing," Sera cried, pulling

a wet but wiggling mass of red fur from the bag and setting it in the grass beside her.

Amanda lifted out a second puppy and gave it a cursory examination. "So's this one." She quickly placed it with its litter mate in the grass and reached back into the sack.

"This one makes three," Sera cried happily, setting it aside while reaching for another. The look that came suddenly to her eyes . . . Carden knew before she got the animal out of the bag. "Oh, God, this one isn't," she said, her voice brittle as she held the limp little body up in front of her face. "Breathe, sweet pea," she begged. "Breathe for me, please."

"Give him here, Sera."

She handed the puppy to him as Amanda lifted another limp pup from the bag and wailed, "This is one isn't breathing, either!"

"Like this, Amanda," he said calmly, gently holding the puppy up and covering its muzzle with his mouth. He blew a bit of air into the creature and then he eased back to add, "Very light and short. Just a puff. Remember that their lungs are tiny. Give them a chance between breaths to cough out the water."

Amanda nodded and followed his instructions as Sera reached back into the sack, pulled out another still pup, and brought it to her mouth.

"Miss Sera, are they going to be all right?"

"We're doing our best, Camille," Sera replied between breaths.

Amanda's puppy spewed water, coughed, spit out a few more drops, and kicked its feet. "He's breathing, Uncle Carden!"

"So is this one," he declared, grinning as it gave a good, hard, healthy sneeze. "That's a good girl," he said, leaning over to put it among the others squirming in the grass. "One more back from the dead. How many more, Sera?"

"Just this one," she said tightly, her eyes clouded with dread. "I can't—"

"Merciful heavens, Carden! What are you doing?"

Honoria. Christ. Couldn't she make a reasonable deduction? Sera handed the limp puppy to him, blinking back tears.

Blessedly, Camille bounded forward to provide her aunt with an explanation. "A mean man tried to drown puppies, Aunt Honoria! He put them in a sack and dropped them in the river. We saw him do it!"

"And Amanda jumped in to save them," Beatrice contributed every bit as passionately. "Camille and I ran up and hit the man with our hoop sticks and took the mama dog away from him and he ran away."

"And Uncle Carden came in after me and the puppies."

"Some of them are drown-ded but Uncle Carden's making them breathe again and they'll be all right."

He wasn't sure he was going to produce the full miracle they expected. The puppy in his hand was the smallest of the bunch and it wasn't coughing out the water as the others had. He tried again to force some air into its lungs.

"Where is your skirt, Amanda?"

"In the river," she replied matter-of-factly, watching him intently. "Uncle Carden had to cut it off me. It kept coming up over my head and I couldn't swim. Not that I was doing very well at it anyway with the bag in one hand."

The color drained from Sera's face. Tears welled along her lower lashes and spilled down her cheeks. She didn't make a sound; she just closed her eyes and buried her face in her hands. He watched her rock back and forth as he tried one more time to bring the puppy back to life.

"Is it breathing yet, Uncle Carden?"

Damn, he hated to admit defeat. Knowing when to do so had been one of the hardest lessons in life he'd ever had to learn. That he was going to have to be the one to teach it to the girls . . . "No, Bea, it isn't. I'm afraid that we weren't able to save this one."

"It's dead?" Camille asked, her voice quavering.

He heard the desperation in her question and wished with all his heart that he could give her the miracle she wanted. He remembered all too well how it felt to have hope crushed. "Yes, sweetheart, it's dead," he said as gently as he could. "I'm so very sorry."

Amanda took the lifeless body from him and cradled it in her arms. "Poor little puppy," she crooned, smoothing the wet, rumpled fur. Tears rolled down her cheeks.

Carden silently cursed the bastard who had created such suffering and sorrow. Wanting with every fiber of his being to give the son of a bitch a sound and thorough beating, he looked around, hoping to find the man lurking about. But if he was there somewhere, he was well hidden in the crowd of onlookers that had gathered around them. The bloody ghouls, Carden silently railed. Willing to gawk at tragedy but too proper and genteel to step in to avert it. Heaven forbid they should summon any courage. They'd left it to a child.

"Bea," he heard Sera say softly, "you may let the mama go now. She needs to be with her babies."

Beatrice did as instructed and the dog instantly went to her surviving puppies, sniffing them, nudging them. Camille and Bea quietly went to their sister's side, knelt down, and reverently touched the lost little soul. Bea's eyes blazed in silent rage as they welled with tears. Camille's lips quivered for a second and then parted to emit a wracking sob. Sera rose to her knees and gathered them into her arms and held them tight.

He couldn't take any more. Swallowing down the prickly lump in his throat, Carden pushed himself to his feet and retrieved his coat and the shell of his walking stick. Sheathing his small sword in the latter instantly brought Sera's gaze up to meet his. She looked so young, so very vulnerable, so determined to be strong and brave. Something deep inside him twisted and he tore his gaze from hers, trying to make the pain go away.

It was still there as he draped his coat over Amanda's shoulders and Camille said softly, "We have to have a funeral."

A funeral? His heart lurched and then sank into his stomach. Oh, Jesus. No, not a funeral.

"Of course we do," Sera agreed, releasing Bea and Camille to scrub her cheeks with the palms of her hands. "I'm sure there's a place in Uncle Carden's garden that the puppy will like." She unbuttoned her jacket and shrugged out of it, adding, "Now let's get these poor little creatures home so that we can see them dried and warmed. We'll put them in this and let Uncle Carden carry them to the carriage for us."

"You're coming to the funeral, aren't you, Aunt Honoria?" Camille asked as the others placed the surviving puppies into Sera's satin-lined jacket.

Honoria dabbed at her nose with a lace-edged handkerchief. "Only if no animals attend."

Christ on a crutch. It was a family affair? Would the staff be invited, too? His stomach clenching, he decided that the only thing to do was expedite the matter. The sooner it was done, the sooner he could drown his demons. "Honoria, may Beatrice and Camille ride back to the house with you?" he asked, tucking his walking stick under his arm before scooping up the jacket and puppies and more than a few blades of grass. "There won't be room in mine for all of us and the animals, too."

"Thank you for not asking me to transport the dog."

"I thought about it."

"Of course you did. Come along, my dears," she said, offering her hands. As the girls dutifully took them, she glanced between them and asked, "Now which of you is Beatrice and which is Camille?"

Sera saw the sparkle in Beatrice's eyes and knew what the child intended to do. Under other circumstances, she would have intervened and spared Honoria the confusion. But she had other matters to attend at the moment, Bea wasn't wrapped in grief and anger, and Honoria needed to learn that her nieces were neither angels nor passive china dolls. No, Honoria was on her own.

And so was she, she realized with a start. Carden was heading toward the fountains and their waiting carriage. Amanda, awash in his coat, was going with him, still carrying the lost puppy in the cradle of one arm. The mother dog trotted along between them, her attention on her puppies and her makeshift leash trailing along the path behind her.

"Never mind me," Sera muttered with a dry chuckle. "I'll be along." As though he'd heard her, Carden stopped and turned back to watch and wait for her, a chagrined smile quirking up one corner of his mouth.

Sera quickly gathered the girls' abandoned hoops and sticks, retrieved Carden's boots, and then paused to glance around to see if she'd missed anything. What she saw were shoes, pant legs, and hems. A good number of them. And in something approximating a half-circle. She brought her gaze up, knowing and dreading what she would find.

Yes, they'd drawn a sizable crowd. Which, thank heavens, seemed to have realized that the free show was over. As they turned and started off in their own directions, she did the same. She'd taken only a single step when a movement at the edge of her vision stopped her in her tracks. Her heart racing and her stomach cold, she turned to look squarely at the man. He was moving away, his stride long and deliberate, his head bowed and angled away from her.

No, it wasn't possible, she told herself as she hurried

to join Carden and Amanda. Her imagination had been overstimulated by the ordeal of the puppies. All those fears had simply allowed an older, stupidly persistent one to percolate to the surface. Gerald was dead.

CHAPTER 11

Sawyer had warned him at the front door, but actually seeing John Aiden Terrell leaning against his desk—dry, clean, warm, wearing boots, holding a brandy glass in hand—and then—on top of all that—knowing why he was there . . . There were limits to what a man ought to have to endure in the course of a single goddamned day.

"Good Lord, Carden. What happened to you?"

"The door bell rang," he snarled, pouring himself a full glass of whiskey, "and I opened it to find Seraphina Treadwell standing on my step."

"I meant the sopping clothes."

He tossed half the whiskey down his throat in one quick movement. The fire was still burning its way to his empty gullet when he answered, "And she had three little girls with her."

Aiden was staring at him and he was throwing the other half after the first when Sawyer arrived, clearing his throat and then saying, "The Bible, sir."

"Do you know where the ashes to ashes part is?" Carden asked, refilling his glass.

"Of course, sir."

He filled a second glass. "Good. I don't, so consider yourself temporarily ordained." Sawyer was standing there slack-jawed when Carden thrust the other glass into his free hand, saying, "Here, have a drink. You're going to need it. The crocodile tears and stoic sniffling will rip your heart out."

Aiden straightened. "I gather there's been a death?"

"Some bastard tried to drown a litter of pups in the Long Water," Carden answered as the first slug of whiskey connected with his senses. "We managed to save all but one of them."

"Bully for you, Carden!"

"Yes, indeed. Very well done, sir."

"Well," he drawled as the second dose began to slide in over the first, "in a few moments, my one failure is going to be center stage. How goes the chaos, Sawyer?"

"Lady Lansdown is in the parlor with a sherry, a fresh handkerchief, and decidedly pink eyes. Anne brought down sheets and an old blanket out of which Mrs. Blaylock and Mrs. Treadwell are fashioning a bed to the side of the hearth for the dog and her remaining pups. Cook is heating water for baths—including one for the dog—and preparing a concoction he swears will have the animals as—he says—plump and pleased as piglets by sunset tonight."

"And the girls?" he asked, the edges of his senses beginning to go very nicely numb.

"They have gone with Anne to find and prepare a suitable coffin, sir. I believe that once they conclude that task, they intend to select a site for the interment."

With any luck, he'd be sufficiently fuzzy by then that he could get through it without being really conscious of anything in particular. "I suppose I should stand by with the shovel, shouldn't I?"

Sawyer handed back the untouched glass of liquid memory-killer, saying, "I shall ascertain their progress in that direction, sir," and promptly left.

Carden drank the contents of his glass, set it aside, and

then drank half of Sawyer's, thinking about what a god-awful thing grave-digging was to do. Filling it in was even worse. That made it all so final, so damn undoable and forever. All the words that hadn't been said and never would be. All the things you wished you'd known and hadn't until it was too late. All the things you wished you'd done . . . A nice coffin, quoting Scripture, planting flowers . . . None of it was ever enough to make the pain of loss and the sorrow of regret go away. And cherubs. You couldn't forget the carved cherubs.

"God," Carden muttered darkly into his glass, "you don't suppose they'll want a headstone, do you?"

Aiden laughed. "For a man who has absolutely no experience with children, you're doing quite well at this, you know. You and Sera ought to have a houseful of your own."

Sera. The words rippled slowly through his rapidly clouding awareness. In a vague sort of way he knew they had a significance. But fully and firmly grasping it just wasn't possible. He'd have to think on it later. Much later. Right now, there were some things he needed to set straight with Aiden. "Are you here to ask Seraphina to attend the Martin-Holloway dinner with you?"

"Yes," his friend replied slowly, warily. "Unless you have a reasonable objection."

"No objection. Just a caveat." Carden drained the glass and set it aside. Meeting his friend's gaze squarely, he smiled and said, "Lay a hand on her, Aiden, and I'll *break* it."

"Are you making a formal claim to her?" his friend asked incredulously.

Formal? Hell, he didn't know. Being unaware was the whole point of drinking hard and fast. And since he didn't have a sufficient number of his wits about him to see the maze Aiden was asking him to navigate, he opted for covering familiar ground instead. "You may escort Seraphina out for an evening, but you'll treat her like one of your sisters."

"There will come a day when you get bored with her, you know."

And Aiden was licking his chops in anticipation. The bloody scoundrel. He could damn well cool his heels. "Well, it's not going to be today or tomorrow. Or even the next day."

"How about three days from now?"

Which was when the Martin-Holloways were having their dinner party. Aiden could only hope and dream. "Sorry to disappoint you," Carden replied smugly, "but I rather doubt it."

Something about the way his friend was looking at him—something in his smile . . . Whatever it was, it was damn irritating. And unsettling, too. "What?" he demanded.

Aiden shrugged, but his expression didn't change. "I was just thinking about digging holes. Shouldn't we be about the one for the puppy?"

That was one of the problems of drinking; you knew in your gut that there were layers to what people were saying, but your mind wasn't sharp enough or fast enough to figure out what they were. He'd remember, though, and think on it later. Perhaps tomorrow, he decided, heading for the door—when it would be safe to be sober. Or, better yet, the day after when his head stopped pounding.

Sera glanced around the foyer and, seeing Sawyer nowhere in sight, decided that the only polite thing to do was to see Honoria out herself. "I'm sure you'll feel better when you get home, Honoria," she said, pulling open the heavy front door. "It was very nice of you to endure for the sake of the girls."

Honoria sniffled daintily and dabbed at her nose with

a lace-edged handkerchief. "It was a lovely service." She raised a silver brow to sniffle again and add disapprovingly, "Despite the fact that Carden's attention was awash. He drinks entirely too much, you know."

"But far less than other men," Sera countered firmly, "far less often, and he isn't mean when he does. There's a great deal to be said for that."

"It's still a bad habit and doesn't . . ." Honoria silently struggled against the urge to sneeze again and then pressed the handkerchief to her face a mere fraction of a second before it overwhelmed her.

"Bless you."

"Thank you. Reflect well on him or the fami—"

Another sneeze interrupted her discourse and Sera seized the opportunity to put an end to it altogether. "Bless you again," she said, pulling the door wider and stepping aside. "Do feel better, Honoria. And thank you again for attending."

Honoria nodded, sneezed twice in rapid succession, waved her hand in hasty farewell and fled. Sera waited until the carriage door was closed before doing the same with Carden's front door. As she turned away, her gaze passed over the foyer table and the walking stick Carden had flung there as they'd entered with the puppies.

Curiosity niggling at her, she picked it up and examined it, marveling at how very ordinary it appeared. The shaft was of some sort of dark, almost black wood that started at a smallish silver-tipped end and gradually widened up the length until it came to a long, relatively thick and heavy piece of silver with ripples along one side. She slipped her hand around it, noting that her fingers instinctively fitted into the grooves. With one hand on the shaft and the other on the grip, she pulled in opposite directions, starting at the sound of metal hissing against metal, at the speed and ease with which the small sword fully cleared the scabbard. Shaking her head in amazement, she carefully sheathed the sharp-edged instrument and laid it back on the table.

"You did that very well, Seraphina."

She looked over her shoulder to find Barrett leaning against the jamb of the parlor door. "I wasn't aware that you'd come to visit," she said brightly, glad that Aiden wouldn't have to manage the situation entirely on his own. "Carden's in his study."

He grinned. "Sawyer says that I have impeccable timing and, yes, I've already seen the rapidly declining state of Carden Reeves." He pointed to the walking stick. "It's an interesting little toy, isn't it?"

"I thought it was an ordinary walking stick."

"That's the intention. You always want the element of surprise on your side."

Sera chuckled. "I didn't realize that Hyde Park was such a dangerous place."

"It's not, generally speaking." His smile faded by slow degrees as he considered her, his mind clearly working through a decision. "But once you acquire the habit of being armed," he said carefully, "you feel a certain vulnerability without a weapon easily at hand. Carden has always favored the cutting weapons. Myself . . . I'm much less personal about my violence. The pistol is my weapon of first choice."

"I didn't realize that there were different kinds of violence," she admitted, sensing that Barrett had both an objective for their conversation and a reason for it.

"I was already with Her Majesty's engineers in the Transvaal when Carden was assigned to the regiment," he went on, still leaning against the doorjamb. "Our commanding officer at the time was a bureaucrat who fancied himself a man of considerable technical talent and expertise. A combination that made our work extremely—and quite unnecessarily—dangerous.

"We were spanning a gorge and he and Carden had a

strong difference of opinion as to how it ought to be done structurally. Carden, being a subordinate, lost the contest. And when the trestle collapsed—just as Carden said it would and despite his every effort to keep it from happening—we lost seventeen good men."

Sera held her breath and watched Barrett gaze back into the horror of the past. After several long moments, he shook his head and straightened, saying bluntly, "Carden went after him bare-handed." He held up his own hand, a mere sliver of space between his thumb and forefinger. "And came this close to beating him to death."

Her heart was racing and she had to swallow before she had the poise to ask, "Did they lock him away for attacking a superior officer?"

Barrett fastened his gaze on hers and coolly, very pointedly, replied, "There were no witnesses to support the commander's accusations."

She knew—to the center of her bones—otherwise. And that Barrett was entrusting her with a long-held and most valuable secret.

"I would have shot the bastard from twenty paces and been done with it," he continued with a shrug. "Carden, on the other hand, made sure he knew that every blow was on behalf of a man who died because of his incompetency and pomposity."

"He made it personal."

Barrett nodded. "Death is very personal for Carden. Not his own, of course. Some of the men who have worked with him would tell you that heights don't bother him. Others—the slightly more observant ones—would tell you that he actually likes them. But the truth is that it's not about heights at all. It's about edges. Carden enjoys danger."

"He flirts with death," she observed softly, uncomfortable with what she was hearing, but not overly surprised by it.

"An excellent way of putting it. Sometimes, he even taunts it. The things I've seen him do . . ." He shook his head and chuckled as a wide smile brightened his face. He leaned against the doorjamb again and crossed his arms over his chest.

"The first task when building a span is to establish a pulley cable between the two anchor points. Men and materiel move out and back and across in a basket that hangs from the cable. If the cable slips from the pulley or jams . . . It's often a very long way down.

"I was in the basket at the midpoint and over fifty meters up when the cable jammed. I hadn't taken a harness out with me and I was too far out for one to be flung to me. Carden disappeared and came back with one of Cook's rolling pins. I sat—exceedingly bored when not horribly embarrassed—in the basket while the rope fell short time after time, a vicious storm rolled in on us, and Carden sat on a truss, calmly whittling on that rolling pin."

"He whittled while you hung over an abyss?"

With a low laugh, Barrett nodded. "The lightning was cracking all around us when he finally put his knife away, walked to the end of the cable, dropped the harness for me over his shoulder, settled the rolling pin on the cable, and stepped off the edge. He laughed all the way out and dropped into the basket with me as though he'd done nothing more than ride a horse down Rotten Row and then hopped off."

"He wasn't wearing a harness himself, was he?" Sera guessed.

"Carden never wears a harness."

"It would take away the edge," she observed with a sigh. "How did he get back to the point?"

"With my weight lowering the point end of the cable, he rode back on his rolling pin."

"Laughing."

"He's not completely foolhardy," Barrett assured her.

"He simply sees risk differently from most men. For him it's a grand game."

Carden's life, as much as she'd seen of it, was a far cry from the one Barrett had described. "There's hardly any great danger in building houses and conservatories. He must be terribly bored these days."

"He's had some practice for it," he countered with another shrug. "Military life is frequently more tedious than it is exciting. One has hours on end to fill as best one can. We invented a great many games to amuse ourselves and pass the time. In fact," he said, stepping away from the jamb with a wink, "I'll show you one of them. Wait right there."

He went to the parlor and returned a few seconds later with an apple. "Here, toss this," he instructed, putting it into her hand and then pivoting to stand beside her. "In any direction you'd prefer and whenever you're ready."

She had no idea what he was going to do—perhaps catch it in his mouth—but she adjusted her hold on the heavy piece of fruit, tossed it straight up into the air above their heads, and then instantly stepped back so that she could more easily watch him. He moved so quickly that she wasn't quite sure what he'd done, but there was a most definite flash of silver just before the apple tumbled out of the air and landed on the marble tiles by the door. She could only stare in openmouthed amazement as Barrett strode over, snatched it up, and pulled the knife out of it.

"Carden would have cut it cleanly in two," he supplied, wiping the blade on the sleeve of his suit coat. The entire knife disappeared up his left sleeve as he added, "He's much more proficient with knives than I am. With a sword, he'd have quartered it."

"Of course," she said, shaking off her surprise. "Swords and knives have dangerous edges."

"I've never thought of it that way. You're right."

"Since I haven't seen any chopped fruit lying about . . .

What is Carden doing for diversion while he endures the tedium of his life?"

"When he's not drinking far more than usual to dull it," Barrett replied, his eyes twinkling, "he's engaged in an exquisitely civilized and highly refined variation of hunting."

"In other words," she rejoined, "he's finding his danger and excitement in being a rake."

"There is a definite edge to it."

"Particularly when you encounter a woman who doesn't appreciate being viewed as game."

"That's very true," he admitted. "There was a—" He swallowed the rest of the story and shot her an apologetic look. "Never mind."

She looked past him and down the hall to the open doorway of Carden's study. How much longer would it be, she wondered, before he couldn't stand the boredom any longer and went back to dancing on high edges? As much as the thought of his casual risk-taking concerned her, she couldn't help but think that it was a better way to go through life than drinking himself into oblivion.

"Barrett?" she began softly. "If it wouldn't be prying to ask or a betrayal of a confidence to answer . . . Why is Carden drinking so heavily today?"

"Ghosts, I suspect," his friend answered quietly, also looking at the open door. "He's never said why he does these dives, but in all the time I've known him, I've never seen him at a funeral sober. We've been to far too many funerals together, Carden and I.

"I think he sees a death as the consequence of a failure on his part. That if he'd tried harder or done something differently, it would have been averted. He hates to fail at anything and takes it hard when he does. Not that he's ever talked about all of this, you understand. Carden holds his secrets like he does his cards, close to the vest."

How very sad, she thought, to have secrets that you

couldn't share with anyone, not even your best friend. There couldn't be any kind of loneliness deeper than that. Laying her hand on Barrett's arm, she waited until he looked down at her before saying, "You're a very good friend to understand and accept that, Barrett."

"He doesn't ask about mine, so we're even," he countered with a most dismissive shrug. He cocked a brow and added, "And then we also share a good number of secrets between us."

"Such as who might have attacked your commanding officer," she supplied.

"That would be one. And all things considered, a relatively minor one among the bunch."

Minor? Good Lord. She didn't want to know what they might consider major. "You're both lucky you aren't in a jail somewhere, aren't you?"

He laughed and grinned. "They haven't built one that could hold us. If you'll excuse me, I think I'll go see if he's still standing."

She nodded her assent, thinking that men were the strangest creatures; they'd risk their lives for each other, lie for each other, follow one another around the world to keep each other from stupidly getting themselves killed, and never feel the least bit put off by the fact that what they knew about each other didn't go any deeper than the experiences they'd shared. They really were altogether another species of animal.

"Oh," Barrett said, stopping and turning back. "The reason I came out here looking for you in the first place . . . Lady Hatcher's ball is in a few days. As the son of a prominent financier, I'm considered useful to know and so I'm invited to these sorts of affairs. Mother always insists that it's my duty to attend. Might I prevail on you to make the evening a pleasant one for me?"

Her instincts squirmed, suggesting that accepting was an unwise thing to do. But Honoria had cornered her into accepting an invitation from Aiden and to turn down Barrett's would likely embarrass him. She couldn't do that to him. Sacrificing good judgment to kindness, she summoned a smile and replied, "I'd be pleased to attend with you, Barrett."

With a smile of his own, he bowed, said, "My sincerest appreciation, Seraphina," and then turned and went on his way.

She frowned down at the walking stick, an odd mixture of exhilaration and disquietude stealing over her in the silence. The source of her concern was patently obvious: she was not only contemplating an affair with an admitted rake who had a penchant for living boldly and recklessly, but she had—in the span of less than a single hour—accepted invitations out from both of his friends. Friends who were every bit as rakish, bold, and reckless as he was. It all very strongly suggested that she'd forgotten to crate up her good sense when she was leaving Belize.

Her sense of elation wasn't equally discernible in any respect. There was a bit of a hopeful feeling to it. And an undercurrent of what almost felt like contentment. Or perhaps it was a sense of homecoming. At least as she'd always imagined what a homecoming would feel like. Whatever it was, there was certainly no reason for any of it. She had no home. She had nothing whatsoever to be hopeful about beyond the likelihood that she'd have something to eat tonight. And content? No woman attempting to juggle relationships of one sort or another with three men had cause for anything approximating contentment. Not a sane woman anyway.

Sera shook her head and decided that she had better uses for her time than trying to solve elusive puzzles. It had been days since the girls had done an arithmetic lesson. On slates the numbers were as defined as the sums and differences were always clear and certain. At the moment, she could truly appreciate that kind of predictability and assurance.

CHAPTER 12

Sera stopped in the kitchen doorway, lamp in hand, not at all certain what she should do. She'd come to check on the puppies and hadn't expected to find Carden with them at this late hour. She wouldn't have thought that he would be in any condition to put one foot in front of the other, much less able to get himself down the stairs and into the kitchen. But there he was, sitting on the floor beside the bed they'd made for the dogs, his back against the hearth surround, a puppy in his lap, both of them seemingly sound asleep.

He'd bathed and put on clean clothes since she'd last seen him that afternoon. And shaved. Apparently himself, judging by the nicks in his jaw. Given his state of inebriation when John Aiden and Barrett had finally hauled him up the stairs, it was a wonder he hadn't slit his throat.

He had a wonderful throat. Neck, chest, and shoulders, too. Since that first morning when he'd answered the door in his dressing gown, he'd hidden himself behind starched collars and fashionable silk ties. He hadn't bothered tonight and, improper though it was, she couldn't help but appreciate it. His shirt was open—buttoned only halfway up, in fact—allowing her to view a broad expanse of his well-muscled and darkly furred chest. He'd rolled up his sleeves, too, to allow her to admire the strength evident in his thickly corded forearms. And at the end of his very long, trousered legs . . . he had beautifully shaped, perfectly proportioned feet.

He wiggled his toes. Afraid that she'd been caught in her bold appraisal, Sera quickly looked to see if he'd awakened. His eyes were still closed and she smiled. She liked his hair ruffled. It looked as though he'd come out of the bath, rubbed his fingers through it, and declared it good enough. It was so boyish—innocent in a way—and such a contrast to the stark virility of the rest of him. How could any woman resist him? Why would any woman even try?

"Do you see anything of interest?"

She'd been caught! Her heart pounding and heat fanning over her cheeks, Sera ignored the question and replied, "I didn't mean to wake you."

His eyes remained closed, but a smile played at the corners of his mouth. "You didn't. I was trying to think. Sometimes it helps to close your eyes."

"What are you thinking about?"

His smile broadened. "How badly my head hurts."

She eased forward, saying, "I've always wondered why people drink if it makes them so dreadfully miserable afterward."

His smile fading, he opened his eyes and considered her. After a long moment he replied, "It's that you get to choose your misery. This one tends to make you forget the others."

She wondered what particular miseries he was trying to forget, but he didn't give her a chance to ask.

"The puppies look to be none the worse for their dunking," he said, gently lifting the pup from his lap and placing it back at its mother's side.

As strange as it seemed, she thought the same thing might be said for his day-long plunge into the bottle.

She'd never seen him so . . . Relaxed wasn't quite the right word. Resigned wasn't, either. But she liked this slightly rumpled version of Carden Reeves. She liked it very much.

"Cook says that it's the broth he made," she shared, placing the lamp on the kitchen table. Tightening the sash on her wrapper, she knelt beside the padding to stroke the dog's head. "He gave the mama a bowl of it and spooned a bit into each puppy. He claims it can cure any ailment from whooping cough to leprosy."

"It probably can. At least I hope so," he said, holding up a thick china mug for her to see. He took a sip and returned it to the floor beside him, saying, "He often did better at treating us than the regimental surgeon did, you know. When it comes to needles and threads, he's better than Mr. Gauthier could ever dream of being. Cook's a true wizard at stitching men back together."

"I hope that you've never had an occasion to personally benefit from his surgical skill."

"Cook believes that small stitches make for cleaner scars," he said, pushing his shirt sleeves higher and leaning forward, angling his arms into the soft light. With a fingertip he traced a long, thin white line from the wrist upward on his left arm, adding, "He put sixty-three in this arm." He showed her a somewhat shorter one on his right. "Only thirty-five in this one."

She'd seen enough scarred men in Belize to know a knife or sword wound from any other. He who lived by the sword suffered by it, too. "They must have been very painful."

He somberly gazed off into the near distance as though remembering. Slowly, the corners of his mouth turned up. He tilted his head to look at her, his eyes sparkling. "Cook put forty-one in my upper left thigh. Would you like to see that scar?"

It was the most thoroughly, outrageously improper offer any man had ever made her. And for some reason, instead of being offended, she was incredibly tempted to accept. "Perhaps some other time," Sera replied, her heart racing frantically. She forced herself to swallow. "How were you cut?"

His smile instantly faded and his eyes darkened. He shook his head, instantly winced, and reached for his cup. "It's not a tale for tender sensibilities," he said around the rim, his gaze holding hers assessingly.

"I assure you that mine were toughened quite a long while ago. Life on the Mosquito Coast is a far cry from genteel and pleasant. I doubt that there's anything you could tell me that I haven't either seen or heard of before."

He believed her. And maybe it was because his brain was still slightly numb around the edges, but her willingness to share his burdens touched something deep inside him. The words were out before he could think better of it and stop them. "Harry Dennison, fourth son of the eighth or ninth Earl of Dennison, has a passion for little girls. He kept it hidden well enough that no one suspected until the day the daughter of our washwoman . . ." The day, that one hideous moment, returned—as always—with gut-clenching clarity. He could see the vultures, feel the heat, hear the flies and the smell . . . The blood was everywhere. Carden deliberately shook his head, saturating his senses with the bright light of pain.

"Neither Cook nor Dr. Phinster could repair the damage and she bled to death," he finished, reaching for his cup of broth. "She was the same age as Bea. And every bit as innocent."

Her eyes were huge and bright with outrage as she asked, "You challenged Dennison, didn't you?"

It was more statement than question. "That's a nice way of putting it. The blunter version is that I tried to kill him. And, despite Harry's spirited self-defense, I would have succeeded if Barrett hadn't been afraid I'd bleed to death before I got it done and decided to intervene. Or if the first weapon at hand had been a pistol instead of a rapier."

"I'm glad Barrett didn't let you die, but I am sorry that Harry Dennison survived, as well."

Oh, he liked her spirit. It was so much like his own when it came to the matter of vengeance. "Of course, violence between officers being frowned upon as it is, one of us had to go, and since Harry was engaged to the colonel's daughter, I was the one asked to resign my commission."

"That was hardly fair," she observed. "Justice wasn't served."

"Yes it was," he countered, smiling. "Cook put over fifty stitches in his face. And they weren't small ones, either. For as long as Harry Dennison lives, the very sight of him will make children run away."

"Good. And I hope the colonel's daughter had the good sense to break off their engagement."

He had no idea what the colonel's daughter had done. She hadn't displayed that much wisdom in accepting Dennison's marriage proposal in the first place. The woman sitting on the floor with him wouldn't have given the bastard so much as the time of day. Sera wasn't just beautiful, she had uncommon good sense. She was compassionate, too, and strong and brave. She was the kind of woman who would make the perfect—

Good God Almighty. He'd pickled his brain more deeply than he'd thought. At least he'd caught himself before he'd said or done something irrevocably stupid. He smiled at her and cocked his brow in his most roguish way. "Are you sure you don't want to to see the scar on my thigh?"

She blushed and blinked and took a long slow breath. The hollow at the base of her slender neck thrummed with the rapid beat of her heart as she softly said, "In all the confusion and activity of the day, I've neglected to thank you for all you did. I don't know what I would have done had you not been there to pull Amanda from the river. And making the puppies breathe . . . It all could have so easily turned out to be a terrible tragedy. I'll be eternally grateful that you took matters so masterfully in hand."

Eternally grateful? He wasn't too pickled to see the benefit in that. He grinned. "I live to be of service."

"No you don't," she countered, smiling softly, knowingly. "But when circumstances make it necessary, you can be a most noble and honorable man, Carden Reeves."

How clearly she'd seen through his carefully constructed façade. "A character flaw that, thankfully, I'm able to keep hidden most of the time," he quipped, hoping to make light of the revelation. "I'd appreciate it if you'd say nothing of it to others. My reputation is at stake, you know."

"And you've worked very hard to cultivate your rakish image, haven't you?"

This was the most amazingly honest conversation with a woman he'd ever had. Even more amazing was the fact that he found it refreshing. "It requires some persistence," he admitted, "but it's not an altogether unpleasant effort. It does have its rewards."

Her smile told him that she knew precisely what kind of rewards he was talking about. The fact she smiled at all was just as telling. She wasn't afraid of him. And she most certainly wasn't running away in a missish dither. No, Seraphina Treadwell was quietly, seriously intrigued. And there was nothing on earth more tantalizing than a curious, honest woman.

"Why would you choose to be a rake, Carden? There are so many other ways to keep the days interesting. Why deliberately do things that encourage people to talk about you? You live a life that simply invites scandal."

"Which is precisely the point and the intent," he confessed with a shrug. "And there's nothing simple about it.

They're going to talk anyway and it's better to have some control over what they're saying than to let them make up their own stories."

"Are they truly that vicious?"

His heart clenched. Yes, they were and that Sera didn't know that for herself frightened him. He did live inviting scandal, and in inviting her to his bed, he was asking her to bear the price of it along with him. It occurred to him that a better man would back away and let her go rather than subject her to the almost certain gossip.

But he couldn't. He'd wanted her the minute he'd seen her. And in the days and hours and minutes since, the wanting had become a hunger so deep that he ached with it night and day. No, walking away from Sera was impossible; he wasn't that strong. But if she had the strength to do it, he could at least summon the resolve to accept her decision.

She had to know what taking up with him was going to cost her. It was only fair. And he owed her to be man enough to tell her. But God, the risk of losing her was terrifying. More terrifying than the memories he'd spent the day drowning. The past was the past and nothing could be done to change it. Sera was today.

Swallowing down his heart, he shifted about until he sat cross-legged in front of her. He held out his hands and she placed hers in them, her gaze gently searching his as he drew a steadying breath. "My mother was an actress," he began. "And almost forty years younger than my father. They'd been married barely six months when I was born."

"And people talked about all of that."

"Oh, yes. They still do, actually. Whenever I walk into a room. Mostly they talk about my mother's questionable virtue and the identity of my sire. The general opinion is that my father—in his doddering old age—was tricked into giving his name and financial support to another man's bastard."

"Surely your father didn't believe that," she suggested softly.

"Obviously he didn't at the outset or he wouldn't have married my mother. But at some point the lies became his truth. I remember that they lived very separate lives and that what few dinners we ever shared were always excruciatingly silent ordeals. My father was seldom home, seldom sober. My mother never went out. No one ever came to call."

He looked down at their hands. Sera's were so small. "All we had was each other," he whispered, remembering how his own hand had once looked in his mother's. "She was my first and my best friend."

His throat thickened and he cleared it before he embarrassed himself. "Then," he said, pushing on, threading his fingers through Sera's, "when I was seven, something brought about a thaw in their relationship. Mother became pregnant again and—in the dead of night—we were sent to live at the country house."

He looked up to meet her gaze again. "Derive what you will from those facts," he offered. "Personally, I've always thought that the opinions of his fellow peers mattered more to my father than anything else. He packed us off to the end of the earth rather than summon the courage and dignity to face down speculation and scandal."

"It must have hurt your mother very much to have been exiled like that."

"The midwife said that delivering a stillborn child killed her. I think she simply didn't want to live anymore and gave up trying."

"I'm so sorry, Carden."

What did it say about his life, he wondered, that Sera was the only person who had ever offered a condolence for his mother's passing? Twenty years, a legion of staff, what everyone else called a family . . .

"After she died, did your father regret what he'd done and bring you back to London?"

She wanted to hope for a happy ending, but didn't; he could hear it in her voice, see it in her eyes. Sera knew. He stroked his thumbs over the backs of her hands. "The night he put us in the carriage and sent us away was the last time I ever saw him. The staff and I were the only ones at her funeral."

The memory of that day returned, clear and dismal. The wind, the rain, the mud, the gaping hole in the ground, and the looks of impatience all around him. But the whiskey had done its work and it didn't hurt as badly as it had earlier in the day. He tightened his hold on Sera's hands and deliberately stepped farther into the pain than he'd ever allowed himself.

"The son of a bitch didn't even buy her a headstone, Sera." His throat tightened again but he continued on, angry enough not to care. "So I sold my pony to get the money to buy her one myself. And I made the carver put cherubs on it."

She gently pulled a hand from his grasp and cupped his cheek. "You were a good son, Carden," she said softly, her eyes shimmering with unshed tears. "A far better son than your father was a husband and father."

The words slid deep into the center of his soul, filling a void he hadn't known existed. The weight of it was solid, comforting. But it was the kindness and compassion of their offering that overwhelmed him. He didn't dare thank her for the gift; he wouldn't be able to hold the tears at bay. Instead, he took her hand back in his, pressed a lingering, grateful kiss to her palm, and then lowered it to his lap again.

"Anyway," he said, desperately forging ahead, "I lived at the country house until he died and Percival inherited it. He and Honoria wanted a rustic playhouse like all the other peers and so my bags were packed and I was sent off to school.

"Every now and again I was summoned for an appearance—when I had to account for my outrageous behavior and promise not to scandalize the Reeves name any more than my mother already had. I think, in all, that I spoke with Percival only a dozen times in my life. Arthur even less. He was always out of country on one adventure or another."

Sera wanted to cry for him, for the loneliness and cruelty of his childhood. Honoria was right; he had become a far better man than anyone could have expected. He'd become a good person despite the miserable examples those around him had provided.

"I saw what they did to my mother, Sera," he said earnestly, tightening his grip on her hands. "I learned from her misery that it's better to exercise some measure of control over what they say than leave them to their own devices. It limits the damage they can do, the pain they can cause."

And, she realized, it was their willingness to inflict it that lay at the heart of why Carden Reeves didn't want to be a peer. He didn't want to sit in the House of Lords and hear the whispers, didn't want to have anything to do with the people who had all but driven his mother into the haven of death. "That you've inherited your father's title is the darkest, meanest twist of fate, Carden."

He smiled weakly. "In all honesty, there's a part of me that's thrilled with the notion of my father spinning in his grave. But the larger part of me . . ." He sighed. "To be part of what has been the cause of so many heartaches and all the resentment in my life . . . I've never wanted anything less, Sera. If I could hand the title to someone on the street, I would."

"Perhaps," Sera countered, breathless with the simplicity and ease of a suddenly realized solution, "you could ask Victoria to take it back and give it to someone who wants it. That's possible, isn't it?"

"It's an idea," he agreed, his eyes sparkling and his smile returning, wide and bright. He drew her hands toward him until the rest of her body was drawn with them. "I have a better oné, though," he murmured, looking up at her. "Rakes never pass up an opportunity to kiss a beautiful woman."

"And you're a very good rake," she observed, easing her hands from his to place them on his shoulders.

"Yes, I am. Practice does indeed make perfect."

If perfectly stunning her was his intent, he succeeded beyond her wildest expectations. His hands didn't go to her waist as she'd thought they would. They came up between the two of them, to the uppermost button on her night rail. His fingers worked quickly, seemingly effortlessly, down the row of small oyster shells. His gaze held hers all the while and she could hear his voice in the dark depths of his eyes. *Do you dare, Sera? How brave are you?*

She was trying to decide when his gaze slowly slid downward and his fingertips skimmed over the bare swells of her breasts. She stopped thinking altogether when he leaned forward to press a languid kiss to an inside curve. He drew back ever so slightly, whispered, "Beautiful Sera," and then kissed the other side of her cleavage.

He eased away from her, his gaze coming back to hers as his fingers worked their way farther down the row of buttons. *Still daring?* she heard him silently ask as he undid the sash at her waist. His fingertips brushed over her skin as he drew her gown wider. *How far will you let me go, Sera?*

"I'm afraid that I'm quite out of practice," she confessed, her breath catching, her heart trying to hammer its way out of her chest as he cupped her breasts in his hands.

Shall I kiss you again, Sera? Ever so slowly, he scraped his thumbs over her hardened nipples. *Here?*

She was on fire, her insides thrumming and molten. Time. She needed time to gather her wits, to remember how she was supposed to move so that Carden didn't think her a complete novice. "Not that I was ever really very good at it, mind you," she admitted, desperate to temper his expectations. "At kissing, I mean. And lovemaking, too. I didn't mean being a rake. Women can't be rakes."

They could, Carden knew, but people didn't call them rakes. They called them whores. And that gender made such a difference in people's minds was precisely what Sera needed to understand. It took every measure of his conscience and self-restraint to still his hands and ask, "Sera, are you willing to pay the price for satisfying your curiosity? They *will* talk. About you. Me. Us. It will follow you for the rest of your life."

She smiled and drew her fingers through his hair. "*If* they find out."

God, what he wouldn't give to have fallen so far from honor that he could declare her naïve hope good enough. "No, Sera," he protested, his throat tightening as dread clawed at his chest. "You can hope for the best, and we can do our utmost to be discreet, but you have to be willing—right this minute—to accept the consequences of the worst."

She wasn't; he could see the flickering shadows of doubt in her eyes. He closed his own, unwilling to let her see the depth of his disappointment. Swallowing against the knot trying to strangle him, he released her breasts with a lingering, regretful caress, and then drew the edges of her night rail over the sweetest temptation he'd ever known.

Her hands slipped from his hair, touched his shoulders just for a moment, and then were gone. He felt them brush against his own arms, heard the sound of sliding satin as she tied her sash into place.

"I think I had best be going back to my room now,"

she said, rising to her feet, her voice sounding every bit as sad as he felt.

God, what a pathetic excuse for a rakehell he was. A decent one wouldn't have a viable conscience. It shouldn't matter one whit whether the woman at hand was making an informed, intelligent decision. A willing body was a willing body. The problem was that he'd spent far too much time talking with Sera. He'd come to know her and, in doing that, he'd come to respect her and want what was best for her. She wasn't a nameless, soon-to-be-forgotten stranger who existed simply to warm his bed and give him pleasure. Yes, no more miserable, worthless excuse for a rakehell than Carden Reeves had ever existed in the history of sex. Wanton and mindless or otherwise.

"If you change your mind about wanting to see the scar on my thigh," he called after her, thinking to make at least a pretense of maintaining the standards, "my room is at the far end of the hall. You needn't knock."

She laughed and the sound somehow made his sacrifice feel less forever and more endurable. He opened his eyes to see her standing by the door, the lamp in her hand, the edges of her night rail open just enough to remind him of how close he'd come to paradise.

"Good night, Carden," she said with a wistful smile and turned away.

"Seraphina?" he called after her. He waited until she looked back over her shoulder to smile at her and add, "Your parents named you perfectly. Sweet dreams, angel. Dream of me."

Sera nodded her assent and went on, knowing that reason and fear held no sway in the world of sleep. Carden would come to her in her dreams and she would lie with him. She would awaken aching and feverish and regretting with all her heart that the heady dream could never be made real. It didn't matter that people would talk about the fact that they were lovers. She would actually feel a most immodest sense of pride about that.

No, what she couldn't bear to hear them say—today, tomorrow, forever—was how blindly, laughably foolish she'd been to fall in love with a man whose only true commitment in life was to bed women and walk away.

Tears spilled over her lashes as what had been a brief, elusive, and unnamed hope withered and died.

CHAPTER 13

He'd suggested that Seraphina wear the red dress knowing that she'd choose the blue just to oppose him. But if she'd also harbored any hopes about the relatively plain gown's allowing her to fade into the Stanbridges' dining room wallpaper, she had to be supremely disillusioned. She was absolutely, stunningly beautiful with her dark hair piled atop her head, loose ringlets framing her face, and no jewelry whatsoever except for the diamond brooch in the décolletage of her gown.

But then, Sera didn't need adornments. There wasn't a man present who hadn't looked long and appreciatively when he'd brought her into the Stanbridge home. What initial tension that had caused among the women had completely dissipated before the introductions were completed. Sera was Sera: gracious, sincere, and wholly unaffected by her beauty. Everyone adored her.

Melanie Stanbridge—every five-foot, happily plump, pin-curled inch of her—was especially delighted with Sera. Not five minutes into the general parlor talk, he'd watched her slip away to quickly rearrange the seating at the dining room table. It hadn't surprised him at all to find himself seated opposite Sera and with Melanie on his right.

What bothered him, though, was that their hostess had put her son on Sera's left. Her intent wasn't lost on him. Or on Barrett. And while his friend hadn't done or said anything that could be construed as even slightly flirtatious, he knew Barrett and what he was thinking. One false move, one inattentive moment, and Barrett would step into the breach and try to charm Seraphina away from him. They'd done it to each other countless times in the past and it had never mattered to their friendship. It was a good-natured competition, a game of sorts with a prize they usually ended up passing to the other. But not this time, Carden silently vowed. Not with Seraphina.

"So tell me something about your life in Belize, my dear Sera," their hostess chirped amid the general buzz of dinner conversation. "I should think it would have been utterly fascinating."

"I'm afraid it's not much of a tale," Sera replied with a dismissive shrug of one delectably bare shoulder. "My father planned for us to be there only a few months and so we lived in a tent just outside Belize City. My mother spent her every waking moment trying to keep the bugs and creatures from overtaking it and, while she attended to a spirited home defense, my father and I hiked out into the wilds every day. He collected plant samples and made copious notes. My task was to make detailed paintings of the various specimens he assembled."

"How long were you there?" Barrett asked.

"A few months stretched into a year and a year into two," Sera supplied, turning her head to meet Barrett's gaze and smile. "As you might well imagine, we amassed an incredible catalog of information in that time. The conditions of the tent being what they were, especially in the rainy season, our work was always in danger of being wrecked in one way or another."

"Was it?" Carden inquired, determined to deprive Barrett of her attention.

"No, thankfully," she said, her smile seeming brighter for him than it had been for Barrett. "Arthur and Mary were kind enough to offer to store everything for us in the relative safety of their clapboard home. It was Arthur who convinced my father that he should submit his notes and my paintings for publication."

She laughed softly and added, "I've often thought that Arthur made the suggestion largely out of a sense of self-preservation, to simply get the mass of paper out of his house. Had it ever caught fire, it would have burned for a week."

Barrett shot Carden a look across the table, cocked a brow, and asked, "And was your father's work ever published?"

"If it was," she answered, looking back at him, "we never received news of it."

Melanie Stanbridge innocently intruded on the contest by asking, "What was your father's name, my dear?"

"Geoffrey Baines Miller."

So much, Sera thought darkly, for Carden's assurance that Melanie Stanbridge wouldn't let her make a misstep. The woman's eyes had widened to the size of the bread plates and the gentle hum of dinner conversation had abruptly dropped into the abyss of dead silence.

"Baines Miller," Barrett said, chuckling softly. "Of course."

"Can you believe it!" someone down the table whispered.

Suddenly, heads bobbed and murmurs rippled. Everyone kept glancing at her and smiling shyly before looking away to murmur and nod some more. And Carden . . . he was no help in terms of providing an explanation, much less an assurance, wordless or otherwise. Her devilishly handsome, always-in-control escort was too busy trying to choke down whatever had gotten caught in his throat.

"Oh, my dear girl," her hostess said breathlessly, "you truly don't know, do you?"

"Apparently not," Sera admitted, wishing someone—anyone—would be brave and considerate enough to share what was apparently, to everyone except her, common knowledge.

"Barrett, darling, in the—"

"I'm well ahead of you, Mother," he threw back over his shoulder as he strode out of the dining room.

Still at a loss, she met Carden's gaze across the table. He'd recovered, but the look in his eyes sent a tendril of fear snaking through her frustration. He didn't like what was happening at all. She had the distinct impression that he wanted the floor to open up and swallow everyone but the two of them. "Carden?"

"No, I won't say a word," he answered, finding a faint smile for her. It disappeared as he glanced around the table, adding, "And neither will anyone else. We won't ruin the surprise for you."

"As I mentioned to you just the other day, I've never been particularly fond of surprises. I'd prefer to know in advance, please."

"Too late," Barrett announced cheerfully, returning with a huge, leather-bound tome in hand. He held it out to her, grinning. "Your father's book, Seraphina."

Stunned and holding her breath, she took it with both hands, her gaze skimming over the front cover. Her father's name was there, across the bottom, in large gold-embossed letters. Her own was beneath his, in smaller gold letters, italicized, naming her as the illustrator. It seemed real and yet it didn't. She opened it to a random page and instantly recognized the picture, remembered the day she'd painted it. On the facing page were the words, not in her father's hand as he'd originally set them down, but in a formal type. She read the first line and finally believed. "I can hear his voice," she whispered. "It's as though he were here."

Carden saw the shimmering veil of tears come to her eyes and knew that she'd be horribly embarrassed to have them fall with everyone watching her as intently as they were. "Look at the fly page, Seraphina," he instructed, breaking the taut silence, hoping to draw her from her memories in time. "Tell us what it says."

She gently closed the book and reopened it, casting him a quick glance of appreciation as she turned to the proper page. "It was published the same month as my father's death."

The same month? Carden frowned, suspecting that this surprise was going to lead to a considerable number of other surprises and that not a one of them was going to be pleasant.

Sera looked up at him. "And it's had ten printings?"

"Oh, probably more," Melanie Stanbridge declared with a wave of her hand. "I've had that copy for well over a year. Almost two."

"And I should imagine each printing is quite large," Cecil Stanbridge offered from the head of the table. "It's a required text at university, you know. In public school, as well. Every botany student in the empire has a copy."

"Every person with a conservatory has one, as well," someone else contributed.

"Two, in most instances," said another. "One for the excellent reference it is and a second for disassembling so that the pictures can be framed and displayed throughout the house. They're simply stunning artwork. Anyone with any taste at all has at *least* one or two on the walls of their homes."

"Haven't you noticed those on my walls, Seraphina?"

Sera glanced at the wall high above the sideboard. Two prints of her work, in ornately carved and heavily gilded frames, hung from the crown molding, side by side. She had come into the room without looking up and there was nothing to do but be honest about it. "I'm sorry, but no, Mrs. Stanbridge, I haven't before just now. I've been too preoccupied trying to remember everyone's names, who is here with whom, and what everyone's interests are."

"You're forgiven, my dear," Melanie said breezily. "It was such a delight to see you learn of it the way you did. I shall never forget this evening for as long as I live. Seraphina Baines Miller learned of her celebrity in my home, at my table."

Sera looked back down at the book and shook her head sadly. "If only Father had lived long enough to learn of it. He would have so enjoyed knowing that his life's work had been of help and interest to others."

Cecil Stanbridge snorted and laughed. "I'd think that he would have also enjoyed knowing that he was leaving his family a most impressive bank account."

Sera looked up at their host, her brows knitted, and Carden knew that until that moment the notion of money had never crossed her mind. All she'd cared about was her father's dream having come to fruition. It was so very Sera. "Seraphina?" he said gently, calling her gaze to his. "As your father's only heir, you're entitled to the royalties."

"Which," Cecil observed, "I would hazard to guess to be at least twenty thousand pounds."

Sera laughed, closed the book, and wrapped her arms around it. "You're exaggerating, Mr. Stanbridge. That's an obscene amount of money."

"No he's not, Sera," Carden quietly assured her. "And twenty thousand is no doubt a conservative estimate." He gave her a moment to catch her breath, to digest in small part the staggering reality of it all, and then added, "I think that whatever plans you may have for tomorrow should be set aside. You need to pay a call on your father's publisher."

Yes. Yes, she did. There were several questions she wanted to ask, several answers she desperately needed.

And beyond those more personal ones, there were undoubtedly others that she should ask. What precisely they were, she didn't know offhand. The publishing business was a world she had never so much as glimpsed before. "Would you be willing to accompany me, Carden?"

"If you'd like."

"I would very much," she admitted, relieved. "Thank you."

"While you're there," Barrett said, "you might ask them why it is that they never communicated their decision to publish and why there have been no royalties paid to date."

"Perhaps," his mother suggested, "they couldn't find Seraphina."

Across from her, Carden shook his head. "She was precisely where she was when her father's work was submitted. They could have found her had they tried to do so."

"My late husband was my father's agent. Perhaps . . ." Her voice faded into the frantic pounding of her heart as possibilities tumbled one over the other in her mind, all of them dark and mean and frighteningly twisted by the memory of the man hurrying away in the park.

"Surely your husband—God rest his soul—would have mentioned such an extraordinary coup had he known of it," Melanie offered.

The old icy shadow of dread wrapped around her heart. Sera swallowed hard and forced herself to smile. "Yes, surely he would have."

I want to go home, Carden.
Don't be afraid, angel.

They'd done no more than was required by civility, stayed no longer than to be perfectly polite. With the copy of her father's book in the crook of his arm, he handed her into the carriage, stepped in behind her and closed the door, asking simply, "Are you still cold?"

"To the center of my bones," she confessed, wondering how he knew. She thought she'd done so well at pretending to be normal.

He took off his coat, draped it over her shoulders, then sat next to her and drew her into the circle of his arms. Sera snuggled closer, burying her cheek against his shoulder and finding comfort in the solid warmth of his presence and in his willingness to offer it. The tiny voice of good judgment suggested that she was courting an advance, but she ignored it. She needed his strength tonight and if a kiss or a caress were the price she had to pay for it . . . Price? Integrity demanded that she be honest. She enjoyed Carden's physical attentions. To a dangerously tempting degree.

"Seraphina Baines-Miller Treadwell," he said as the carriage began to roll down the Stanbridges' drive. "That's one long name."

"Seraphina Maria Louisa Baines Miller Treadwell. And that's just the English version. The ride home isn't long enough to do the Spanish one."

He laughed and hugged her tight. "It's nice to hear the sparkle back in your voice. Are you feeling better?"

"A little," she admitted, bracing herself for what she knew was coming. Carden had seen the darker implications of her fame long before she had. "At least I'm warmer."

"Do you feel up to answering some questions for me?"

"I thought you would have some," she said with a sigh, easing away from him. She was instantly chilled, but not as deeply as before. And, somehow, she felt stronger for being able to see the chiseled planes of his face and the hard line of his jaw. "Go ahead, Carden. Ask me whatever you want."

"All right. To begin, tell me about your husband. Where did he come from? How did you meet him?"

It was precisely where she'd thought he would start. "Gerald was a financial agent for William Walker," she began. "Are you familiar with the name?"

"I can't say that I am."

"Walker is an American. Twice in the last four years, he's attempted to invade and overthrow the rightful government of Nicaragua. His vision is to create American slave states along the Mosquito Coast."

"And the American government doesn't approve," he guessed.

Sera nodded. "And because of that, Walker's forced to acquire private financing. Gerald's responsibility was to seek out individuals who had money to invest in the enterprise. It was after Walker's first failure to conquer Nicaragua that Gerald arrived in Belize and eventually approached my father about managing his publishing affairs."

"And your father thought this was a good idea?"

"Oh, Carden," she said, deeply regretting that he would never get to meet her father, would never know him for the interesting, loving person he had been. "My father was a good man. But all he wanted to do was his research. The writing and the organization of his notes were the interesting parts of it to him, but none of the rest of it appealed. And what didn't appeal to my father, he delegated to someone else. Since he felt that conducting business with London publishing houses was inappropriate for a female mind, he rejected my offer to attend to it and happily turned over all responsibility to Gerald."

"Your father didn't know about his connection to this Walker fellow, did he?"

"No," Sera assured him, pleased that he'd assumed her father to be the honorable man that he had been. "No one knew until after my father died and one of Gerald's former compatriots came to Belize hoping to enlist his assistance in planning yet another invasion of Nicaragua. Gerald was out when the man arrived and, not knowing that Gerald had kept his past a secret, he told me everything over tea and biscuits while we waited."

"Assuming that since you were married to the man, you approved of Walker's goals."

Sera nodded again. "But I'd been with Gerald long enough by then to realize not only the wisdom of keeping my opinions to myself, but also in pretending they were in sympathy with his own. He had accepted the Walker offer when Arthur and Mary heard the rumor about the ancient ruins and asked him to guide them into the interior."

"Did—"

"Yes," she hastened to assure him. "I had no secrets from Arthur and Mary. They were my friends. I told them everything."

"And yet Arthur asked him to be their guide?" he asked. "Had he taken complete leave of his senses?"

"Arthur wanted to find his ruins and Gerald represented his best chances for doing so. It was a purely pragmatic decision on your brother's part. I desperately tried to talk him out of it, but Arthur was just as single-mindedly blind about his work as my father was."

He muttered under his breath, but Sera couldn't tell whether it was over Arthur's priorities or the fact that the carriage had drawn to a halt in front of his house. She watched in silence as he opened the door, vaulted out, and turned back to assist her. Though moonlight softly gilded his face and shoulders, it did nothing to soften the hard light in his eyes. Scooping the precious book from the seat beside her, she took his hand and joined him on the walkway. He gave her a smile and, still holding her hand, led her to the front door and inside.

In the silence of the sleeping house, Carden gazed down at her, wanting to gather her into his arms, kiss her slowly, thoroughly, and tell her that they were done with thinking and talking, that they were going to pretend that the world beyond the walls of Haven House didn't exist and that they were safe.

But he couldn't. Only a fool closed his eyes when he sensed danger prowling in the shadows. "We're not done talking, Sera," he said quietly as he closed the door behind them.

"I know," she whispered, giving him one of her bravest, steadiest smiles of the evening. "We've yet to come to the heart of the matter."

"Would you care to sip on a brandy while we do?"

"I don't recall ever having had a brandy. Will I like it?"

Oh, if he were a truly predatory man . . . "It's quite a bit headier than sherry," he explained, leading her toward his study. "I'll pour you a small glass." And do battle with his conscience if she smiled at him and asked for more.

He was pouring and congratulating himself for self-restraint when she slipped his coat from her shoulders and laid it over the back of a chair. He paused, remembering the day she'd arrived here and how he'd vowed to put her in gowns befitting her beauty. Having so spectacularly achieved that goal, he couldn't help but recall the others he'd made regarding her. Having her willingly in his bed. And inside a week. The latter possibility was gone; life had swept away the days without his being consciously aware of their passage. But taking her to his bed . . . God, he wanted her more now than he had that first day, more than he'd ever imagined he could want any woman.

She looked over at him, smiled, and glided toward him, the lamplight soft on her burnished skin, lost in the lusciously sweet valley between her breasts. His loins tightened and he heeded the warning, marshaling enough of his wits to hand her a glass and admonish, "Slow, small sips or it will go straight to your head and make you regret it."

Following his instruction, she sampled. And then, as though testing his control, she languidly touched the tip of her tongue to her lower lip. "I like it better than sherry," she said, softly interrupting his fantasy. "It feels like liquid velvet."

Carden dragged air into his lungs and forced himself to think past the shimmering heat of desire. Sera wasn't willing to brave scandal for him. He'd given her a choice in the kitchen and she'd made it. She didn't want him with the same kind of hunger and desperation that he wanted her. He couldn't force her. Not and live with himself.

He expelled a long, hard breath and deliberately focused his thoughts on the complexity of the world that had sprung up around her in the last hour. After several long moments he said, "Sera, I don't how to say this gently."

"Bluntly will do," she replied, taking another sip of brandy.

He was going to hate himself in a few minutes. "I believe there's a distinct possibility that Gerald either abandoned or murdered my brother and his wife in the jungle and made his way to Walker's camp to rejoin the cause. I think he's probably still alive, Sera."

"And as ugly as those possibilities are, I think there's even more," she added evenly, stunning him with her calm. "If, as my father's agent, Gerald knew of the acceptance and publication of his work . . . and if it's indeed the financial success that everyone says that it is . . . the royalties would make for a very handsome contribution to Walker's cause, wouldn't they?"

"Or to Gerald Treadwell's own pockets," he suggested, beginning to pace. "You're supposed to be in Belize, awaiting his emergence from the jungle. As he left you, he was reasonably certain you'd never discover that you'd been cheated of your inheritance. He couldn't have anticipated that a man named Percival Reeves falling face first into his porridge would bring you to England less than a year later or that you'd attend a dinner party a fortnight after your arrival and learn of the duplicity."

Sera took another sip of the brandy and waited, not wanting to tell him what she had to.

"I know it all sounds terribly far-fetched, Seraphina, but . . ."

"No, it doesn't, actually," she countered. "I think I've seen Gerald."

He whirled on her so fast the brandy sloshed over the rim of his glass. "What?"

"In the park, the morning we rescued the puppies," she supplied, her heart thundering and her chest aching. "I saw him walking away at the back of the crowd that had gathered about us."

"Why, for the love of God, didn't you mention this then?"

He was upset by the news? He didn't even know Gerald! "What was I supposed to say, Carden?" she demanded. " 'Oh, by the by, there goes my dead husband'?"

His shoulders slumped. "Damnation, Sera," he said, rubbing his forehead and somehow looking both furious and dejected.

"I thought I was merely imagining things at the time," she offered in her defense. "But, now, given what I've learned this evening . . ."

"Do you think he saw you?"

He was grasping at straws and as much as she wished she could let him hold the hope, she couldn't. "How could he have *not* seen me, Carden? Seen all of us? We provided everyone in the park with a grand performance."

"I'm going to hire Barrett to find the bastard," he announced just before tossing the remaining contents of his glass down his throat.

Her heart tripped and her blood raced cold through her veins. She drank all of her brandy in the same fashion as he had and then went to refill her glass. "I would much prefer to leave Gerald Treadwell forever in the past," she said, pleased with the calm she heard in her voice as she turned back to face him. "Please, Carden, if you care anything at all for me, don't prod the snake."

He crossed to place his empty glass on the desk beside her. And stayed. Leaning his hip against the corner and crossing his arms as he always did, he said quietly, gently, "I don't have any right to ask and you certainly don't have to answer. But . . . why did you marry him, Sera?"

She knew the course their exchange would follow and resolved to be honest with him no matter how poor the light of truth made her look. There was nothing to be done but face the past squarely and hope he understood she'd done the best she could in the circumstances in which she'd found herself at the time. And perhaps, when she was done, he'd understand why she needed the past left in the past.

"My parents were dying and they knew it. Both were worried about what would happen to me after they passed away. Gerald was fairly well educated and charming and they saw in him a deliverance for me."

"You married him to please your parents?" he asked incredulously.

"To give them peace in their passing, yes." She sipped the brandy, fortifying her determination. "But I'd be lying to you, Carden, if I were to claim that I didn't have concerns of my own. I knew that when my parents died, I'd be stranded in Belize without a shilling to my name. Being the wife of Gerald Treadwell, while less than an ideal situation . . . It was never a romantic relationship, but, when sober, he was at least well-spoken and reasonably attractive. You have no idea what a rarity that is on the Mosquito Coast."

"If only you'd known about your father's book," he said ruefully. "They'd already accepted it. They were probably setting the type as you were saying 'I do.' "

"It's what you didn't know at the time that always makes the difference in looking back," Sera observed. "I might have chosen prostitution over marriage had I known beforehand of not only Gerald's association with Walker, but also of his excessive drinking and flagrant womanizing. Gerald becomes physically aggressive when intoxicated and I didn't like being struck any more than I liked having women encamped on my doorstep with one of his babes in their arms."

"God, Sera."

She didn't dare look at him. If she saw pity in his eyes, she wouldn't be able to get the rest of it said. She drank the brandy in two heavy swallows. "There isn't a great deal of formal social structure or expectation in Belize, but all of it was, nevertheless, sufficiently humiliating. It didn't take me long to fully regret having tied my life to his. But even quickly was too late. Arthur and Mary, once they realized how we had all been fooled by him, tried to intervene as much as they possibly could. I can't tell you the number of times they literally hid me from him."

"Why didn't Arthur buy you passage out of Belize?" Carden asked, angry that she had been allowed to remain in a situation where hiding her had even been necessary.

"He offered to. As I've said, your brother was a kind man." She shrugged her beautiful shoulders. "But where would I have gone and what would I have done for a living?"

"Anywhere you wanted to go, and you're a very talented artist."

Her smile was bittersweet. "I wasn't as brave in those days as I am now. When Arthur and Mary didn't return, I had no choice but to stand on my own two feet and make a way for myself and the girls. If I could go back and do it all again, knowing what I've learned about myself in the last year . . ." Her eyes shimmered with tears and she turned away, lifting her chin and saying, "Things would have turned out very differently, Carden. For all of us. I just learned too late, especially for Arthur and Mary."

He rose squarely to his feet, took her face gently between his hands, and brought her gaze to meet his. Her eyes were dark and sad and his heart ached for her. "What happened to them isn't your fault, Sera. Arthur knew what kind of man was leading him off into the jungle. He made the choice to follow, no one else. And I promise you, even if it takes the rest of my life, Gerald Treadwell will be found and held accountable for his actions."

She instantly tensed and the sadness in her eyes was replaced by the unmistakable light of fear. "Please don't go looking for him," she pleaded, her voice quavering. "I don't want him back in my life."

"I don't have a choice in the matter, angel," Carden said gently but firmly. "He saw you in the park. He knows you're here, knows you'll discover the truth sooner or later. Whatever house of lies he's constructed will collapse the moment you walk into the publisher's offices. He knows that, too. He can't afford to ignore you. If I don't find him, he'll find you."

He could feel the coldness that came over her, the sudden lurch of her heart.

"And assert that he's my husband and that he has every lawful right to control me and my father's estate in my best interest."

"No, Sera," he said slowly and carefully. "He can be denied that right if it's proven that he's misappropriated and misused the money in the past. The fact that you haven't received a single tuppence of the royalties is proof enough for that. And it will also be sufficient grounds for you to petition for and be granted a divorce."

Divorce? Was it possible? The scandal of it be damned. Could she actually escape the net that had ensnared her so long ago? Was Carden telling her the truth? Or was he giving her hope where none truly existed? Oh, dear God, how she wanted to believe him.

"Trust me, Sera," he whispered, smiling at her, tracing the curve of her cheeks with his thumbs. "I'll see you through this."

He would. She knew it to the center of her soul. Everything would be all right. Warmth flooded through her, and as the horrible tension was washed away, her knees weakened and the world around her began to slowly spin. "I feel . . . dizzy."

His hands went to her shoulders, steadying her as he chuckled and teased, "I have that effect on some women."

"I think it's the brandy," she countered, closing her eyes and pressing her forehead into his chest. "You warned me about drinking it too fast."

The world moved again, not around as before, but upward in a smooth, easy arc. Carden . . . She smiled and twined her arms around his neck, burrowed her cheek into his shoulder and let him carry her up the stairs. What she'd ever done to deserve such a wonderfully caring man, she didn't know, but she was glad that the path of her life had met his. She tried to tell him so, but the words tangled on the tip of her tongue and were lost. As they drifted away, a soft cloud of warmth stole over her senses and she surrendered with a contented sigh to the whisper of a kiss and the promise of sweet, dreamy sleep.

"Someday, angel, I hope you'll let me carry you all the way to the bed at the end of the hall."

Yes, she hoped so, too.

CHAPTER 14

Her head didn't really hurt. She was just very much aware of the dull knot in the center of her forehead. And that her entire body had felt a hundred pounds heavier than normal since the moment she'd awakened that morning. Carden had laughed at breakfast and told her that she shouldn't plan to make a habit of drinking brandy. She wasn't quite so sure. There was one most decidedly positive aftereffect: it took considerable concentration to move her limbs with anything approximating grace. Talking took even more focus. And as a consequence, she was too busy thinking to be the least bit nervous as they walked into the offices of Somers and Priest.

The publisher's secretary looked up from his work as they came to a halt in front of his desk.

"We would like to see Mr. Somers, please," Carden said, his hand slipping reassuringly to the small of her back.

A thin, dark brow slowly rose above the rim of the man's glasses. "Do you have an appointment, sir?" he asked haughtily.

Sera knew it wasn't to go well even before Carden very coolly replied, "We do not."

The man sneered—sneered!—and went back to his

work, saying dismissively, "I'm afraid that Mr. Somers has a full day on schedule."

Three long seconds passed before Carden calmly countered, "I'm sure he'll be willing to take a few moments of his time for us. Please tell him that Lord Lansdown and Miss Seraphina Baines Miller wish to see him."

The man's head came up so abruptly that Sera held her breath, certain that it was going to snap off his neck and tumble to the floor. His eyes widening, he sputtered, "B-B-Baines Miller?"

Having already had one experience with such a reaction to her name, Sera was able to smile and say serenely, "I am the daughter of Geoffrey Baines Miller."

"She's also," Carden contributed, amusement evident in his voice, "the artist whose work illustrates the text you have published under her father's name."

The secretary came out of his chair as though he'd been shot. His hands flew about and he fairly vibrated in place as he gushed, "Please, please have a seat, Miss Baines Miller, Lord Lansdown. I'll inform Mr. Somers that you are here." And then he just stood there, gaping at her.

"Today would be nice," Carden quipped.

The man jumped and whirled while in the air. Unfortunately, his feet didn't come down quite squarely under him and he stumbled into the glass-windowed door some ten feet behind his desk.

As she and Carden watched him knock—quite unnecessarily—and fumble with the knob, Sera quietly observed, "That's the very first time I've heard you introduce yourself as a peer."

"I thought it would be useful in opening the door for us." He chuckled as the secretary all but fell into his employer's office. "I was woefully mistaken."

"I simply can't get over how awed people are at the mention of my father's name. It's such an unexpected thing."

"Sera," he countered, his voice sober, his words quick and firm, "your father's work appeals to horticulturists. Your work, on the other hand, appeals to everyone. It is you of whom people are in awe, not your father. It is you who are responsible for the book's excellent sales. Bear that in mind as you speak with Mr. Somers. He'll most certainly be aware of it."

A man came out of the office, his coattails sailing behind him. He cast Sera a quick look and then hurried away. The secretary came out next, instantly stepped to the side and flattened himself against the oak filing cabinet.

Not a half second after that a portly gentleman with a wreath of pure white hair stepped through the doorway and bore down on her, his smile broad and his hands extended. "Miss Baines Miller!"

With her portfolio in her left hand, she was able to offer only her right.

"It is a rare, rare honor! Please come into my office," he said, both hands wrapped around hers and drawing her forward even as he issued the invitation. His gaze darted past her for a split second. "Lord Lansdown."

"Somers," Carden replied coolly, following in their wake.

"Please," Somers said, motioning to a pair of upholstered chairs opposite his desk. He waited until she had set down her portfolio and was seated before taking his own and continuing. "What may I do for you, Miss Baines Miller? Name it and it shall be done."

Sera smiled, feeling more in control of the situation than she had any in her life. "Let me begin at the beginning. A fortnight ago I arrived in London as the escort of Lord Lansdown's three orphaned nieces. It was at a dinner party in the home of Mr. and Mrs. Cecil Stanbridge last evening that I discovered that you are the publisher of my father's botanical work."

His chin lowered and he swallowed before saying ever so distinctly, "Discovered?"

She nodded. "I wasn't aware until yesterday evening that my father's work had been accepted for publication. In the Stanbridges' copy, I noted that it has undergone at least ten printings since its original date of publication."

He swallowed again. Harder this time. "How is that you were unaware of the book or its success?"

"I've come here today to ask that very question," she replied calmly, very glad for having had brandy the night before. "How is it that I have not been informed of this matter?"

"And if I may insert myself at this point to ask a far more pertinent question," Carden said. "How is that Miss Baines Miller has never received so much as a single shilling in royalties?"

Somers threw him a most unpleasant look and then turned a paternal smile on her. "Perhaps your father has decided for some reason to withhold from you the information of his success?"

It was a reasonable suggestion—had her father been any sort of a secretive man. And then, of course, there were the other facts. "My father and my mother died just over two years ago," she explained. "In the same month in which you published his work. I've been told—by those who know how publishing is done—that your acceptance of that work most certainly came some months prior to putting type and ink to paper. And I can assure you, Mr. Somers, that my father knew nothing of it at the time of his passing."

He blinked several times and drew a long, slow breath before saying, "This is a most awkward situation."

"Isn't it, though?" Carden contributed dryly, settling deeper into his chair and crossing his legs.

Somers shot him another dark look. A shadow of it lingered in his eyes when he met her gaze, smiled thinly, and said, "I find myself having to ask a question with the most unpleasant implications."

"Oh?" Carden drawled, clearly irritated.

"Ask whatever you'd like, Mr. Somers," Sera hastily offered, anxious to forestall open acrimony. "I'll gladly provide you answers to the best of my ability if it will help you do the same for me."

"Very well, miss," Somers agreed, sitting back in his chair. "How am I to know you are indeed the daughter of Geoffrey Baines Miller and the artist of the work included in his volume? How do I know that you are not some impostor attempting to defraud the author?"

Carden bolted forward in his seat. Sera reached over and laid a hand on his arm to stay him while replying, "I assume that you still have the original manuscript and paintings in your possession?"

"Of course. They're kept in the vault."

"Have you happened to have studied the paintings yourself?"

"I have."

"Then you're aware of the notations on the backs of each?"

He nodded slowly and she saw that he understood where she had been leading him. "I am."

"If you'd like to retrieve the manuscript from the safety of the vault, I'll allow you to test my recall of those notes. Many of them are more personal than scientific in content."

"Retrieving the manuscript itself won't be necessary," he declared, pushing himself up and moving quickly toward the rear wall of his office.

Sera watched him over her shoulder and grinned when she saw his destination. As he took the picture off the wall and started back to his desk with it, she met Carden's gaze and winked. He cocked his brow and settled back into his chair, obviously not altogether confident but apparently willing to let her have a go at it.

"This one is my favorite," Somers said, setting the edge of the frame on his desk so that she could see the picture. Standing behind it, he added, "I chose to keep it in my office so I could see it every day. Do you recall what you wrote on the back of this one, miss?"

"I noted that my father believed it to be an undiscovered species and that he wanted to name it in honor of me. I also noted that while I appreciated his attempt to have my name recorded in the scientific annals for all time, I preferred that he choose a plant that didn't smell like dreadfully dead fish."

He didn't even bother to look at the back of the picture. He simply smiled and set it on the floor beside his desk, saying, "I am satisfied, Miss Baines Miller. No impostor could have known that."

Carden looked over at her. "Does it really smell like dead fish?"

She laughed. "I know it's hard to believe that something so beautiful can make a good acre of jungle impossible to endure, but I honestly thought I might retch before I completed that particular painting."

"As she also noted on the back," Somers added, his smile fading.

Carden's did as well. "Since she's ably passed your examination, Somers, we return to the lady's question of why she learned of the publication at a dinner party only last evening and to mine regarding the whereabouts of what must be the considerable royalties due her as the heir."

Somers swallowed twice and visibly gathered himself. "My sincerest condolences on the loss of your parents, Miss Baines Miller," he offered smoothly. "Your father was a rare intellectual gift to the world and I will be eternally grateful for having had the honor of being his publisher. We are most fortunate that you remain to gift us with your artwork."

It was prelude, she knew; sincere in its message but also intended to buy the publisher time to think and plan. "Thank you, Mr. Somers," Sera said graciously, waiting for the real response to begin.

"How very tragic that your father never knew of his success. But I find it most strange to think that Mr. Carter failed to pass such important information on to him or to you."

"Mr. Carter?" she repeated, caught completely off guard.

"Yes. Mr. Reginald Carter. Are you not familiar with the name? At the time of acceptance, Mr. Carter was residing in Belize."

"I don't know a Reginald Carter," Sera rejoined, her wits snapping back to center. "I've never heard of or from him. And Belize is not so populated that he would have been lost in a crowd of humanity. Had he indeed been there, I would have been aware of it."

"Oh, dear," Somers said softly, as though to himself. "This would appear to be a most tangled and sticky web in which we find ourselves."

Blessedly, there wasn't the slightest hint of confrontation in Carden's manner or voice when he asked, "Have you been regularly sending the royalties in care of this Reginald Carter?"

Somers considered him for a long moment and then relaxed. "On three occasions, yes. Once, general delivery in Belize City. Then twice more to an account he established here in London to make the transaction more secure. Distances and the mail being what they are, you understand. This past autumn, Mr. Carter presented himself to me personally and with credentials that satisfied me as to his identity. He has personally accepted the bank drafts ever since."

Sera could almost hear the mental wheels clicking in Carden's head when he asked, "And he provided you with documentation that led you to believe that he is a legitimate literary and financial representative of Geoffrey Baines Miller and his heirs?"

"Of course. I wouldn't have consigned the monies to him if he hadn't." Somers looked at her. "I can produce it if you'd like, Miss Baines Miller. As is customary, it was placed in our legal files."

God help her. What if her father had actually signed such a thing? "I would very much like to see it, Mr. Somers," she managed to say with entirely feigned aplomb.

He rose from his desk again and bowed slightly. "If you'll pardon me for a brief moment."

She lowered her chin in silent assent and then watched him hurry out of the office. The instant he was out of earshot she turned to Carden. "It's Gerald, isn't it? Reginald Carter is really Gerald."

"Oh, I'd wager the house on it," he laughingly replied, his eyes sparkling, his manner easier than it had been all morning.

"Why are you so delighted by this?"

"I'll tell you later. Let's get through this first." Sobering only slightly, he said, "If the document seems legitimate, let me take it from there. But if you recognize it for a forgery, say so. But don't mention that you know who Reginald Carter really is. If Somers goes to Gerald asking questions, we're better off if Somers knows nothing of any value. That way he can't inadvertently confide a detail that might tip our hand."

"Agreed. Do you have a plan?"

He grinned. "No, but I will before the day's out."

She was about to point out that she didn't find much comfort in that when Somers returned, a piece of parchment in hand. He passed it to her on his way to his chair. She looked first at the signature and then, her heart in her throat, at the date. It took a long, torturous second, but realization, when it came, brought instant, merciful relief.

"Mr. Somers," she said, handing the paper back to him as he settled into his chair. "I'm afraid that I must tell you that this is not my father's signature. It's a forgery. A very good one, but a forgery nonetheless."

The color drained from his face and there was a decidedly tight sound to his voice as he stared at the paper and replied, "I'll have to have proof of your assertion before I can seek any sort of legal action."

She paused for a moment, wondering how she could do that. Realization came much more quickly this time. "I hadn't intended to use my father's last bit of work to this end," she said, turning to reach into her portfolio. She extracted the thin stack of paper and shuffled through the notes and pictures, adding, "And it's certainly not why I brought it with me today, but . . ." Finding the ones she wanted, she handed the entire stack across the desk.

She gave him a moment to study them before beginning. "Please note the day on which the agenting document was allegedly signed."

His gaze slid over to it. "Yes."

"In your hand, on top, are my father's field notes made the same week. As you're no doubt aware, he was meticulous about noting the dates and times of his observations."

She hadn't thought it possible, but even more color drained from the man's face. He shuffled through the papers. "He was failing badly, wasn't he?"

"Yes. I brought the specimens to his bedside so that he could work. It made him feel as though there was still purpose to his life when the days and hours were growing dim."

Holding the notes in one hand, Somers picked up the parchment and looked back and forth between them. A bit of bright pink color was rising above his starched collar when he said, "Your father couldn't have signed his name to this document on this day."

"No, he couldn't," she agreed, releasing a breath she hadn't known she was holding. "What you have on the agent document is a fairly good version of what his signature was like in far better, more hopeful days."

He laid all the papers down and laced his fingers on top of them. Pursing his lips, he considered her for a long moment. Finally, he sighed and said, "Miss Baines Miller, you appear to have been defrauded."

"A conclusion that was reached at last night's dinner party," Carden commented quietly. "Which brings us to the true crux of the matter. What's to be done about it?"

Sera couldn't tell whether he'd been thinking of this eventuality all along or if it was simply a matter of the publisher being in his natural element. In either case, he didn't hesitate to respond, "All current royalties owed to the estate will be delivered to you on the next date due. Mr. Reginald Carter will no longer be recognized as the agent of record."

Carden was every bit as quick. "And what about all the money he's stolen to this particular date?"

The red creeping higher on his neck, Somers drew himself up and squared his shoulders. "I will personally see that criminal charges are filed against him. We will use all available legal resources to bring him to justice and see that any remaining monies are turned over to Miss Baines Miller without delay."

"And if Mr. Carter hasn't left anything to be turned over to her?"

Sera watched as Somers swallowed yet again and what color had been on its way to his face receded. "Then . . . I . . ."

Carden didn't give him a chance to stumble or stammer any further. "To my thinking you bear some responsibility for Seraphina having been defrauded by this Reginald Carter person," he said kindly but with great firmness. "It was you who accepted his credentials and you who delivered—personally—her money to him. Many a time, apparently. She shouldn't have to bear the financial loss for your failure to exercise due diligence."

Sera had no idea what "due diligence" was but the words seemed to have considerable impact on Mr. Somers. He rallied and found a tight smile. "I'm sure our respective barristers can come to some sort of mutually acceptable agreement on the matter. We have an established, professional association with Miss Baines Miller that we wish to continue to nurture and grow. I certainly wouldn't want the Carter issue to come between us."

Carden nodded, apparently satisfied with the offer of dueling barristers. She was less concerned with that aspect of Somers's reply than with another. "*Continue*, Mr. Somers?"

"My dear woman," he said, beaming as he picked up the papers she'd handed him moments ago. "You have just handed me a folio of botanical artwork that clearly stands as some of the best you've ever produced. I would be very honored if you would allow me a few days to prepare a bid for its publishing acquisition."

He wanted her work? On its own merits? Once again she feigned a degree of calm she didn't feel. "That would be fine, Mr. Somers."

"Of course, I'd have to ask that you grant me exclusive rights to the property until such time as I can render the bid. If we cannot come to terms, then I would—most sadly and regretfully, of course—relinquish that right to another house."

She nodded, knowing that she'd accept whatever he offered. To have her own money . . . It wouldn't be much, though. He had only a few pieces of her work. "Are you interested in only those paintings you have in hand?" she asked, trying not to sound too hopeful, "Or would you also care to see the ones I made following my father's death and for which there are no accompanying botanical notes?"

His eyes widened and it took him a moment to snap his lower jaw into place. "There are more?"

"Perhaps as many as a hundred and fifty. Perhaps more," she explained, knowing that he was no doubt going to consider her the greediest woman who had ever walked into his office. "It was my habit to paint every day and I found comfort in it when I needed it most. I've never really stopped to count them."

"A hundred and fifty," he whispered, his gaze focused off in the distance. "Three volumes. Maybe four." He brought his attention back to her abruptly. "How soon may I see them?"

He didn't seem to be the least put off by her blatant effort to make all the money she could. In fact, he looked quite happy about it all. Taking heart in that, she replied, "I have yet to unpack them and they do need to be arranged into some semblance of presentation order. Would the end of the week be soon enough?"

"It would be perfectly fine, Miss Baines Miller. Take all the time you need."

"And while she prepares her work for your consideration," Carden interjected, rising from his chair, "you'll see to the complaint against Reginald Carter?"

Somers also rose. "Consider it done."

And with that Sera knew the ordeal was also done. Taking Carden's hand, Sera allowed him to assist her to her feet. She picked up her portfolio and smiled at the man on the other side of the desk. "Thank you for your time and assistance this morning, Mr. Somers. I look forward to our next conversation."

"As do I. It has been my pleasure to be of service." He bowed slightly. "Good day, Miss Baines Miller."

"And to you, sir."

"Lord Lansdown," he added crisply, with no bow at all.

Carden smiled and presented her with his arm while drawling, "Somers."

And then it was well and truly over. She floated out of the office at Carden's side, knowing that her happiness had absolutely nothing whatsoever to do with brandy.

Carden grinned. He took back every disparaging remark he'd ever made about God, the saints, and anything even remotely associated with the divine. You had to when you were able to walk off the field with both a clear victory and the woman on your arm. Life was good. And it was going to get better yet.

"Stay to the left of the stairs," he instructed, chuckling as he led Sera out the front door and down toward the walkway and their waiting carriage. "Somers will be bolting forth at any moment."

"To go in search of Reginald Carter?"

"Ha!" He opened the door and paused before handing her in. "He'll send a neckless minion to squeeze what's left out of Gerald. No, Somers will be at his club within the hour to brag that Seraphina Baines Miller has arrived in town with the art folio of the century and that he holds exclusive bidding rights to it."

"I'm flattered that everyone thinks so highly of my work, but they're just pictures."

"Pictures that every publisher in town will want," he countered, finding her humility refreshing. "By sundown tomorrow the word will have rippled forth and you'll have at least two confidentially submitted offers by the end of the week."

"But they won't know anything of the quality of the work or of how many pictures the collection contains. They'd be bidding blindly."

"The quality is certain and the number doesn't matter," he assured her. "What does matter is that they take the publishing glory—and the profit—away from Somers. They'll simply offer to double or triple his best bid. Whatever it is."

She frowned for a moment and looked up at the building they'd just left. "Carden? In general terms . . . Just roughly estimating . . ."

He grinned, knowing that what she expected to be offered was only a fraction of what would eventually come her way. "At *least* five thousand pounds."

"Honestly?"

Such an innocent about some things, so wise beyond her years in others. Carden nodded. "Heaven only knows how many thousands Gerald's stolen over the last few years. Whether you ever see so much as a farthing of that, you're still a wealthy woman, Seraphina Baines Miller."

She sighed and considered him with pursed lips. "Gerald isn't going to shrug his shoulders, walk off, and let me strip him of his gold mine. He'll go to drastic measures to protect it."

"The game is over," he countered, offering her his hand. Helping her into the carriage, he added, "Somers knows that he's not a legitimate agent, Sera. Gerald's financial river has already dried up and, try as he might, there's nothing he can do to make it flow again."

"You don't know Gerald. I do," she protested from her seat. "Obviously he's willing to engage in forgery to achieve his goals. What's to prevent him from forging documents to support a claim of being my husband? If he—"

"Sera, stop," he commanded from the walk. "You're torturing yourself. Not ten minutes ago you proved him to be liar, a thief, and a forger. Which, by the by, my dear, you accomplished in a single masterful stroke. I stand in awe of the smoothness of your execution."

"Thank you."

"Gerald Treadwell. Reginald Carter. It doesn't make any difference what name he chooses to use," Carden went on, pulling up the curtain at the window. "He has no credibility. No one would believe anything the man said or accept as legitimate any document he produced. His game is up. You have nothing to be concerned about beyond where you're going to invest your great wealth."

"What if he steps forward claiming to be my husband just to live with me, to have me support him?"

He closed the door and leaned his forearms on the window edge. "Angel, if you say you've never seen the man before, who's going to take his word over yours?"

"I'd be lying. That wouldn't be at all honorable, Carden."

God, Sera was just too good to be true. "We're done discussing this."

She considered him and the closed door. "Aren't you coming home?"

"I'll leave you to your sorting and arranging," he replied. "Let the girls assist you. Have them help you think of ways to enjoy all that you've earned, Sera. I'll be back in time for dinner. You are not to give Gerald so much as a passing thought while I'm gone. Is that clear?"

"Spoken like an earl."

"Oh?" he countered, chuckling. "And just how many earls have you heard speak?"

"Several. In Jamaica. They tend to pontificate wherever they go."

He laughed outright and eased away from the door. "Enjoy yourself today, Sera. It's a new beginning for your life."

"Where are you going, Carden?"

"To my club. It's just around the corner."

"To tell John Aiden of the famous artist living in your house?"

He signaled his driver. "Something like that," he called as the coach began to ease its way into traffic.

He stood there, smiling and watching until the carriage was swallowed up in the sea of other vehicles. Then he turned on his heel, let his smile disappear, and set out for his club knowing that if anyone would understand the necessity of retribution, it was Barrett Stanbridge.

CHAPTER 15

Barrett was with Aiden at the back of the club playing a game of chess and drinking. Carden glanced at the grandfather clock on his way through the maze of tables, thinking it was too early in the day for imbibing, and furrowed his brow. Half past noon? He detoured to the bar and ordered himself a double scotch.

Aiden looked up and grinned as he approached. "Carden! This is a surprise. We thought you'd given us up. What brings you to the club today?"

Barrett settled back in his chair and stretched his legs out under the table, saying, "He went with Seraphina to the publishing house this morning and discovered, just as we suspected last night, that something is rotten in London."

Carden nodded, pulled up a chair, and sat. "I need your professional help." He couldn't resist taking a good-natured jab at his friend. "Assuming, of course, that you're free to take on an assignment."

"I think I can fit you in," Barrett countered, chuckling. "Tell me what you learned at the publisher's."

Carden drank a bit of scotch and considered the various ways of approaching the explanation. Not everything he'd learned recently had been in Somers's office. It didn't really matter where he'd found what kernel of information, though. What mattered was that he laid out what he knew in a fashion that formed the clearest picture. He looked between his two friends and decided that he might as well get the most central piece of the puzzle on the table straightaway.

"First off," he said, unable to think of a way to gild the essential truth. "Sera isn't a widow."

Aiden swore beneath his breath. Barrett took a sip of his whisky, then drawled, "Well, that slightly complicates your interest in her, doesn't it?"

He bristled, resenting the suggestion that he was too shallow to understand that Sera was different from all the other women any of them had ever known. Sera wasn't just a conquest. And she wasn't going to be the subject of any men's club casual conversation, either. "My relationship with Sera is none of your concern. And it has absolutely nothing to do with why I'm here and what we're talking about."

"No offense intended, Card," his friend offered in the way of apology. "I simply wanted to see the way the wind was blowing these days. I thought perhaps you might be developing some genuine feelings for Seraphina."

"I haven't given it any thought," he countered curtly, drawing the line again. "Quite frankly, I don't have the time or inclination to do so at present. Sera's husband is here in London and he's been masquerading as her father's literary agent for the past three years."

"And," Barrett supplied, "she hadn't heard of the publishing of the book or received any royalties because he's been stealing her blind from the very beginning."

"A true prince among men," Aiden observed. "Do you have any idea of where the son of a bitch is?"

Satisfied that they'd moved away from the consideration of Sera's worth, Carden relaxed into his chair and took a sip of his scotch. "No. But he's using the name Reginald Carter."

Barrett nodded. "What does he look like?"

"Seraphina described him as being reasonably handsome and charming when he chooses to be."

"That's half the men in London," Aiden groused.

"How tall is he?" Barrett inquired. "What color are his eyes? His hair? Does he have any scars or peculiar habits?"

Carden shrugged. "He's a mean drunk, a womanizer, and a sloppy forger."

"There's the other half of London," Aiden said with a sigh. "This isn't going well, you know."

Carden ignored him. "And he's an American. According to Seraphina, prior to arriving in Belize, he was a financier for a military adventurer, a fellow American named William Walker."

"Walker?" Aiden repeated, his whisky glass frozen halfway to his mouth. "The man's a lunatic. Persistent, determined, and dedicated to his grand and glorious dream. And a *lunatic*."

Barrett shook his head. "Can't say that I've ever heard of him."

Aiden quickly explained, "He puts together private armies and invades small countries along the Mosquito Coast in hopes of expanding the number of American slave states."

"I gather," Barrett said, "he hasn't had any success to date."

"None, despite two attempts."

"He's apparently planning a third," Carden supplied. Aiden rolled his eyes. Barrett cocked a brow. "Sera says that one of his former associates came to Belize City and asked him to go back into the financing business on Walker's behalf and he accepted. That was just before he led Arthur and Mary off into the jungle."

"Never to be seen again," Aiden finished darkly.

Barrett stared at the far wall and chewed the inside of his cheek before saying, "The timing of it all is certainly interesting."

"Well, I'm relieved to hear that I'm not the only one whose suspicions were triggered."

Aiden swirled the whisky in his glass. "So do you think Sera's money is being used to finance another Walker invasion?"

"I think it's a distinct possibility," Carden conceded. "As is his keeping the money for himself. I'd be willing to wager on either. Scruples and loyalty don't seem to be his long suits."

Barrett continued to stare at the wall. "He's not going to be all that difficult to find. I'll be able to shorten the time even more once Seraphina provides me with a more detailed physical description of him."

"She's to know nothing of this," Carden instructed. "You're not to speak with her about it, Barrett. Not even in the vaguest of ways."

Barrett's gaze slid to his. "This requires an explanation, you know."

"She's afraid of him. At the slightest provocation, she obsesses over what he might do to her in order to keep his control of the money."

Aiden snorted. "Well, I'd say she has just cause for concern, Carden. Greed can make men desperate. And there's nothing quite like carts of money to make them greedy. Don't you think Sera might be comforted to know that we intend to find the man and . . . and . . ."

"A bit slow," Barrett drawled, shaking his head, "but he eventually catches up." His eyes darkened and the corners of his mouth deepened. "What *do* you intend to do when we find him?"

In the blackest recesses of his heart, he wanted the man dead. The civilized part of his brain wanted him hauled into the dock and off to prison, publicly branded the scoundrel, thief, and murderer he was. But a larger and more demanding part of him wanted Sera happy and free as easily and quickly as possible. "I'm hoping to convince the lying bastard that his best interests lie in developing a sudden but very permanent case of amnesia."

Barrett studied him for a long moment. "And if he refuses to be so pleasantly accommodating?"

Then he'd have to choose between the dock and murder. "I'll cross that bridge when I come to it. And I'll cross it alone."

Barrett's gaze slid away again. "We'll discuss it further should we find ourselves there. Another question, if I may?"

That Barrett was seeking permission didn't bode well. The hairs on the back of his neck prickling, Carden asked, "Strictly professional?"

"Highly personal, actually." He didn't give him time to refuse. "It concerns the issue Honoria raised the first night Sera was here. Everyone left my parents' dinner party last night gleeful at the prospect of being the one to tell others that the renowned artist Seraphina Baines Miller is in London."

Aiden nodded. "I'd heard about it before I got to the club this morning and Barrett could fill me in on the details. My housekeeper told me before breakfast."

Barrett let that sink in for just a moment before he continued, saying, "You know perfectly well what's going to happen, Carden. Just as it happened to you, before sundown tonight she'll have invitations to every significant social affair of the season."

"Which," Carden snapped, not liking the conversational turn, "solves my problem of finding a suitable companion and hers of acquiring an escort."

"I'll concede that positive consequence," Barrett said, lifting his glass and studying the color of his whisky. "But it has some decidedly negative ones, as well. What was only a quiet problem when Seraphina was an unknown, unattached woman living under your roof will now become a huge public one. You know how people are, Carden. They'll assume the worst and the speculation will be vicious. Sera's reputation is going to be seriously damaged if you don't move to protect it. Don't you think it would be wise to move her and the girls into Honoria's townhouse as soon as possible?"

Wisdom had nothing to do with it. He wanted Sera in his house where he could be with her without having to abide by socially established calling hours, where he didn't have to stand in a queue and beg for a few minutes of her time. Yes, it was selfish and no, he didn't care.

"I'll think on it," he offered flatly, knowing he'd done all the thinking he was going to do on the matter. Sera was a delight and she was his and he wasn't giving her up.

"You'll think on it?" Barrett growled. "What's there to think about? Why would you want her scandalized?"

The speculation about the governess living under his roof would be forgotten in the scandal of a court trial and a divorce. Sera was damned if she did, damned if she didn't. It was only a matter of degrees. If she was with him, then he could at least hold her and help her endure it. He looked between his friends and something deep inside him cringed at the thought of being that honest with them.

"We're collaborating on a conservatory plan," he offered, scrambling to think of anything that he could use to justify his decision. "Being in different residences would make it much more difficult to do. And then there are the puppies, too. Honoria's nose becomes a spigot whenever she's anywhere near dogs or cats. And her eyes swell up to give her a decidedly unattractive piggish look. She's never been able to tolerate animals in the house.

The puppies couldn't go with the girls and they wouldn't leave without them."

"Not that I mean to be unfeeling and inhumane," Aiden said, "but I think Seraphina's reputation should come before the care and feeding of rescued puppies."

It did. Feeling a trap closing around him and desperately wanting out of it, he offered another flat pronouncement in the hope it would end the discussion. "I'll present the options and leave the decision up to Sera."

"With all due respect," Barrett countered sharply, "Seraphina isn't at all capable of making an informed judgment on the matter. Yes, she has social graces. Yes, she's obviously been raised to be a gentlewoman. But she knows absolutely nothing about the expectations of the rarefied social world into which her celebrity is about to thrust her.

"She honestly thinks that everyone—with the possible exception of her husband—is as good, open-hearted, kind, and generous as she is. They'll go after her for sport and she'll be devastated by the cruelty of it. No, you have to make the decision for her and there's only one you can reasonably make."

Carden threw the rest of his scotch down his throat and rose to his feet, saying, "I'll explain it all so that she understands it clearly."

Barrett snorted. "All the while assuring her that you'll protect her from the groundless accusations."

They weren't entirely groundless. Not if hope counted for anything. If Sera came to him and asked to share his bed, he'd take her there and not think twice about it. And it would be a hell of a long time before he even considered letting her out of it, too. The world beyond them be damned.

"You can't, you know," Aiden insisted. "The more you defend her, the more guilty she'll appear. I really do think Barrett's right. She has to go to Honoria's. As much as

I'm loath to admit it, in this situation appearance is everything."

"Think of it as a personal challenge," Barrett added, his tone suddenly light and easy. "Seducing her while she's under your roof is really just too much like fishing in a barrel."

It took conscious effort to keep his fists at his sides. Through clenched teeth, he warned, "You're about to cross the line, Barrett."

"I'm aware of that," his friend retorted, meeting his gaze squarely and in open challenge. "And the choice to walk up to it is deliberate. You too could stand to make some deliberate choices of your own. Some selfless ones would be nice for a change. You don't have to make a lifelong habit of it if it chafes, but you really ought to give it a try just once. Just for Sera's sake."

Barrett was his friend. They'd been through many a rough patch together. They owed each other their lives several times over. They could get through this contest and still be friends, but only if he resisted the urge to knock Barrett's teeth out. Carden took a step back. "If you have any real concern for Sera, you'll find her husband."

Something akin to disdain flickered in Barrett's eyes. It was there in his voice as he said, "Falling in love isn't the worst thing that can happen to a man, Carden. Throwing it away is."

"I am *not* falling in love," he declared, turning to leave.

"Give Seraphina our best," Barrett taunted in parting.

"Tell her," Aiden hastily added, "that I'm claiming the second dance with her at Lady Hatcher's ball."

Carden stopped in his tracks, his mind racing through the implications. He turned back. "The second?"

Barrett lifted his glass in salute and smiled. "I have the first."

It took every measure of his will and pride—every

memory of what he owed Barrett Stanbridge—to keep his fists at his sides, then turn and walk away.

Sera stepped back from the line of easels and squinted at the pictures she'd arranged along the trays. Too many reds, she decided. By the time her eye traveled the length of the row the individual features of each flower were becoming blurred, lost in the color similarities. Perhaps adding some yellows and oranges would break up the pattern sufficiently. Blues and violets would be even more dramatic, more effective. There were several particularly striking ones that would do nicely.

She eyed the oilskin pouches still stacked in the wooden crate she'd put at the end of the chaise and wished that she'd thought to record the contents of each as she'd stuffed them full. But then, there hadn't been time, she reminded herself; the ship wouldn't have waited for her to be so organized. She'd been fortunate enough to find the bags in the corner of the storage room, even luckier that they'd accommodated her entire collection. She was just going to have to go through each one of the pouches to find the pictures she wanted and be glad that the oilskin had perfectly protected them.

The glass walls of the greenhouse shook and Sera instinctively looked up, afraid that the roof was going to shatter and rain down on her.

"Where are the girls?"

Carden. The harshness of his tone brought her around to face him, her heart hammering. He was angry; angrier than she'd ever seen him, angrier than she'd known he could be. Was Gerald there to take her away? "They take a nap every day at this time," she supplied breathlessly, trying to summon some courage and calm. "What's wrong, Carden?"

He advanced on her, his eyes blazing. "Have you been asked to Lady Hatcher's ball?"

Puzzlement replaced fear. Was this truly why he was angry? "Yes," she answered honestly, her brows knitted. "Barrett asked me to attend with him."

"And you said you would go?" he demanded, pacing around her.

She turned with him, watching him warily. "I didn't want to hurt his feelings by declining. You said that he would invite me out and that you would be gracious if I accepted."

He came to a sudden halt, took a step toward her, and fairly growled, "I said I would *try* to be gracious."

"Clearly you're having difficulties with that," she observed softly, taking a half-step back.

"Yes, I am," he admitted hotly, closing the distance she'd tried to put between them. "I've discovered that I'm not particularly good at sharing. I don't want to share you with anyone." He swung his arm outward, toward the world beyond the greenhouse walls, as he added, "Especially my friends. They're rakes!"

"So are you," Sera countered, her puzzlement swept away by astonishment.

"But I'm an honorable rake."

"There's no such thing," she declared, her hands going to her hips as astonishment evaporated in the heat of indignation. Did he really think she was that gullible? That stupid? "A rake is a rake. You use women and then toss them aside."

"I've never tossed anyone aside," he said, looking terribly shocked and affronted that she'd cast such an aspersion his way. "That would be callous and cruel."

"Well, then let me rephrase it," she retorted, undaunted, indignation building toward true outrage with every beat of her heart. "You use women and then gently set them aside. You seduce one, thank her kindly for her favors, and then blithely go in search of another. You are a rake, Carden Reeves. That part of who you are isn't contrived for the benefit of wagging social tongues. You truly enjoy the hunt, the conquest."

He took another step closer and leaned down so they were eye to eye. "Every man does," he asserted, his voice quiet but granite-hard. "Tell me that women don't enjoy being pursued. Tell me that you cringe at the idea of letting me catch you. Go ahead, lie to me, Sera."

She was caught. One didn't fall in love with a rake. And if you had the poor judgment to do so, you certainly didn't confess your folly to him. Her heart racing, her breathing ragged, she gazed into his eyes and knew that he was forcing her to choose between surrender and survival. "I won't," she said firmly, lifting her chin. She deliberately turned away from him, adding, "But we're very different people and—"

He caught her arm and hauled her back. "Different how?"

She didn't want to fight him, didn't want to destroy what relationship they had. But surrender was impossible. "I'm a married woman and—"

"I don't give a damn about Gerald Treadwell," he snarled, grasping her shoulders. "You don't owe him fidelity. He left you, Sera. He stole from you and abandoned you. His greed and meanness set you free. No, don't you dare put Gerald Treadwell between us, Sera. It's cowardly and dishonest."

Deep inside her a dam gave way and a lifetime of accepting and enduring came to an end. She shoved her arms up between them and then flung them outward, breaking his hold on her. Free, she held her ground, tilting her head back to meet his stunned gaze.

"All right, I'll give you an honest answer, Carden," she vowed. "I am a coward. I don't want to be swept off my feet and then thanked and set aside for another woman.

No, Gerald never seduced me. I submitted because that's what a wife is expected to do. And no, he never once thanked me for my favors. But he set me aside for other women, Carden, and it hurt. Not my heart. I was never fool enough to give him that.

"It was my pride that he battered. And yes, I'm very much aware that pride is nothing more than a tin shield, but when it's all you have, you cling to it for dear life. As much and as deeply as I'm attracted to you, Carden Reeves, I *will not* surrender what pathetic little defense I have and let you hurt me."

"Sera," he whispered, reaching for her.

The sadness, the wanting and regret, in his eyes almost undid her. She stepped back and went on, determined to drive him away before he realized that she'd withheld the most important truth. "I thought that I could. Early on, when we were strangers. I thought that if it was my choice to be set aside, I could satisfy my curiosity and walk away unscathed. But we aren't strangers anymore and somewhere along the way I lost my courage. I'm sorry if I led you on and let you think that there could be more between us. I shouldn't have."

He didn't try to close the distance between them. He simply stood where he was as he quietly asked, "If we're not strangers, what are we, Sera? Governess and employer?"

"Yes."

"But more than that?" He didn't wait for her to admit it. "Are we professional associates?"

"Just barely."

"Friends?"

"I don't know," she answered, struggling to breathe as she sensed the walls closing in around her.

"Sera, we're lovers in all but fact."

He was right and she hated him for it. She wanted to throw something at him and scream at him at the top of her lungs. She desperately, with every fiber of her being and every beat of her heart, wanted to fall into his arms and hear him tell her that he loved her even more than she loved him. God, she couldn't breathe. The world was starting to spin. And the tears, damn them, were crawling up her throat.

"I'll make you a promise, Sera," he said, his voice grounding her. "I'll stay with you until *you* set *me* aside. The ending will be yours to choose."

She considered the lure and the trap beyond it. And then saw the escape it afforded her. She drew a steadying breath and committed herself to one final attempt. "What if I never want it to end? What if I want to be with you always?"

He blinked and for a moment seemed to lose his balance. He swallowed, cleared his throat, and rubbed the palm of his hand over his lips. "I don't know," he finally answered. "I honestly don't know."

Made brave by his confusion, she pressed further. "The idea frightens you, doesn't it?"

"Yes, it does."

"Carden, I'm just as afraid of being set aside as you are of being shackled."

His breathing quickened and grew shallow. His gaze drifted off to the far wall as his pulse pounded in his temples and the muscles in his jaw clenched and unclenched. It took what felt like an eternity before he whispered, "Impasse."

By sheer force of will she kept herself from sagging in relief. Her secret was safe. Her heart was safe. But the price was more painful than she'd ever imagined it would be. Telling herself that someday she'd look back and know that it had been worth paying, she offered Carden what solace she could, saying, "Let's agree to be kind to each other and graciously accept that we're ill-suited and ill-fated."

He didn't look at her. "I don't like it."

"I'd prefer a different outcome myself," she admitted, her heart aching and battered, "but I don't see one as being even remotely possible."

He wanted to ask her if she thought one was possible with Barrett. Or if Aiden was the man who would offer her all she wanted. But he couldn't. He couldn't bear the thought that she might say yes. He couldn't stay here with her, pretending that the loss wasn't tearing him apart inside. If he didn't go and go now, he was going to offer her the moon and the stars and in six months they were both going to hate him for his weakness and stupidity.

"My appointment with Lady Caruthers is tomorrow," he said, staring out the window. "Will you have the paintings done by then?"

"I put them on your desk an hour ago. You will let me know what she thinks of them, won't you?"

He nodded, turned sharply on his heel, and walked away, praying he could get to the door before what little self-control he still possessed deserted him. His hand was on the doorknob when the sound of Sera's tears softly reached him. He faltered and then resolutely, blindly went on.

CHAPTER 16

Carden looked down into his empty brandy glass and decided that he really didn't want anything more to drink. The first two scotches at his club had sufficiently diluted Lady Caruthers's sickly sweet lemonade by mid-afternoon. The four after that had been largely for the sake of having somewhere to be and something to do other than come back here and chance meeting Seraphina in the hall. And it was a damn good thing that he'd been successful at doing that, he silently groused, tearing off his stretched collar, because he'd utterly failed to figure out what he was going to do about her.

There were so many ways to go. All of them had merits. And drawbacks. He pitched his collar on top of the drawings, unbuttoned his shirt tab, threw himself into his chair, slammed his feet up on the desk, and considered his dilemma yet again.

Yes, packing her and the girls off to Honoria's at first light still appealed to his bruised pride. Going out to find himself another woman—any woman—definitely still appealed to his ego. And his loins. He'd have already done it if his gut wasn't being so damn persistent about telling him that he wasn't going to be fully sated unless it was Sera he took down into the sheets. And his bloody conscience . . .

He vaulted up out of the chair, deciding that he did need the brandy after all. He was adding another splash for good measure when Aiden Terrell walked jauntily into his study.

"What are you doing here?"

"Well, hello to you, too," Aiden quipped, utterly unfazed by the rudeness. "Tonight's the Martin-Holloway dinner. I've come to collect Seraphina. Have you forgotten?"

"No," he lied, dropping the stopper back into the decanter. *The day just gets better and better.*

"I still remember the threat so there's no need for you to repeat it."

"That's good," Carden replied, pulling open the next two buttons on his shirt as he returned to his desk. "I gather you've just come in."

"You gather correctly," he said, dropping back into his seat. Putting his feet up, he added, "Although I may go out again. I haven't decided."

"Is there any particular reason for the testiness this evening?"

And for the miserable night before and the whole wretched day, too? "Just thinking about Lady Caruthers's conservatory and how long it will take to get the damn thing done."

"If it would brighten your mood to know . . . Barrett thinks he's on to the trail of Reginald Carter."

Yes, it did brighten his mood. Beating the hell out of someone would make him feel so much better in so many ways. He nodded and took a healthy drink.

"Carden," his friend said, eyeing him warily, "is there anything you'd like to tell me? Anything I can do to help you out of this?"

Go to hell and take Seraphina with you? He took another drink. "No, I'm fine, thank you."

"Well, you don't seem fine to me."

He felt her presence, felt her gaze sliding over him. He looked up to find her standing in the doorway—just where he'd known she would be. She was wearing—not the conservative blue gown she'd worn when they'd gone out together, oh, no—but the bright green one with the crystals sprinkled over her bodice. The crystals that winked and dazzled and said, "Look! Wouldn't you like to touch?"

"Good evening, gentlemen," she said quietly, her gaze darting away from his. "Sawyer told me you were in here. I hope I'm not intruding."

Aiden—the drooling weasel—smiled and gushed, "You look ravishing, Seraphina."

"Thank you," she said, somehow managing a blush. She looked back at him and touched that pretty little tongue of hers to her luscious lower lip before asking, "How did Lady Caruthers receive the presentation today?"

"She adored the plan and gave me carte blanche," he replied, raising his glass to her. "Just as you said she would."

"I'm happy for you, Carden. When do you actually start the project?"

He shrugged in reply, glad that she sounded every bit as tense and miserable as he felt.

Aiden looked back and forth between them several times, sucked in his cheeks, then gushed again, saying, "Well, I think we should probably be going, Seraphina." He crossed to her and presented his arm, adding, "Dinner is at eight."

She took Aiden's arm blindly, her gaze on his as she said, "The girls are in the kitchen with the puppies. They're trying to think of names. Anne will be down for them shortly and see them tucked in for the night."

"Enjoy your evening," he drawled, hoping Aiden would trip on her hem on their way out. He waited, listening, and when the only sound that came was that of the front door closing, he snarled and tossed the last of the brandy down his throat.

If Sera was going out on the arms of other men, then, by God, he wasn't going to sit at home and pine over it. There were plenty of women in London who would be more than happy to spend an evening—a whole damn night!—in his company. He'd have one more brandy to celebrate his reentrance into the world of successful seduction, get himself something to eat and a quick shave, and then he'd go find a woman who not only understood, but truly appreciated the considerable merits of purely recreational sex.

Aiden's discomfort hadn't been lost on her, and as he settled into the opposite carriage seat, Sera knew that it was only a matter of time before he began to ask questions. Despite the jading influence of rogues like Carden Reeves and Barrett Stanbridge, he was such a caring and empathetic young man. Somewhere out there in the world was a young woman who had no idea how incredibly lucky she was going to be someday.

"Seraphina," he predictably began as they edged out into the evening traffic, "even a blind man could see that something's gone terribly wrong between you and Carden. What happened?"

She was tempted to tell him that unless they were driving to Edinburgh, there wouldn't be time for the story. Instead, she smiled and replied, "I appreciate your concern, Aiden. I truly do. But it's personal."

She expected him to make another attempt—he was too kind to abandon the effort after only one—and he didn't disappoint her. "Would it help to talk to another female about it? I could take you to see Lady Lansdown."

"Oh, Lord," she half-gasped, surprised by his choice of

tack. "Thank you, but no thank you. Honoria's the very last person I'd talk to about Carden."

"What's he done? Maybe I could prevail on his good sense. If that fails, I could probably get one good punch in on him."

"Just one?" she asked, amused and hoping that he'd allow the conversation to go in another direction.

"Maybe two," he amended, grinning. "Any more than that would be by sheer dumb luck. I may be younger and faster than he is, but he's more experienced and considerably meaner. In the end, he'd win. But I'd be more than willing to sacrifice myself if you'd just tell me what he's done."

Nice *and* persistent. Nicely persistent, actually. "He hasn't done anything."

"Is that the problem? He hasn't done something you hoped he would?"

Hoping someone would love you didn't obligate them to do so. "Oh, Aiden," she replied, shaking her head, "it's very kind of you to offer to help, but as I said, it's personal."

He leaned forward, his elbows on his knees. "Please talk to me, Seraphina," he asked earnestly. "I can't fix it for you if you won't tell me what's gone awry."

"It can't be fixed," she admitted, remembering the caged look in Carden's eyes as he'd considered spending forever with her.

"Nonsense. Did you do something?"

What hadn't she done? She'd accepted—no, invited—Carden's advances. She'd stepped to the very edge of an affair with him and then scrambled away, hiding behind pride and anger and an incredibly dubious claim to virtue. And when he'd reached for her, tried to ease her fears, she'd struck out at him, knowing where his weaknesses lay and deliberately aiming for them. She'd intentionally battered him in her effort to escape the consequences of her own decisions.

And to punish him for not loving her.

The tears came, spilling in hot rivulets down her cheeks. Suddenly Aiden was beside her, his arm around her shoulders as he pressed a handkerchief into her hand and whispered, "What, Seraphina? What did you do? Tell me and I'll set it right with Carden."

"You can't set it right," she cried, flinging her hands up at the futility of it all. "It can't be undone."

"What did you do?" he asked again, his patience clearly at its end. "Spit it out!"

"I foolishly, blindly, utterly, and completely fell in love with him!"

He stared at her, his mouth slightly agape, and she looked away, scrubbing his handkerchief over her cheeks and silently daring him to tell her that he could do something about *that*.

His laughter caught her completely off guard. She'd barely turned her head to look at him when he hugged her tight and buoyantly declared, "That's not a bad thing, Seraphina. That's not bad at all. In fact, it's wonderful. The best news I've ever heard."

She put her hands flat against his chest and pushed herself away so that she could see his face. "Falling in love with a confirmed, committed rake is good news?" she asked incredulously. "You've lost your mind, Aiden."

He laughed again and shook his head. "Carden's days as a rake are over. He just doesn't know it yet."

She stared at him, not knowing what to think, what to believe, what to say. "Honestly, Seraphina. He's so in love with you he can't see straight. Which is the problem at the moment. He's so in love that he doesn't know that he's in love. Does that make any sense?"

It did. And her heart so wanted to hope that it was true. But in knowing Carden, she also knew that hoping would only compound her folly and deepen the pain. Wisdom lay in accepting the truth. She wiped the last traces of tears from her cheeks, saying, "He doesn't love me, Aiden. He never will. He can't."

"You're wrong, Seraphina," her companion countered, settling back into the seat beside her, his arm still comfortingly draped around her shoulder. "Barrett and I've been watching him tumble for you since the minute you walked into his life. He'll come around in the end. Trust us on this."

"Trust you?" she said, confounded yet again. "If you're both so sure that he loves me, why have you both asked to escort me out? Don't you consider that a betrayal of your friendship and his feelings?"

"You've accepted our invitations," he pointed out. "Don't you consider that a betrayal of your love?"

Sera carefully chose her words, needing to explain but not wanting to bruise his pride. "If you're the only one in love, the only betrayal is of that of your own hope. And I was willing to do that to avoid embarrassing either you or Barrett by declining your invitations."

He blinked and then knitted his brows. "You accepted out of pity?"

"I didn't say that," she protested, knowing even as she did that she was splitting hairs. "I was concerned for your feelings."

He tried to look injured, but couldn't control the smile tickling the corners of his mouth. "Well, whatever your motives, they're dovetailing perfectly with Lady Lansdown's plan."

She started, once again caught off guard. "Honoria? Honoria has her fingers in this mess?" Sera closed her eyes, remembering the day Honoria had come upon them in the park. "I should have seen it," she muttered. "I shouldn't be the least bit surprised."

"It's a good plan," Aiden assured her. "Really."

She knew otherwise. "And just precisely what is this plan?" she asked. "What are you hoping to accomplish?"

"Lady Lansdown proposed it the first night you were here and described it as 'time-honored.' It's a very simple one, actually. Barrett and I take you out and about and make Carden jealous enough to realize that he loves you."

Oh, dear God. The plan had been put into play and the damage had already been done. Why hadn't she seen what was happening in time to put an end to it? Why, why, why?

"And our part of it's working very well," Aiden continued, apparently taking her horror for disbelief. "Carden was furious about your going out with me this evening. And when he found out yesterday afternoon that Barrett's escorting you to Lady Hatcher's ball . . . I thought Carden was going to kill him right there on the spot. I really did."

"Instead he came back to the house and we had a hideous row," she countered, angry that they'd been manipulated into a disaster. "Whatever bridges we might have been able to build were burnt to ashes, Aiden."

"A row over what?"

There was no point in mincing words. "Thanks to Honoria's timeless, simple plan, it began with the fact that Barrett asked me to the ball and I accepted. It progressed from there, rather brutally, I might add, and ended when we arrived at bitter reality."

"That bitter reality being . . . ?" Aiden pressed. "Friends are honest with each other, Seraphina."

But for the good, woefully oblivious intentions of friends . . . "The truth is that I can't bear the thought of being a temporary lover and Carden can't bear the thought of being lovers forever."

"And I don't suppose," he drawled, "that it occurred to either one of you to compromise and let love and time work things out between you?"

Her anger fled, humiliated in the face of the memory.

Carden standing there, offering her all he dared to give, more than he'd undoubtedly ever offered any woman. "He tried," she murmured, her heart tearing.

Aiden sighed long and hard, then shifted on the seat beside her, withdrawing his arm from her shoulder to take her hands in his. "Seraphina," he said calmly but with great firmness, "there are no absolute certainties in life. If you don't risk anything, you risk everything."

His words burrowed slowly, inexorably, into her heart and soul. If she didn't offer Carden her heart—and take the chance that he would break it—there would be no hope of his ever giving her his heart in return. Risk not, gain not. Risk greatly, gain the world.

It was a simple, fundamental truth. And she would have never realized it had Aiden not laid it right in front of her and demanded that she open her eyes. She met his gaze, searching for the words to express the depth of her appreciation.

"I know," he said quietly, his smile assured. "I'm not nearly as naive as I let most people think I am." His smile widened into a grin. "Which reminds me. Please don't ever, *ever* tell Carden that I put my arm around your shoulders or that I held your hands. If he finds out, you'll be able to bury what's left of me in your reticule."

Yes, some woman, someday, was going to be very lucky, indeed. "The secret is safe with me," she promised. "It's the least I can do to thank you for your friendship and your wisdom."

"You'll think on what I've said?"

"Yes, Aiden. I already have."

"Good," he declared happily, giving her hands a little squeeze before releasing them. "Now," he added as their driver opened the carriage door, "let's get this dinner done so you can go home and square things with Carden."

Sera smiled as he stepped out and turned back to offer his hand. She took it, marveling at how smoothly he'd managed and timed their conversation. And to think that she'd once worried about what he might learn from Carden and Barrett. John Aiden Terrell was a masterful rogue in his own right. And while he'd used his skills to her incredible benefit this evening—for which she would be forever grateful—she couldn't help but feel a little sympathy for all the women who didn't see the danger he posed until it was far too late. God help the one who set out to settle him down.

He froze in the doorway, only then remembering what Sera had said to him in parting. Any chance of backing away and escaping unnoticed was dashed when Bea glanced up and saw him standing there.

"Hello, Uncle Carden!" she exclaimed. "Have you come to help us name the puppies?"

Recovering quickly enough to smile and lie, he replied, "I thought it sounded like a wonderful way to pass the evening." He sucked in a deep breath and committed himself to getting through it. Sera had said Anne would be down shortly; the girls were already in their night rails and dressing gowns. Playing the good-natured uncle wouldn't delay him all that long.

"How far have you gotten?" he asked, joining them on the floor beside the dog and her pups.

Camille picked up one of the puppies and held it, fat little tummy toward him, saying, "We've decided that this one is Tippy because of the little white tip on his tail."

It was a "her," but he didn't see any reason to correct the mistake. Tippy was one of those names that went perfectly well either way. "Very logical. It'll be easy to remember."

Beatrice picked up another, and holding it the same way, announced, "And this one is Bootsie."

"Because of the slightly darker feet," he guessed as he

noted another significant feature. "If I might make a small suggestion? It's a boy dog. With a name like Bootsie the other boy dogs are likely to pummel him. Maybe you could call him Boots so his life would be a little easier?"

"Boots is fine with me," she said, silently looking between her sisters for approval. They nodded and she put Boots back in the bed with his mother.

Carden scooped up one of the remaining three. "How about this one? What are you thinking for . . ." He took a quick, discreet peek at its underside. "Her?"

"Miss Sera," Camille suggested. "Because her eyes are blue like Miss Sera's."

"Puppies' eyes don't stay that color, sweetheart. In just a week or two they're going to turn brown."

Camille's eyes widened. "Are Miss Sera's eyes going to change color, too?"

"No. Sera is always going to have blue eyes." *Beautiful blue eyes.*

"We could call her Fluffy," Amanda suggested.

Camille looked at her sister and frowned. "Miss Sera?"

"No, silly," Amanda countered, huffing in disdain and putting her hands on her waist. "The puppy. Miss Sera isn't at all fluffy."

No, never would anyone think to describe Seraphina as fluffy. She was beautiful, yes. She was intelligent and artistic, too. But deep down inside, she had a core of steel and a wanton streak that men would kill for the privilege of unleashing.

"Tippy, Boots, and Fluffy," Beatrice said, interrupting his thoughts. "That leaves these two and the mama. I think we should call one of them Lucky. They all are, you know."

"How about this one?" Amanda suggested, scooping one up to hold it in front of her face and coo, "Hello, Lucky."

Camille puckered her mouth and frowned for a moment

before asking, "Is it a boy dog or a girl dog, Uncle Carden?"

He considered Lucky to be in the same category as Tippy and he certainly didn't want to do anything that might—however innocently—prompt one of them to ask how he could tell the males from the females. "A girl," he guessed.

"A girl named Lucky?" Beatrice said, her upper lip curling in obvious displeasure. "I wouldn't want to be named Lucky."

"What about Lucky Lucy?" Amanda offered, turning the puppy in question to face her sister and inspection.

Carden inwardly cringed. He'd guessed correctly. A female pup. Who was going to go through life with a strumpet's name if he didn't quickly make another suggestion. The problem was how to phrase it so he didn't have to explain matters he didn't want any of them to ever know about.

Amanda turned the puppy so he could see the animal's poor little embarrassed face and asked, "Isn't Lucky Lucy a good name for her, Uncle Carden?"

"It's a perfectly good one," he agreed, deciding that he'd shorten it to Lucy and hope the girls eventually did the same. Lucy was going to owe him for the rest of her life.

"That leaves this one," Camille announced, picking up the last puppy. She turned toward him with it—thank God, belly boldly first—and asked, "Is it a boy or a girl, Uncle Carden?"

"It's another girl." He and Boots were severely outnumbered. They were going to have to stick together.

"Let's call her Beauty," Bea proposed.

Amanda snorted. "That's a dumb name."

"It is not."

"Then when we take her to the park," her elder sister

retorted, "you can call out 'Come here, Beauty!' and let people laugh at you."

"Well, at least they'd laugh at me," Beatrice shot back. "They'd just feel sorry for—"

"What about Furball?" Carden tossed out to derail the argument. "She's furry and shaped something like a ball."

They all three looked at him as though he'd turned into the village idiot. Beatrice laid her hand on his knee and gently said, "I'm sorry, Uncle Carden, but that's what cats cough up."

"She's red," he observed, hoping to improve their opinion of him. "Maybe we could just call her that. Red."

Beatrice shook her head and curled her lip again. "One of the sailors on our ship was named Red." She looked between her sisters. "For his beard, remember?"

Camille nodded and wrinkled her nose. "He always had *stuff* in it, Uncle Carden."

He could imagine. Which he really preferred not to do. "It sounds most unappealing," he replied. "It's never wise to give something a name that reminds you of unpleasant people, places, or things."

"Well, so much for Mr. Hopkins," Amanda said, throwing up her hands in a gesture that would have implied frustration if she hadn't been grinning.

"And *La-dy* Matthews," Camille contributed, putting her nose in the air and wiggling her shoulders.

Beatrice stared off into the distance and very somberly said, "And definitely Mr. Treadwell."

Camille froze. Amanda started, then gave Beatrice a quick shove in the shoulder before pinning his gaze and saying breezily, "There were a great many unpleasant people in Belize, Uncle Carden."

"Apparently," he said, thinking that Gerald Treadwell ranked as the most unpleasant.

"I miss Belize," Camille admitted on a sigh, hugging

the puppy close. "It was very pretty there. And warm and sunny."

"Since you have good memories of Belize," he suggested, hoping to avert a slide into melancholy, "why not call the puppy that? Belize would be a good name, don't you think?"

They instantly brightened and nodded and each took a turn petting the shiny red coat.

Tippy, Boots, Fluffy, Lucy, and Belize. It had a cadence to it. As Camille put Belize back with her sisters and only brother, Carden reached out and began scratching the mother dog behind her ears. "What should we call the mama?"

"Every time someone says 'mama,'" Camille said very quietly, "I think of Mama and Papa and miss them all over again."

"Me, too," Bea whispered.

Afraid that they were about to dissolve into tears, he hastily offered the first alternative that popped into his brain. "We could call her Queenie."

"Why?" Camille asked, her grief mercifully evaporated by curiosity.

"I don't know. Lots of people name their female dogs Queenie."

"The queen's name is Victoria," Bea mused.

"I don't think she'd be flattered," he countered. Ruffling the fur on the dog's head, he said, "Patience, girl. We're working on it."

"Patience!" Amanda exclaimed. "That's perfect!"

Bea grinned from ear to ear. "And the next time Miss Sera tells us that we have no patience, we can say, 'Yes we do!'"

"How long till she comes back, Uncle Carden?" Camille asked, wiggling and clapping her hands. "How long?"

"It will be a while. I think you're going to have to

be . . ." He paused and looked pointedly between them, struggling to contain his grin. "Patient."

They groaned in unison.

"Patience is a virtue," he laughingly reminded them.

Amanda clutched her stomach and groaned, "I'm going to retch."

"Well, do it in your room," he chuckled as the upstairs maid stepped into the kitchen doorway. "Anne's here to see you tucked in."

They scrambled to their feet and each planted a quick kiss on his cheek before bounding off. "Good night, ladies," he called after them.

Amanda paused in the shadows of the dining room, then turned and came back to the doorway. "I miss Mama and Papa, too, but not always," she said, her expression so solemn that she suddenly seemed far older than her years. "Sometimes, with you and Miss Sera, it feels very much as though we're still a whole family. Good night, Uncle Carden."

"Good night, Amanda."

With you and Miss Sera . . . Carden sighed and climbed to his feet. It had been a smoothly executed ploy, but if Amanda had had any deliberate thoughts of it being sufficient to keep him at home tonight, then she really needed to learn something about—

"No, on second thought," he muttered, heading for the larder, "Amanda doesn't need to know anything about the needs of men."

CHAPTER 17

He found a chunk of cheese and slab of roast apparently left from dinner and took them to the butcher block in the center of the kitchen. By the time he'd pulled a knife from the slotted holder, the dog was at his side, her puppies temporarily abandoned in the hope of sharing his impromptu meal.

He cut two slices of the roast, tossed one in the air, and popped the other into his mouth with a smile as the first was seized—and consumed—before it even came close to hitting the floor. Two more slices of roast and six of cheese followed after that.

He was slicing another chunk of the roast and thinking about seeing if he could make Patience do a half-turn in the air for it when she suddenly looked at the back door, her ears perked forward. He listened with her and watched her hackles slowly rise. She was growling quietly, low in her throat until the knock came, and then the growl became a furious bark as she charged the door on stiff forelegs.

Through the glass he could see the unmistakable outline of Barrett Stanbridge. Holding Patience by the scruff, he opened the door and then dragged her back to the central table, saying over his shoulder, "She appears to be an excellent judge of character." He'd no sooner uttered the words than Patience eyed the roast on the table and settled with a hopeful look in her eyes.

Barrett smiled. "I came by for three reasons. The first is to let you know that Reginald Carter has apparently gone to ground. Until recently he was living high and well in a Chelsea townhouse. According to his staff, he walked out the door the morning before last and they haven't seen or heard from him since. My guess is he's gone into the no-man's-land of Newcastle or Southwark. It's going to be the devil to find him, but I've got good men on the task."

"I don't care what it costs," Carden said, flinging a slice of meat for Patience. "I want him found."

"It won't cost you anything until he is. I don't pay men for looking, just for finding. It tends to motivate them to get the job done efficiently."

Perfectly sensible. He hoped Barrett's men were either the greedy sort or had a lot of mouths to feed at home. "And the second reason you're here?"

"I went by the club this evening and had a drink or two with Rob Tompkins."

"I had drink or two with him this afternoon," Carden shared, slicing himself another bite of the roast. "Was he still upright? Still sobbing into his cups?"

"He was not only upright, but quite happy, actually. He said you'd agreed to come look at the problems they're having with a patch of the underground, that you'd taken the drawings from him and were going to go over them."

"He was so miserable I took pity on him. They're on my desk."

"I just wanted to say that I'm glad to hear it, Card. You're wasting your talent on conservatories."

But better conservatories than feeling like a rat burrowing beneath the city. And none of it compared with feeling like a bird on a soaring, long-span trestle. "And the third reason you're here?"

"I was heading to Covent Garden for some sport and wondered if you wanted to go along."

So that Barrett might—at some critical juncture and ever so accidentally—mention the occasion to Sera. "I can't," he said, wondering if Barrett really thought he was that feebleminded. "I promised Tompkins I'd have some ideas for him first thing tomorrow morning." He hadn't made Tompkins any promises at all, but as excuses went, it was the perfect one.

Barrett shrugged and took the doorknob in hand, saying, "Work should come before play, I suppose. If you get done sooner than you anticipate or just change your mind . . ."

"I know where to find you," he said, tossing a piece of cheese for Patience.

Barrett left without another word and Carden snorted as the door closed. Hell would freeze and the Prince Consort would go out in a dress before he made the mistake—no, the fatal error in judgment—of meeting Barrett anywhere and chasing skirts with him.

He wasn't willing to give up on his hopes for Sera just yet. He'd behaved like an ass yesterday, raging at her like some cuckolded husband, pushing her too hard and too fast. Of course she'd retreated behind the façades of pride and propriety; he hadn't given her much of any other choice. And by the time he'd realized his blunder, the damage had already been done.

The question now was how to smooth things over with her, how to reach past her fear and draw her back to his side, to get her to look up at him, smile, and invite his kisses. Just one soulful kiss; that's all it would take. Sera always melted when . . .

Carden closed his eyes and shook his head. How thick could a man be? He was a master of seduction who had ignored every damn rule of the game. He'd allowed their relationship to wander into the realm of the mundane and everyday. He'd asked Sera to come to his bed by conscious choice. He'd negotiated terms. Jesus. It was no wonder he was home sharing his meal with the dog and she was out to dinner on the arm of his friend.

Well, by God, that was going to change and change before sunrise. He'd ignore her evening out with John Aiden; just pretend it hadn't happened. It was of the mundane and had no place in the world of enchantment he was going to weave around her. He'd apologize for his behavior in the greenhouse and ask her to forgive him. When she lowered her defenses to do so, he'd draw her into his arms and kiss her. And when she looked at him, lost and searching for her way, he'd whisper to the wanton in her. Of decadent pleasures. Of dangerous delights and wicked satisfactions. He wouldn't give her time to think, time to talk. And Sera would come to him, wanting and trusting and so very willing.

All he had to do was bide his time until she came home. Tompkins's drawings would do for distraction. But the minute Seraphina came through the door . . . Carden grinned and tossed Patience what was left of the roast.

He unrolled the drawings and flipped to the ones for the section Tompkins had said they were presently constructing. The problems were small ones and, in and of themselves, no more than an aggravation. But when combined, they were consuming man hours and delaying forward progress. And time was money. Great wads of it.

Carden studied the design and could see nothing wrong with it. The designing engineer had been a thoroughly competent one. Judging by the general approach, Carden could see that the man had come to the underground project with considerable experience in building aboveground railways. There was nothing wrong with the plans. But given the problems as Tompkins described them . . .

Carden frowned and flipped back to the drawings for the section most recently completed. There was nothing amiss there, either. He went back another section, to a portion of the line nearly a half-mile from where workers were now trying to shore walls, support overheads, and lay track while what should have been solid ground shifted and crumbled by small degrees all around them.

He sighed and shook his head as he studied the design of the girdings, at the foundations, at the elevations. There was nothing wrong anywhere that he could see. Structurally, there was no reason at all for the problems they were having. Which meant that the source of the problem lay somewhere outside the design and construction of the structure itself. And that "somewhere," he knew, could be anywhere in the unseeable, unknowable mass of soil and rock that lay between the streets of London and the top of the tunnel.

"Somewhere" was within the midnight-black realm that was the responsibility of the geologists—who were either doddering old men or peach-faced boys who made nothing more than educated guesses. If he had a gold sovereign for every time one of them had been wrong, he could buy the throne, Carden silently groused, turning back to the page with the geological drawings and notes.

There was nothing there to suggest that the ground hadn't been undisturbed and perfectly stable for the last eternity. Nothing to suggest that it wouldn't be equally stable for all of the next.

He flipped back to the uppermost of the drawings and considered the *x*s Tompkins had made to note the most problematic areas of the site. With a few exceptions, they were down the north side and fairly well distributed from the top to the bottom.

"It has to be water," he muttered. "Has to be. But from where?"

He returned to the geology reports, looking for any references that might have been made to ancient streambeds, old wells, or abandoned underground cisterns. And he found nothing. Which really wasn't all that surprising. He'd never encountered a university-educated geologist who could find and track underground water sources with anywhere near the accuracy a good witcher with a divining rod could.

Frustrated, he went back to the top drawing and read the platting description, trying to put it within the context of the city above. When he had it fixed in his head, he leaned back in his chair and closed his eyes, mentally sorting through the buildings there, searching for one that could be a source of a water mass sufficiently large to flow through the underground strata and eat away at the tunnel. Finding no suspects, he began stripping away the current structures and putting in their places the ones he remembered from earlier years, buildings and businesses that had been the victims of the drive to raze the old and build newer and better. There had been a spectacular fire there when he was a boy, he remembered. It had started in one of the—

Carden bolted upright and flipped through all the sheets Tompkins had given him, mentally drawing the route aboveground, hoping he was wrong.

He wasn't. The tunnel was following a line just south of where the old foundries had been. At least a dozen of them and each with a huge underground cistern to hold the water needed to cool forged metal. He remembered how fast the charred remains had been cleared away, how quickly the new had risen from the ashes. No one had taken the time to tear out the cisterns. They'd simply been covered over and forgotten, the wood allowed to slowly rot, the metal to rust away. And every time it rained, every time the snow melted, the cisterns had continued to do what they had been designed to.

Carden looked at the xs and knew with dreadful certainty that the old caverns were finally giving way, that the accumulated water was flowing out of them, and that it was only a matter of time before the weight of water and mud and rock brought not just the current section of tunnel down, but at least the last four. It was a miracle that it hadn't happened already.

Snatching up the drawings, he rolled them as he strode from his study and to the servants' quarters. "Sawyer!" he barked, flinging open his butler's door. "Wake up!"

Sawyer barely raised his head from the pillow and lifted one side of his sleeping mask to ask, "Are there flames, sir?"

"No. But there's going to be a tunnel collapse. I have to go."

Pulling off the mask and pushing aside the bedcoverings, Sawyer sat up. "And my role in averting this disaster, sir?"

"Tell Sera where I've gone and that it may be a day or two before I get back here. If she looks the least bit rumpled when she comes in this evening, take John Aiden aside and tell him that he's a dead man. And send a note to Barrett telling him that I want one of his men watching this house while I'm gone. Tell him that I'm willing to pay men to look. He left for Covent Garden just a while ago. Monroe will find him there if he hurries."

"Good luck to you, sir. I shall see to it all and keep the home fires burning."

"Just make sure Seraphina and the girls are safe," Carden called back over his shoulder. "I don't much care about the rest of it."

God, he hoped Tompkins was still at the club. If he wasn't, he was going to be dragged out of bed. In fact, before the hour was out, there were going to be a hell of a lot of men rousted from the comfort of their beds and homes. And their assumptions.

Lying along the bracing timber, Carden looked along the top half of the tunnel, back into the completed sections, searching in the dim light for any signs of bulging plate or bowing timber. Deciding that all looked well at the moment, he turned his head to look the other way, resting his cheek against the tarred wood as he scanned the entirety of the newest section—the one still most in danger of being structurally compromised. Two days. Two days and nights and they were *still* hauling in metal plate and timbers, still battling to keep the ground in place.

He glanced along the crown, finding some comfort in the fact that there were no longer tiny rivulets of water seeping through the seams between the iron plates they'd hoisted up and pinned into place with whatever would do for a support column. As engineering went, it was a visual nightmare of cobble, slapdash, and make-do, but it was, apparently, working well enough to keep the roof off the floor. There was definitely something to be said for that.

"Now, if we can keep the foundations intact," he murmured, leaning over to study the scene below. The noise was thundering, the light miserably dim, and the air smoky and ominously damp. But he could see that the braces were still coming down the ramp from aboveground on sleds, their descent swift and efficient as teams of filthy, grim-faced men fed the ropes through the pulleys and called for the next hauling team to stand ready. The beams, wood and iron alike, were still being dragged down the tunnel floor by another army of equally resolute workers and left for the teams that were hefting them up one by one, working their way toward the ramp, positioning the ends against the stone foundations and then sledging them into place.

Carden shifted, moving forward on the beam to see around a column, and studied the north wall, hoping that the steel plate and prop supports they'd desperately thrown up the first night would continue to be sufficient for the task. Water trickled through the seams and he swore softly, glaring at the crown above him and wondering if the pumping crews were emptying the cisterns with a god-damn teaspoon.

Knowing there was going to be no rescinding the orders to prepare for setting mid-level braces, he visually marked the wall in regular intervals from the end of the section to the ramp. It was when he reached the end of the course that he saw him.

He was tall. He was massively shouldered. But mostly Barrett Stanbridge stuck out because he was the only man in a clean white shirt. Carden studied him for a minute, trying to tell by his demeanor why he'd come down from above. He didn't seem agitated or even slightly concerned about finding him with any sort of haste. Actually, he seemed more interested in analyzing the bracing structures than anything else. Which, in all likelihood, meant that nothing horrible had happened to Sera or the girls.

He'd no more than framed the thought and sighed in relief when Barrett looked up and met his gaze. His smile instant and wide, he shook his head and started forward. Carden leaned out from the timber, grasped the edge of a vertical support steel beam, and then half jumped, half pulled himself fully onto it. Barrett was waiting for him at the base when he slid to a halt.

"Seraphina sent me down here to check on you and make sure you're not doing anything risky or foolish," he explained. "I think that particular maneuver might be something I should keep to myself. She can't fret over what she doesn't know."

Sera was worried about him? Was she worried enough that she'd already forgiven him for being an oafish ogre?

"Well," he drawled, bringing his attention back to Barrett, "I can't very well put my own life and limb before those of others. Neither can I point to a problem, wish them the best of luck in solving it, and walk away."

"Agreed. Leadership by example and all of that," his friend said as they started toward the ramp together. "Do you need another set of hands and a bit of brawn?"

Carden shook his head. "There's sufficient brawn. Simmons and Franklin are the bracing-crew leaders. They mustered out a month after we resigned our commissions. And I think enough water has been pumped topside and we've done enough strategic shoring down here to stave off an imminent collapse. If, however, I'm wrong in the longer run, I'd rather have you on the outside."

"Any particular reason other than you're a selfless friend?"

Carden stopped and waited until Barrett had turned to face him before saying, "I'm assuming that, as my friend, you'll see that Sera and the girls aren't left alone to make their way in the world."

"I'm not the only one capable of doing so. John Aiden would see to it, as well."

"Yes, but it would never cross John Aiden's mind to marry Sera. You, on the other hand, have already given the notion some thought."

"Oh?" Barrett countered with a cocked brow and a guilty smile. "And what have I decided?"

Carden grinned. "That it's a damn good thing women like Sera are a rarity because they can actually make horrible fates—like marriage—look appealing."

Slowly sobering, carefully studying him, Barrett bluntly asked, "Are you considering it?"

"It's flitted through my mind once or twice," he admitted. "Both times when I'd had too much to drink. But in a cold, sober light . . ." He shook his head. "No. She's held my interest longer than any other woman, but reality being what it is . . . Forever is a damn long time, Barrett. I'm not a forever man and I know it."

"Neither am I," his friend countered, "so try not to get yourself killed so that I don't have to seriously contemplate such somber possibilities."

Carden considered the water trickling out of the north wall and how to answer. He couldn't very well tell Barrett not to worry, that everything would be fine; Barrett was an engineer and could see for himself that matters could go to hell in a heartbeat. "How is Sera?" he asked instead.

"Quite distracted."

"By whom?" he asked dryly. "You? Or Aiden?"

"You and your dash into dangerous pursuits," Barrett shot back. "Sawyer says she spends a great deal of time pacing and looking out the windows. Which explains why the girls tell me that she's making no progress whatsoever on getting her pictures sorted for the publisher. You failed to mention the other day at the club that she's been asked to submit them."

"I was more concerned with finding Reginald Carter. Have you?"

Barrett looked away. "We're getting closer."

And he was frustrated for not having already accomplished the task. Carden abandoned the subject, asking, "Do you have a man watching the house as I asked?"

"Two. One front, one back. Both well armed."

"I appreciate it, Barrett," he said, clamping a hand on his friend's shoulder. "Thank you. With any luck, I'll be out of here tomorrow and free them to go back to looking for Sera's soon-to-be-former husband."

They resumed their course toward the ramp, walking in companionable silence until Barrett cleared his throat and asked, "Would it trouble you greatly if you heard that Gerald Treadwell had been found dead?" Without giving him a chance to reply, he stepped over a foundation brace, saying, "You know just as well as I do that violent ends are common in Newcastle and Southwark. His timely demise would save Seraphina a great deal of heartache and scandal. And no one will be unduly suspicious unless he dies *after* you're known to have met with him."

Barrett's approach would be neat and clean; the problem quietly and permanently solved before it could grow any uglier than it already was. But creating a problem in solving one wasn't an acceptable solution. Barrett had nightmares enough already and he wouldn't add to them simply for the sake of making his life—or Sera's—easier.

"It's a risk I'll have to take," Carden replied, as they stepped over another brace. "Honor requires that he have a chance to make right some of the wrongs he's done to Sera."

Barrett snorted. "And if he atones and wants Seraphina back as his wife?"

"I won't let that happen. He'd have to kill me first."

"Well, as the barristers always say, self-defense is the best defense. And it would solve the problem. The scandal will be horrific, though. Neither you nor Seraphina would ever live it down."

"Well, as I always say," he countered, unable to keep the bitter memories from edging his tone, "better scandalized than dead."

Barrett was looking at him askance when Simmons strode over and barely kept himself from saluting. "Cap'n Reeves," he said, "I thought you'd want to know that we're about ready to put in the first mid-level brace." His gaze snapped over to Barrett and he nodded crisply, adding, "Leftenant Stanbridge, it's good to see you, sir. Have you come to give us a hand, too?"

"Yes," Carden answered for his friend, "but we don't need it. He's just leaving."

Simmons checked another salute, disguising it by pulling on the brim of his wool cap, and walked off toward the north wall.

"I'll give Sera your regards," Barrett said, studying the plates and supports already in place. "Should I give her a kiss from you, too?"

"Only if I die in here," he quipped. "Touch her while I'm still breathing and you're going to die out there."

His friend's smile was weak and fleeting. "Be careful, Carden," he said solemnly. "Mind the walls. If they shift even the littlest bit more, *get out*."

Carden nodded and watched Barrett make his way up the ramp, knowing that if the walls caved in a lot of men were going to die. And he stood a damn good chance of being among them. No matter how fast he ran or how high he climbed. Carden cocked a brow as he realized that for the first time in his life he wasn't inclined to simply shrug his shoulders over the possibility and go on.

Barrett disappeared into the patch of bright light that was the world above and Carden turned away. He had a good number of things he intended to do if he was lucky enough to get out of this alive. And at the very top of the list was getting on with seducing sweet Seraphina. Nothing, no one, was going to stand in his way. She was worried enough to send Barrett to check on him. Sera cared. If she hadn't already forgiven him, she would. And he was going to make sure that Sera remembered the delight in her surrender for as long as she lived.

He grinned and joined the team lifting the brace, thinking that it was nice to have something worth surviving for.

CHAPTER 18

He was finally home. He was standing there, behind his desk, in a patch of late afternoon light, with a brandy in his hand, his shirt and trousers filthy, his sleeves rolled back to above his elbows, and his chin and cheeks shadowed with the growth of three days' beard. She'd never seen him more handsome.

"Are you all right?" she asked, drinking in the sight of him as she advanced into the room.

"I'm fine, Sera," he assured her, his gaze just a bit unfocused as he stifled a yawn. "I have a few nicks and a couple of bruises, but nothing to be at all concerned about."

Sera waited for his eyes to sparkle and for him to offer to show them to her. Instead he yawned again. Telling herself that his failure stemmed from exhaustion, not disinterest, she swallowed down her disappointment and went on. "I've been so worried about you. Did you save the tunnel?"

"Certainly not by myself and there were a few times that I wasn't quite so sure it could even be done. But in the end, we pulled out a miracle or two." He smiled. "Tunneling is a nasty, dirty business. They don't pay the men who work down there nearly enough."

Oh, his smile. She'd so missed his smile. That she might never see it again had been her constant fear for the last three days. And now that he was home again, she didn't want to miss a single chance to be with him. There were so many apologies to offer, so much she needed to explain.

Not the least of which, she realized, was how they were being manipulated in the name of good intentions and friendship. "Tonight is Lady Hatcher's silly ball," she began. "I tried to beg out of it, but Barrett said I couldn't—unless there was a death in the family—without Lady Hatcher considering me incredibly rude."

He rubbed his forehead, yawned hugely and deeply, and then said, "I thought it was tomorrow night. I've lost track of time. Being underground does that to you."

Sera considered him for a long moment and knew that while she could explain all she liked, he was simply too tired to fully comprehend it. Or, she realized, her blood running cold, it could be that in the aftermath of their horrible fight he'd decided that she wasn't worth the frustration and chosen to relinquish the field to Barrett.

"Would you prefer that I conjure up a dead relative and stay here with you?" she asked, her heart hammering and the dreadful school of mullet churning in her stomach. "I'm sure Barrett could quite easily find someone else to escort."

He studied her and in the depth of his eyes she could see the decision being carefully measured and weighed and, finally, made. Slowly, he shook his head. "Thank you, but no, Sera. I'm longing for a bath and a shave and a meal that isn't served cold on a tin plate. After that . . . I'm going to fall down and sleep for a week. There's no point in your missing the party. Go out and enjoy the evening."

"Are you sure?" she asked, unable to keep the quaver from her voice.

"I'm positive, Sera. Go be a princess."

He was handing her off to Barrett. At least he'd hesitated a second or two. But hoping to hear regret in his voice was hoping for too much. She nodded and bravely lifted her chin. "All right," she said. "If you insist."

He started to smile but it was lost in another deep, body-shuddering yawn. She backed away, wanting to promise herself that—tomorrow, when he was rested—she'd make another attempt to rekindle the fire they'd once had and she'd so foolishly stamped out. But she couldn't. The hurt in being set aside so absently, so indifferently, was bad enough. To invite a more deliberate and pointedly final ending was more than she thought she could bear with any sort of dignity at all.

Carden checked his watch once more and then tucked it away. He hadn't actually lied to her; he'd simply compressed a week of very necessary sleep into six good hours. It was all about timing and so far he was spot on. Now if the rest of the world would just cooperate with his grand strategy. Bypassing the gatekeepers at the front doors, he slipped in through the kitchen entrance, smiled and winked at the maid as he snagged a canapé from the tray on his way past, and headed for the central part of the house. As he'd hoped and planned, the stairway was empty and he bounded up the brightly lit steps. Too late for the public production of formal entries, too soon for the parade to the dining room. Just right for sliding unnoticed into the great whirl of glitter, conversation, music, dancing, and casually meandering guests.

Barrett was where they always stationed themselves at these sorts of affairs—standing, champagne glass in hand, beside a potted palm at the rear of the ballroom. A position that not at all coincidentally afforded one an unobstructed view of both the punch bowl and the dance floor and was close enough to both that one could easily swoop down on an unsuspecting morsel.

Sera, he noted, wasn't with him. He looked out over the dance floor and found John Aiden smiling down into the face of a laughing redhead. Sera was nowhere in sight. With decidedly mixed feelings about that, he made his way to the potted palm.

Barrett's gaze continued to sweep the dance floor as he said by way of a greeting, "What are you doing here, Carden? You didn't say anything about accepting Lady Hatcher's invitation."

"That's because I didn't make the decision until this afternoon," he replied, also watching the dancers. "Bad form, I know, but I'll apologize, and if I promise to be gone before another place setting has to be added to the table, Lady Hatcher will forgive me. Have you found the bastard yet?"

"No, but we're much closer than we were when you were underground. It's narrowed down to the south side of Newcastle. I think we'll have the rat cornered in his burrow sometime tomorrow. Do you see the brunette in the yellow gown just to the left of the violin section?"

Carden nodded. "A nice little tiff going with her escort. You might be in luck tonight after all. Where's Sera?"

"I don't know," Barrett answered with a shrug. "The last I saw her, she was over by the balcony doors."

He'd barely leaned in that direction when Barrett added, "In the interest of keeping you from creating an awkward situation and embarrassing her . . . she was talking with Lord Fraylee at the time."

Pulling up short, Carden turned squarely to his friend. "And you didn't step in to get her away from him?"

Barrett abandoned his study of the brunette to meet his gaze and drawl, "All they were doing was talking. She's allowed to do that, you know."

"Fraylee has fast hands," Carden reminded him. "And

Sera has absolutely no skill at beating them off."

Barrett smiled and cocked a brow. "Is that personal experience speaking?"

The taunt rolled off his shoulders; he was too focused on his plan to care about anything else. He smiled and observed, "You can be a real son of a bitch, Barrett."

"Agreed," his friend said, chuckling. "But it trumps stupid in any game. Please try not to plow over anyone on your way to find her. And be nice to her when you do. The bold statement of the red dress notwithstanding, for some reason—probably *you*—she's a bit fragile tonight."

Shows what a great lot you know, Carden silently retorted as he walked off. *Sera isn't made of fragile stuff.* The red dress. Well, he'd known this afternoon that he was taking a chance in sending her out with Barrett when she didn't want to go. Whether she'd chosen to wear the red gown in defiance or hoping the color would give her courage didn't matter. He'd bought her that particular gown because he'd intended to strip her out of it. And, by God, before the night was done, he was going to make that fantasy real. And bless Seraphina for, however unwittingly, doing her part.

He stepped out onto the balcony and quickly surveyed it from end to end. It was empty at the moment, although it wouldn't be for much longer—not if Barrett got to the brunette before her escort could make amends. He glanced out over the moonlit garden below but saw no movement, heard no sounds beyond those of the night.

Where was Sera? She had to be out here somewhere. If she'd been in the ballroom, he'd have known it the minute he'd walked in. Lord Fraylee wasn't the only one who recognized a beautiful woman when he saw one. Sera would have been surrounded by predators clamoring for a place on her dance card. No, she had to be out here.

He looked farther, out past the gardens toward the small lake, then down the sweep of stone stairs toward the ends

of the house. And then he smiled, knowing exactly where
Sera had gone.

Sera set her empty champagne glass on the floor beside
the chaise and closed her eyes, breathing in the heady
mixture of scents. Gardenia. Azalea. Hibiscus. Orange and
lemon. Rosemary, basil, and bay. The air was thick with
it, borne on warmth and moisture and soft moonlight,
wrapping around and lulling her senses. If only there were
a breeze to brush over her skin, to rustle through the lush
growth of palms and whisper her to sleep. And if she were
sleeping in Carden's arms . . . Paradise under glass.

"Found you," the breeze murmured lushly over her
nape.

She started and bolted to her feet, whirling around to
find him standing on the other side of the chaise. "Carden," she said, her voice barely louder than the frantic
hammering of her heart. "What are you doing here?"

"That," he replied, casually strolling around the end of
the chaise, watching her intently, "seems to be the standard opening remark of the evening."

Sera moistened her lips and tried to swallow. "And the
standard reply is . . . ?"

"It depends on who I'm talking to," he supplied quietly
as he slowly moved around the edge of her skirt, his gaze
holding hers. "If I'm cornered by Lady Hatcher, I'll say
that I simply couldn't resist attending one of her renowned
parties. I didn't feel the need to give Barrett any explanation at all."

Because Barrett knew why he was here. Her heart skittered as she realized that she was seeing Carden—for the
first time—at his rakehell best. And she'd thought that he
was good at kissing. Good Lord. He was an incredibly,
thrillingly dangerous man. "And how are you going to

answer me?" she asked, watching him over her shoulder and trying to breathe.

He stopped and smiled at her ever so leisurely, ever so deliberately. "I came here to find a woman to share my bed tonight."

Her blood heated and surged. "Then I'd suggest that the greenhouse isn't the best place for you to look," she replied, desperate to tamp down her soaring hope. "You'd have far wider prospects in the ballroom."

"I'm not interested in wider prospects. I've already narrowed them down to the only woman who will do." He cocked a brow. "Unless, of course, you're meeting someone here. Am I intruding?"

She'd been marked and served notice that he was going to take her unless she bolted for the door in the next two seconds. "No." She forced herself to swallow and add, "I came out here to escape the constant, empty prattling and the thinly veiled propositions."

"I've never believed in thin veils," he said softly, "unless it happens to be all a woman is wearing. Then it's rather exciting."

He started back around her, again easing along the line of her hem, his gaze still holding hers. She couldn't look away, didn't want to run. She'd never felt more alive, more in peril of being consumed. The mixture was more potent than the sweetest nectar.

"Do you know what else is exciting, Sera?" he asked, stopping squarely in front of her. He lifted his hand and gently trailed a single fingertip over the swell of her breast. "Making love," he said, watching her eyes, "in someone else's conservatory and then going back to the ball pretending that you didn't."

Her heart jolted. Here? Now? Was he truly serious? A primal heat ignited low in her abdomen and her knees weakened. "That would be a rather difficult illusion to maintain, wouldn't it?" she asked, trembling as he withdrew his hand. "You can pretend all you like, but I think rumpled gowns, wrinkled, muddy suits, and debris in your hair would tend to give you away."

One corner of his smile eased upward. "No rumples, no wrinkles, no mud or debris. Would you like me to show you how it's done?"

Yes, he was serious. Most serious. Oh, God, did she dare? *If you don't risk anything, you risk everything.*

"I can see the curiosity in your eyes," he whispered. "You're tempted, aren't you, Sera?"

There was no denying it. And she didn't want to. "Are there any terms of surrender?"

"Just one," he said, his smile fading and his eyes disappearing into the darkness. "The going out on the arms of my friends is over as of tonight."

"Will you be free to offer your arm to other women?" she countered.

"No, I'll be faithful to you."

For as long as he could, she silently added. For as long as she could be as boldly daring in private as she was primly proper in public. *Risk greatly, gain the world.*

"Well, Mr. Carden Reeves," she said, lifting her chin and placing her hands on her waist. "I don't think it's at all possible to make love in someone else's conservatory without rumpling a skirt. You're going to have to prove it to me."

He'd expected her to ask to make her surrender at home, but had come prepared to fully accept wherever she might choose to give it. That she was boldly willing to take up his challenge right here, right now . . . He was the luckiest damn man who had ever drawn a breath.

"You're not expecting slow and easy, are you?" he asked, grinning and unbuttoning his trousers.

Her smile was wide, her eyes bright. She laughed softly and arched a brow as her gaze dropped to his hands. "I gather I shouldn't."

Laughing with her, he pressed a quick kiss to her lips and then dropped down onto the chaise, saying, "Not this time, angel. Pretend you're going to step across a wide puddle."

"How wide?" she asked, lifting her skirts as he took the protective sheath from his pocket. Her lips parted as he covered himself and he heard her breath catch as full realization struck her.

"Second thoughts?" he asked, watching her face and gently taking her wrists. Beneath his fingertips, her pulse raced. "It's not too late to stop."

"Yes it is," she countered laughingly, her gaze meeting his and holding it. "But I've never . . ."

"Ridden?" he guessed, grinning and drawing her across him, adoring her easy honesty.

Settling her knees on either side of him, she teased, "And if I should fall off?"

"Not to worry," he promised. Sliding his hands under her voluminous skirts, up her silk pantalooned thighs and to her hips, he whispered, "I'll hold you tight. Trust me, angel."

Seraphina looked down at the moonlit angles of his face, into the dark wonder of his eyes, and knew to the center of her soul that Carden Reeves was the only man on earth who would ever possess her heart, the only man for whom she would risk all things. Releasing her skirts, she slipped her hands to his shoulders, and murmuring, "I wouldn't be here with you if I didn't," she leaned forward and languidly trailed the tip of her tongue along the curve of his lower lip.

Had they been anywhere else, he'd have let her tease and torture him forever. But in the constraints of the situation, he had no choice but to silently promise them another time and place, gently take her shoulders, and push her upright. Slipping his hands to her waist, holding her firmly, he shifted beneath her and positioned her hips, then arched up, drawing her closer, watching her eyes as he found the slit in her pantaloons and mated them in a single slow, smooth stroke.

She gasped quietly, her eyes widening and a joyous smile lifting the corners of her mouth as a tiny shudder rippled through her body. Her obvious surprise at the pleasure thrilled him, filling his heart and somehow intensifying the luscious heat of her welcome. Seraphina. His exotic, ever-so-innocent, boldly daring angel. There was no other woman like her; not in his past, not in all of Britain. And she was his for the taking. For the giving. For as long as he could make her gasp, smile, and shudder with delight.

"Ride, angel," he whispered, shifting his hips as he lifted hers. He brought them back together, hard and fast, straining upward, driving deep, and then instantly backing away. His breath caught as she seized control of the rhythm, drawing and joining, sending wave after glorious wave of sharply building sensation through him. His blood pounded hot into the center of his being and from deep in his throat he moaned, "God, yes, angel. Just like that."

Closing her eyes, Seraphina's world contracted into a breathlessly new, brilliant, and all-consuming awareness. The heat, the friction, the strength and fierce power of possession . . . Hers of him. His of her. It was wicked. It was holy. And it was everything and undeniable; riding the upward spiral of sweet fire was all that mattered, all the reality that existed in her universe. She fisted her skirts tighter and yielded to the pulsing rhythm of the blazing tide that engulfed her. It surged and swelled, relentlessly bearing her up, and she rose on the wave, gasping at the pureness of the pleasure, crying out at the desperate need that coiled through her and fueled the thundering heat searing her senses.

She was magnificent. Beautiful with unstinted passion, honest in her wanting. And he wouldn't deny her hunger and need for all the world. Tightening his hold on her hips, he drew her close, holding her there as he increased the force and cadence of their ride.

Seraphina moaned and surrendered to the thrumming flood of potent sensation, letting it carry her forward and ever up, until, gasping and molten, she was hurled into a glittering universe of wondrously shuddering, body- and soul-shattering completion.

He held his breath, straining to control the crest, trying to stave off his own attainment to prolong and savor the stunning depth of hers. She was just easing back to earth when he caught the movement at the edge of his vision and delay became impossible. He arched up, driving deep, filling her, and surrendered his own control.

"Carden!" she gasped, tightening around him again, arching into his possession.

Fulfillment came hard and swift, tearing a moan from the center of his soul and saturating his senses. He desperately struggled to breathe, to claw his way back to the reality of where they were, to clear his vision so he could save her from certain ruin.

"I feel compelled," she said softly, her breasts rising and falling in winded cadence as she smiled down at him, "to point out that my skirt is bunched in my hands. I'm afraid I've thoroughly rumpled it."

God, that he had an eternity to savor the wonder of her. But he didn't. "It takes time for wrinkles to set. And we're out of time."

"No," she said, settling her hips closer.

The friction was exquisite, the temptation every bit as compelling as the danger was looming. "Yes," he countered, quickly lifting her hips and shifting beneath her so that common sense had a fighting chance. "I can see the steps from here and Lord Fraylee is leading another man's wife down this way."

She squeaked and started and he caught her arms to

keep her from tumbling to the floor in her haste to leave him. Choking on his laughter, he crushed her lips with a quick kiss and then set her onto her feet even as he turned her toward the rear of the greenhouse and whispered, "Out the back door. Now! Hurry! I'll be right behind you."

Sera ran, her skirts high above her ankles, her heart in her throat, her legs wobbly and weak beneath her. The door opened without resistance and she dashed through it and into the cool night air beyond. A small copse of trees lay straight ahead and with her last measure of strength she dashed into the safety of the shadows. Her hands braced against the smooth bark of an elder, she gulped air and waited for her panic to pass and her nerves to settle. She was insane. Completely, utterly, certifiably insane. And she had never, ever in all of her days felt as wildly, wickedly, deliriously happy.

The giggle rolled up her throat and she quickly clamped a hand over her mouth, desperate to contain the sound. Another rolled in its wake, growing into a full-fledged peal of laugher. She covered her mouth with both hands and tried to choke it back. And failed. They came in waves, rippling through her body and bringing tears to her eyes. Good Lord, she couldn't breathe again. That realization went a small way toward sobering her, but not enough. She was still trying to contain her merriment and catch her breath when Carden loped into the shadows and caught her around the waist.

Whirling her about, he planted his back against the tree and pulled her hard against the length of him. She flung her arms around his neck and looked up at him, at his unholy grin, and then sagged into him, laughing silently as she buried her face in the front of his shirt.

"Are you all right, angel?" he asked, caressing her back and planting kisses to the top of her head, his heart hammering every bit as frantically as her own.

She looked up at him. "I hate corsets," she rasped, mercifully too breathless for her giggles to make any sound.

Carden drank in the unbridled joy in her eyes, reveled in the sweet satisfaction of holding her in his arms. There was no other woman on earth like her. God only knew why she'd accepted him as a lover but he wasn't going to risk losing her by looking for an answer any better than that.

"I'll have you out of that corset as soon as we get home," he promised. He cast a quick look at the house over his shoulder. Lady Luck had smiled on them so far, but he knew that with every second they tarried, they tried her patience.

"But right now," he said, giving her a quick kiss, "you have to get back to the dance before Barrett decides to play protector and come looking for you. I'd really rather get through the evening without my nose being smashed."

She didn't want to go back to the loud and too bright world of Lady Hatcher's ball, didn't want to step out of the wondrous circle of his arms. But it was the price to be paid before he could fulfill the promise of being together again. She nodded and eased away, letting her hands slide down the solid strength of his chest.

He caught them and lifted them to his lips. Brushing a kiss over the back of each, he smiled and released them, saying softly, "Turn around, angel, and let me fix your hairpins."

She obediently turned and let him set the loose pins, realizing that it was an intimacy no man had ever wanted of her before. Because Carden had no equal among all the men she'd ever known. And, no matter how long she lived or how hard she looked, she would never meet another man like him. "Carden? Thank you."

"For fixing your pins?"

"That, too. But mostly thank you for making me feel so . . ." Sated. Wild. Gloriously special. She sighed. "Wonderful."

He slipped his arms around her and nuzzled the curve of her shoulder. "So you'd be willing to do that again?"

"Oh, yes," she said, looking up at him over her shoulder. "Can we?"

His grin was wicked. "I'd be more than happy to oblige you."

"When?" she pressed, turning in his arms and threading her arms around his neck.

He laughed and gently set her from him. "Try not to look so deliciously blissful and find Barrett. Plead a headache or something, but get him to take you home. I'll meet you there."

Her eyes brightened. "In the conservatory?"

He must have sold his soul at some point and just didn't remember it. No, Sera couldn't be a gift from God. Only the devil would have given him the woman of his every hedonistic fantasy.

"I'll be waiting for you at the front door. I'm not promising any room in particular." He grinned and added, "Although I can think of several distinct advantages to a feather bed and satin sheets."

She stretched up on her toes and pressed a soft, lingering kiss to his lips. The slow touch, the luscious taste of her, reignited the heat of desire.

"Go, Sera," he said, firmly setting her away and holding her at arm's length. "Now. If you don't, I'm going to lay you down right here."

"As threats go," she observed, leaving him, "that's not much of one, Carden Reeves."

He laughed and Sera walked on, back toward the bright lights of Hatcher House. It didn't matter if he loved her, she decided as she went. He made her happy with whatever portion of his heart he could give. It was enough. She was going to cherish every moment she had with him. And when the joy stopped shining in his eyes, she'd walk away with the most precious memories any woman ever possessed.

CHAPTER 19

She stopped when she saw the two of them standing together beside the potted palms. Singly, either one of them wouldn't have been daunting, but Barrett and Aiden together would require a great deal of mental agility and she wasn't quite sure she was up to the challenge. Whatever chance she might have had of slipping away unnoticed was dashed when John Aiden turned, saw her, and grinned.

"Give me strength," she whispered past a brave smile as she made her way to them.

"Seraphina!" Aiden exclaimed. "Every time I see you, you look more beautiful than the last. You're positively glowing this evening." He looked over his shoulder. "Isn't she glowing, Barrett?"

"She is, indeed," he answered, struggling to control his smile. "Moonlight walks in the garden seem to agree with her."

She could feel the heat fanning over her cheeks and realized too late that she should have given the pretending-that-you-haven't part a bit more consideration than she had. There appeared to be far more involved in the façade than smooth skirts and perfectly coiffed hair. Whatever that aspect was, she clearly wasn't executing it very well at all. They both knew. She could feel it.

"Did Carden set a time for having you home?" Barrett asked, his smile breaking free.

She blinked, not certain how to respond, not sure just how far the pretending extended. Was she supposed to claim that she didn't know Carden was there? Or that they'd accidentally met in the greenhouse and done nothing more than exchange pleasantries about the weather? Was she supposed to give up the pretense at the first suggestion that it was a failure?

She hadn't thought to ask questions and Carden had assumed that pleading a headache would be sufficient. Looking back and forth between them, she confessed, "I honestly don't know what I'm supposed to say."

The two men exchanged a quick look and then Aiden took a tiny step back and gestured for Barrett to proceed.

"Seraphina," he began, "I know Carden. I don't always approve of the things he does, but most of the time I understand why he does them. He would tell it differently, but the fundamental truth is that he came here this evening because he couldn't bear the thought of your being out with anyone but him. And, most importantly, to put an end to it in his own inimitable fashion. He would have seen to the resolution the night Aiden escorted you out, but the tunnel business interfered. I just hope that you had the good sense to make some demands of him while you two were in the gardens setting matters straight."

"Demands," Aiden added quietly, "of a non . . . romantic nature."

Sera considered them, realizing the full ramifications of having male friends. They didn't pretend ignorance or that physical attraction didn't exist. They minced only what words they had to in order to preserve the essence of her female sensibility. And all they asked of her in return was that she trust them and approach matters in the same way.

"Seraphina," Aiden pressed, "did he at least promise you fidelity?"

She nodded and then bravely admitted to her single fear. "Not that I expect it to last overly long."

"I think he might surprise us," Barrett offered, looking decidedly pleased.

"As his friends and yours," Aiden said, "we'll do all that's in our power to see that he doesn't throw away the best thing that will ever happen to him."

Barrett nodded in silent affirmation.

"Thank you both," she whispered, deeply touched and knowing that, male or female, she'd never in her life had such good-hearted and devoted allies.

Barrett glanced toward the main entry and a mischievous grin stole over his face. "What do you suppose he'd do if I didn't get you home until the wee hours of the morning?"

"Or, better yet, noon tomorrow," Aiden posed, joining the game.

"Carden should be the least of your concerns," she counseled, putting a quick end to their sport. "I'm the one who will do injury if I'm not spirited away from here in the next few minutes."

"Our coach awaits us," Barrett said, laughing softly and offering his arm. "Shall we go make some excuse to our hostess?"

"Don't plead a headache, Sera," Aiden suggested. "No one is going to believe it. You look entirely too . . ." He smiled at her and winked. "Glowing."

She laughed even as the blush swept over her cheeks and Barrett led her off to find Lady Hatcher.

It was an impulsive decision and not without potential consequences, but Carden leaned forward and rapped the end of his walking stick against the wall of the carriage anyway. As it rolled to a stop alongside the queue of other waiting vehicles, he opened the door and vaulted onto the roadway.

Sera saw him and the brilliance of her smile evaporated what few qualms he'd had. Barrett on the other hand . . . His step faltered and, judging by the quick frown and the speed at which he turned Sera away and spoke to her . . . No, Barrett wasn't pleased with the change in plans; he was focusing on the possible repercussions.

With Seraphina's back to him, he couldn't see her face as she looked up at his friend, couldn't gauge what she was thinking, what she might be saying. But when Barrett scowled, cocked a brow, and then sighed, Carden knew that she'd won the contest. He'd never had a doubt.

Glaring the entire way, Barrett brought Sera to him.

"What a timely and convenient coincidence it is for us to meet like this," Carden said, offering Sera his hand. "Since Sera and I are going to the same place, it would be ridiculous to have two carriages make the trip. I'll see her home, Barrett."

Barrett didn't say anything and Sera filled the taut silence, saying graciously, "Thank you for the lovely evening, Barrett. I do hope you'll go back and enjoy what remains of the party."

Summoning some grace of his own, Barrett managed to sound almost genial when he replied, "It was my pleasure, Seraphina. And yes, I will."

Handing Sera into the dimly lit carriage, Carden knew that Barrett was biting his tongue and waiting. He closed the door and stepped off to the side, half expecting his friend to swing a fist at him.

Instead, Barrett leaned close and in a low growl announced, "You and I are going to talk tomorrow."

Knowing precisely what the concerns were, Carden nodded and quietly replied, "How is early in the afternoon for you? In your guest room as I'm putting away my things?"

It took several long seconds, but Barrett finally eased back, having apparently recognized the proposal as a serious one. "That's a capital idea," he said, still openly assessing him. "The best you've had in quite some time. Congratulations. And thank you."

"I'm not doing it for you or me," he pointed out, reaching for the door handle. "And if I could think of any other way, I wouldn't be doing it at all. I'll see you tomorrow afternoon."

With that he opened the door, climbed inside, and promptly closed the world away. As much as he wanted to drop down on the seat beside Sera and take her into his arms, he listened to the voice of reason and chose the opposite seat. There were issues they needed to discuss, hard realities that had to be faced and accepted, and he wanted them disposed of before they reached Haven House. None of it was coming with them into his bedroom.

As the carriage began to roll, she settled back into the cushions and slowly moistened her lower lip with the tip of her tongue. "I thought you were going to wait for me at the front door."

His loins tightening, he gave her what was becoming a many-layered truth. "I decided that I couldn't wait that long to see you again."

"Barrett says we're courting scandal in being seen leaving together, that a lady never leaves a social affair with a gentleman other than her escort without inviting tawdry speculation."

"He's absolutely right," he admitted. "Does it bother you?"

Sera considered him, knowing that her initial instincts were correct; he didn't intend for the ride home together to be another breathless, mindless seductive interlude. This time was for taking care of the more businesslike aspects of their relationship. And since it had to be done sooner or later . . . Carden was right; sooner was probably better.

"As I pointed out to to Barrett on the walkway . . . Whatever scandal arises from my being seen leaving in your carriage as opposed to his will be completely forgotten in the scandal that erupts when they learn that my husband is still alive. That scandal will be completely unforgettable."

"Yes, it will, and there's nothing we can do short of murder to avert it. But, for the sake of the girls, we'll do everything we can to temper it. To that end, I considered having you all move to Honoria's house, but decided that I didn't much care for the notion of Honoria as a constant chaperone."

"Thank you."

"So the next-best solution," he went on crisply, "is for you and the girls to stay in the house with the staff and I'll go live with Barrett until I can find another townhouse of my own."

Sera arched a brow. "And allow the gossip mongers to drive you from your own home? That hardly seems fair or right."

He seemed to mull over the notion and then countered, "Or until we can buy or build you your own house."

Her own house. It was a notion she'd never contemplated. Largely, she knew, because it had never been even the remotest of possibilities. "That's what men do for their mistresses," she mused aloud.

"Mistresses are dependent on their lovers for financial support," he clarified, his voice pensive. "You're a woman of independent mind and means, Sera. If you want a dozen residences, you can afford them. You don't need me for anything."

"Yes I do, Carden."

"For what?" he quietly taunted. "For what do you need me? Name one thing."

She needed to see his smile, to hear the rich timbre of

his voice and the heady joy of his laughter. She needed to see him with his shirtsleeves rolled up and holding a glass of brandy in his hand, to know that no matter what happened he would keep everyone safe. She needed the way she felt when he made indecent proposals, when he touched her, when he looked deep into her eyes and dared her to be wanton. She needed, with all of her heart, to love him and hope that he would come to love her in return.

And she knew that that most fragile hope would be crushed and all of it would be lost if she answered him honestly. It was the one risk she wasn't willing to take. But he did deserve an answer. If for no other reason than to spite him for thinking she'd fail in her search to find one for him.

His heart tripped. The light in her eyes . . . the sweet, deliciously predatory shadow of her smile . . . He watched her slide forward on her seat, his blood surging hot and wild. Her hands went to his knees and he instantly, fully hardened.

"Do you want me to tell the driver to take the long way home?" he asked, his heart pounding furiously as she moved into the space between his legs.

Her hands slid slowly up his thighs. "The advantage in that being?"

Setting aside his walking stick, he took her wrists in hand and gently stopped the progress of her magnificent torture. "I'll have time to get you out of your hoops."

She leaned forward and pressed a lingering kiss to the hollow beneath his ear. "And the advantage of taking the shorter way?" she whispered.

That he could last that long. Why the hell had he given her a choice? "We'll have a little more time than we had in Lady Hatcher's greenhouse. But not much."

She grazed his cheek with a kiss as she drew away, easing her wrists from his grasp as she settled on the edge of her seat. Her breasts slowly rising and falling, she smiled at him knowingly. "You're a libertine, Carden Reeves."

"I know. And you're a thoroughly wanton angel. The short way or the long?"

"The short," she declared, her smile delightfully wicked as she gathered up her hems. She paused and arched a brow. "Unless, of course, it will make the feather bed and the satin sheets less enjoyable when we get there."

"It won't," he assured her, unbuttoning with one hand as he reached into his coat pocket with the other. "There are distinct advantages to quick preludes."

"What kind of advantages?"

"With the sharper edges of hunger sated, you have the patience to go slowly enough to appreciate and savor every pleasurable sensation."

Slowly enough to savor. She smiled as Carden settled his back against the wall of the carriage and stretched his legs along the seat as best he could. He was covering himself with the protective sheath when she reached up and snuffed out the carriage light.

"Do rumples and wrinkles matter any more tonight?" she asked into the darkness as she eased across the space that separated them.

"No." His hands gently grasped her wrists, drawing her closer, holding her steady as the carriage gently rocked on its springs and she slid her leg across him.

"Good," she whispered as his hands slipped beneath her skirts and skimmed upward to her hips. When he shifted and tried to draw her down, she switched her balance to the foot she'd left on the floor and resisted his effort.

"Because," she added, smiling at his scowl, "I think I'd very much like to rumple you. And savor every moment of it."

"Sera . . ."

A hint of willingness to play to the game. A hint of wariness, too. "I can see distinct advantages in being the one who's riding," she murmured, ever so slowly lowering herself onto him.

The fullness and heat were heady; the deliberate friction lusciously exquisite. And the unpredictable movement of the carriage made it all that much more breathtakingly provocative. Carden's hands tightened on her hips and she heard him drag a ragged breath into his lungs as he arched up, trying to draw them fully together. She held back, determined to slow her spiraling ascent this time, wanting to make the pleasure last for as long as she could.

If ever there was a woman who could drive a man mad with pure wanting . . . She was so right, so perfect in every way that mattered. Halfway simply wasn't possible with her. And neither was any sort of detachment or patience. Sera was an all-or-nothing woman. And he wanted all of her. *Now.* His body desperately aching and straining, his mind frantically raced through the ways in which he could seize control of the moment from her. But none of them were subtle or the least bit gentle and he couldn't hurt her. He wouldn't even risk it. Not now. Not ever.

"Oh, God. Sera."

She heard the warning of frustration.

"Please don't deny me, Sera."

Undone, she granted them both mercy, surrendering her mind, body, and soul to the surging sweep of ecstasy, to the joy of loving Carden Reeves.

Carden leaned his head back against the wall of the coach, closed his eyes, and sighed in contentment. Gerald Treadwell had walked away from this woman? The man didn't have a brain in his head or blood in his veins. Truly a case of one man's folly being another man's gem. Or something like that. It was hard to think beyond the amazement of how quickly and deeply Sera could satisfy him. Damn hard to think at all, actually. She'd melted his bones and turned his muscles to jelly. He'd never felt more drained or alive in his life.

She shifted and he tightened his hold on her hips. "Where are you going, angel?"

"The carriage has stopped," she answered, clearly concerned.

He opened his eyes and smiled at her. "So?"

"If your driver climbs down to open the door . . ."

He was about to assure her that his driver knew better than to open the door, but bit the words back, realizing that any mention of the understanding they had . . . No, he didn't want the specter of other women sharing the carriage with them. He didn't want Sera thinking about his past in specific terms, never wanted her to wonder how she compared to the others. Not that making a comparison was even remotely possible.

"All right," he said, releasing his hold and helping her back to her feet. "We'll observe just a bit of caution for a change."

She settled on the opposite seat and watched him remove the sheath and button his trousers, thinking that the recklessness of their evening was largely an illusion. Yes, they'd risked scandal in being caught, but Carden had seen to it that the risks were minimal. And each time they'd come together, he'd put the sheath between them, protecting them both from a multitude of complications. Carden Reeves took chances, but not without careful calculation. She found that vastly reassuring.

There was no denying, however, that Carden's conscientious use of the sheath saddened her, too. That the regret sprang from a well utterly foreign to her awareness made the feeling all the more troubling. She'd always considered the sheepskin barrier a godsend, had always insisted that Gerald wear one. But with Carden there wasn't the usual comfort of knowing that it stood between her and irrevocable consequences. She didn't want to be protected; she wanted children.

She closed her eyes and willed the sharp pang to pass, reminded herself that children should come from promises of forever. Carden didn't love her and hadn't promised her anything more than an affair. There was no forever with him. She'd known and accepted that reality when she'd stepped into his arms. And she had to accept that it was for the best that there would be no children, either.

She felt him move, heard the door latch click open, and found the courage to open her eyes and take his hand, to smile and pretend that her heart wasn't aching.

Something was niggling at her; he'd caught a glimpse of the ephemeral shadow in her eyes as they'd come into the house. It flickered there again as they reached the top of the stairs and started down the hall. Was she having second thoughts about going to his room? he wondered. About actually making love with him in a bed? Good God Almighty, why? They'd already . . . Fully clothed.

That was the problem, he decided. She was anticipating—no, dreading—the deliberate removal of their clothing, the peeling away of all the layers and letting him see her naked. And of her seeing him naked, too. He smiled, knowing that it wasn't going to be the awkward process she thought it would be and that by the time he had them both stripped she wasn't going to feel anything but overjoyed at the freedom.

"Let me peek in on the girls," she whispered, pulling her hand from his and stopping at the girls' bedroom door.

"For God's sakes, don't wake them," he warned even as she turned the knob and pushed it open a crack. He held his breath, willing her to look quickly and then close it.

Instead she pushed it wider and started forward. "Where are you going?" he whispered, alarmed and catching her arm to stay her.

"Mrs. Miller has fallen out of bed," she explained softly over her shoulder. "If Camille wakes up and can't find her doll, she'll cry."

"If you wake her, *I'll* cry."

Her smile could have lit a ballroom. "Wait for me here."

Hell, he wasn't about to go anywhere without her. He held his breath again as he watched her silently glide across the room, pick up the doll and tuck it back under the covers beside the soundly sleeping Camille. The sigh of relief caught in his lungs when she bent down and feathered a kiss to the top of his littlest niece's curly head. For a second there was only the sensation of tightness, of a breath held unnaturally, and then it twisted into a palpable ache that spread through him like liquid fire, igniting a ravenous, demanding need.

She moved silently back toward him, smiling softly, unwittingly fueling the fire already consuming his every intention for patience and slow seduction.

"There," she said quietly, easing the door closed. "That didn't take long, did it?"

"An eternity," he confessed, sweeping her up into his arms and starting down the hall. Laughing, she draped her arms around his neck and stretched up—intending, he knew—to kiss his cheek. He turned his head and met her lips with his own. The touch was soft and tender and her sigh tore like a gale wind through what was left of his resolve.

Kissing her deeply, greedily, he blindly opened the door to his room and carried her inside. He was kicking the door closed behind them when the back of his head exploded with a searing, world-obliterating pain.

CHAPTER 20

His groan ripped through her in the same instant that she felt the strength, the spark, in him go out. As he crumpled to his knees, Sera desperately rolled out of his arms, frantically scrambling to catch him, trying to break the last of his fall.

"Carden!" she sobbed as his weight overwhelmed her and drove her down and back. "Oh, God. Carden! What's happened?" she cried, wrapping her arms around his shoulders as they collapsed to the floor together.

The pain encircled her upper arm, hard and biting, and she *knew*. The scream caught in her throat, lodged behind her thundering heart, as she was hauled, struggling and gasping, from beneath Carden's still form.

"Hello, Feenie," he snarled, dropping her on her feet and then yanking her around to face him. "Remember me? Gerald? Your husband?"

She had never forgotten him; how he looked, how his hands bruised her flesh. How afraid he'd always made her feel. What he smelled like when he'd been drinking. The memories were all there, still the same. Except now she hated him with every fiber of her being.

"Aren't you going to ask why I'm here?"

She moistened her lips, drew a steadying breath, and answered evenly, "I already know."

"Good. That will save us some time." His grip on her arm tightened. "Where are your pictures?"

She wouldn't cower, wouldn't cry out or beg him to stop hurting her. Never again would she give him that satisfaction. Never. "In the conservatory," she answered through clenched teeth. "In oil pouches in a wooden crate at the foot of the chaise."

"Then let's be about getting them," he snapped, flinging her toward the door. "Go."

She stumbled and caught her hem, tearing the fabric and scattering beads as she staggered into the solid oak panel. Catching herself with her hands, she instantly pushed herself back and squarely onto her feet. She wrenched open the door, then stepped aside and whirled on him. "I just told you where they are," she declared. "You don't need me to retrieve them for you. Just take them and leave."

He laughed, darkly, unevenly, and so quietly that her skin crawled. "I'm not going anywhere without the goose that lays the golden eggs."

Suppressing a shudder, she held her ground. "And I'm not leaving this room with you."

He lifted his arm and her blood ran cold. "Your compliance, Feenie," he said blithely, pointing the muzzle of the pistol at Carden's head, "or I'll put a bullet in your lover's brain."

Shaking, chilled to the marrow, Sera tried desperately to get her mind to work, to see a way out that protected Carden. A shot would make noise and rouse the house. A sane man wouldn't risk it, but she wasn't sure that Gerald would put sanity before spite and vengeance. He might shoot Carden whatever choice she made. Unless he didn't have the time.

She bolted, sprinting for the stairs, past the girls' room, her hems up around her knees. Only a vile curse and the heavy thud of footfalls came in her wake. Choking back a sob of relief, she raced on and started down the stairs, struggling to breathe in the confines of her corset, her gaze fixed on the foyer table below, on Carden's walking stick.

Gerald was closing on her. Even over the pounding of her heart, the rasping of her breath, she could hear him, feel him, and smell him. The impact came just as she reached the last step, the momentum propelling her off her feet, forward and down.

She heard herself cry out and then perception slid into a haze. A crash, a jarring pain rippling through her body, the breath leaving her lungs in a single hard rush, the panic of not being able to drag another one in. Her brain screamed that breathing didn't matter, that she'd broken free of Gerald's hand and that she had to move while she could.

Her gaze raked the floor even as she brought her hands under her shoulders and pushed herself up. The table had been overturned. Gerald was trying to right and raise himself. Wood splinters, flowers, china shards, water, the little silver tray. And by the front door, Carden's walking stick. She scrambled toward it, her skirts and hoops tangling with her legs, her desperation catching high in her throat.

The tray crashed and china crunched and Sera lunged for the stick. She caught it with the barest tips of her fingers and dragged it into her grasp just as her ankle burned with the pain of Gerald's furious grip. In the vaguest way she realized she was being hauled back from the door, that she was being flipped from her stomach onto her back. The larger, clearer reality was the hiss of the metal as she cleared the sword from the scabbard.

Kicking at him, she sat upright and swung the blade, not caring what part of him she struck as long as he paid a price in pain. The blade whirled as it sliced air and hummed as it sheared through the cloth of his jacket. It sang as it opened the flesh of his shoulder.

He swore and jumped back, releasing her ankle, and

Sera swung the blade again, madly determined to drive him further. It whirled and sang again and the lower half of his pant legs sagged, his flesh parted and the white of bone flushed red.

He roared and she brought the blade back, preparing to strike again. But he didn't back away; he stepped to her and she screamed in rage as his hand clamped around her wrist. She kicked at him, tried to pull herself from his grasp and accomplished nothing. He squeezed her wrist and turned it until her hand opened and her salvation clattered to the floor.

And then she was flying up, her wrist, elbow, and shoulder on fire, the foyer a blur. When the motion stopped and the bright edge of pain faded, her back was pinned to his hip and chest, held there with the iron band of his arm encircling her waist. Ahead of her, filling the passage that led to the rear of the house, was Sawyer. And Monroe. Both wide-eyed, gaping, and nightshirted.

She twisted and kicked, trying to break free, and she saw quick flashes of white as Carden's men started forward. The cold pressure of the muzzle at her temple froze them all.

"Thank you," Gerald sneered. "Gentlemen, you will move aside and let us pass." He bent to press his chin against the side of her head. "And if you fight me in the slightest way, I'm going to put a bullet into the old man. Or maybe the other one. Do you have a preference, Feenie?"

Gulping what air the arm around her midsection allowed, she met Sawyer's furious, helpless gaze. "Do what he says," she instructed. "And when we're past, go see to Carden."

"Ah, ever the self-sacrificing lover," Gerald growled in her ear. Her stomach roiled at the stench of alcohol. "Gentlemen," he barked, pushing her forward. "Move to your right. Keep to the wall and your hands up where I can see them."

"Take me in the lady's place," Sawyer offered.

"Move!" Gerald snarled.

Sawyer and Monroe obeyed, slowly, reluctantly, and Gerald half pushed, half carried her into the vacated opening, turning, always keeping the muzzle to her head and her body between him and Carden's men.

A movement on the stairs caught her eye and she looked up and past Sawyer and Monroe. And into the terrified gazes of Amanda, Beatrice, and Camille. Behind them stood Anne, her hand over her mouth and her face as white as her night rail.

Sera's heart wrenched. She couldn't reassure them; to do so would draw Gerald's attention to them and put them at risk. And so she smiled for them bravely and did what she could to keep his awareness sharply focused on herself. "Can you not move any faster?" she snipped. "I swear to God you're the slowest kidnapper in the history of crime."

Mercifully, he reacted as she'd hoped he would. "Do anything stupid, gentlemen," he snarled, "and I'll kill her. Or you." And then he spun around, dropped her fully to her feet, and shoved her ahead of him. "Get your sweet ass to the conservatory and don't even *think* about trying to get away."

She went, grateful to lead him away from the girls, to give Sawyer and Monroe the chance to reach Carden and tend his wound. Oh, dear God, please, please let Carden be all right.

"Gather it all up and be quick about it," Gerald snapped, shoving her toward the chaise. Her foot caught again in her hems. More fabric tore, more beads spilled. Catching herself, Sera hiked the tattered remnants of her skirt and went where she was supposed to go, did as she was ordered.

Scooping up the paintings she'd begun to sort, she haphazardly stacked them and dropped them into the top of the opened crate, atop the oilskin pouches that held the rest of her collection. A flicker of white by the door caught her eye as she worked and her heart went into her throat and tears welled in her eyes. *No, not me,* she silently railed. *Don't worry or risk for me. Take care of Carden.*

Afraid that Gerald might also see their follower, she ignored the pain in her wrist and hefted up the crate, boldly, defiantly lifted her chin, pinned his obsidian gaze, and asked, "And where would you like this hauled, my dear husband?"

"Out the back," he snarled, motioning with his head to the rear door of the greenhouse, the muzzle of the pistol trained on her chest. "There's a hack waiting in the alleyway. Go straight there and don't drop anything along the way."

More beads spilling around her and the wormy old wood of the crate crumbling in the palms of her hands, Sera complied, kicking her skirts ahead of her to keep from tripping over the uneven hem. She half hoped the crate would fall apart in the center of the yard—just for the satisfaction of making Gerald fear for the safety of his precious damn golden eggs. The bastard. If it did fall apart . . . Even if it was the last thing she ever did, she was going to pick up a sliver of wood and drive it through his black heart.

But the crate held and she made her way across the yard without a chance of escape or vengeance. The gate at the rear was open and beyond it, sitting in the alley just as he said, was a rented hack. Its door stood open as well and she didn't wait to be pushed or told what to do. She placed the crate on the floor and slid it inside, her gaze darting from one end of the alley to the other, looking for a place to go, someone who might come to help if she screamed.

It wasn't a heavy blow, but her head snapped forward just the same. And then snapped even more violently back. Her scalp burned and her eyes watered as he twisted his fist tighter in her hair. "Get in."

She didn't have a choice, didn't have to make any more effort than to lift her skirts. Gerald did the rest, hefting her up by her hair and her arm and shoving her forward. She fell across the crate as he released her and she scrambled up to pack herself into the farthest corner of the rear-facing seat. The door slammed shut and the carriage shot forward, pitching Gerald into the opposite cushions. He swore and righted himself. Glaring at her in the darkness, he laid the hand holding the pistol in his lap and reached behind him with the other.

A more than half-full bottle appeared in the next instant, the glass glinting in the moonlight, the contents dark and sloshing. Whisky, she knew, watching him pull the cork with his teeth. He spat it aside and said, "You're going to pay for cutting me, Feenie. You're going to wish you had never laid eyes on me."

She'd wished that years ago but knew better than to say so, to say anything. If she was quiet, if she didn't look at him, didn't challenge him in any way, he'd focus on the whisky and forget she was there. And when the bottle was empty, he would close his eyes and forget the world was there. It was then that she could slip away. She'd done it hundreds of times. She knew how to be patient, how to survive.

The inside of his head was white-hot but the disgustingly vile smell drew him through the pain and forced open his eyes. "Jesus," he growled, his voice raspy as he roughly pushed away the hand holding the nasty little vial.

"No, it's Sawyer, sir."

He knew that, but he was too busy collecting his wits

to frame words. He was in his room, on the floor, the back of his head pounding like holy hell. The last thing he remembered was coming through the door with Sera in . . . His stomach clenched and his blood turned to ice.

"Please do not attempt to rise just yet, sir," Sawyer protested, pushing his shoulder back toward the floor. "You have been dealt a heavy blow to the back of your head."

"I know that," he retorted through bared teeth, shoving Sawyer's hand aside and struggling to sit up. "Where's Sera?"

Sawyer slipped an arm around his shoulders and assisted in the effort.

"Dammit, Sawyer," he demanded as his butler helped him gain his feet. The world swayed and he grabbed the front of Sawyer's nightshirt to still the two of them. "Where's Sera?"

"She has been taken, sir. By force."

His stomach churned and heaved. He stared into Sawyer's face, focusing on the man's eyes, on what he had to know to get Sera back. "Keep talking."

"I immediately despatched Monroe to find Mr. Stanbridge and Mr. Terrell. Assuming that they were still at Lady Hatcher's, they should be here momentarily, sir."

He didn't give a damn about any of that. He gave Sawyer a shake. "Who took her? Did you see him?"

"Very clearly, sir. A tall man, rather thin for being the brutish type. A Yank, clearly of their most disreputable class."

"Gerald," he muttered, his fists tightening in Sawyer's nightdress.

"There were no introductions, sir."

"Was Sera all right when he took her out of here?"

"She was most distressed over your situation, sir."

God Almighty, there were times when he wanted to strangle the man. Widening his stance, strengthening his balance, Carden pulled him closer. "Sawyer, forget you're a goddamn butler and tell me straight out. Had he hurt her?"

"Physically, sir, she appeared to have been knocked about a bit, but she was still quite capable of struggling against him."

She hadn't been carried out. She'd been whole and sound enough to resist. The flood of relief sent the world reeling again. He released Sawyer and staggered to the armoire, grabbed the top edge and let it anchor him.

"Her willingness to do so, however," Sawyer went on, "was tempered appreciably when he brandished his pistol and threatened to shoot Monroe or myself. I am sure he would have included Cook and Mrs. Blaylock as well were it not their night out, sir. The Yank was quite indiscriminate in whom he threatened."

Oh, God. Sera. He knew the look that had been in her eyes as she'd faced the muzzle of that pistol. She had been afraid, but determined to be brave. He knew Sera. And he hadn't been there for her. She'd faced it all alone. She was still alone.

"What the hell happened down in the foyer?"

Aiden. A small wave of relief came at the sound of his voice. His question, his obvious agitation, tempered it with apprehension. Carden turned his entire body to look at him. "The foyer?"

"It was the crashing of the table that awakened me," Sawyer supplied hastily. "Monroe as well. When we arrived in the foyer, your lady was in the clutches of her assailant. It is purely speculation on my part, sir, but I believe that prior to that unfortunate turn of events, she attempted to run the Yank through with your walking stick sword."

"Judging by the amount of blood," Aiden added, stepping around him to gingerly examine the back of his head, "she slashed him good before he took it away from her. You have a helluva knot, but you'll live."

He'd already surmised as much. Watching Sawyer's eyes, he pressed, "Are you sure she wasn't cut?"

"I saw no indications of such an injury, sir. Her assailant was the one bleeding."

Thank God. And good for Sera.

"Although, I must say, sir, that he seemed to be largely unaware of it. I detected the unmistakable odor of alcohol about his person."

Yes, drunks didn't feel much pain. He was going to let the bastard sober up before he exacted justice. And when that was done, he was going to show Sera how to use the sword effectively. The next time she needed to defend herself, one clean swipe would be all she would need. But he had to find her first and, with every second that passed, she was farther and farther away. Letting go of the armoire, he took a broad stance and squared his shoulders. His head throbbed, his teeth and eyes ached, but he focused beyond it all. On what it was going to take to find Sera.

"I have one man down and unconscious and another missing."

He turned to see Barrett striding into the room, his eyes hard and lethal. Another small wave of relief stole over him. This one, though, came with confusion. "Man?" Carden asked.

"I didn't know you were back from the tunnel until Seraphina mentioned it on the way to Lady Hatcher's this evening," he explained, stripping off his evening gloves. "I hadn't pulled my men, Carden. They were still on post. Obviously one ran afoul of Gerald Treadwell. Monroe's tending him. I have no idea where the other one is."

Sawyer cleared his throat. "Might he be a decidedly small, wiry, furtive fellow, sir?"

All three of them turned to the butler, but it was Barrett

who asked, "Have you seen him in the last hour or so?"

"The Yank took Mr. Reeves's lady out through the conservatory and then the service gate. Monroe had already been despatched for help and I followed after them, hoping that I might see an opportunity to effect her rescue. Unfortunately, I did not and she was forced into a waiting hack which was quickly driven away.

"The fellow I described slipped from the bushes some distance down the alleyway and dashed after it on foot. I assumed it was an urchin attempting to catch a free ride. I would be immeasurably relieved to know that I assumed incorrectly, sir."

"You did, Sawyer," Barrett assured him with a clap on the shoulder that practically drove the man's knees to the floor. "Joseph O'Mara is one of my best men, Carden. He won't lose her and he'll send word as soon as Gerald Treadwell lights somewhere with her."

"And I'm supposed to sit here and wait until then?" he asked incredulously. Sera was being held at gunpoint and he was supposed to twiddle his thumbs?

"There's nothing else you can do," Barrett countered. "And getting angry with me about it isn't going to make things move one bit faster."

"Sorry," Carden muttered, swallowing down his frustration and his heart.

Sawyer cleared his throat again. "Your pardon, sir. But there is one matter that needs your attention as soon as you are able to address it."

Carden painfully cocked a brow and his man continued, "Monroe and I were not the only members of the household awakened by the scuffle in the foyer, sir. Your nieces were witnesses to your lady being rather brutally hauled away."

Something else for which Gerald Treadwell was going to pay dearly. "Where are they?"

"In their room with Anne, sir."

"I'll go talk to them," he said, starting in that direction despite not having any idea of precisely what it was that he was going to say when he got there. Aside from apologizing and begging their forgiveness for not being there to protect Sera.

"Sir?"

He turned back to find Sawyer at the foot of the bed, carefully holding a silver-plated dueling pistol in his hand.

"I confiscated this from Miss Beatrice," the man explained, bringing it to him. "Do be careful. It is loaded."

Carden expelled a long, hard breath and tried to calm his skittering pulse. "Where did she get it?"

"I have no idea, sir. I was returning from the garden, on my way up here to ascertain your injuries, when I encountered Miss Beatrice in the dining room. I have not the slightest doubt that she intended to find and shoot your lady's attacker."

Oh, sweet Jesus in Heaven. Bea? For crissake, she was only seven years old!

Aiden shook his head. "Don't ever stint that girl's allowance."

"If you have no further questions of me, sir," Sawyer said, "I shall see to preparing a cold compress for your head wound. If there is anything I can do to assure the speedy and safe return of your lady, you need but ask, sir."

As the man started away, something in the deepest recesses of Carden's abused brain softly clicked. "Sawyer?" he called, stopping his butler. "I do have one more question. When did Sera become 'my lady'?"

"The day she walked into this house, sir."

With a brief bow, Sawyer walked off, leaving him standing there, swaying on his feet and struggling to pull a full breath into his lungs.

"Carden?" Aiden called quietly. "We *will* get her back."

It was a possibility. But only one among many and he knew it. Sera had warned him of her husband's brutality, of his ruthless determination to achieve his ends. Carden hadn't believed her, had dismissed her concerns and assured her that everything would be all right. And he'd been wrong; as wrong and as blind as a man could be. Sera had known what danger stalked her. She had feared for her life and now—too late—he did, too.

He looked between his two friends. "Alive? Unharmed?" They said nothing and in the silence, he added, "Don't offer me hope you can't guarantee."

He handed the pistol to Aiden and then walked away, saying, "Don't unload it. I'll be taking it with me when we hear from O'Mara. I'll meet you both in my study when I'm done talking to the girls. Interrupt if word comes."

Pausing in the doorway, he turned back and considered the two of them again. He owed them honesty. "You both need to know . . . When I find Gerald Treadwell, I'm going to kill him. If you don't want to be a party to that, I understand."

They each met his gaze in turn and, although neither said a word, he saw their commitment in their eyes, their willingness to stand with him through it all and to the end. With a nod of thanks that became an involuntary wince, he left them, heading to comfort his nieces as best he could.

CHAPTER 21

Sera had never been so cold. Or in so wretched a place as the narrow, deserted strip of street on which she stood, clutching the crate of her paintings. Pale light glowed here and there from the windows of rickety buildings that towered and teetered up from the cobblestones. All manner of waste and refuse littered the walk under her feet. Her stomach clenched at the smell and it took all of her resolve not to gag.

There was nothing she could do to suppress the shudder that wracked her body as Gerald clamped his hand around her upper arm. He pushed her ahead of him, toward a dark set of stairs that led down into the walk. She went, using the crate to hold her tattered hems above her feet and silently, desperately hoped that Gerald would lose his footing and fall.

He was drunk by the standards of most men, but not those unique to Gerald Treadwell. His speech was slurring, his gait unsteady. But slightly less than half the whisky remained and he wouldn't stop until it was gone. And the time between the half and one-quarter marks was the most dangerous. He could still move, think, and, because his thoughts tended to be mean then, strike.

But once he passed the quarter mark . . . Just a few seconds would be all she needed to get away. He could come after her, but he wouldn't be able to catch her. Not then. All she had to do was keep quiet and bide her time. She'd be home before daybreak. She'd be back in Carden's—

Memory shredded her hope. The sight of Carden lying still and silent on the floor. The single second in which the vitality of him had been snuffed out like a candle. Tears welled in her eyes and she desperately blinked them back, knowing that if Gerald saw them, they'd earn her a slap.

Don't look back, Sera. Don't look back.

They reached the door at the bottom of the stone pit and he released her arm only to plant his hand between her shoulder blades and hold her against the door as he unlocked the rotting wood panel. It swung open on rusty, sagging hinges and he roughly pushed her through the opening and into a small, barely furnished room.

Two small windows, one on the street side, one on the alley side, provided just enough light for her to make out the outlines of a small iron stove, a cluttered wall shelf above it, a narrow bed, an oil lamp sitting on an upended crate, and a straight-backed chair.

"Put it down there," Gerald snapped, pointing with the pistol to the space between the end of the bed and the coal stove.

She did as he told her and then straightened, waiting for another command, knowing better than to act on her own.

"Sit!"

She moved to the chair quickly and sat, dropping her hands into her lap and silently watching him put his bottle of whisky and the pistol on the upended crate beside the bed. If he turned his back . . . She saw the blow coming, tried to block it, and failed. The world reeled and went gray. Adrift in the fog, she felt the rough fibers of the ropes, knew that she was being tied into the chair. And no amount of fear or desperate realization could make her limbs move to resist.

She closed her eyes and let her head fall forward so that Gerald wouldn't see the tears threatening to overwhelm her. She heard the scratch and smelled the sulfur, knew that he was lighting the oil lamp. Then he shuffled to the end of the bed and she heard him grunt just before there was a cascade of falling paper, followed by three heavy thuds. She started at the crash and risked lifting her head and opening her eyes just long enough to see what he was doing.

"Goddamned cold country," he muttered, yanking open the stove door. "I haven't been warm a day since I've been here." He shoved a handful of the splintered crate onto the faintly glowing coals inside and then began to turn.

Sera closed her eyes again and listened to him make his way to the upended crate. The bed groaned and then there was the unmistakable sound of sloshing and long hard swallows. And then there was only the faint crackle of the stove.

She peeked through her lashes and her heart lurched as her gaze met his and a smile slowly spread over his beard-shadowed face. Her stomach churning, her pulse skittering, she lifted her head and resolved to do the best she could.

"Did ya miss me, Feenie?"

She bit her tongue and tamped down her loathing. "What did you do to Arthur and Mary?"

"Killed 'em. Just a mile or two inside the jungle. You'd have found 'em if you'd really looked." He put the bottle to his lips, tilted it back and took a long drink. "Or maybe not," he added, wiping the arm of his jacket across his mouth. "The jungle eats quick."

"Why did you kill them, Gerald? Why didn't you just leave them to fend for themselves?"

"Because," he replied, smiling at the bottle, "ol' Arthur

put his nose an' his hands where they didn't belong. And there wasn't any way to explain the fistful of money he pulled from my pack. It was either kill 'em or give up the plan." He shrugged. "Wasn't 'bout to give up the plan."

"And what have you been doing with my money?"

He lifted the bottle in salute. "Livin' well an' supportin' just causes." To her frustration and disappointment, he didn't take another swallow. Instead, he rested the bottle on his thigh and reached over to snatch a handful of the loose paintings scattered across the foot of the rumpled bed. Holding them out for her to see, he asked, "How much has Somers offered ya for these?"

"Nothing," she lied. "He hasn't seen them."

He snorted and took a quick, short drink. "Yer gonna send him a note in the mornin'. He gives ya two thousand pounds or he never sees 'em. Understood?"

"Yes," she answered, her mind racing. The note would have to go by courier. Somers's offer had been for over twice that much. He'd know something was wrong. If he thought to ask questions of the courier—

"Yer too damn easygoin'," Gerald said, leaning forward to squint at her. "What ya thinkin', Feenie? How ya gonna wait till I pass out an' run away like ya always did before? Gonna take the chair with ya this time?"

He tilted his head back and laughed, hard and loud. Sera tugged against the ropes binding her wrists to the chair and glanced at the level of the whisky in the bottle. Almost to the quarter mark. Almost.

His laughter ended on a choke and he lunged forward to wrap his fingers around her throat. His gaze bored into hers and she closed her eyes, tried not to breathe in the sour odor of him, desperately hoped that her heart wouldn't explode.

His fingers tightened. "What ya thinkin', Feenie? Talk!"

She hated him. Hated him more than she'd ever known

it was possible to hate. Through clenched teeth she answered, "When Carden finds you—"

"Yer lover," Gerald sneered, releasing her and dropping down on the bed again. "He can't be much of one if . . ."

He hesitated and even in the haze of her anger and fear Sera knew that he'd momentarily lost the train of his thought. A tiny hope flickered inside her.

"The likes of you." He snorted and took another drink and then pointed the top of the bottle at her as he added, "He's not comin' after ya, Feenie. I laid him out real hard. Woulda shot him dead if ya hadn't bolted like ya did."

It was the one and only answer she truly cared about. The relief was intense and it took every measure of her determination to keep it from showing. "Which is precisely why I bolted."

"Think yer so smart, don'tcha? Always thought ya were . . . smarter than me. Better." He took another quick drink of whisky and then flung aside the stained pillow. "If yer so smart, Feenie," he demanded, waving two strips of paper at her, "tell me where these tickets are to."

He didn't give her a chance to reply. "Don't know *that*, do ya? Ya think yer lover will come a-lookin' for ya in Ar . . . Ar . . . gin—"

"Argentina."

He glared at her. "Yer gonna paint when we get there. Yer gonna paint me real goddamn rich."

Her anger sparked, hot and too quick to contain. "Didn't it occur to you when you left Belize that you were leaving the golden goose behind?"

He laughed and took another drink. "Didn't know jus' how damn golden ya was till I got here. Was gonna come back for ya, figurin' ya had more paintings by now, but then ya turned up in Hyde Park." He lifted the bottle in salute again and grinned. "Thanks for savin' me the trip, Feenie. Much obliged."

She held her tongue, knowing that she didn't need to

say anything more. He'd reached the quarter mark. From this point on, he would supply her side of any conversation.

"Yer not goin' to run away anymore, Feenie. No sirree. I close my eyes, yer gonna close yers, too." Setting the whisky bottle on the crate, he heaved himself to his feet, swayed precariously for a long moment, and then lurched toward the small shelf on the wall above the stove.

He took a bottle from the clutter and staggered back. Standing in front of her, he swayed and smiled and pulled the cork from the blue bottle. "Laud'm," he said. "Keeps yer wife at home where she belongs."

She understood what he intended to do and what it meant to her fragile hope of escape. "You have me tied," she pointed out, trying to keep the desperation from her voice. "I can't go anywhere."

"Gonna make sure," he said, pressing the mouth of the bottle to her lips. "Swallow."

Sera clamped her mouth shut and turned her head, refusing to take the drug.

He glared down at her, swaying on his feet. With a half-turn, he snatched the pistol off the crate. The muzzle pressed hard against her breast, he held the bottle to her lips again. "Do as you're told!"

She had no choice. Choking back a sob, Sera closed her eyes and parted her lips. He poured the liquid in faster than she could swallow and it ran out and down over her chin. He kept pouring.

"Again! Swallow!"

Only when she gagged and spewed it back on him did he stop and back away. Tears coursing down her cheeks, she struggled to breathe, to break free of the ropes binding her to the chair.

"Don't think I've for . . . forgotten that yer gonna pay for cuttin' me," he taunted, putting the pistol and the bottle on the crate beside the bed. "Haven't, ya know. Tomorrow, Feenie. When I can make it hurt bad. After ya write the note."

He picked up one of the paintings and considered it as he swayed forward and back. A smile lifted the corners of his mouth just before he crumpled it into a ball and turned to her. Again she saw his intent and tried to evade it. And again she failed. Catching her jaw between his thumb and fingers, he squeezed until her mouth opened. He stuffed the painting in and then released her.

"Go 'head an' scream for help, Feenie," he mocked, staggering to the end of the bed. He laughed and scooped up another handful of splintered wood and stuck it haphazardly into the stove. "Scream 'way."

She was caught; her every last hope had been taken away. But the laudanum was stealing over her and the realization came softly and without concern. There was nothing more she could do. She had tried. Gerald had won.

She stared at the mouth of the stove, watching the flames dance and the embers pulse inside. He hadn't put the wood in right; ends of the splinters stuck out the opening. The fire would crawl up and they would fall to the floor. Her mother had always warned her about the danger in that. Fire killed so many people. She'd always been so careful. She'd never thought that she would be one of them.

The movement was quick and she knitted her brows. She watched it drop from the end of the splinter to the floor and then dash for the end of the bed, its yellow legs a whir of motion.

Sera blinked and tried to shake her head. She was seeing horrible things that weren't really there. He'd given her too much laudanum. At least she wouldn't feel the flames. That would be a blessing. Her eyelids were leaden and she fought the urge to drift away. It took conscious effort and all of her will, but she turned her head and focused on the bed.

Gerald lay sprawled on his back across it, the whisky bottle in his hand, his blood-crusted legs dangling over the side. Her paintings and the empty oil pouches lay scattered around him. And from them came the bright yellow whirs of rapid motion. One, two . . .

Her eyes drifted closed and she abandoned the count. If only Carden would come for her before it was too late. She didn't want to die without telling him that she loved him.

All three girls were standing at the window, staring silently into the night. Anne sat in a chair in the corner, crocheting by the soft light of a lamp. She looked up at his arrival, nodded crisply as she laid aside her work, and soundlessly slipped from the room.

Carden considered his nieces, still wondering what to tell them and how to say it. The decision was taken from him when Camille looked over her shoulder and saw him standing there.

"Uncle Carden!"

All three of them turned to look at him. Amanda's gaze slipped past him for a moment and he knew that she'd hoped to see Sera coming through the door in his wake. Camille, hugging Mrs. Miller to her with both arms, looked up at him as though she expected him to do something wondrous at any moment. Beatrice . . . Lord, if ever there was child old beyond her years. Bea didn't have to be told how wrong things could go in the next few hours. Amanda and Camille needed to have their hopes settled while Bea needed to be assured that hope was possible. How the hell he was supposed to accomplish both goals at the same time . . .

"It will be all right," he promised, carefully balancing firmness and optimism. "We're going to get Sera back."

"When, Uncle Carden?"

"Soon, Amanda. We're waiting for a man to bring us a message and then Mr. Stanbridge, Mr. Terrell, and I will be leaving to get Sera."

"It was Mr. Treadwell who took her."

"Yes, Bea, I know," he said, easing down onto the edge of the bed so that he was level with her. "What I don't know is where you got the pistol that Sawyer took away from you."

"It was Papa's," she supplied evenly. "He had two of them in a box. He took one of them with him when he went away. We brought the other with us when we came here. I found it when we were unpacking and I hid it in my trunk. Miss Sera doesn't know I took it."

"Why did you take it, Bea?"

She swallowed. "Because I was afraid that Mr. Treadwell would come looking for her. And he did." Her lower lip quivered as she added, "But I didn't get the pistol loaded in time to stop him from taking her." She didn't make a sound as huge tears spilled over her lashes and down her cheeks.

He wasn't going to ask her how she knew about loading a weapon. That could wait until later. He gathered her into his arms and hugged her tight. "It wasn't your responsibility to protect Sera," he told her, cradling her head against his chest. "It's mine, Bea. Mine alone. What happened isn't your fault. Do you believe me?"

It took a few moments, but she eventually sniffled and nodded. "Good," he said, taking her shoulders in his hands and holding her out so he could look her squarely in the eyes as he laid down the law. "You are never to touch a pistol again. Is that *clear*?"

"Yes, sir."

He had his doubts and would have pursued them, but Camille sidled up beside him and put her hand on his arm.

"Uncle Carden?"

"Yes, Camille?" he asked, as Bea slipped away to discreetly scrub the tears from her cheeks and Amanda sat down beside him.

Camille climbed up to perch on his leg, Mrs. Miller tucked tightly under her arm. "Anne says that you were hit on the head really, really hard."

"I was."

"Does it hurt?"

"Hurt" didn't begin to describe the pulsing pain. "Yes, it hurts."

She looked at him earnestly. "Are you going to cry?"

His throat closed and his chest tightened. Not from the pain; he'd endured worse. But from the certain knowledge that he'd let Sera come to harm. He coughed softly and swallowed and smiled for his youngest niece. "I feel like it, sweetheart," he admitted. "But I won't. Crying doesn't help anything."

"But it's all right to cry when it hurts, Uncle Carden. Miss Sera says so."

"Yes, well . . ." Not when you were a grown man and the pain was your own damn fault, he reminded himself as his chest tightened another degree. Not in front of your nieces. And not when you had to save your woman.

There was a quick knock on the door before it opened. Aiden stuck his head inside, said, "O'Mara's here," and then disappeared, leaving the door ajar.

It was time. The ache in his chest evaporated and his blood raced in his veins.

"I have to go now," Carden said, lifting Camille off his lap and setting her on the bed. He stood and looked among the three of them. "You all will stay in this room. Anne will come back to be with you. And I'll come see you when I return."

"With Miss Sera," Camille added brightly.

"With Sera."

Amanda squared her shoulders. "We'll say a prayer for you both, Uncle Carden."

"Thank you," he replied, turning and striding across the room.

"And one for the soul of Mr. Treadwell, too."

He stopped with the handle of the door in his hand and looked back into eyes that he knew were the mirror of his own. "You and I are going to have a talk, Bea."

"Yes, sir."

No flinching, no wavering. And she'd die before she apologized for how she felt. God help the world, he thought, pulling the door closed behind himself. And God's mercy on Gerald Treadwell. It was the only pity the bastard was going to get.

"You'll let me go first," Barrett said as the coach pulled hard to the side of the roadway. "He has one shot and it won't do Seraphina any good if you take it."

"Then you damn well better move faster than I do," Carden retorted, wrenching the door handle and vaulting out in one smooth motion even as the carriage slid to a halt. Stars danced in front of his eyes but he blinked them away just as O'Mara jumped from the box and landed on the walk, pointing to the stairs leading down. Carden started forward only to have his shoulders suddenly yanked back.

"Go!" Aiden barked, holding him by the fabric of his coat, keeping him upright but off balance. The jarring sent streaks of white-hot pain shooting through his skull, but he ignored them and struggled to pull himself free.

Aiden held fast, forcing him to watch Barrett sprint to the railing surrounding the stairwell, grasp it with one hand, and clear it to drop into the blackness. Wood splintered in the next second and only then did Aiden let him go.

He dashed forward, knowing his head wouldn't let him jump the distance as Barrett had, and took the stairs two at a time, the pain pounding to the rhythm of his frantically beating heart. He careened through the door and slid to a stop. Barrett was stamping out coals on the floor. Treadwell lay sprawled and motionless across the bed. Sera was slumped—

He darted to her, his heart frozen with dread. "Sera!" he called, lifting her head, fighting back the tears as he saw the bruises around her neck, the sides of her face, her arms. He pulled the gag from her mouth and laid his hand on her chest to feel for her breathing. So shallow. So slow. But blessedly there.

"Sera!" he called again, cradling her head as he pulled the knife from his sleeve. "Just open your eyes for a second, angel. Just a second. Let me know you're all right."

Her eyelids fluttered and her lips parted and it was enough to send his heart soaring in gratitude. Gently, he eased her back and released her long enough to slice the ropes binding her to the chair.

Barrett stepped to his side. "This is the story, Carden. The pictures were stolen. You hired me to find them. John Aiden assisted me in the search. We found Reginald Carter just like this. That's the story I'm telling the constables. Seraphina was never here. You were never here. Understood?"

He did, but he also saw a potentially fatal flaw in it. "Yes, but—" The thought evaporated at the sight of Sera's raw and bloody wrists. Rage, primal and white-hot, shot through him. He straightened and whirled toward the bed, determined to wreak vengeance for every bit of pain Sera had endured.

But Gerald Treadwell couldn't feel any more pain than he already did. His face and neck were hugely swollen; his tongue protruded from his mouth, bloated and blue. His chest rose and fell in the erratic, labored cadence that spoke of hovering death.

"Get Seraphina out of here, Carden," his friend said

softly. "Take her home. Take care of her. We'll do what needs to be done here." Over his shoulder he said crisply, "John Aiden, go find what passes for a physician in this neighborhood. And be quick about it. We don't have much time."

Carden nodded and slid his gaze away from the dying man. As he did it passed over an upended crate beside the bed. On it lay Arthur's dueling pistol, the mate to the one taken from Bea and that was now safely tucked in the small of his back. Dark certainty settled over him and he swallowed down a surprisingly deep sense of loss and regret.

"Sco . . . lo . . ."

Carden spun at the faint sound. Her eyes were barely open and she was struggling to keep her head up. Relief flooded through him, wide and sweeping and glorious. He bent beside her and cupped her face in his hands, saying softly, "Don't try to talk, Sera. I'm taking you home."

Her brows knitted. "Pendra," she whispered, her voice strained with a heart-wrenching urgency he didn't understand.

"No one moves!" Aiden ordered crisply and with sufficient conviction and force that Carden held his breath.

Aiden stepped close and smoothed a lock of Sera's hair from her cheek. "What, Seraphina?" he asked gently. "Say it again."

She knitted her brows and on a shallow breath said, "Sco . . ."

"Scolopendra?"

Sera relaxed into his hands and Carden looked up into Aiden's wide eyes, silently demanding an explanation.

"Nastiest, meanest frigging bug in the tropics," Aiden supplied quickly. "Moves fast and eats meat. Viciously. If you're even the least bit sensitive to the venom, you end up like Gerald Treadwell."

Aiden turned away and stared at the bed, at the litter

of Sera's paintings. "It's here somewhere and we damn well better find it before one of us is the next meal. Carden, shake out Seraphina's skirts. And shake them well. Check her hair, too. The son of a bitch can climb and it can cling."

Carden eased Sera back in the chair, made sure she was balanced, quickly ran his fingers through her hair, and then took out his knife again.

"It would help to know what the thing looks like," Barrett snarled from behind him.

Aiden held his hands up about eight inches apart. "It's about this long, dark brown, hundreds of yellow legs. Don't put your hands where you aren't looking. Don't lean up or even brush against anything."

Carden swore under his breath, slipped the blade inside Sera's bodice and drew it toward himself, cutting the fabric all the way down to the hem.

"And when we find it?"

"Knock it to the floor with something and step on it. *Fast*. And hard."

Barrett looked over at him just as he finished slicing open the waistband of Sera's hooped crinolines. "What are you doing?"

"Aside from ending any possibility that one of the goddamn monsters could bite her . . ." Slipping an arm around her shoulders, he lifted her enough to shove the crinoline down over her hips. She murmured in protest, but he hushed her and pushed it down past her knees. It fell to the floor around her feet and he slipped his other arm under her and lifted her up to cradle her against his chest.

"What if someone sees a woman in a red dress being carried out of here?" he asked, his mind arrowing back to his earlier concerns about Barrett's plan. "There were red beads all over the floor when we came through the door, Barrett. Even the thickest constable could put it together. It's a big hole in your story."

"What if people saw her being hauled in here?"

"She left before you two got here. They just didn't see her go."

"All right. It's believable."

"There's the bastard!"

It took Aiden two stomps before he was finally fast enough to catch it between the sole of his shoe and the floor. "That was a small one," he declared over the popping crunch. "There's probably more of them. Keep looking. And be careful about it."

Barrett looked at him askance and swore.

"Put the gown and what's left of the ropes in the stove," Carden instructed, carrying Sera toward the door. "When Aiden goes out to find the physician, have him toss her hoops somewhere along the way. I'll see you at the house later. And bring that pistol lying on the crate with you."

He left them to their tasks, carried Sera up the stairs, and into Barrett's waiting carriage. O'Mara waited until he'd dropped into the seat with his precious cargo before slamming the door closed behind him. The driver instantly snapped the whip and they were on their way.

"Sweet Sera," he whispered, dragging the carriage blanket over her, tucking it close around her, kissing her brow. "My sweet, sweet Sera."

She shifted slightly in his arms, her cheek burrowing feebly against his shoulder. "I'm here, angel," he assured her, drawing her closer. "I have you. We're going home."

"Cold."

He shifted about, keeping her covered with the blanket as he opened his coat and drew her inside. Resting his cheek on her head, he savored the scent of her, the feel of her cradled against him. How close he'd come to never holding her again. "I was so afraid," he whispered, his chest aching, tears welling in his eyes. "I thought I'd lost you, Sera."

With a contented sigh, she melted into him and softly

murmured his name. The fullness in his chest bloomed and flooded through him. There was no resisting the power of it, no retreating from the truth. And he didn't want to.

He gathered her close and shared the truth with her. "I love you, Sera. I love you with all my heart."

CHAPTER 22

Sera awakened with a start and then, seeing the comforting familiarity of her room, eased back into her pillow. It was nice to be among the living, she thought, looking up at the ceiling. She moved her arms and legs, stretched her shoulders and her neck, and decided that she didn't hurt too badly—especially considering all she'd been through the night before. Her wrists and ankles burned a bit; not enough to bring tears to her eyes by any means, but enough that she doubted that she could tolerate stockings or cuffs for a day or two.

She lifted her arm and studied the bandage wrapped and tied around her wrist. Carden must have done that for her. After her bath. It had been dark and he'd talked to her softly. He'd kissed her and told her to dream of him. She'd slept so deeply after that.

There were other snippets of memory. None quite as clear. There was a vague recollection of Mrs. Miller being tucked under her arm, of Anne tending the fire in the hearth, and of Sawyer checking her brow.

But there were no memories of how she'd come home. Nothing after she'd seen the scolopendras racing over the bed. Which was a blessing, she knew. Before that moment, though . . . No, she wasn't going to look back, wasn't going to remember. It was done. She and Carden had survived. That's what mattered.

And that she get herself out of bed and back into life, she admonished herself. She glanced over at the windows, at the slit of light peeping past the draperies. The soft light of mid-morning. Yes, she needed to be up and about.

She stretched languidly, happily, then pushed aside the coverings and sat up. There, lying at the foot of the bed, was her wrapper. Lying atop it was a shiny new hand spade tied with a bright red ribbon. Grinning, she slipped from bed and scooped it up. One end of the ribbon had been passed through a paper tag.

You'll find the rake in the conservatory.

Laughing, she quickly saw to her morning ablutions, pinned up her hair, slipped her feet into her mules, snatched up her wrapper, and set off to find him.

It was the most amazing thing she'd ever seen. Yesterday the conservatory had been barren and brown, a disgrace to horticulture. And today . . . The palms grew to the very roof, green and lush and thick. The air was moist and warm and scented with flowers, their colors splashing vividly from front to back, top to bottom.

The only thing that remained the same was the furniture and it was where she'd arranged it. And sitting in a chair, his bare feet propped up on the wicker table, sat her handsome rake. He had the most beautiful smile, the most wonderful eyes. Closing and laying aside his book, he rose and came to her, his gaze never leaving hers.

"Good morning, angel," he said, taking her in his arms and kissing her lightly. "How are you feeling?"

Safe. Treasured. Loved. "Hardly as sore as I expected to be," she replied because she knew that was the kind of answer he wanted. "What happened in here?"

"Lady Godwin, she of the spit-and-twig conservatory, decided she needed a new one if Lady Caruthers was getting one. And since her old one has to come down before the new one can go up, there was a question of what to do with her jungle in the meanwhile. I very generously offered to keep it for her."

"All of this has been moved since yesterday afternoon? How, Carden?"

"It's been two days, two nights, Sera. The doctor said we should just watch you and let you sleep off the laudanum. So we did." He bent his head and brushed a kiss over her lips. "And while you were dreaming of me, I had Paradise moved for you."

Her heart filled to overflowing, she gazed up at him and wondered at the marvel of his kindness, his caring. "Have you slept at all?" she asked softly.

"A bit here and there. But enough," he replied with a shrug. "Would you like a cup of tea?" His smile widened. "I'd offer you a brandy, but aside from it being a bit early in the day, the doctor also said neither one of us should be drinking spirits for a least a week. So far, I've been very good about heeding his advice."

She cupped his cheek and searched his eyes. "Are you all right? What did Gerald do to you?"

He cocked a brow roguishly. "I have a rather healthy knot on the back of my head. Would you like to see it?"

"Yes." She started to step out of his embrace, but he held her tight and turned his shoulders so that she could see the nape of his neck from just where she was. The knot was the size of an egg. "Oh, Carden," she whispered, thinking of the pain he must be enduring.

He turned back squarely to her and the light in his eyes had nothing whatsoever to do with pain. "Camille says kisses make bumps feel better."

"She's right." Stretching up on her toes, she kissed him,

reveling in the taste of him, in the wondrous way his lips fit against and welcomed hers. Heaven was kissing Carden Reeves. She could easily spend a lifetime doing it, she decided, drawing back.

"Don't tell Camille, but your kisses work much better than hers do."

She laughed and traced a fingertip over his lower lip. He kissed it and then said, "I have something to show you."

She arched a brow. "The scar on your thigh?"

Laughing, he took her hands in his. "Close your eyes and trust me."

Sera had never trusted anyone as deeply and unconditionally as she did him. He drew her forward and she went knowing that he wouldn't let her stumble. A sound caught her ear and she tilted her head to better hear. "Carden, is that water falling?"

"Lady Godwin's former gardener is a stickler for creating what he calls the proper atmosphere. He's also aces with pipes and rocks."

"Former?" she asked, her wrapper brushing a gardenia in passing.

"He's my gardener now."

"When am I going to meet him?"

"Not today. He has the day off. He's definitely earned it."

If the man had moved the contents of an entire greenhouse and established it in another over the span of two days, he deserved not only a day off, but a medal, too. They were nearing the waterfall; the sound was becoming clearer. It was over to her right. It couldn't be a very big one; the splashing wasn't loud enough for the water to drop from a height any greater than half a meter.

He stopped, saying, "Just stand here and don't peek." He released her hands and she let them fall to her sides. Yes, the waterfall was there, just ahead and off to the right as she'd thought. Carden had moved behind her.

His hands went to her shoulders and he gently adjusted her until she was facing the waterfall straight on. "All right, angel," he said quietly. "Open your eyes and tell me what you think."

Sera gasped in amazement and brought her hand up to cover Carden's as she tried to take it all in. It was a room, thickly walled in greens, splashed by all the colors of the rainbow. The waterfall was there—on the far side—just as she'd expected. But it was so much more. At least three meters high and half again as broad, the water rippled silently down the face of black stone until it broke over a ledge and cascaded into a wide basin. And slightly to the left and before the fall was a high four-poster bed, draped in netting and appointed with bright white linens.

"Are you pleased?"

"Oh, Carden," she whispered. "It's my fantasy."

"Do I play any part in this fantasy of yours?" he asked, sliding his arms around her midriff and pressing a lingering kiss behind her ear.

"A most prominent one," she happily admitted.

He kissed the curve of her neck. "You'll tell me if I do anything wrong?"

"Of course," she murmured, knowing that any way he touched her was perfection.

Kissing his way back to the hollow behind her ear, he untied the sash of her wrapper. "How am I doing so far?" he asked, his hands gliding up her torso to cup her breasts through her night rail. Suckling her earlobe, he slowly scraped his thumbs over her hardened nipples.

Her body thrumming, her core going molten, she desperately asked, "Where are the girls?"

"Walking in the park with Honoria," he answered, kissing his way back to her nape, his thumbs sending shivers of delight coursing through her. "After which they'll be going to luncheon together. It will be late afternoon before they return."

"And Sawyer?"

"Off on errands. With a very extensive list."

Oh, Lord, her bones were dissolving. "Aiden and Barrett?"

Nuzzling beneath the edges of her wrapper and night rail, he kissed the curve of her shoulder. "Aiden is busy with his ship business. Barrett is on an investigation of some sort. I did invite them to dinner this evening, though."

Her senses were flooding, the heady spiral bearing her upward. "You've seen to everything."

"I pride myself on being thorough."

She could feel his smile against her skin. She had to do something about slowing his thoroughness or—in less than a minute—she was going to be a sated puddle at his feet.

"I've noticed," she said raggedly, turning in his arms and placing her hands flat on his chest, "that you pride yourself on a great many things, Carden Reeves."

She was riding close to the edge, trying to keep from tumbling over; he could see it in the light of her eyes. "I happen to be very good at a great many things," he said, resting his hands on her waist, giving her a temporary reprieve. "And false modesty is so annoying, don't you think?"

"There's a difference between modesty and humility."

He grinned. "I'm not inclined to be humble."

"So I've noticed," she countered, laughing softly.

"What else about me have you noticed, Sera?"

"You're a talented architect," she answered, her gaze dropping to his chest as her hands moved to the center of it. She opened the button of his shirt.

He mentally counted. Only three were fastened before his shirt met the waist of his trousers. "And?"

The next button opened beneath her fingers. "Despite your declarations otherwise, you're also very good with children."

"And?"

The next one parted with the buttonhole. She looked up at him. "You're very, very good at kissing."

"Yes, I am," he agreed, lowering his head to prove it. He moved his mouth over hers, possessing her gently as his hands slipped down her hips and back to cup her. She arched her back, pressing her breasts against him, and parted her lips to catch his lower one and slowly stroke it with the tip of her tongue. Delight rippled through him and he drew back to smile down at her. "And you're very good at it, too."

"You inspire me."

The look in her eyes . . . "Oh?" he taunted, his heart racing.

"To do the most wicked and wanton things." She opened the button on his trousers.

"That's *my* fantasy."

She smiled and arched a brow, opened the next button. "Shall we combine yours and mine and see what happens?"

He knew what was going to happen. This time. The next. Today. Tomorrow. Every day for as long as he lived. He was going to love her. With his heart and soul. His body was never again going to be his alone to command. She was going to shred his intentions every time they came together. She would drive him mad and past restraint and he would let her because she was the only one who could, because he was powerless to stop her. And because he would never feel as whole, as complete, as he felt when joined with her.

"Love me, Sera," he whispered. "Please love me as much as I do you."

Her every dream, her every hope. "I do," she answered,

her heart overflowing, her soul on wing. "I love you, Carden Reeves."

He smiled and bent to whisper a kiss across her lips as his hands went to her shoulders. He pushed her wrapper aside and she released him to let it slip down her arms, past her fingertips, to pool on the ground at their feet.

His fingers trailed up the curve of her shoulder, the length of her neck, and he tenderly cradled her face in his hands. "Tell me what you want, Sera."

"You."

The light in his eyes was wicked, thrilling. "Any particular way?"

"Naked would be nice," she answered, slipping her hands between them.

He cocked a brow and grinned, took a half-step back and held his arms out to the sides.

His surrender sent a fiery jolt of heat into her core. Breathless, she opened his trouser buttons with trembling, impatient fingers. His shirt buttons, too. She skimmed the palms of her hands up over the rippled contours of his abdomen, the hardened planes of his chest, and to his massive shoulders. She found his gaze and held it as she pushed his shirt aside, as he lowered his arms and let it slide away.

She drew her hands down along the same chiseled path, watching him, reveling in the dark spark of anticipation she saw come into his eyes. *Watch me dare, Carden Reeves.*

With deliberate patience, she slowed her touch at his hips, deepened the friction between the palms of her hands and his skin. His breath caught and his chin came up. He grasped her shoulders, holding her there, holding himself steady.

His smile disappeared and he closed his eyes as she stroked down his thighs. He stopped breathing as she started back up and came to the center. And when she took him into her hands, he moaned hard and deep and tightened his hold on her.

It was the most magnificent of tortures and Carden surrendered himself to the pleasure of it, to the mastery of her touch, knowing that he couldn't long control the urgency coiling low in his loins.

"Sera," he warned, "you're pushing my limits."

"I know."

The laughter rolled up from deep in his chest and he opened his eyes to find her smiling up at him in unholy joy. He took the front edges of her night rail in his hands and tore the thing straight down the center. Her eyes lit up and her mouth formed the most inviting little O.

"That's it," he declared, chuckling and drawing the gown over her arms and letting it fall away. "You don't get slow and gentle this time."

She slipped her hands to his hips and the trousers slid down as she arched her brow and laughingly countered, "Perhaps I don't want slow and gentle."

The line was fine and she was daring him to hold it. His blood heated another impossible degree. "Oh, angel," he taunted, moving slowly behind her. She watched him over her shoulder just as she had in Lady Hatcher's greenhouse.

"You're going to get slow after all," he whispered, cupping her breasts. Slipping her hardened nipples between his fingers, he gently squeezed them. "Do you like that, Sera? Does it feel good?"

"Yes."

Suckling her earlobe, teasing it with the tip of his tongue, he rolled the peaks between his thumbs and forefingers. "And that, Sera? Do you like that?"

Her knees melted and she closed her eyes, leaning into him and trusting him to keep her from falling. The hard length of him pressed into her flesh and through a shudder of pleasure she gasped, "Yes."

He trailed the tip of his tongue along the curve of her ear and then released her nipples to place his hands on her waist. Turning her, he swept her up into his arms, carried her to the bed and set her on the edge. Her eyes were bright, shimmering with desire, and he looked into the depths of them as he took her breasts back into his hands.

Scraping the pads of his thumbs over the crests, he leaned forward and brushed his lips over hers. She closed her eyes and sighed and he came back for another kiss, this one deeper and more possessive. Her arms twined around his neck and her lips parted in invitation. He accepted, gently invading, touching, stroking. She moaned and, beneath his thumbs, her nipples hardened another degree.

Drawing back, he feathered kisses at the corners of her mouth and then moved deliberately downward, kissing and gently suckling the slender column of her throat on his way to the feast of her breasts. She drew a long, hard breath as he neared a rosy summit and he paused for just a moment before he slowly drew his tongue over it.

"Oh, Carden," she whispered raggedly.

He blew gently on the wetness, smiling as she started, moaned, and arched toward him. "Do you like that, Sera?" he asked, his lips a mere breath away from the treasure. "Do you want me to do it again?"

Her answer was wordless, but undeniably clear and direct. She drew her arms from his shoulders and placed them behind her on the bed, arched her back and brushed her nipple across his lips. Reveling in her forwardness and happy to reward her, he obediently, languidly licked her. Once, twice, three times. And then she shifted, turning slightly to offer her other breast.

He obliged her. And himself. Lapping her ever so slowly once, twice. "Tell me if you like this," he whispered, taking her gently between his teeth and rapidly flicking her with the tip of his tongue.

"Oh, Carden."

Releasing her, he kissed his way to the other breast and paused. "Was that a yes?"

"Yes," she declared, pressing her nipple to his lips. "Don't stop."

Taking her offering between his teeth, he answered, "At your command," and then teased her, pleasuring her with his tongue. Then, true to his word, he didn't stop. He took her peak wholly into his mouth and suckled her, pulling at her deep and hard and not at all gently.

He released his prize only to claim the other just as deliberately. She moaned and arched closer and his patience with slow seduction frayed. Aching with want, he clung to what little control he still possessed. Easing back and straightening, he lifted his gaze to her face. Her eyes remained closed, her breathing ragged and fast as she leaned forward to lightly brush her breasts against his chest. Watching her, he slipped his hands up the length of her thighs. As he neared her hips, she murmured a wordless plea and arched her head back.

He leaned forward to kiss her throat. "Do you like this, Sera?" he asked, his lips grazing her skin as his fingers found and stroked the heated wetness of her. "Or shall I stop?"

"No. God, no."

She was close, so close to the edge. "Ah, Seraphina," he said, easing away from her. "I think maybe I should."

"Carden!" Sera cried, tumbling back from the crest, frantically catching his arms. "Don't you dare leave me like this!"

His smile was wicked and wide, his eyes bright with knowing triumph. "Afraid that I'd deny you, angel? Never."

Her heart was thundering, so full that she knew it was going to burst. She loved him. Loved the way he made her feel, the way he knew her and teased her and pleasured every fiber of her body and soul. "You're shameless, Carden Reeves," she breathlessly accused.

"And you love me for it," he countered, adoring her, craving her, as he drew her to the very edge of the bed and fitted himself between her legs. "You like being a wanton."

"Only with you."

"Yes, Sera," he murmured, taking her hips in his hands. "Only with me."

He filled her leisurely, hard and deep. She moaned and slowly shuddered, seizing him, welcoming him, holding him fast in the slick, wet heat of her body. He drew back only a bit and then pushed forward, filling her again, driving himself as deep into her as he could. She dug her fingers into the bedcoverings and arched up, soaring on the spiral, panting. "Carden!"

They were both too close. It was too soon. "Only me, Sera," he repeated, gasping, struggling for control as he drew back and bent down to gently capture her lower lip with his teeth. "Only me. Promise it."

She touched her tongue to his lips, arched up. "Only you, Carden."

"Always," he gasped, desperately releasing his claim to her mouth and stilling her hips. "Always, Sera," he pleaded. "Look me in the eyes and promise me always."

"Always, Carden. Only you."

Lifting her up, he filled her with every measure of his desire, every measure of his being.

She tumbled over the edge with a strangled cry, the heat and the power of her fulfillment gripping him and pulling him hard to the hilt. His own release building and beyond stopping, he surrendered to the tide that sated his need and flooded his heart and soul with the love of Sera.

• • •

She drifted in dreamy contentment, wrapped in the strength of Carden's arms, warmed and cradled against the length of his body. Water splashed at the edge of her awareness, an accompaniment to the sweet lullaby of Carden's heartbeat, the even measure of his breathing.

Always. He'd asked her for always. Sera smiled and nestled her cheek closer into the curve of his shoulder. Someday there would be— Her heart tripped with sudden realization.

"What's wrong?" he murmured, pulling her closer, pressing a kiss to her temple.

She shifted, pushing herself up on her elbow and swallowing back her trepidation. "We forgot the sheath."

Tracing her lip, he smiled. "I didn't forget, Sera," he said softly. "I very deliberately chose not to bring them into Paradise."

No woman on earth had ever been happier, more completed than she was. "Thank you."

His eyes sparkled with devilment. "You'll have to marry me, you know. The scandal will be horrendous if you don't."

"Well, I certainly wouldn't want your reputation to suffer."

"I was referring to yours," he countered, chuckling. "Mine's already an irredeemable disaster."

"They can say whatever they like," she assured him, settling back in beside him, her head in the cradle of his shoulder, her hand lying over his heart. "About either of us. I don't care."

He threaded his fingers through hers and whispered, "Thank you for loving me enough to be patient with me."

"I would have waited forever and a day for you, Carden Reeves."

Yes, forever and a day. With Sera. With her at his side, anywhere would be Paradise.

Turn the page for a sneak peek at

THE PERFECT TEMPTATION

By Leslie LaFoy

COMING JULY 2004
FROM ST. MARTIN'S PAPERBACKS

Alex took her seat in the cab, folded her hands in her lap, and sincerely regretted that she hadn't had the courage to throw something of a dignified tantrum. Barrett Stanbridge was everything that Emmaline had said he was: urbane, gentlemanly, the epitome of professional. His associate, however, was another matter entirely. John Aiden Terrell was a man barely civilized.

His hair was too long and too sun-bleached to even approximate fashionable. And it was unruly, too. Most men combed their locks into a deliberate style of one sort or another. But not Terrell; he simply let it tumble wherever it wanted. Which happened, she silently groused, to somehow perfectly accentuate the most beautiful, intensely green eyes she'd ever seen. In the first moments they'd quite simply taken her breath away. And then she'd noticed the sardonic, knowing glint in them. Combined with his easy, graceful movements and his massive shoulders . . . She'd thought of tigers, of the danger that lurked beneath the indolent manner, and it had taken every bit of her self-discipline to suppress the gasp. It hadn't been easy, but she'd studiously ignored him and eventually recovered some measure of her composure.

He, of course, seemed to have spent the rest of the

interview trying his best to ruffle it. Positioning himself so that he half-reclined against the desk with his well-muscled thighs within casual glance! It was patently obvious that he had abandoned the major tenets that ruled the public conduct of gentlemen. The man was a rake at best. At worst, an unabashed hedonist.

Yes, she should have spoken up when asked if she had any concerns about or objections to the arrangements Mr. Stanbridge had made. She should have said that she preferred to avoid being in the presence of John Aiden Terrell if at all possible, that he made her feel really quite . . .

Well, frightened wasn't entirely accurate. He was so very different from all the other gentlemen she'd ever met that she couldn't help but be a bit intrigued by him. Her heart skittered when she met his gaze and she held her breath every time he opened his mouth to speak. And the way he moved . . . Good God, the man was nothing short of a feast for brazen eyes. It was all most unsettling. Yes, Alex decided, unsettled was the proper word. John Aiden Terrell made her feel horribly unsettled. She should have said that when Mr. Stanbridge had asked for any objections.

But she hadn't said anything of the sort. Terrell had goaded her until stubborn pride and dignity had seized control of her better judgment. Now she was stuck with him for the immediate future. The only recourse was to make the best of the situation, to remember that protecting Mohan came before all other considerations. If Terrell proved himself to be anything short of stellar at the task, she wouldn't hesitate to send him packing back to his employer. With any luck at all, he'd be on his way before sunset.

The door of the rented carriage opened, and Terrell, his sun-burnished head uncovered, bounded in and dropped unceremoniously onto the opposite seat. "I presume," he said, stuffing his hands into the pockets of his greatcoat, "that you've instructed the driver as to your address?"

The vehicle began to roll even as he asked and so she refused to dignify the question with an answer. Instead, having decided that there was no time like the present to firmly establish her authority as his employer, she said, "I wish to be absolutely clear on one point at the very outset, Mr. Terrell. While in Mr. Stanbridge's office, you referred to my situation as desperate. It's not. It's merely vulnerable. There's a significant difference between the two."

One tawny brow slowly rose to disappear under the hair tumbling over his forehead. A wry smile lifted one corner of his mouth and dimpled a handsomely chiseled cheek. "The difference, Miss Radford," he countered dryly, "between vulnerable and desperate is generally about a half second. Which is roughly the time it takes for someone to pull a trigger."

"No one from India is going to use a firearm," she replied, struggling to contain her irritation. "A blade of one sort or another would be the weapon of choice. It's tradition."

"And does that bit of reality make you feel better?"

"I have been trained in the defensive arts," she supplied, meeting his gaze unflinchingly.

"Are you proficient enough that you could turn an attacker's weapon against him?"

It depended entirely on the skill and determination of the assailant. A small child or a cripple might have reason to think twice before launching an assault against her, but no one else would. Still, she wasn't prepared to share the truth with the likes of the tiger in the opposite seat. "I assure you, Mr. Terrell," she said evenly, "that I would be able to delay any attacker long enough to afford Mohan the chance to escape capture."

He considered her as a smile tugged at the corner of his mouth. Finally, he asked, "Would he take it or would he stay to help you?"

The man had all the persistence of a rat terrier. And none of the charm. "Mohan has been instructed to run away under such circumstances."

"You didn't answer the question," he observed with a slight shake of his head. "You have a habit of doing that, you know." He leaned forward to rest his elbows on his knees. His gaze boring into her own, he firmly asked, "Is Mohan the type of child who thinks of himself before others?"

She had no idea why he considered the matter to be worth such dogged pursuit, but since she also couldn't see any danger in honesty, she answered, "I suspect that in a threatening situation, Mohan would act foolishly and try to protect me."

"There's something to be said for gallantry and bravery," he countered, settling back into the seat again. "Too many young people today think only of themselves."

"Mohan can't afford the luxury of such lofty ideals," Alex felt compelled to point out. "He's to be the raja one day. His survival is far more important than being well-considered by others."

"What good is a raja who's a coward?" he scoffed. "Who would willingly follow him? Assuming, of course, that he even possesses the strength required to lead."

And what did John Aiden Terrell know of the qualities of leadership? He was nothing more than an underling to be hired out to anyone who would pay. "Mohan will someday make a very competent and courageous leader."

The brow inched up again. "Will he be a wise one as well?"

"It's my responsibility to see that he has the knowledge and experience necessary to exercise his power for the betterment of his people."

He sighed, compressed his lips, and contemplated the tops of his boots. After a long moment, he lifted his gaze to meet hers. "Is it a custom in India to avoid answering questions?"

"I beg your pardon?" Alex asked, genuinely confused by his sudden change in conversational direction.

"There," he said with a wave of his hand. "You just did it again. You have a very difficult time providing direct answers, Miss Radford. In the short span of our acquaintance, your willing responses have been of three types—half the truth, a truth unrelated to the inquiry, or an overt attempt to change the subject entirely. You aren't fully honest unless you're absolutely forced to be. Why is that?"

Because it's how one survives in a royal Indian household, she silently answered. Pushing aside the jumble of memories and ignoring the odd and unfamiliar sense of melancholy welling inside her, Alex lifted her chin and squared her shoulders.

"I don't see that my personal behaviors are any of your concern, Mr. Terrell," she declared in the voice she used to squelch dissension in the schoolroom. "You've been employed for the sole purpose of protecting Mohan. And while your duty and mine are temporarily the same, our association doesn't require the development of anything more substantive than a purely business relationship."

"A half-related truth. That makes a fourth way you can answer. I'm impressed."

He had to be the most insufferable man in all of London. In all of England. Perhaps even the entire British empire. The possibility of enduring his questioning and derisive comments for the foreseeable future was more than she could bear. "Is there some particular reason why you have this apparent compulsion to needle me, Mr. Terrell?" she demanded, determined to resolve their contest one way or the other. "Do I remind you of someone you especially dislike?"

"Well, you certainly don't appear to have any difficulty in asking a direct question."

"A related truth, Mr. Terrell," she shot back. "Perhaps even an attempt to change the subject. But not an answer."

His smile was easy and broad, crinkling the corners of his eyes and sending a hard jolt into the center of her chest. "And you don't appear to like evasion any better than I do, Miss Radford. Shall we call a truce? Or shall we just continue to verbally fence until one of us actually succeeds in drawing blood?"

A truce? Dear God, no. Not under any circumstances. She needed to keep as much distance as possible between them; he had a way of undermining her concentration, of stirring feelings that she suspected might grow to be uncontrollable.

"I don't much care for your manner, Mr. Terrell," she admitted. "You're disrespectful, sarcastic, and appear to be, at best, only marginally interested in the task to which you've been assigned."

He snorted softly and his smile widened. "I've been assigned to the task for less than fifteen minutes. The majority of that time has been spent trying to pry straight answers out of you. And not altogether successfully, I might add. Which means that, to this point, anyway, you haven't earned my respect." His smile faded and his eyes darkened to the color of a storm-shadowed sea. "As for sarcasm . . . I don't like being treated like a boot-licking minion, Miss Radford."

"Especially by women," she clarified, her pulse racing in the face of prodding his obvious anger.

"Mostly by spinsters with an inflated sense of self-importance."

There it was, the unvarnished truth of it. He'd accurately concluded that she wasn't the sort of woman who would ever wrap herself around his ankles and beg him to deliver her from evil. And since she didn't meet his standards of femininity, he wasn't obligated to meet the expectations of a modern St. George. It certainly wasn't the first time she'd been declared insufficiently female, but that truth didn't dull the pain. In fact, inexplicably, the barb seemed to have gone deeper this time than ever before.

Summoning every shred of her dignity, Alex found what she hoped passed as a serene smile and said, "It's apparent that we're not going to be able to work well together, Mr. Terrell. I think it would be best if we had the driver turn back."

Terrell settled his broad shoulders into the corner of the carriage, stretched his long legs out, folded his arms over his chest, and grinned. The pit of Alex's stomach tightened even as her skin warmed and tingled.

"You said that you put the injured guard on a boat for India three weeks ago," he began. "Given your determination to protect your ward, I'm guessing that you haven't spent the last three weeks forgetting to hire a replacement guard. I think you've made the rounds and went to Emmaline for a recommendation only when the obvious, more publicly known choices didn't meet your standards. Barrett is a very private investigator. You only know about him by personal reference. So, following the deductive logic to the end . . . You have two options, Miss Radford. It's me or go it alone."

He might actually do a decent job of protecting Mohan. His mind worked with surprising precision and clarity. Not that she was about to share that bit of appreciative insight with him. And not that she was willing to surrender control of any situation to him, either. "What credentials and experience do you have, Mr. Terrell?"

He laughed silently and she knew that he was thinking, *change of subject.* Blessedly though, he found some grace and didn't torment her. "Relatively few, actually. I was once ten years old and have younger brothers so I do have a basic understanding of what goes through the minds of boys. Beyond that . . ." He shrugged. "Barrett has decreed that I shall spend my life productively. I've discovered that, for the time being, it's easier to acquiesce than fight him on the matter."

"Do you always take the easiest course?"

"Rarely, actually. I'm reforming at the moment."

Alex arched a brow, wondering just how much of an improvement she was seeing.

"No, not happily and not by much," he supplied, apparently able to read her mind. "But since a child's life is in danger, I'll manage to trudge along."

She understood the edgy resignation she heard in his voice; she'd spent all of her life trudging through one duty after another. Nevertheless . . . "I don't find that attitude very reassuring, Mr. Terrell."

His smile faded slowly and, as they had the last time she'd prodded him, his eyes darkened. "I'll do what I must to protect Mohan for as long as necessary. How you feel about me in the process really doesn't matter one whit."

Why on earth that taunt bothered her—and bothered her deeply—she didn't know. It was, however, quite liberating if not completely honest to counter, "Which sums up perfectly my sentiments concerning your opinions of me, Mr. Terrell."

"Good," he said, openly assessing her. "We have an agreement. Our first."

"And quite likely our only one."

"No. One more is absolutely essential. I'm responsible for the child's protection and I'll make decisions in that regard. You'll agree to respect them."

"Only if I consider them wise ones, Mr. Terrell. I won't surrender my good judgment to you or anyone else."

There was a long moment of silence during which the rented carriage slowed and drew out of traffic. As it eased to a stop in front of Emmaline's shop, Terrell leaned forward in the seat, took the door handle in hand, and said, "I'm a fairly reasonable man. I'm willing to discuss whatever issues may arise, but only to a certain extent. When I draw the line, it's drawn and I won't tolerate dissension or resistance from either you or Mohan."

"How very imperial of you," Alex observed icily.

He grinned, dimpling his cheek and sending another jolt into the center of her being. "I can go toe to toe with the best. You've met your match, Duchess." Then he winked, popped open the door, and vaulted out onto the snow-covered walk.

WELCOME TO THE DELECTABLE LIAR'S CLUB . . .

. . . an elite group of renegade spies who work in the service of the Crown. By day, they are gentlemen with a notorious fondness for games of seduction. By night, they embark on missions that are difficult, dangerous, and always undercover. They are the bad boys of England—and women cannot resist their scintillating charms . . .

The Liar's Club Series
by Celeste Bradley

THE SPY
THE IMPOSTOR
THE PRETENDER

"Totally entertaining."
—*New York Times* bestselling author
Julia Quinn on *The Pretender*

"Bursting with adventure and sizzling passion to satisfy the most daring reader."
—*Romantic Times* on *The Pretender*

**AVAILABLE WHEREVER BOOKS ARE SOLD
FROM ST. MARTIN'S PAPERBACKS**

Visit Celeste Bradley's Web site at: www.liarsinlove.com

MY *Scandalous* BRIDE

CHRISTINA DODD
STEPHANIE LAURENS
CELESTE BRADLEY
LESLIE LaFOY

*Four scintillating tales of love and desire
by some of today's hottest romance stars!*

Christina Dodd, "The Lady and the Tiger"

Laura Haver must pose as the wife of notorious rogue Keefe
Leighton, the Earl of Hamilton, to discover her brother's killer.
But things go too far when Keefe engages Laura in an artful
game of seduction.

Stephanie Laurens, "Melting Ice"

Once, Dyan St. Laurent Dare, Duke of Darke, dreamed of making Lady Fiona his bride. Now they're together again—at a
scandalous dinner party where debauchery is the menu's main
course.

Celeste Bradley, "Wedding Knight"

Alfred Knight will do anything to avoid a scandal—even marry
a woman he barely knows. But his bride has a most titillating
secret.

Leslie LaFoy, "The Proposition"

Rennick St. James, the Earl of Parnell, has four days to seduce
London's most popular widow into becoming his wife—or else
she'll marry another man. It won't be easy . . . but Rennick is
determined to have his way . . .

AVAILABLE WHEREVER BOOKS ARE SOLD
FROM ST. MARTIN'S PAPERBACKS

MSB 9/03